Kraken Calling

Kraken Calling

a novel

ARIC MCBAY

SEVEN STORIES PRESS
new york • oakland • london

SEVEN STORIES PRESS
140 Watts Street
New York, NY 10013
www.sevenstories.com

College professors and high school and middle school teachers may order free
examination copies of Seven Stories Press titles.
Visit https://www.sevenstories.com/pg/resources-academics
or email academics@sevenstories.com.

Library of Congress Cataloging-in-Publication Data

Names: McBay, Aric, author.
Title: Kraken calling / Aric McBay.
Description: New York, NY : Seven Stories Press, [2021]
Identifiers: LCCN 2021035231 (print) | LCCN 2021035232 (ebook) |
ISBN 9781644211441 (trade paperback) | ISBN 9781644211458 (ebook)
Subjects: LCGFT: Dystopian fiction. | Novels.
Classification: LCC PR9199.4.M388 K73 2021 (print) | LCC PR9199.4.M388
(ebook) | DDC 813/.6--dc23
LC record available at https://lccn.loc.gov/2021035231
LC ebook record available at https://lccn.loc.gov/2021035232

Printed in the USA.

9 8 7 6 5 4 3 2 1

"We are what we pretend to be,
so we must be very careful what we pretend to be."
—KURT VONNEGUT

"Belief
Initiates and guides action—
Or it does nothing."
—OCTAVIA E. BUTLER, *PARABLE OF THE SOWER*

2051

Evelyn was summoned by her supervisor just as the overhead lights dimmed for midday power-down. She quickly finished collating the sheaf of paper in front of her; the pages felt slightly damp, as always in winter, but fingerless gloves kept sensation in her digits. She knocked on her boss's door with one hand, tucking the other into her pocket to warm it.

Her breath hung visibly in the air for the moment before he called her in. His corner office was warmer than the secretarial pool where she worked. He faced a window, suede-gloved hands behind his back, observing the city street below.

"It's a beautiful morning, isn't it, Miss Park?" he asked, without turning to look at her. A haze of charcoal smoke hung in the air, shot through with shafts of sunlight from a mostly overcast sky. A four-story brick building down the street, once a library, was being demolished by a large crew of workers—all red tags, no doubt—with picks and sledgehammers. Dust from their labor mingled with the airborne smoke. Loose piles of brick and lumber radiated from the work site across an empty street, an explosion in slow motion. Evelyn could see workers swinging hammers, the sound of each strike delayed by distance and muted by the office's thick window glass.

"Very pretty," she answered.

Her boss went over to a small potbellied stove in the corner. Atop it, a pot of coffee percolated the same grounds it had been boiling all week. Evelyn's boss put a few scoops of charcoal into the stove. Evelyn knew immediately something was wrong; she had never seen him dirty his hands filling the stove himself. He would always ask someone else to do the job, all the while muttering about rations and bandits and the shortage of charcoal from the north. Not today.

He sat down at his desk and spoke without making eye contact. "I'm sorry, Miss Park. We can't give you the promotion you asked for."

Evelyn kept her face blank, but her disappointment was deep. At home, Sara and Sid had eaten the last of their apples, and winter was still in its early days.

"I have people to take care of," she said. "Rations have been smaller."

He nodded, lips tight, eyes averted. "We don't have the budget for it. Health Care Records Administration just isn't profitable. We need to *cut* costs, in point of fact." He fiddled with the lapel of his old but tasteful suit, adjusting the green plastic card that peeked from his breast pocket. "I've just laid two people off."

Evelyn bit her lip. "I'm fast; I do my job well; I catch other people's mistakes. I'm worth a raise."

He sighed. "The problem isn't just here. We're at the bottom of the heap, but it's like this all across the public sector. Except Triage Administration, of course."

"So send me there," she said, surprising herself. She knew almost nothing about Triage Administration except that it was famously tight-lipped, that compensation was generous, and that they were short-staffed after a spate of cyberattacks.

He made eye contact with her for the first time, eyebrows raised. "I can't give up one of my star employees."

She weighed her words. "If I'm one of your star employees, think of what they would give you in exchange."

He stared at her, mouth half-open, in silent cogitation. Then he smiled, picked up his phone, and—as she sat across the desk from him—effusively praised her to some Triage Administration bureaucrat, before explaining how much of a budget boost he would need to be willing to part with her.

When he hung up, he looked deeply satisfied with himself. "Great demand at Triage Administration these days. Very busy. Excellent revenues."

He stood abruptly. "You start today. They're waiting for you. Good luck."

She stood, thanked him politely, and shook his gloved hand. "Go by Human Resources for your paycheck before you leave," he added.

There was a line in the Human Resources office; Evelyn wasn't the only one leaving, but at least she wasn't being laid off. As she queued up, the person at the front of the line argued with an HR staffer.

"This isn't the right amount," said a woman in her forties who appeared flushed and sweating despite the chilly air. "I worked two and a half days this pay period. You're barely paying me anything."

"YEA service charges are weekly," explained the staffer in a calm, nasal voice. "You get charged flat fees every week for basic services, same as everybody else. Vaccine surcharge, infrastructure upkeep, security patrol, epidemiology service, triage administration—"

"It's not fair to charge me all at once and use my whole paycheck," the woman protested.

"You can come back tomorrow to work out a payment plan," he said.

"I can't *get in* here tomorrow; my pass is only good if I work in this zone!"

"Then wait until I've dealt with this line," replied the staffer. "Next!"

When Evelyn was called up, the HR staffer swiped her debit card, depositing her miniscule paycheck, and inspected her triage tag. "Triage Administration is Green Zone, so I'll need to flash your card." Evelyn handed over her yellow tag, a thick plastic card that displayed her photo and a bar code. The staffer inspected the scuffed and worn card skeptically. He opened a safe, put Evelyn's old yellow tag inside, and retrieved a shiny new white one. "Do you live in the Green Zone?" the staffer asked.

"Yellow Two," Evelyn replied.

"Once you're at Triage Administration, you should move," the staffer advised. "There's a freshly renewed neighborhood nearby. Green Zone's much nicer once you can afford it," he added, touching the new white card to a panel on the desk. There was a beep, and the card turned green. "Have your travel papers updated at Triage Administration today or you'll have trouble at the checkpoint tomorrow morning," he said as he passed her the green tag. Evelyn inspected the new tag; as she watched, her face, name, and bar code appeared on the front. She clipped the tag onto her shirt.

Evelyn bade good-bye to her coworkers, made perfunctory promises to stay in touch. From a hook she collected her coat, a dark jacket her partner, Sara, had made for her. She retrieved her lunch from the cold room—literally an office with no heating that they used as a refrigerator—then walked down three flights of stairs and out the front door. The air outside was cool and damp and smelled faintly of acrid smoke.

On the street she heard the sounds of the red-tag demolition crew, the ring of steel on steel and the dull clunk of hammer on brick. She walked in the opposite direction, toward the Triage Administration building a few kilometers away. The street was mostly empty this time of day; adjacent buildings had been sealed off for quarantine. She saw a handful of other pedestrians and a few couriers on bicycles. From a parallel street she heard the rumble of automobiles and big trucks, but none was in sight.

Evelyn passed a cluster of armband-wearing public safety officers as they emerged from a quarantined building. They were low-level contractors, yellow tags with a ragged look. Their "uniforms" were not uniform at all but patched-together ensembles combining police garb, military fatigues, and black leather jackets scrounged from any number of picked-over military supply depots, thrift stores, and garbage piles. Some wore mismatched kneepads and oversized boots. They were armed variously with police batons, metal pipes, and bowie knives strapped visibly to their hips. One had a handgun in his belt, though it was hard to imagine that a rough-looking street-level contractor possessed more than a handful of ammunition.

They stared at Evelyn as she went by. She didn't make eye contact.

Evelyn soon turned onto a larger avenue, passing through the wide gate in a recently built brick barricade, topped with razor wire. The brick was the same color as that of the demolished library. The city was filled with such walls now, though this new gate was unguarded as she passed through it. A few tattered propaganda posters had been affixed to the wall by the Emergency Authority. They bore mottos like *Watch for Signs of Infection! Prosperity Restored!* and *Say YES to YEA!* Evelyn shook her head. Even she could have come up with better slogans.

On the avenue there was more foot traffic: single pedestrians like herself, green-tag businesspeople walking in pairs, and two crews of red-tag laborers on their way to a job site. Evelyn heard a clang some distance behind her. She glanced over her shoulder to see that the gate she had passed through moments before was now closed and locked. On the far side was one of the ragged guards she had passed. She shook off a skin-crawling sensation and picked up her stride; she started to wonder if she should have chosen a different route.

Before sixty seconds had passed, an old school bus painted dull green pulled across the road a hundred meters in front of her. Several public safety officers exited the front doors. One of them retrieved a coil of razor wire from the side of the bus and began to unspool it across the road: a surprise checkpoint. Evelyn's pulse quickened. Her documentation was in order, but she hated checkpoints. She gave a cursory glance up and down the street. The alleyways and side streets had been permanently blocked off, and anyone who lived on the avenue would have locked their doors upon seeing the arrival of the bus.

Evelyn saw public safety officers manning the checkpoint, all wearing blue latex gloves and white medical face masks. The first officer wore the crisp black uniform of Armor Security and questioned each person in line as they approached. He passed their ID cards off to a similarly dressed officer—a commander of some sort—who stood slightly to the side, staring blankly into the glow of his electronic goggles as he scanned the cards that were handed to him.

The third safety officer was a guard of the yellow-tag variety, barely old enough to shave. He apparently didn't rate a helmet and was wearing a scratched hard hat with the York Emergency Authority logo stamped into the front. On one arm he held a chipped police riot shield. The rest of his mismatched clothes made him look as though he had fought a battle to defend a Salvation Army—and lost.

The first two pedestrians were green-tagged professionals, so well dressed that they didn't bother to wear their passes. Evelyn slowed unconsciously as she approached the checkpoint queue, as if the soldiers would tire and decide to leave before she reached it. Instead, she simply became the last person in line. By the time she reached the queue, the people in suits had passed through. Two people in regular clothes had been quietly detained and placed on the bus. Its diesel engine had been shut off to save fuel; she could see through a window that one detainee, a woman in her sixties, was shivering slightly near the back of the bus.

The line moved forward, and an old man a few paces in front of Evelyn reached the officers. "I've already gone through two checkpoints this morning!" he complained. "You can't open new checkpoints wherever you please!"

"Sir, that was a Homeland Patrol checkpoint," said the second in command. "More than one company has a franchise in this neighborhood. Please show me your proof-of-health card."

"I want to go through!" insisted the man. "Soldiers stopping people in the streets—we have civil rights in this country!"

The commander seized the man's wrist. "Sir, everyone has the right to fair triage by a qualified expert. And we're not soldiers, we're public safety officers. Show me your papers, or I'll have to take you in for triage." The man tried to pull away, began shouting. The other guards promptly handcuffed him and hustled him onto the bus. The commander flipped up his goggles for a moment to rifle through a cloth bag the old man had dropped. Evelyn could see it was full of groceries.

"Contraband!" said the commander in triumph, waving a bruised-looking banana. He flipped his goggles back down and snapped a photo with them. "No wonder he wouldn't cooperate." He confiscated the groceries and placed them in a locker built into the side of the bus. The commander turned on a voice amplifier in his helmet—unnecessarily, since only three people still waited to pass the checkpoint—and addressed them. "People, we don't want any trouble. I need you to have valid papers *in your hands*. Be ready to have your bags searched. If you don't want to do that here, we can take you down to the triage station and do it there."

Evelyn double-checked her new green ID and her proof-of-health card, which bore a recent and valid stamp. As she waited, a Homeland Patrol truck drove past the checkpoint on the far side; its driver flashed Armor Security a middle finger.

The two guards returned from putting the old man on the bus and began searching the person at the front of the line. The man directly in front of Evelyn—bundled up in a high-collared black coat, cloth mask, and knitted watch cap—began to sidle sideways slightly, fiddling with the straps on his backpack. The youngest soldier noticed and raised his riot shield slightly. "Sir, I need you to stay in line," he said.

The man in the high collar muttered an excuse about being late for a meeting. The young soldier stepped right up to the man, pushing his chipped riot shield into the man's face. The man stepped backward, nearly stepping on Evelyn's shoes. The soldier shouted, "Don't give me any trouble!"

There was a sudden, sharp scuffle; the young soldier was thrown to the pavement and across Evelyn's feet, knocking her backward onto the ground. Evelyn saw the man with the high collar pivot away from her and toward the commander. She heard a sharp bang and flinched. The officer's goggles shattered, and he fell to the ground. The black-clad man pivoted again—Evelyn saw he held a pistol—and shot the next officer twice in the chest.

The man in the coat spun back around, and for an instant Evelyn had a glimpse of his dark and deep-set eyes. The man held his gun on the young soldier, who stared back wide-eyed from the ground. The man in black took a few deep, heaving breaths as he held the guard in the sights of his pistol. Then he turned and ran through the checkpoint. As the man's footfalls faded, the young soldier groaned, rolling into a fetal position and pulling his riot shield over himself like a blanket.

Evelyn tried to sit up. She heard a tearing sound, felt something tug at the back of her jacket. She realized that she had fallen back into a coil of razor wire. She slid away from it, to the sound of tearing cloth, and sprawled on the pavement, gasping in shock. Her head spun. She stared up at the slate-gray sky as snow started to fall.

Somewhere, an alarm began to whine.

—⚡

The sheep were out again. Addy could see tufts of wool they'd left on the fence wires as they squeezed underneath. The electric fence charger had failed, no doubt. Addy scanned the frosty fields nearby and then the border of woods along the pasture. She saw no sheep, but there was a track of disturbed grass leading north. The sheep must have snuck out of their paddock to find winter forage—oyster mushrooms, perhaps, or some clearing with an ungrazed thatch of yellowed grass.

"Adelaide!" called a voice nearby.

Addy turned and smiled. "Carlos," she greeted him. He jogged toward her from the cluster of buildings that made up the farmstead.

"Fence is off," he said. "Sheep went up the ridge."

"So I see!"

"We'd better catch them before they walk off a cliff."

Addy grabbed a shepherd's crook from a nearby fence post and, with Carlos, walked swiftly toward the forested ridge. The weather was well suited to chasing sheep. The frozen ground was firm, and there was just enough frost to follow the flock's footprints.

In a few minutes they neared the small flock of sheep, who were snuffling curiously near a copse of oak trees. The sheep nosed under a layer of fallen leaves, now frozen and crunchy. Addy and Carlos slowed so as not to startle them.

"You get the ram by the collar," whispered Carlos, "and then I'll . . ." He trailed off and furrowed his brow as he looked into the distance.

Addy grabbed his sleeve and pulled him back gently behind a cedar. She could make out a figure less than a hundred meters away. She heard footfalls on the frosted leaves—slightly uneven. She wished for a pair of binoculars. Her breath hung in the air as she stared.

"YEA scout?" whispered Carlos, staring wide-eyed at the approaching figure.

"We haven't seen a drone in weeks," said Addy. The figure wasn't wearing a uniform and seemed to be alone. Addy guessed it was a woman; the figure stared at the ground as they walked, face obscured by a hood. The stranger was getting close, nearly to the sheep.

Addy stepped out from behind the cedar tree, ignoring Carlos's hissed discouragement. "Hello?" she called softly. Then louder: "Hello?"

The face snapped up. A woman, indeed, but her face was smeared with dirt, and she was bleeding from several scratches under her right eye. A few drops of blood were frozen to her collar, still bright red.

"Please," the woman said. "I need your help."

Addy stepped closer and reached out to take the woman's hand.

—⚓

Evelyn finally arrived at the Triage Administration building barely an hour before closing time, having been delayed and questioned at the checkpoint as a witness to two homicides. She was met by a friendly, blue-gloved receptionist in the main foyer of the limestone building. "The director likes to meet all the new employees," the receptionist explained. The receptionist ushered Evelyn upstairs; on the way they passed several fashionably dressed employees of the Triage Administration.

The walls sported hand sanitizer stations and official posters blazoned with slogans. *Tropical Fruits Carry Tropical Disease*, proclaimed the banner above an illustration of bananas and pineapples radiating cartoon stink lines. *Everyone Has the Right to Fair Triage By an Expert*, promised a picture of a smiling citizen being examined by a doctor. *Information Hygiene Prevents Digital Epidemics*, read the caption beneath a man tossing a mobile phone into a fire.

The receptionist paused at the threshold of the director's office and pointed a blue finger at the green ID card clipped to Evelyn's collar. "Hon, you don't need to wear your green tag in the Green Zone," the receptionist said in a hushed voice. "Everyone knows if you're here, you belong here." Evelyn blushed slightly and tucked the card into her pocket. "He'll call you in when he's ready." Evelyn took a seat and waited, still shivering slightly from the day's events.

A YEA radio program played quietly through speakers in the ceiling. "Record-breaking warm weather in December brought relief to households dealing with the high price of charcoal," said a woman's voice.

"I guess global warming wasn't so bad after all!" answered a man.

"You said it, Jack. In light of the good news, fuel rations will be reduced this month by five liters."

The man took over. "Seven hundred people are dead in Cairo after food riots yesterday morning. Police blamed the riots on leftist agitators. And fresh news today on last week's shoot-out between a terrorist cell and members of Armor Security: Forensic investigators found a hidden cache in a nearby building filled with guns, grenades, and illegal drugs. The block has been rezoned as red until it can be properly searched."

A muscular, middle-aged man with a turtleneck and a shaved head approached Evelyn. She stood quickly, nervously. "Good afternoon,

Director Jus—" she began, but he snorted, shook his head at her mistaken assumption, and waved her into the director's office.

The actual director was in his fifties. He was tall; his thick black hair had bursts of gray at the temples. He smiled broadly and—to her surprise—gave Evelyn a bare-handed handshake as he welcomed her into his office. His hand was warm and soft. He didn't let go after the handshake but held her hand for an extended moment as he looked down at her face. "Welcome to Triage Administration," he said. Then he frowned slightly. "You're trembling. There's no need to be nervous." His smiled returned. "We don't bite!"

She pried her hand away gently and averted her eyes. "It's just that I witnessed a . . . shooting on the way over. Two security guards. So I'm a bit—"

"Shaken up," he finished. "Oh, my dear, have a seat." He put a hand on her shoulder and guided her to a chair by his desk. The director smelled faintly of some cologne Evelyn found pleasant. He called to someone outside his office door and gestured, one hand still on her shoulder.

He sighed loudly as she sat. "Terrorists and criminals," he said, shaking his head. "What a horrible thing. And I see they tore your jacket. Animals." He examined the tear in the back of her jacket, where layers of red felt could be seen through the dark outer shell.

Evelyn's partner had sewn many layers of warm felt into the breathable polymer coat. It was cozy in the fall. It couldn't keep out gusts on truly cold days, but felt was better than sheets of newspaper.

"I hope you weren't questioned for long," said the director.

"My Triage Administration transfer—"

"Of course," he smiled. "Even the dimmest security contractor knows we are their bread and butter. When we're around, even Armor and Homeland pretend to get along."

The receptionist entered the office and placed a steaming espresso cup in front of Evelyn. Evelyn sipped at it tentatively, then looked up at her new boss. "Is this—"

"Real coffee." He nodded with a smile. "Despite the ongoing emergency, despite fungal diseases in the tropical plantations, we try to live life as normally as possible. People work hard here, Evelyn. But we are rewarded." He went to the opposite side of the desk and sat. He gave her an appraising look for such a long time that Evelyn began to feel uncomfortable. She focused on the rich flavor of her coffee.

"Evelyn, do you understand what we do here?" He didn't wait for her to respond. "We assess need and assign limited resources. We have an important job. Our society is sick, you see. Not just physical maladies—a sickness of the soul. Your unfortunate experience today"—he waved his fingers at her coat—"is only one symptom. Our people had once prosperity. Some of us work hard to restore a society with strong bodies and sharp minds. But others . . ." He sneered slightly. "Others are unwilling to work, to make the sacrifices we need for progress."

He looked her directly in the eye. "Our job is to know the difference. To separate those who will help restore the health and well-being of our nation from the people who are too sick to do it any good—those who must be quarantined."

"For treatment," she said. "To get them the help they need."

"Yes," he said. "For their own good. I'm glad you understand. Normally I would do a brief interview, but let's leave that for another day. Stanley will show you around the building."

He stood, and beckoned the stocky man with the shaven head from the office threshold. Evelyn drained her last mouthful of coffee and stood as well. The director strode around the desk, putting a hand on the tear in her jacket. "Let me give you a welcoming present. Stanley, would you please have Miss Park measured for a new jacket?" She tried to protest, but he silenced her. "We have resources here that other divisions don't. It's nothing. I'll see you soon."

Stanley jerked his head to indicate that she should follow. She did, noticing the offices were warmer and better lit than she was used to. She removed her jacket. If every floor were so warm, she wouldn't even have to wear a second sweater at her desk. "So, Stanley, are you a tailor?" she asked in an attempt to make conversation. He snorted derisively and shook his head.

As they passed doors and intersecting corridors, Stanley muttered a word or two. "Case Processing," he growled tersely at one doorway. "Statistics," at another. "Requisitioning. Communication. Information Hazards. Electronic Countermeasures." They descended a stairwell near the rear of the building. "Cafeteria." He waved one floor down. Evelyn's stomach growled at the scent of cooking food; rumor was that portions at Triage Administration were so generous that staff took home leftovers. It would make a difference for Sid as he grew.

They passed through a heavy basement door. "Triage Archives." He pointed left but turned right, though a door labelled *Surplus Storage*. Inside was a small office where several women consulted clipboards and updated spreadsheets on archaic computers.

One of them looked up, a middle-aged brunette with tired eyes and a conservative hairstyle. "Take her measurements," Stanley said brusquely. "Winter coat. Warm. Something classy." The brunette woman produced a clothier's tape and measured Evelyn with practiced proficiency. Then she disappeared through a back door. Evelyn caught a glimpse of racks of clothing, bolts of fabric, row upon row of shelving.

There was an awkward quiet. The two remaining women tapped at their keyboards in rapid staccato without looking up. After a few minutes, the brown-haired woman returned and shook her head. "Nothing in that size today," she said.

"So find something," said Stanley as he walked toward the door.

"We'll try tomorrow," the woman answered.

"Will a new shipment be coming in tomorrow?" Evelyn asked as she followed Stanley up the stairs. "Imports from Europe?" Uncomfortable with the continued silence, she pressed: "Or the Protectorate? Or somewhere else?"

Stanley stopped on the stairs so suddenly that she almost ran into him. Then he turned slightly toward her without making eye contact. "Surplus," he muttered. And then he turned away and kept walking.

—⁀

The walls of the long-abandoned dining room reverberated with her anger. "What the fuck did you think you were doing?" she demanded.

Layth sat back in his chair and stared at her across the dimly lit table. She had a head of close-cropped gray hair and thick eyebrows. A scar above her left eyebrow intensified her gaze. She was a foot shorter than him but, standing with her palms firmly on the table, she loomed over him.

"Do you realize that they red-zoned twelve blocks after your little show? We've got half a dozen contacts trapped inside and about a thousand people without electricity or water. What were you thinking?"

"I had no choice," Layth answered. "It was a surprise checkpoint. I was penned in."

"So you shot three people?" demanded the woman.

Layth unzipped his backpack and dumped out its contents; shrink-wrapped packages clunked heavily onto the table. A few contained small-caliber ammunition, coated in translucent machine oil. Another held rechargeable batteries, still in their original Japanese packaging. A third contained orange pill bottles, labelled neatly by hand; a fourth was full of small blank coins and labelled *Samizdata*. Another held rolls of cash wrapped with rubber bands.

"I shot *two* people," he corrected. "And I only had one chance to get this cache, X. Armbands were searching the whole block, building by building. If I waited any longer . . ."

She inspected the packages, picked up the bag holding rolls of hundred-dollar bills, and threw it on the floor next to a pile of empty soy sauce containers. "I wish you had left the cash and retrieved things of value."

"There *were* no more valuables," Layth answered. "The caches were nearly empty. Even the grenades were gone."

X shook her head. "Damned cowboy," she sighed. "This is what happens when you put a meathead in charge of a resistance cell. That idiot gets them all machine-gunned, but not before using up most of my supplies. Felicity!" A young woman with a notebook entered the room.

X swept the materiel to the edge of the table with one arm and sat. Felicity joined them at the table and counted the supplies, making brief and cryptic notes. After a moment, Layth pulled a foil-wrapped pouch out of his pocket and threw it on the table. "Oh, and there were these," he added. "Alibis."

X opened the foil packet and dumped out a small stack of unflashed white ID tags. Their digital ink displays were blank, their embedded RFIDs fresh and empty. "Well," she said, "I guess that's something."

"Are these all antibiotics?" Felicity asked. "No gansufloxacin? No MultiSpec V?" Layth shook his head. Felicity and X exchanged brief looks of concern.

X tapped an index finger thoughtfully on her formidable nose, then spoke. Her voice was softer. "I'm glad you made it out in one piece, Layth. I'm glad you retrieved this cache. But do I need to remind you how grim things are? We're running out of basic supplies. We lost seven people this week alone."

Layth grimaced. "I know."

"We need to be careful," X told him. "We need to be more subtle than ever. Now give me the blow-by-blow."

He gave an account of his day: Rising before sunset to be on the street at the lift of curfew. Sneaking into the target building through an abandoned cargo door to get the cache. Travelling through alleys and hidden corridors to avoid detection, only to be stopped by a surprise checkpoint a few blocks from home. Shooting two soldiers and leaving the last one, merely a boy, alive. Sneaking to the boarded-up Chinese restaurant and reporting to X.

X nodded. "Okay. Go rest." Layth stood to leave.

"But if you have to fight your way out again," X said, "be sure to shoot them all."

—⁂

"Did he hit you?" Addy asked.

The woman across the table hesitated. "He waved his fists. He threatened. But he didn't actually hit anyone."

"What happened to your face?" asked Addy. The scratches on the woman's face were stark red in the late afternoon sunlight that flooded the farmhouse kitchen.

"I walked into a thorn branch on the way here."

"Did he tell you to leave his land? Or did you choose to leave by yourself?"

"He said to leave," the woman said. "Said we weren't working hard enough. Said we ate too much, that if we weren't gone by sunset he would drag us out himself."

Addy nodded thoughtfully, pouring the woman a cup of tea from the pot on the kitchen table. Beside her, Carlos took notes, his callused hand moving slowly across the sheet of paper as he wrote compactly with a pencil stub. A fire crackled softly in the kitchen woodstove.

"What did you take with you?" Addy asked.

"Just what I own," the woman replied, nodding at a small backpack by the door, a pair of worn winter boots, a patched coat on a hook. "The others went to Newbrook with the clothes on their backs."

"Sandra, did he give you a share of dried goods? Money? Anything?" asked Addy.

Sandra sipped from her tea, then shook her head. "He said we owed *him* money. For room and board. Said we were bums if I couldn't pay it. Said we owed *him* for hosting us. When I grew half their food!"

Addy nodded, frowning. "That's all we need for now. Why don't you warm up here for a few minutes, then we'll find your old spot in the women's bunkhouse." Sandra sniffled, looked grateful, and thanked her.

Addy stood, and Carlos followed her lead, tucking his notepaper into a folder on a bookshelf. They donned their coats and stepped outside of the farmhouse. The leaves scattered across the yellow grass were brown and dead, free of snow but coated with frost. The air smelled faintly of wood smoke. Oblique daylight grew red as the sun neared the horizon. They walked around the corner of the barn, which was painted with an enormous, faded image of a thistle. Carlos scratched his beard and spoke softly: "Do you believe her?"

"Of course I do," said Addy. "A woman doesn't walk three hours across frozen fields in the middle of the winter for a place in a crowded bunkhouse if she has another option. Don't you think she's telling the truth?"

"I'm *afraid* she's telling the truth," said Carlos. "We fed Bill Farnham's children for an entire winter. We built them a hand pump and a windmill. We sent them trained homesteaders to board and to work the land. Hell, I planted a willow grove on his farm myself. And now he's kicking out *our* boarders? His family wouldn't have made it through the last ten years without us."

"People forget quickly." Addy sighed. "They grow their own food for a few years and suddenly they don't need the Thistle anymore."

"They *still* aren't growing their own food. If we hadn't sent them workers this summer, they'd barely have anything in the cellar," he vented. "But now that it's winter, he's charging *our* people rent. He never even had to pay them! It was mutual aid!"

They followed a footpath along a cedar-rail fence. A few horses stood on the far side of it, nosing at a pile of hay. The path crossed a small bridge over a shallow stream. The streambed was wide and rocky; only a trickle of water flowed between icy stones.

"We should go down there tomorrow," said Addy, "for his side of the story."

"I can tell you what he'll say," Carlos replied. "It's his land, and he can do what he wants with it!"

"That farm was Haudenosaunee land a few centuries ago," said Addy. "I guess it still is, rightfully. But Farnham signed a land-sharing agreement with us eight years ago. The YEA land registry probably lists that farm as government property due to unpaid taxes." She chuckled. "Probably the only person who thinks that land belongs to Bill Farnham is Bill Farnham himself." Carlos snorted.

Past the stream there was a steep hill covered in small willow saplings. The willows could be cut at ground level every few years; each stem would regenerate into one or two or three new stems the following year. The young, flexible willow stems were turned into baskets, fencing, medicine, and kindling.

Addy and Carlos climbed the path as it switchbacked up the hill through the willows. "We should talk to the community militia first thing tomorrow," said Carlos. "Send a brigade with horses. Tell him: honor the agreement, or we take all the food our people grew."

Addy smiled. "That's appealing but premature. Let's try diplomacy first. Besides, Lieutenant Dumont is out on patrol for another few days."

"I'm not joking," said Carlos. "I'm serious, Adelaide. You let these guys start breaking their agreements, soon enough we'll have landlords and serfs everywhere. *You're* the one who always warns about feudalism. We've got to nip this in the bud."

"You're not wrong," she admitted. "But let's not be hasty." She took his hand. They reached the top of the hill. Past the crest, the trees ended abruptly. On their left was a fifty-foot tower topped by a wind turbine, spinning slowly in the breeze. On their right was a small bench beside a tool shed.

In front of them was a seventy-foot drop into a vast crater that stretched kilometers into the distance; its opposite wall was the horizon. They sat on the bench and stared out at the expanse of bedrock and pools of icy water before them. Carlos leaned toward Addy, who turned and kissed him on the lips before looking back toward the sunset.

"I still can't get over the sight of this." Addy sighed. "How the hell did we let things get this bad?"

2

2028

"There are four hundred people here today!" Helen yelled into the megaphone. "The people of Newbrook are sending a clear message to this government about what we want for our future. We will not let you risk the health of our community's children! We will not let you poison the land! And we will not tolerate companies that put profit before people!"

The crowd roared its approval. Helen lowered the megaphone and stepped down from the bed of the pickup truck she had been standing on. The crowd began chanting—"People before profits!"—and marched slowly forward along the fence of a petroleum depot, its decrepit tanks looming in the distance. A journalist called Helen's name to ask for a few quick photos in front of the fence. She obliged, somewhat reluctantly, brandishing her megaphone as the journalist snapped photos, the rusted white cylinders of the tank farm in the background.

"Can you tell me why your group is marching around the tank farm today?" the journalist asked, scribbling on a tiny notepad.

"This petroleum depot was closed in the first place because it was a hazard," Helen replied, launching into a well-rehearsed sound bite. "It was cheaper to shut it down than repair the leaks. It's ludicrous to reopen it at a time when we must move away from harmful fossil fuels."

She pointed across the road. "And putting an environmental hazard like this across the street from an active elementary school is dangerous and irresponsible." The journalist finished writing and thanked her. He didn't need to check her name or its spelling—the tank farm story had been in the newspaper every week for months.

Helen stepped back onto the hot asphalt of the street, rejoining the body of the march as it circumnavigated the petroleum depot. She weaved through the crowd to catch up with her fellow organizers. A few of them were busily tapping at their phones, while others led chants or waved banners.

"Helen!" Elijah called, looking up from his phone. "Good news and bad news. What do you want first?"

"Good," she said.

"We got the documents from the latest freedom-of-information request back. It's full of useful info about 'industrial revitalization.' I'm going back to the office to check it out."

"What's the bad news?"

"They're trying to roll this tank farm redevelopment into a larger state-sponsored project."

"Fuck," said Helen.

"There's a press conference livestreaming right now."

"Let's all meet after to watch it," said Helen.

"See you then!" Elijah said, returning to his phone screen. Helen threaded her way to the front of the march, where their pilot vehicle— the pickup truck from which she had given her short speech—was slowly leading the way. A few of the march participants who couldn't (or didn't want to) walk the whole way were sitting on bales of straw in the back. Helen walked up to the open driver's-side window.

"Howdy, Helen," said the woman in the driver's seat.

"How's the driving, Gwen?" Helen asked.

"We have some company," Gwen replied, nodding her head forward. A police cruiser—lights flashing—had placed itself at the front of the procession, an unrequested escort.

"Hopefully they won't give us trouble," said Helen.

"Maybe," said Gwen, in a cheerfully doubtful tone. "But some people might be looking for it." She glanced into her side mirror and jerked her thumb backward. Helen looked. Some of the younger, black-clad protesters had decided to expand the width of the march from one lane to two. Their expansion into the opposing lane was being impeded by a pair of bicycle cops who pedalled alongside the march.

"Taavi," said Helen, shaking her head.

"You need to stay in your lane," the bicycle cop told Taavi. "For your own safety."

Taavi rolled his eyes. "There are hundreds of people here. We need both lanes."

"This march doesn't have a permit for two lanes," the cop replied. He got off of his bike and parked it diagonally in front of Taavi, as if to funnel him back into the main march. Taavi just walked around him on the outside.

"This march doesn't have a permit at all," said Taavi. "If you want to make us safe, stop cars from driving right beside the march. There are little kids here."

"Don't bother talking to him," said Andy, who had emerged from the march to walk beside Taavi. "It's no use talking to cops." A young woman followed him out; Samantha wore dark clothing, like Taavi and Andy, but her hoodie was densely packed with political patches and buttons.

"Come on, people, take the whole street!" Samantha shouted to the crowd. She waved her arms to beckon. A few people began to follow them across the yellow line into the opposing lane.

"Stop doing that," said the bicycle cop. "You're inciting a misdemeanor." Andy responded with a middle finger. "I could arrest you for making lewd gestures."

The cop grabbed Taavi, who was closest, by the sleeve. But by this time several dozen people had crossed into the lane, including a number of middle-aged, middle-class-looking people; their disapproving glances made the cop release his grip.

As the march approached its endpoint, Taavi and the others decided to quietly slip away rather than linger with the dwindling crowd and a growing number of police at the rally point. They walked nonchalantly up onto the sidewalk and then cut between two buildings to emerge in a parking lot out of sight of the departing march.

"Hey! You're under arrest!" shouted a voice—the bicycle cop. He had seen them depart and followed them to the next street. The trio ignored him and kept walking, but their route was promptly cut off by a police cruiser with flashing lights. A second cruiser was speeding toward them down the street.

"Shit," said Taavi.

~

"How do you know you can trust me?" he asked.

Dee stared evenly at the young man across the table from her. She had chosen the meeting time and location carefully; one had to be cautious when hiring a hacker to penetrate a powerful network of companies. The Lucky Lion café was packed, in the midst of its Saturday-morning brunch rush. Dee had arrived an hour early to scout the place, had spent ten minutes watching the young man from across the room after he arrived. Watched him order green tea and a peanut butter cookie, as she had instructed him to, before she approached.

Dee considered his question thoughtfully. How did she know she could trust him? The answer was not straightforward.

When Dee was four years old, her family's minivan was in a ten-car highway pileup. Her mother and two siblings died within minutes. Dee's father, who was on one of his frequent business trips overseas, returned to find her in the ICU. She was unconscious for three days. Sitting at the bedside of his one surviving child, Dee's father vowed never again to be away from her.

They recovered slowly, together. Dee's father had been almost forty when he met Dee's mother; nearly fifty at the time of the crash, he had no interest in remarrying. Dee became the center of his life, and he the center of hers. So when Dee's father began to work again, to travel, he took her with him.

Her father's job title was "fair trade prospector"; he travelled around the world trying to find new products that were *almost* ready to be put on the global market as "ethical products." Once he found them, he used his connections to call on investors and distributors and marketers. He helped popularize shea butter from Mali. He got funding to create the second-largest coffee cooperative in Costa Rica. Over five years, the investors he brought in doubled the export of fair-trade-certified handicrafts from Bangladesh, where his family was from.

Dee's father homeschooled her some of the time, but she could not remember doing a single exercise out of a textbook. He taught her to read with posters and newspapers and travel brochures in half a dozen different languages. He taught her math by letting her spend rupees and francs and pesos at street vendors and cafés around the globe. He encouraged her to write down her thoughts in journals, to photograph or draw the things she saw in Sydney or Bangkok or Caracas.

Critical thinking she learned from her father's constant questioning of potential business prospects. *Can production really be scaled up? Will delivery deadlines be met? Is the product consistent and uniform enough for international sale?* (Later, as her father's business sense paid off and his early investments matured into real wealth, she learned from him a deeper form of introspection as he agonized over who benefited most from the deals he brokered between international capitalists and subsistence farmers.)

For social studies, the world was her textbook. By the time she was twelve, Dee had met and interacted with a greater variety of human beings than 99 percent of the people on the planet ever would. She could speak three languages with reasonable fluency, but she could *communicate* with almost anyone. She learned to read faces, body language, and the nuances of vocal tone. With her father's help, she learned to dig deeper. From expression and emotion, she could derive character. Her father had made so many business deals through interpreters that he learned to judge whether a person was honest or trustworthy without words. Soon she could do the same, and by her teen years she had surpassed her father.

So when Simón, the hacker, asked how she knew he was trustworthy, she almost laughed. How could she not? She nodded at one of the tablet users at an adjacent table. "That computer, how fast is it?"

He scoffed. "Very slow. Older dual-core processor underclocked to stretch out battery life. And integrated graphics, so . . ."

"And you could tell this just by looking at it?"

He nodded. "I know the make and model. But humans aren't manufactured. You can't tell what's inside by looking at the outside."

She glanced at another patron of the café, an older man likewise reading on a tablet. "Can I run any software I want on that thing?"

He frowned. "That's iOS, so everything is locked down and approved. But that's—"

"Both of those machines just look like black rectangles to me. I couldn't tell them apart if I were holding them. But you can tell from a distance what's inside of them, look at the screen to tell what software is running—"

"You can tell from the window chrome that—"

"See, I don't even know what that means," she interrupted. "But the way you tell from a glance what's going on in inside a computer? It's the same for me with people, from their body language and their faces. I could watch a video of us having this conversation and tell that you are trustworthy even if the sound were muted." She could sometimes tell even *more* without sound—words could obscure true feelings.

"But you look like a teenager," he said.

"My apparent youth is exactly how I avoid detection," she said simply. There was an awkward silence as she gazed at him without elaborating.

"Did you bring the, ahhh"—he glanced around the room in a manner that was obviously conspiratorial—"*materials?*"

Underneath the table she had placed a backpack containing two thousand dollars and an encrypted USB key with further instructions and a list of targets. She had asked him to bring an identical backpack, empty.

"The deposit is there," she replied. "Once you finish these jobs, I'll have more business for you." She shifted in her seat, getting ready to stand. "This is the only time we'll ever meet in person."

Before she could stand, he reached partway across the table, stopped short of actually touching her. "I just want to you know, I'm not just in this for the money," he said. "I want to work with your organization. I believe in what you're doing. If there's more I can help with . . ."

She picked up the empty backpack and stood to go. "I'll pass it on to the higher-ups," she said with a tight smile. "I'm just a courier."

⌇

When Taavi got home to his basement apartment that night, his mother was waiting. "Where have you been? It's so late!" she said the moment he came through the door.

"I went to the protest, Mom," he replied.

"That was hours ago. I saw you on TV arguing with a cop!" she said.

He rolled his eyes as he took his shoes off. "Yeah, we got arrested, so that's why I'm late."

"Jeez, Taavi, you got arrested?" she said, "You'll never get a job with a criminal record."

Taavi was parched, so went to their tiny kitchen and opened the fridge. He poured himself a glass of soy milk.

"It's those friends of yours," she said. "Everyone else got a summer job after graduation."

"Mom, the unemployment rate for youth is like thirty percent. The rest have jobs so boring they want to kill themselves or get drunk every night." This was a conversation that they had repeated many times in different variations.

"Your friend Samantha did the vegetable-growing thing for the city; can't you do that?" his mother asked.

"That was a summer program for high school students, Mom," he replied.

"Taavi, you need structure in your life! You need something to do other than stay up late. You know, if you had a steady job the girls would respect you more. Or the boys, or whatever."

"Oh my god, Mom."

"Not that's there's anything wrong with seeing boys or girls. But your father wishes you'd make up your mind."

Taavi slapped his own forehead. "Mom, you're sharing relationship advice from the guy you divorced?" Taavi shook his head and walked toward his bedroom.

"I printed out some job ads and left them on the table!" she called. Taavi went into his room and closed the door more quickly and more loudly than necessary.

Dee took four different buses and three subway routes on her way home. She employed her usual countersurveillance techniques—jumping on and off busses, paying fares in cash, donning or removing cloth face masks of various colors, changing jackets in crowded subway cars, taking a detour through a mall—so it was well after supper when she arrived home. She put the battery back into her phone as she walked up the driveway.

When she arrived, her father was asleep on the couch. The television was on, showing a nature documentary about kangaroos. She turned the volume down, waking her father.

"Adita!" He smiled. "How was the library?"

"It was good!" she said, sitting down beside him and hugging him. "I got a lot done."

"I tried to call you about dinner," he said, his face looking drawn and pale, "but it went to voice mail."

"My phone ran out of battery," she lied.

"Ah, my brilliant daughter," he said with genuine love on his face, "who memorized a French phrasebook in ninety minutes but can't remember to charge her phone. I ordered Chinese. Leftovers are in the fridge."

She went into their house's large kitchen and pulled the cardboard containers from the fridge. She frowned—the food was from the Lucky Lion, where she had met Simón. It was most unlucky to have a personal connection to a place where she had held a clandestine rendezvous. She made a mental note to never again visit the Lucky Lion. In the fridge there were also two older bags of takeout that had been pushed to the back. Dee sniffed them, then threw them in the garbage.

Dee microwaved a plate of chicken fried rice and went to sit beside her father. He had switched the television to the news. "Your morning cup of joe could get a lot more expensive if agronomists can't control a new coffee fungus spread by global warming," warned the anchor. Few of the stories were what Dee would consider good news: A dispute in the East China Sea after a Japanese warship collided with a Filipino fishing boat. A court battle in which the White House was trying to limit Chinese investment in North American energy infrastructure.

Climate-induced crop failures in four countries. An increase in out-breaks of antibiotic-resistant tuberculosis. Glowing coverage of how warrantless vehicle tracking by police was "a net gain for public safety."

There was an interesting story about a community fighting to keep a decrepit petroleum depot closed to protect groundwater. "That might be a good cause to donate to, Adita," her father said. "You could look into the Friends of the Watershed."

"I'll do that," Dee said. "I just made a donation to a government transparency researcher"—Simón the hacker would be amused to hear himself described in such terms—"but I was also thinking more about that idea we talked about, the fair-trade café with the bookstore."

"You know I like the idea of you starting a business, Adita," her father said. "It's important not to be complacent, not to live off the money we already have. But a bookstore? In this day and age? No one buys books anymore."

"It wouldn't be just paper books," she said. "There would be tablets and e-readers. We would recommend books, sell hardware, set people up. I know people who can run it; they just need some seed money and a signer for the building rental."

"If that's what you want, I'll support you," her father said. "You could wait until you are older, but why waste time? Life is short. I wish I hadn't waited so long to have you. Sometimes getting a job done will take just as much time as you give yourself."

Dee nodded. "I'll look at some venues tomorrow."

"All right," he said. "But I want to see a business plan by the end of the week!" They went back to watching the news; a few minutes later, he was asleep. Looking at his face, Dee could see he had lost more weight. She pulled a blanket over him and went to her room to review her long list of action items.

~

After the march, Helen and the other organizers sat down at the Friends of the Watershed office to watch video of the government press conference. On the screen, a state spokesman stood confidently at a podium. Business suit, immaculate. Blue tie, iridescent, with full

Windsor knot. Blond hair, carefully brushed and neatly parted. Shutters clicked; flashbulbs strobed irregularly.

"We've had a tough few years in this country," the spokesman said. "Hard-working people have lost their jobs. Everyone has struggled to make ends meet.

"But our government is here with a solution—a solution that will bring prosperity back to our country. That will stimulate our economy while creating thousands of new jobs. That will lower energy prices, and make consumer goods more affordable, by enabling us to make our own energy right here at home." A handpicked audience of supporters applauded loudly.

"The Industrial Revitalization Initiative will invest billions of dollars. It will expand the infrastructure we need to supply fuel and electricity to our growing cities. It will provide good, stable employment for many years to come." More applause. "And it will bypass the crippling environmental and zoning legislation that has caused our country to fall behind in the global marketplace." Generous applause came over the speakers.

"By using advanced forms of clean coal and hydraulic fracturing, we can obtain the energy that our country runs on. New, safer pipelines will bring crude from the oil sands for refining and manufacturing in our own backyards. Tax breaks for job creators and a streamlined approval process for new industrial facilities will ensure that construction can begin now, when we need it—to keep the engines running, the lights on, and the future bright for our children." Thunderous applause.

The image froze, and the applause went silent. "I think we've all heard enough," said Helen. She turned to the others—Tom, Gwen, Teresa, Elijah, and Apollo—for their thoughts.

"Same old talking points," said Tom. "Jobs, technology, stimulus. A few people will get shitty jobs for a few years, and then they'll be back in the unemployment line with more benzene in their bloodstreams."

"The scale is new," said Teresa. "He looks polished, as always, but I think they're really panicking this time. Their poll numbers are starting to look as bad as the NASDAQ." A chuckle passed through the room.

"I don't want to be a party pooper, kids," drawled Gwen, "but this is a big thing to take on. Shouldn't we focus on the tank-farm fight?

I mean, we're run ragged just organizing marches and petitions and town hall meetings and what not."

"That's why I wanted to talk while I have you all together," said Helen. "I'll be quick. But here's the executive summary."

Helen clicked a key, and a map appeared on the projector screen. It was highly detailed and centered on an area around the Great Lakes.

"This is Elijah's best guess of what the IRI will look like," said Helen, gesturing to the screen. "Not all of it has been publicly announced, and some ongoing projects will be folded in. But you get the gist." The map was color coded: Upgraded electrical lines were rendered in a deep blue, spiderwebbing out from the cities. Planned pipelines were red, tentacular clusters with thick nodes at industrial parks and factories that connected to fracking sites. New industrial extraction sites were shaded yellow, some of them bigger than the towns and villages they neighbored.

"So this is what our enemy looks like," said Apollo. Helen suppressed a frown. She admired Apollo's ability to zero in on pressure points, to find places of leverage, but she was sometimes repelled by his adversarial attitude. Apollo continued: "Big isn't always bad. They can't defend every industrial site. The more places they have to work, the more places we can show up and cause a ruckus."

"We're *all* busy, Gwen," said Teresa. "But this project is huge. It affects the integrity of everything: soil, water, air, biodiversity. If we stop the tank farm but don't stop this . . ." Teresa trailed off and shrugged.

"I don't disagree, kid," said Gwen. "But I'd rather focus on a cause we agree on than stretch ourselves too thin and fall apart."

"That's a concern for me, too," said Helen. "If we want to organize a bigger coalition to take this on we should start soon, before they build up too much momentum. Focus on the petroleum depot, but keep IRI in the long view. What do you think?"

"We fight it," said Apollo. "What else can we do?"

Tom nodded in agreement and joined in the chorus. "God knows what kind of future we'll leave for our kids if we don't."

3

2051

Layth sat across the table from X in the boarded-up restaurant. An old fluorescent light flickered faintly overhead.

"You must be joking," said Layth, scrunching his nose in disgust. "A Catholic priest? Are we that desperate for allies?"

"The Catholic Church has a . . . mixed history of social justice," X replied. "But when the European old guard was gutted by epidemics, the ranks filled out with liberation theologists from the global south." She paused. "And yes, we *are* that desperate for allies."

"Is this priest heavily armed? Is he bringing us guns and rockets? Grenades? Antibiotics? Medicine? Or just a few copies of the Good Book?"

X shifted uncomfortably in her chair and rubbed the scar above her eyebrow. "He's on a fact-finding mission." Layth snorted, but X continued. "What he reports back to his superiors could win us supplies and support. In the Second World War, resisters snuck reports out of concentration camps to the Allies—you've never heard of Witold Pilecki?"

Layth sighed. X was always like this. You couldn't win an argument; she would cite little-known, century-old examples. The only way to win was to list even more obscure counterexamples at even greater length, something that Felicity had accomplished twice, and Layth exactly zero times.

He changed tack: "How am I supposed to do my job *and* hand-hold a Bible-thumper?"

"Simple," she replied. "Meet him upon his arrival. Escort him *without incident* to his destination."

"How do we know we can trust him?"

"We have assurances," X said, "via Gertrude. Besides, Layth, there's a history of clergy supporting liberation movements. Think about the priests in Nazi-occupied Europe who helped smuggle refugees to freedom. Or the American churches that protected Latinx refugees from deportation."

"Catholic churches?" Layth asked.

X waved that away. "If you want to talk about the Catholic church, look at the autonomous Catholic Worker houses that campaigned against war and inequality for over a century. Or the liberation theology movement in Latin America! Priests like Archbishop Romero in El Salvador. Surely you know his story."

Layth sighed again and leaned back in his chair to indicate that he didn't. X leaned forward without breaking eye contact.

"In the nineteen-seventies, the country of El Salvador was ruled by a right-wing military government. Grassroots social movements were fighting for basic human rights: labor unions, accessible health care, and freedom of expression. US-backed death squads terrorized the poor and the left, imprisoning and torturing activists. One of the death squad leaders, trained by the US military, was nicknamed 'Blowtorch Bob'—do I need to explain how he got the name?"

"Please don't."

"Archbishop Romero spoke out against the death squads, called for compassion and relief for the poor. And people listened—he had a weekly radio show that was heard by half the country."

Layth raised an eyebrow. "So the death squads gave up?"

"In nineteen-eighty, Romero gave a speech calling on government soldiers to heed the will of Jesus Christ and respect human rights," X said. "Immediately afterward, he was assassinated in broad daylight by a US-backed death squad. A quarter of a million people attended his funeral. It was the largest demonstration in the country's history."

Layth let out a slow breath and stared at the ceiling for moment before he could look back at her. "And then things changed?"

"And then President Reagan sent the death squads more guns," replied X. "Were you hoping for an easy victory? Things got worse before they got better. But they did get better, slowly. Point is, it's dangerous to do the right thing, even as a priest. So you'd better keep this priest safe."

"What if it turns out we *can't* trust this priest?" Layth asked. "What if he turns out to be another infiltrator?"

"Then, *after consulting me*, ensure he can do our movement no harm," she replied. Layth was silent. "I'll take that as agreement."

Layth said nothing.

X stared at him for a long while. "We need to talk about what happened. About losing people."

"We don't need to talk about it," said Layth.

"He's dead, Layth. You'll have to accept that," she said. "It's thin comfort, but it's better to know, in a way. Someone I was very close to, a lover, went to prison many years ago. He languished there, and when things got rough, he was simply disappeared."

"I just want to get on with my next mission," he said without looking at her. "We can talk about our feelings after we win."

She sighed. "There are still people in this movement you care about, yes?" asked X. "So don't get reckless." She reached into a folder and handed him a map. "Don't let the priest out of your sight until he's delivered. Success is essential. But his request is unusual—and dangerous."

Layth shrugged. "Where do I meet him?"

—⁓

Adelaide switched the radio to something classical and settled into the library alcove that served as her map room. Visitors were often surprised that the Thistle had a map room. But to Adelaide it made perfect sense. What better way to be situated on land, to know it deeply, than to map out past, present, and future?

The main glass cabinet held archival surveys, charts of Indigenous language families—the world as it had been. There were maps of colonial expansion, terrain scattered with farmsteads, churches, and mills. Maps of the farm showing crop rotation and grazing plans back to the 1960s. Delicately folded soil maps of rocky highlands bounded by long belts of sandy loam and low, flat zones of rich clay, their details rendered obsolete by quarries.

There were maps of the Thistle, each building outlined in black, fields and pastures, fence lines, buried pipes and wires. Maps of the Thistle's regional allies and intern placement programs, hand-drawn overtop county roadmaps from the 2010s. Climate maps showing record temperature increases and uneven precipitation.

The wall *above* the cabinet contained Addy's attempt to compile a picture of the world as it had become—her cartography of the present, on three successive sliding cork panels. She flipped on a light to better see the maps as, outside, twilight faded to darkness.

The first panel held a world map, sparsely annotated. She had tried to record major events and border changes since the map's printing in 2025. In green ink were a swath of early food riots across Latin America and northern Africa, with subsequent riots encroaching into China and Eastern Europe.

The most up-to-date annotations—yellowed by a decade of aging—reported populist and fascist coups along with outbreaks and epidemics. "Borders sealed," she had noted on the fringes of China and the European Union. After that, news from far-flung places had become unreliable. Major independent news sources had been censored, shut down, or co-opted.

She turned up the radio—was that Stravinsky playing?—and slid the world map aside to access the second panel, a map of North America. This map was more up-to-date. The western coastal region was outlined in red, showing the borders of the Chinese Protectorate. An orange blob—a hand-drawn radiation symbol—obscured part of northern Alberta. The seceded states of Texas and Vermont, along with the former province of Quebec, were outlined in yellow. A few sovereign Indigenous communities and the independent Dakota territory were marked, as were a handful of UN peacekeeping bases that once dotted the eastern seaboard, though she doubted they were still present.

She slid the panel to the third map, a detailed rendering of the Great Lakes region along with the northeast (formerly united) states. A blob of red encompassed the core cities of the York Emergency Authority. Addy had drawn concentric dotted lines showing the expansion of the Authority's borders, documenting them as a physician might track the spread of sepsis. She also recorded the alignment of various municipalities and client cities under the sway of the Authority, along with skirmishes between YEA forces and local rebels. Most such flare-ups were short-lived, but a few lingering hot spots persisted.

Addy crossed her arms and stared, still contemplating this map, as a voice came over the radio. "You're listening to the official York Emergency Authority music channel, bringing you—" She reached out to tune the set to a different channel. But every station was either jammed, yielding only buzzing noise, or playing some official Authority broadcast.

She turned it off and went back to her map of the YEA front.

Some minutes later, Carlos walked in. "Ten years ago, the Emergency Authority was three hundred kilometers away," he observed. "Now they're triaging within fifty kilometers and making promises to landlords even closer." He shook his head and rubbed his bearded jaw. "How many drone overflights have there been in the last year alone? Lieutenant Dumont says the numbers have tripled."

"They must have half the city's garrison in the field to occupy so much territory," said Addy. "Obviously not afraid of an uprising at home."

"Maybe they're too desperate for food and charcoal to worry about resistance in the city," said Carlos. "At least they're still on the other side of the river."

Adelaide said nothing, just stared at the map, her eyes hooded.

"These rent conflicts will be the least of our problems," he said. "In a few years—maybe months—we'll have triage officers and soldiers in the village, or walking right up our driveway. What are we going to do then?"

—⫰

The old docks still stunk of diesel, though Layth doubted the fuel tanks had been used in twenty years. A dead complex of concrete silos and warehousing loomed in the evening smog, barely visible in the deep-blue light that penetrated the overcast sky. Layth squatted near a tangle of overturned shipping containers that had been rusting for nearly as long as he had been alive.

At the appointed time, he heard the scrape of paddles along gun-wales and a gentle swishing of water. He stood and stepped toward the icy dock. A moment later, he could see the canoe approaching, silent and dark, three shadows seated within. A figure at the bow grabbed the edge of the dock as they approached but did not tie up the boat up or step out—appropriately cautious in a city barely an hour from curfew.

The figure in the middle climbed from the canoe onto the dock. Shouldering a bag, he whispered a few words to the people who had delivered him. Then he approached Layth and held out a hand to shake.

"That'll give you away," said Layth, refusing the proffered hand. "Few here would offer to shake bare hands with a stranger."

The man lowered his hand and offered a slight smile instead, showing an even row of white teeth. "I am Father Silvio."

"Another bad habit," said Layth. "Don't introduce yourself to people you don't know. How do you know who I am?"

"You are Layth," said Father Silvio. "Archie, in the boat, told me so."

Layth inspected Silvio carefully. The priest was shorter than Layth and from his face presumably slim, though he looked well-rounded in several layers of warm clothing. Layth guessed that he was in his mid-forties, with dark eyes and weathered skin. The priest wore, as all of them did, a thin cloak of reflective, silvery polymer meant to frustrate infrared drone cameras.

"You're clean-shaven; that's another problem for your cover story," said Layth. "Come on, let's get you dressed." They headed into an abandoned warehouse as the canoe pushed off behind them. "We don't have much time before curfew. Do as I say and move quickly."

"I will do my best to follow your instructions," said Father Silvio. His speech had the precision of a well-educated person who had learned English as a second language, with just a hint of a Spanish accent.

Inside the warehouse Layth led Silvio through a dark and cavernous space. The floors were littered with the splinters of shipping pallets, the pallets themselves having long ago been broken up and burned as fuel. They entered a small room where Layth had stowed several bags and a battery-operated lamp. He clicked on the lamp and took a closer look at Silvio's clothing. It was dark and dignified, though without an obvious priest's collar. That was something, at least. The man wore a thick black coat. "Is this wool?" asked Layth, pinching the material.

"Alpaca," Silvio replied. "It was a gift from my parish on my departure for the cold northern climates."

Layth inspected the coat briskly and pulled a small black rectangle from one pocket. "A phone? Are you joking?"

"It's off," protested Silvio, "I thought—"

"What you thought doesn't matter," said Layth. "They consider any phone without their spyware installed to be a foreign cyberwarfare device. The YEA can track any wireless signal that reaches over a kilometer. They shut down internet access and open cell networks years ago. You use this, they'll find you in minutes and make you *wish* you were in a triage camp."

"I see," said Silvio.

"Don't use their phones, either. You won't be allowed one in the camp, and even if you could find one, it would be tapped. They have a supercomputer that scans every communication for subversive content. As for the coat, it's no good," added Layth, to Silvio's obvious surprise and disappointment. "It doesn't match your cover story. Too new. Too clean. Too . . . nice. Same for your shoes, your hat. I need to you take those off. Actually, take everything off."

Silvio sighed, but then obediently stripped in the frigid air. In a few moments he was in his underwear, standing on a pile of his own clothes so as not to step on the freezing, grimy floor.

Layth sighed. "Even your underwear looks brand new."

"I have had this for many years," said Silvio, crossing his arms over his chest and shivering slightly. But Layth shook his head.

"Elastic band is still stretchy. Dead giveaway." Layth found an appropriately aged and threadbare set of socks and underclothes in one of his bags. The priest changed reluctantly as Layth looked away.

Layth assembled a new outfit for the priest, mixing clothing he had brought with the priest's own articles. He allowed the priest to keep his own dark sweater but rubbed it on the floor until it was thoroughly soiled. A pair of well-worn sneakers, a hole in the left toe, replaced the priest's shiny leather shoes; a dingy hoodie and jean-jacket combo substituted for the alpaca coat. Even Silvio's dark hat was exchanged for a woven acrylic toque that was slowly but obviously unraveling.

"Perfect," said Layth as he took in the new ensemble. "You'll fit right in. Now let's go. It's forty-five minutes to curfew, and we're in the wrong part of the city."

⚓

Evelyn was still dazed from the afternoon's events when she reached her apartment complex that evening. A smoggy orange sunset silhouetted the high-rise towers and the clusters of antennae atop them. On the nearest roof she saw a YEA sniper looking over the edge, smoking a cigarette.

Authority guards clustered around the door to her building, ready for shift change. Their uniforms were not new but had been neatly patched. These men were responsible for guarding and maintaining the nest of telecom gear—jamming, transmission, and listening antennae—atop Evelyn's building. Unlike low-level armbands, they wore thick overcoats with embroidered Armor Security logos. Evelyn slipped past them without making eye contact and entered her building.

Once inside, Evelyn heard YEA radio playing in the lobby. "A rebel town surrendered to Authority forces this afternoon after a prolonged battle that began when terrorists attacked a charcoal convoy. The battle left twelve people dead, but the surrender is expected to relieve high charcoal prices.

"And two apartment buildings were quarantined today after yet another outbreak of antibiotic-resistant staphylococcus. Officer of Public Health Todd Buchanan blames the outbreak on rampant use of black-market antibiotics by residents of the buildings. 'People have to understand that there are consequences for using dangerous contraband drugs,' he explained. 'It's everyone's duty to report illness or signs of drug trafficking.' The quarantine is expected to last for several months."

The lobby was tidy and well kept, if dim in the light of flickering fluorescents. Old layers of paint—once a cheerful spring green—

flaked from the walls, but any loose bits had been swept up and disposed of. The yellowing tiles of the floor were chipped, and several were missing, but the floor itself had been recently mopped. A bulletin board with community notices—neatly arranged messages and requests for blankets and batteries—hung on the wall between the elevator doors and the stairwell. Evelyn could see a note addressed to her from her downstairs neighbor, Mrs. Schmidt, who often enlisted Evelyn's help in filling out health-care fee waiver request forms. Evelyn tucked the note into her pocket.

The only graffiti in the lobby was on the large, yellowing Third Pandemic Act poster. Someone had scratched at the heading "Pandemic" until only the letters "Pan ic" remained. Where large print warned that gatherings of more than eight people were forbidden, someone had added "unless they are asshole cops." The graffiti's creativity diminished from there.

Evelyn walked past the elevators and into the stairwell. She lived on the twelfth floor, but elevators were strictly for YEA guards. When she was six floors up, she heard the rumble of the elevator as the night shift ascended to their rooftop post. As she passed the eighth floor, she heard someone strumming away on a guitar with a broken string.

When she stepped out onto her own floor, she sighed heavily and began to relax for the first time in hours. She unlocked her apartment and stepped in. Compact fluorescent bulbs flickered overhead, their fixtures damaged by prolonged brownouts. "Hello?" she called.

She heard tiny footfalls, and a little boy came careening around a corner, flinging himself into her arms. "Evelyn!" he yelled excitedly.

She lifted him up and spun him around a few times, smiling widely. "How was your day, Sid?" she asked.

"We harvested carrots!" he said, grinning back. He had missing baby teeth where his adult teeth were coming in.

A woman followed him into view. "We didn't harvest them, Sid," she said. "We just took them out of the cold cellar. Hello, roomie." She kissed Evelyn warmly on the lips and they embraced, all three of them holding close.

"I hate it when you call me that," said Evelyn, smiling into Sara's hair.

As they hugged, Sara felt the tears in the back of Evelyn's coat. She pulled away, her face concerned. "What happened to your jacket?"

Evelyn lost her smile. "Incident at a surprise checkpoint today. They were searching everyone and some guy freaked out and"—she glanced at Sid and then spelled the word—"s-h-o-t some guards."

Sara's eyes widened. "Oh my god. Are you okay?"

"I'm fine," said Evelyn. "Shaken up. It was a heck of a day. I just need a glass of water."

"The water is rustier than usual," said Sara. "Take your shoes off and sit down, and Sid will get me that cider from the fridge." Sid opened the sliding door onto the balcony, which required his full strength. On the chilly cement of the balcony were several bags of carrots, a few jars of kimchi and pickled vegetables, and a plastic jug of apple cider. Sid picked up the jug of cider, slid the door shut, and handed the bottle to Sara. Sara sniffed it, shrugged, and poured some of it into a saucepan to heat on the electric stove. Evelyn sat on the couch, Sid by her side, and recounted what had happened at the checkpoint, mouthing certain words so that Sid couldn't hear.

Sara sat down next to Evelyn and caressed her arm gently. "I'm so sorry you saw that, baby. I'm glad you're all right."

"That's not even the weirdest thing that happened," said Evelyn. "I got stuck in the checkpoint because I was being transferred to Triage Administration."

Sara's hand froze, and her body stiffened. "What?"

"Yeah," said Evelyn. "Complete surprise. I didn't get the promotion—not enough funding. So they sent me over to Triage. And I have to say, those people are really nice. Made me feel at home. Nice warm building, well lit . . ."

"Evelyn, don't you know what they *do*?" asked Sara, her brow furrowed in concern and disbelief.

Evelyn frowned. "They keep disease from spreading. They give people medicine. They take care of sick people."

"They also quarantine people who don't want to cooperate with the Authority," replied Sara. "Who do you think pays collection bounties to the security franchises?"

"Sure, the triage system is flawed." Evelyn shrugged. "But if the people who work there are more compassionate, the system will be more compassionate. We can't fix problems by just complaining about them. We've got to fix them from the inside. Where do you want me to work?"

Sara was shaking her head. "You don't understand. The rumors about what they do in that building . . . They *change* people."

"They aren't going to change me, Sara."

"That's not what I mean," said Sara. "They change people's *minds*, they alter their . . ." She trailed off as she glanced at Sid. "These people, the system they run, it's monstrous."

"Sara, they aren't *monsters*," said Evelyn. "The cafeteria serves albacore and chocolate pudding! The water is clear, and the pressure is great. And they dress classy, almost retro. Like it's the forties."

"Obviously," said Sara.

"No, the *nineteen*-forties," Evelyn said. "Rumors aside, we need more money to take care of Sid. He needs better rations, he needs fresh fruit, he needs—"

There was a loud knock on the door. "Public safety!"

Sara and Evelyn stared at each other in surprise. Sid started to say something, but Sara cut him off. "Go play in your room," she said firmly.

Evelyn went to the door and looked through the eyehole. An Armor Security guard with blue gloves and a white face mask was standing at their door along with the building superintendent. Evelyn opened the door halfway but stood squarely in the gap. She was not offering an invitation.

The guard spoke first. "Ma'am, our chemical tests show traces of illegal drugs in this building. Do you know anything about that?"

Evelyn left her face a neutral mask. "I haven't heard anything about that."

"We have positive tests on sewage from this building. One or more people are using illegal drugs. We don't overlook that sort of thing, ma'am."

The superintendent interrupted in a slurring British accent. "I won't have people using illicit drugs here. This is a clean building. No drugs." He seemed slightly drunk and unaware of the irony. "Ask her roommate."

Sara appeared at Evelyn's shoulder. "Is there a problem?"

"Ma'am, the superintendent tells us you give people medications. Herbal medications. Is that true?"

Sara was nonchalant. "Mint tea for a cough. Aloe for a burned hand. Nothing pharmaceutical. Can I ask what drugs you found?"

"Metabolites of tetracycline. Ciprofloxacin. Strictly regulated antibiotics," said the guard. "Under the Third Pandemic Act I have a right to search suspicious residences. Would I find anything untoward if I were to do a search?"

"Nothing but a messy kitchen," Sara replied.

"Well, I might just have a look all the same," said the guard.

But the superintendent shook his head and pointed to his watch. "It's almost evening power-down. I pay a fortune on these winter nights if things run late."

The guard shrugged. "If you see anything suspicious, you be sure to let us know." The two women nodded. The guard and superintendent left.

Evelyn shut the door; they returned to the couch and took each other's hands. Sara was frowning, shaking her head. "That superintendent needs to shut the fuck up. Bringing guards here—what an asshole!"

"It's just a random check," said Evelyn. "They can't monitor every building's plumbing for antibiotics all the time."

"Maybe," said Sara dubiously.

"You'll have to tell Mrs. Schmidt to use the composting toilet," Evelyn said, "until her lung infection clears up."

"I *did* tell her," said Sara. "But she has trouble walking outside in winter. Maybe we can set up a sawdust bucket toilet in her apartment."

Sid emerged from his room. "Evelyn, will you read to me?"

Evelyn nodded. "Get your pajamas on and pick a book. We only have a few minutes before lights out."

⚯

"Why must we walk so far?" Father Silvio asked Layth as they trudged along a dim waterfront path.

"The city is divided into zones with different security levels and contractors doing enforcement," said Layth. "We need to get you to the right zone *without* hitting any checkpoints along the way."

"This zone has many Spanish-speaking Catholics?"

"This company's specialty is a Spanish-speaking, err, workforce," replied Layth.

"And the companies control movement and economics in each zone?"

Layth nodded, adjusting the hood of his anti-IR cloak to better conceal his face from the sky. "It's like a franchise."

"It sounds more like a fiefdom," answered Silvio.

"I guess that's for you to decide," said Layth. "Is this very different from where you come from?"

"Oh yes," Silvio replied. "Very different."

This, Layth decided, was the moment to probe for truthfulness, or perhaps for some mental illness, behind Silvio's reckless plan. "Tell me about where you're from," Layth suggested.

"It is very beautiful and warm," Silvio replied. "Never cold like this. Food grows through the entire year."

"Sounds like everyone is well fed."

"Oh, there has been hunger everywhere, but we have done no worse than anyone these past years."

A vague non-answer. Layth wanted to elicit a more concrete response. "So, I would guess that you're from Ecuador? Or Puerto Rico, maybe."

Silvio chuckled apologetically. "I have been told to not be too specific about my life and home, for safety. My trainers, they call it 'security culture.'"

"No doubt," said Layth. "Your trainers were from the Church?" Silvio was silent. "Did your ship depart from Havana?"

Silvio made a very ambiguous-sounding *mmm* noise.

"What kind of ship was it?"

"A sailing ship," answered Silvio. "A very beautiful one."

Layth knew for a fact that Silvio had not *arrived* on a sailing ship. "Oh, how many masts?"

"My life in the church has not given me the nautical experience to understand ship design," Silvio replied. *Bullshit*, Layth thought to himself. But he changed topic.

"Don't broadcast that you're from so far south," Layth advised. "The fear of tropical disease here is extreme. If anyone asks, claim to have arrived a long time ago. And for god's sake, don't tell anyone you're a Catholic priest; there are evangelical gangs in the camps."

"Under duress, I will claim to be an agricultural worker, brought in before the borders closed," Silvio said with certainty.

Layth wanted to ask more, but clearly Silvio had been instructed to stay tight-lipped. Besides, they had almost reached their target zone. They turned away from the water and paused in a shadowed doorway. Layth faced the priest. "Silvio, you don't have to take this risk. You can't understand what happens in this zone. Urban mining, hazardous-waste reclamation. There are safer ways to get information."

"It's not just information, Layth," Silvio said. "There are people suffering here, and it is my duty to minister to them."

Layth just nodded. "You'll go through this door and turn left," he said. "There's a permanent checkpoint a hundred meters down the road. Just before the checkpoint, there's a redbrick alley on the right. Go into the alley and wait."

Silvio took a deep breath and nodded. "Thank you, Layth."

Layth checked his watch. "Almost curfew. Go now."

Silvio walked through the door and turned left. Layth counted to twenty in his head and followed.

—⚓

Addy stayed in the map room for some time after Carlos had gone out to do his evening chores. She was still staring at maps, well after sunset, when the electric lights abruptly went out. Addy cursed and looked out the window. The whole farmstead was dark. The problem must be at the generator.

She walked downstairs through the kitchen, where a dozen people had been holding a meal-planning meeting before the lights had gone. "I'll check it," she said.

Addy put on her coat and boots, grabbed a windup flashlight, and left the farmhouse. The air was chilly, but the full moon offered some light, illuminating the old mural of a flowering pink thistle on the barn. She walked to the stream and followed it downhill. The heart of the farm was the shallow valley bisected by this creek. On the east side of the creek were farmhouses, a greenhouse, the common hall topped with solar panels, cabins, barns, a root cellar, the militia's small armory, gardens, cropland, forest, and the only access road. On the west side were forest, pasture, hayfield, and the quarry precipice.

Addy reached the bottom of the little valley, where the creek trickled into a small pond. The water level was visibly low; precipitation had been short all year. A few ducks sat near the edge, but the pond itself was thinly frozen over, a round black mirror. She paused for a moment to gaze into it but could not see the bottom.

A buried pipe four inches in diameter ran from that pond, down the steep cliff where farm gave way to the void of the quarry, and through a micro–hydro generator shed at the bottom of the cliff. Addy stared down toward the shed, its roof gleaming faintly in the moonlight, and then carefully began to descend the stairs and ladders that would bring her, ledge by icy ledge, to the bottom.

The generating station was a small shack on a ledge about ten feet above the water level of the quarry. Addy entered the chilly structure. Batteries were stacked on shelves against each wall. Most were very old and had been repaired many times, their failed or damaged cells neatly bypassed with copper wire. There were golf cart batteries, RV batteries, even a few deep-cycle batteries being used for their intended purpose.

The ramshackle system was undamaged, but a voltage gauge showed the battery bank was almost completely drained; their large inverter had shut itself off. The Thistle didn't have an electrical surplus in the winter; short days meant people were inside in the evenings, using lights, stereos, sewing machines, and soldering guns. Their patchwork battery bank just didn't have the storage capacity for the number of people who now lived at the Thistle.

Most of their winter power came from a micro-hydro machine in the shed that was, at that moment, ominously silent and still. A small waterwheel and a nozzle—like something from the end of a fire hose—sat inside a frosty translucent box.

When the water was flowing, the nozzle sprayed and propelled the wheel at several hundred rotations per minute, spinning an attached generator. Instead, Addy saw a thick encrustation of ice around the end of the nozzle, obstructing it completely. To avoid draining the low levels in the pond reservoir, someone had turned down the flow rate; apparently they had overcompensated.

Adelaide opened the box and spent a few moments clearing the ice by whacking it with a wrench. She opened the flow valve to full, but the water in the nozzle was still frozen. "My kingdom for a blow torch," she muttered to herself.

She found the stub of candle in one corner of the shed, then drew a stainless-steel lighter from her pocket and lit the candle. Carefully, Addy placed the candle directly beneath the bronze nozzle, so that the tip of the flame just touched it.

And then she tucked her hands into her pockets, hunched her shoulders, and waited.

The checkpoint was well illuminated under the dark sky. A humming generator powered high-intensity floodlights. A short distance in front of Layth, Silvio was a black silhouette approaching those lights. Just before Silvio reached the gate of the checkpoint, the man turned to the right, ducking into a dead-end alley.

Layth continued to walk up to the razor-wire-topped gate. His heart thumped loudly in his chest. The scuff of his shoes on the pavement sounded awkward, abrasive, amplified.

A blue-gloved guard called out to him. "It's almost curfew. What's your business?"

Layth's mouth felt dry and cottony. "There's a suspicious man lurking around," he said, pointing to the entrance of the alley. "I think he might be trying to sneak around the checkpoint."

Moments later, the gate opened, and three guards rushed out, rifles in hand. They approached the mouth of the alley with guns raised. One entered, and then two. Layth heard shouting.

Shortly, they emerged with Silvio handcuffed and held between them. Silvio did not make eye contact with Layth as he was manhandled into the guardhouse. "Thanks for the vigilance!" a guard said. "But there's no reward unless he has a warrant."

"Just being a good citizen," answered Layth. And then he turned and walked swiftly back the way that he had come. Behind him, the heavy door of the guardhouse slammed shut.

—✐

"I froze my butt off watching that candle for fifteen minutes," Addy told Carlos in the faint glow of their bedside lamp, "until finally the water started to trickle. A few minutes later, the ice was cleared, and the waterwheel was at full speed."

"We'll have to switch between shutting the water off and running it at full speed," said Carlos, "to keep this from happening again." Addy nodded.

"I hope this doesn't come across the wrong way," Carlos continued, "but I'm proud of you for becoming so involved and capable on the farm. When you first arrived, you were so withdrawn. You barely knew how to turn a wrench. Now look at you! You're one of our handiest mechanics, not to mention a great organizer."

"Thanks," she said flatly.

He squinted at her. "What's that look? I don't mean to come across as patronizing or anything, I just—"

"No," she said. "I appreciate it." She kissed him and then turned out the light.

—✐

"Well," said Layth, "the plan worked perfectly."

"He was captured in the appropriate zone?" asked X.

"The successful execution of a terrible plan," Layth replied.

"Even our allies barely believe reports from the triage camps," said X. "Firsthand information is the only way to convince them. He volunteered. It was his idea."

"If they're going to risk using the water route, why not send us something more useful than a single martyr?"

"They send us plenty of supplies," answered X, "as you know. Look, Layth, I know you've been having a hard time lately. When we lose someone close to us . . ." She sighed. "When you're ready to talk about it, I—"

"I appreciate the gesture, X," he said. "But I don't need this right now. I can't . . ." He trailed off and then shook his head once, sharply. "I can't. I don't need therapy, I need work."

"It would be pretty therapeutic to put a bullet in the director of Triage Administration," said X. "Justice is good for the soul, and he's been on my personal shit list for decades."

"If I had the connections," answered Layth, "I would. But right now, I just need my next mission."

X nodded slowly, scratching at the scar over her left eyebrow. "There's always another mission. Check some of the Samizdata branches. We're desperate for new info and new safe houses right now."

"Samizdata," repeated Layth. "New safe houses. Got it."

4

2028

"We spent half an hour crammed in the back of the cop car," said Taavi, "all three of us. And they didn't even charge us with anything!"

"That's good, at least," said Apollo.

"It's such bullshit!" said Andy. "It's just harassment."

"Yeah, it is." Apollo nodded. Four of them sat on the back porch of the community house where Apollo lived. Bicycles were piled against a nearby fence, and chickens scratched at the long, green grass of the suburban backyard.

"They asked us all kinds of questions," said Samantha. "It was an interrogation."

"Yeah," said Taavi. "'Who came with you to the protest? Did you bring weapons? Do you have weapons at home?' But we didn't say anything except name, address, birthdate."

"Good for you," said Apollo. "You did the right thing. Stayed strong."

"They asked about you," said Andy. "Like, 'Did Apollo Papachronis tell you to come here? What did he tell you to do?'"

Apollo rubbed his tattooed forearm and nodded slowly. "Interesting. Thanks for letting me know."

"Weirdly, they left us all together when they weren't questioning us," said Taavi, "instead of keeping us separate."

"Maybe they wanted to hear what we would say," said Samantha, adjusting her thick-rimmed eyeglasses. "Eavesdrop."

Apollo looked thoughtful, then concluded: "I'm glad you're fine. But keep your eyes open. They may pick you out, give you more attention in future. Which reminds me: Are you coming to the IRI town hall next week?"

53

The others exchanged looks of skepticism. Andy said, "That's not really our thing, Apollo."

"I think you should go," said Apollo. "I'm on the panel. It's important that we show the colors, you know? Remind people there are radical alternatives—possibilities for action, and not just business as usual."

"Yeeeeah," said Taavi with reluctance. "But it's boring. People always complain about how the government doesn't listen. What do they expect?"

"Plus," said Samantha, "it's silly to put out these little declarations and pleas and whatever. The rich want to turn the whole planet into McDonald's and open-pit mines. Why pretend the state and corporations are reasonable?"

"So don't pretend that!" said Apollo. "Be radical. But radical movements can still march and wave signs. Look at the Black Panthers."

Sam's eyes brightened. She pulled a thick book from her bag; the cover bore an image of Black women and men in leather jackets and dark berets, fists raised.

"The Black Panthers were amazing," Sam enthused, looking between Taavi and Andy. "They weren't afraid of the police. They fought White supremacy in the nineteen-sixties, when they were denied jobs and basic health care, their communities attacked by cops. They defended against policy brutality and ran kitchens to feed people, and their people supported them."

"Sam's right," said Apollo, a hint of pride in his voice. "If you reach out, you can make the community understand."

"That's different," said Taavi. Apollo raised a questioning eyebrow, and Taavi continued. "The Black Panthers were fighting for *their* community. They all knew racism was harmful. That's different from stopping capitalism or fossil fuels. People at the march today want to stop the tank farm in their backyard, because it affects them personally. But they don't care about abolishing the police or capitalism."

"They *like* capitalism," said Andy. "Even though it's ruining the planet, even though climate disasters are destroying poor countries where brown people live."

"Because *they* don't feel the bad impacts," added Taavi.

Sam reached excitedly into her bag to pull out another thick volume.

Andy rolled his eyes. "More books?"

"Bring the war home!" Sam exclaimed. She passed the book to Andy. "The Weather Underground was a White organization that existed at the same time as the Black Panthers. They fought racism and the war in Vietnam. But most White people didn't care about the war, because it was killing Brown people. So, the Weather Underground decided to 'bring the war home' and blow up things here, like banks and government buildings." Taavi's eyes widened, and she clarified: "They weren't trying to kill people, they just blew up empty buildings."

"To make privileged people understand the impact the war was having overseas," Apollo added, "that America was killing hundreds of thousands of innocent Vietnamese civilians."

Andy frowned. "You can't make a bunch of middle-class people understand something they don't want to."

"You can make connections," said Apollo. "Look, you know the project I'm working on: we're connecting local environmental movements, like the tank-farm campaign, to Indigenous land defenders around the world. We funnel money from people with privilege to the front lines. We've raised nearly a hundred thousand dollars. By the end of the year, we could raise half a million."

"Wow!" said Taavi, genuinely impressed.

Sam looked at the book in her hand. "When the Black Panthers raised a lot of money, the government attacked them, tried to split them up and shut them down."

Apollo nodded. "The government is pissed. One bank already kicked us out, so we started using cryptocurrency for transfers."

"Is that even legal?" asked Andy.

Apollo laughed. "Point is, you have to connect small struggles like the tank farm with bigger struggles like pipeline construction on Indigenous territory. You have to knit different movements together. The government might hate you, they might—they *will*—attack you," Apollo promised. "But if you work together, they can't *stop* you."

The high school gymnasium was crowded with people the following Tuesday. They stood or sat in rows of folding chairs, their overlapping conversations filling the gym with chatter. Along one side were tables with folding displays and literature from a dozen grassroots environmental groups and nonprofits. At the front, on a stage of portable risers, stood a long table with a half dozen microphones and glasses of water. Behind the stage, two women conferred.

"Where's Apollo?" asked Helen. "He's the only panelist who's late. I talked to him after the protest march, and he promised to come."

"You two have a fight or something?" Gwen asked slyly. "Aren't you still flirting with radicalism?"

Helen rolled her eyes in mock exasperation. "I called him twice. No answer."

Gwen checked her watch and shrugged. "He must be running on anarchist time."

"Well, the room is full, and it's ten past," said Helen, patting her own hips with nervous energy. "We've got to start."

"I'll introduce y'all," said Gwen. Helen took a seat on the stage beside Tom, who was wearing a *Solidarity Forever* T-shirt. Gwen stepped to the mic. "Hi, everybody," she said over the murmur of the crowd. People began to settle and take their seats. "Good evening, all."

"Hi, Gwen!" shouted a voice from the crowd. There was general chuckling.

Tom leaned toward Helen and whispered, "The crowd really loves her, eh?" Helen nodded and shuffled her notes.

Gwen smiled at the crowd. "Thanks, everyone, for coming tonight. I'm Gwendolyn Gibson." There was a smattering of applause. "Thank you. I'm here to introduce our panel tonight. They'll have some things to say, we'll have a chance for questions, and then we'll all talk about what ought to be done. Okay?" The crowd murmured its assent. Gwen gestured toward the panelists.

"Elijah Freeman, doctoral candidate in environmental remediation and all-around snappy dresser." Polite applause. Somewhere in the audience, a phone chimed, and then another.

"Folks, I'm gonna need you to turn off your cell phones," said Gwen, "or at least put them on vibrate. Next up, Tom Billingsley, a union rep who understands that jobs don't matter without a decent planet to put them on." Applause. Elijah's phone vibrated, and he looked at the screen.

"Helen Kasym, coordinator of Friends of the Watershed and one hell of a gal." Applause. Elijah scribbled a note on a piece of paper and slid it down the table.

"Teresa Brant, community organizer, Mohawk, and survivor of the first petrol-depot leak—you all may know her dad, in the front row in his wheelchair." Extra applause. Helen read the note: *Apollo arrested plus three others. Maybe more. Terrorism charges.* The word "terrorism" was double-underlined. Several more phones rang in the crowd.

"And we're eagerly awaiting the arrival of Apollo Papachronis, experienced rabble-rouser and veteran organizer."

∽—

Taavi, Samantha, and Andy, in the audience, were growing annoyed at Apollo's absence. "*He* asked *us* to come here," Andy whispered, "and then didn't show up? Come on, man."

"Shhh," said Samantha, "they're trying to introduce people."

Taavi's phone buzzed in his pocket. He pulled it out, hoping for a message from Apollo. Instead, he got a text message *about* Apollo. He stared at it in shock. "Apollo's late because he's been *arrested.*" Taavi showed the phone to Sam and Andy, and they began a whispered conversation about what to do. Their whispers were lost among a growing hubbub in the room.

Gwen was asking the crowd for patience. "Folks, there have been some unexpected events. If you could bear with us for a moment, we'll get things sorted out."

Taavi, Samantha, and Andy stood and walked out of the gymnasium. Apollo's community house was five minutes away by foot. Once outside the school, they started running.

∽—

Dee surveyed the large, open room. Its décor was eclectic, mixing a century of different styles. Some walls were redbrick, others plaster and lath. The ceiling was panelled in ornamental tin. Dee photographed everything.

"As you can see," said the real estate agent, "the building has a lot of character. This aesthetic is very popular among urbanites and young people." He added, with a hesitant smile, "As I'm sure you know."

He walked through the middle of the space, gesturing. "It *was* an upscale clothing boutique, but with the economy, well, you know. Plenty of room for tables or retail shelving. There's a small kitchen in the back the previous tenants didn't use, but the owner wouldn't consent to renovations." He added in a stage whisper: "Never sure they would make it, you see." He showed her the kitchen, the bathroom, storage spaces.

"Back door here for deliveries and staff. Second floor is office space—usually rented along with this retail space. And two more floors of apartments."

"Occupied?" asked Dee, a question she knew the answer to.

"Empty," said the agent. "Owner hasn't been able to keep the retail space filled. And with longtime renters he was barely making any money from the apartments. He kicked out the tenants so he could do some renovations and bring in new tenants. But he hasn't been to *finish* the renos he started up there. Money trouble."

"What with the economy and all," finished Dee.

"Exactly," said the agent with exaggerated empathy. "As you can imagine, he's in a hurry to fill this storefront. We can price it in a range your family will find quite appealing."

Dee nodded and looked around. "How about a discount to rent the whole building, apartments included?"

The agent gave her a sly smile, as if they were enjoying a private joke. "I'm not used to teenagers wheeling and dealing! Why don't you have some *older* members of your family come and take a look at the place? I'm sure the photos you've taken will pique their interest."

"Most of my family is still home in India," she lied blithely. "But they're looking to do more business overseas. They've asked me to keep my eyes open for suitable accommodation, which of course they would want to arrange before relocating."

"Of course," said the agent, a new glint in his eyes. "Well, let's take a look upstairs."

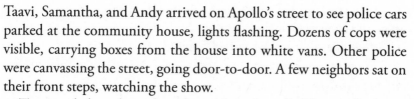

Taavi, Samantha, and Andy arrived on Apollo's street to see police cars parked at the community house, lights flashing. Dozens of cops were visible, carrying boxes from the house into white vans. Other police were canvassing the street, going door-to-door. A few neighbors sat on their front steps, watching the show.

Taavi and the others slowed to a casual stroll. They walked past the end of the street, once, to examine the scene from a distance. Then Taavi and Andy hung back while Samantha talked to one of the neighbors, someone she recognized.

Sam returned a few minutes later. "Cops showed up this morning. Arrested people in the house. They're going door-to-door asking questions. Like, *Did you see anything suspicious at that house? Did you see people going out at odd hours? Did you see people carrying strange packages?*"

Taavi sighed angrily. "There's a hundred neighbors. Someone will say yes no matter what, and they'll report that shit on the news. The other neighbors will think they've been living next to terrorists."

They heard a sharp whistle. They looked for its source and spotted a black-clad man behind a hedge, beckoning to them. They walked over.

"Hey punks," he greeted them. Corben was a recent addition to Newbrook's radical scene, a thirtysomething who frequented punk shows and protests. "You been watching long?" They shook their heads no. "I've been watching all day. Came down to visit Apollo, and there were pigs crawling all over."

"Did you see the arrests?" asked Taavi.

"Nah, that had already happened," said Corben, glancing around the side of the hedge. "You know why they got arrested?"

"News says terrorism," said Andy. "No details. Apollo missed the town hall meeting."

"Yeah, this sucks," said Corben. "Me and Apollo were tight, right?"

They nodded. "You guys better get out of here; place is crawling with cops."

Corben walked away. Taavi, Samantha, and Andy set off in their own direction.

"What are we going to do?" asked Taavi as they walked.

"We've got to push back," said Andy. "Hit *them* where it hurts. Show the cops we won't tolerate this bullshit."

"What does that mean?" asked Taavi.

"Let's go spray-paint the cop shop," said Andy. "Give them a nice big 'fuck you' in five-foot letters."

Samantha shook her head. "The police station is covered in cameras. They'll see us in a second."

"We could find a police car at a coffee shop," said Taavi. "When they get out for some Boston creams, spray it quick, run off."

"But we could wait all night for the right moment," said Samantha, "and there are witnesses at a coffee shop."

"Screw that shit," said Andy. "Let's just go where they park."

"They have cameras at the police station parking lot, too," said Taavi.

"No, listen," said Andy, "there's a garage down the street from my dad's house. It's where they send cop cars to get repaired. There's two or three cop cars all the time and the fence is, like, super old and rusty. We could get in, no problem."

"Awesome," said Samantha. "So when do we do it?"

"Tonight," said Taavi. "We do it tonight."

≻

"It's important to not panic," said Gwen as she stood in Helen's living room. "We don't know what's going on. We don't know why Apollo and those other young people were arrested. We shouldn't act rashly."

Helen nodded. "Let's not rush into anything that would make things worse."

"I don't know," said Tom, frowning. "Terrorism and money laundering? Those charges look really bad. Apollo came to our meetings. He spoke at events with us. What will supporters think when they read about this?"

"I hear you," said Helen. "But we've known Apollo for years. He's a serious community organizer. He wasn't laundering money, he was fundraising for land defenders. This is an attempt to discredit him. There's no real substance behind it."

"It doesn't *matter* whether there's substance," said Tom. "You saw what happened at the town hall. We didn't get anything done after people realized we were short one speaker because he got *arrested by a counterterrorism squad.*"

"If it's an attempt to discredit him, it's working," said Teresa. "And it's working to discredit us, too."

"We should issue a statement," said Tom. "Distance ourselves from Papachronis. We don't endorse his arrest, but make it clear he was only a minor part of this group."

"But he *does* have an important role," said Elijah. "An essential role. It's a matter of solidarity. If we distance ourselves we'll be seen as backing down, which we can't afford."

"We can't afford *not* to," replied Tom. "We can't be seen supporting a suspected terrorist. What will my union's rank and file will think? I support community struggles, but I've got to protect the integrity of my union so we can protect our members."

"You won't protect them by giving in to scare tactics," said Elijah. "Listen, there's nothing new about these tricks. Those in power used to do the same thing to people like you. A hundred years ago, the government accused union organizers of being 'foreign agitators' because they were fighting for the eight-hour day. They put union organizers like the Wobblies in prison camps or had them deported. In the fifties, when unions fought for safer working conditions, the government called them communists!"

"That's completely different," said Tom. "We were fighting for our rights, not breaking the law."

"But they *did* break the law in fighting for their rights," said Elijah, his voice rising. That's how we *get* rights! Listen, in the eighties, your union backed the South African Congress of Trade Unions and the African National Congress in their fight against White supremacy, against apartheid. It's in the archives at the university—you donated funds, you went to rallies, you boycotted South African corporations."

"Nelson Mandela was a hero," Tom answered.

"Who defied the law! When nonviolent activism was supressed by the government, Mandela shifted underground, built an armed wing of his party, began a campaign of sabotage!" Elijah was almost shouting, as if though the force of his voice he could make Tom understand. "They called him a terrorist to make people afraid. To drive groups and unions away from supporting liberation. To try to make you back down!"

"But we didn't back down," Tom protested, balling up his hands in frustration. "Hell, when the ANC office in Toronto was set on fire, the postal union gave them office space."

"Exactly!" said Elijah. "So why are you backing down now?"

Tom leaned forward. "Look, terrorism is just not—"

Gwen interrupted, raising her hands in a *let's calm down* gesture. "We're getting ahead of ourselves," she said.

"Yes," agreed Helen. "Ignore the rumors; he's been arrested for what, eight hours? He hasn't been formally charged with anything. He hasn't been to a courtroom. We won't know until tomorrow what charges are actually filed."

"Maybe," said Tom, "but when the newspaper comes out tomorrow morning, it'll be full of articles linking Papachronis to our committee, our nonprofits, our unions, our fight against the tank farm, *and* opposition to IRI. That's going to look terrible. Helen, you're the one who always says we have to get in front of things instead of being reactive. So, let's do that!"

Helen took a deep breath. "Okay, people. Who would support issuing a statement *today* distancing ourselves from Apollo?" Immediately Tom raised his hand, and Teresa raised her hand a moment later and waggled it, half-certain. "Two people," said Helen. "Who would prefer to wait until we know more?" She raised her hand, and so did Gwen and Elijah. "Well, there it is. We wait."

"This could be a big mistake," warned Tom.

"Maybe," said Gwen, "but for now, I'm more worried about how Apollo and the others are coping."

~

The first hours after capture are critical, Dee read. *In this time, either the prisoner of war will use his training and moral fortitude to establish a firm line of resistance against the captor, or he will begin to crumble. The prisoner must immediately establish a refusal to cooperate with the enemy, including a refusal to give information and a refusal of special privileges not offered to other prisoners. If the POW fails to establish this precedent immediately after capture, he will lose his self-respect and leverage. The captor will identify him as a weak link, encouraging future mistreatment.*

Dee did not usually read training manuals for POWs. She was, after all, extremely cautious and had no intention of getting caught. But the flurry of arrests in nearby Newbrook was unnerving, especially when her network of recruits was expanding so rapidly. So, while she waited for the real estate agent to draft rental papers for the building, she browsed the old manual from a hidden, encrypted partition on her tablet.

The prisoner above all must remember that he is in the right, the text continued. *Captors will do everything possible to weaken the physical, emotional, and mental state of the prisoner. The shock of capture makes these efforts most effective in the first few days. If the prisoner can maintain his strength for that period, he will find that his trials may get easier. Or, at least, he will find himself psychologically grounded and better equipped to deal with mistreatment.*

The first news articles had come out earlier in the evening, cobbled together from police statements and social-media photographs. Dee wondered how many cops, court officials, intelligence officers, and dispatchers had to be involved in these simultaneous arrests. The news claimed more than sixty officers participated in the arrests; so probably more than a hundred people were involved. How could so many people keep such an operation a secret? Surely the state had been surveilling the phones and e-mail of the arrestees. But couldn't that surveillance cut both ways?

The captors will attempt to project power over the prisoner. With small pieces of information—the name of his commanding officer, his unit, or his comrades—the captors will try to create the perception that they are omniscient and that it is useless to hide anything from them. The prisoner of war must defy these attempts. Small pieces of incidental information are easy to gather. The prisoner must neither confirm nor deny, must not give any information except name, rank, and serial number. To give more would encourage interrogation.

Dee began mentally drafting a message to Simón. Surely there was some way to monitor warning signs, to gather information about—

"Here it is!" said the real estate agent. Dee jumped slightly, blanked her screen, and stood with a smile. "This package has everything you need. Just get these signed, and we're in business."

Dee accepted the package and shook his hand. "I can't wait," she said.

~

"That was a close vote," said Gwen, sipping her coffee.

"I hope we aren't pushing the coalition too far," said Helen. "Maybe we need to back off a bit."

"We back off too often. We've got to push ourselves to win," said Gwen. "Think about the future. Think of what will happen if we don't."

"Millions of species will be wiped out?" joked Helen darkly.

"Yes," Gwen answered seriously. "And millions of humans."

"Doesn't that exaggerate the stakes of one campaign?"

"There are thousands of places like our town that are in danger," said Gwen. "As goes the battle, so goes the war."

"As goes the pipeline struggle, so goes the planetary struggle?" extrapolated Helen.

"Exactly," Gwen answered. "Ultimately it's about climate justice. Look at what happens when rulers decide there's not enough to share—not enough food, not enough resources. Humans become expendable. Look at the Rwandan genocide. Look at the genocide of Native Americans. Hell, look at the Nazis."

"Gwen," said Helen, "hard times don't always mean people start killing each other."

"Hard times incubate sociopaths," said Gwen. "Without the Depression, would Hitler have come to power? Would he have been able to convince enough Germans that they needed more 'living space'?"

"That's depressing, Gwen. You can't convince anyone with doom and gloom. If people think the world will turn out that way, they'll just sit at home and watch TV."

"That would be different how?" joked Gwen. But then she added, sadly, "No, you're right. People would stay home rather than take risks. Hence fascism." There was a long moment of quiet.

"Do you think Apollo is all right?" Helen asked.

Gwen gave her a tight smile. "If anyone can cope, he can, kid."

Taavi, Samantha, and Andy heard through the grapevine that the police changed shifts at three o'clock in the morning. Reasoning that few patrols would be out during the shift change, they waited until then to strike.

At sunset, they went to Andy's father's garage to sit on a musty couch and smoke pot, watching an old movie about reptile aliens invading Earth. The aliens pretended to be friendly at first but planned in secret to eat humanity for meat. Eventually humans formed a secret resistance movement, which Taavi and Samantha cheered. Andy had fallen asleep against one armrest, so Samantha slid a bit closer to Taavi.

At three in the morning, they woke up Andy and grabbed cans of spray paint from the garage workbench, stowing them in a black backpack. Then they headed down to the repair yard.

The fence was not quite as decrepit as Andy had suggested. They squeezed through a gap by a tree root. Samantha tore the seat of her jeans on a piece of wire, which Andy laughed at until Samantha told him to shut up for the sake of their covert mission.

There were three different police cars parked behind the garage: two shiny and new, one that looked like it had driven through a concrete flower planter.

"Awesome," said Andy. He pulled out a can of spray paint, popped the top off, and shook it vigorously. In capital letters he wrote *FUCK THE PIGS* all along one side of the damaged car. Excess paint dripped from every stroke.

"Too much paint makes it drip," said Sam. "Move faster or hold it further away." She grabbed a can and approached an intact police car. She painted an enormous red circle-A symbol on the hood, showing artistic finesse in her smooth application of the paint. *Defund,* she added to one side.

Taavi took his own can of spray paint, shaking it, and approached the last car. He painted *Free the Newbrook 4* in black along one side, nearly running out of space at the trunk. When he stepped back to admire his work, he noticed several of his fingers were sticky with paint. "We should probably have gloves," he told the others.

Andy was beyond such subtlety and began to kick his cop car on the front end where it had already been damaged. This yielded a satisfying spray of plastic chips from one of the headlights. Then—with surprising agility and balance for a mildly stoned person—he delivered a precise kick to the driver's-side window. His combat boot shattered the window easily. "Yeah!" said Samantha. She grabbed a pipe from nearby, whacking the windshield of her car until it spiderwebbed with tiny cracks.

Taavi laughed, but all the noise made him nervous. "Maybe it's time to make our escape," he said.

Andy had one more achievement in mind. He jumped onto the hood of his car and kicked the damaged windshield in. Then he unzipped his fly and sent a stream of urine into the car's interior, soaking the upholstery of the front seats. Samantha laughed uncontrollably.

Suddenly, a deep voice shouted from a nearby house. "Hey! I'm calling the cops!"

Andy dismounted hastily, almost falling on his face. The three of them ran for the gap in the fence. As they squeezed through, they tossed their used spray-paint cans into a bush. Then they ran as fast as they could, not stopping until they reached Andy's garage.

5

2051

Evelyn slept poorly, dreaming of checkpoints and violence. She would take a different commute that morning—into the Green Zone—but her experience the previous day left her anxious and distracted.

She left her building just before sunrise, as usual. At the bus terminal checkpoint she found herself nervously eyeing other people in the queue. None seemed particularly suspicious, but Evelyn wondered if *her* nervousness would show. Spend too much time staring at fellow citizens, and the guards would flag *her* for suspicious behavior. Anxiety fomented anxiety.

She took a deep, slow breath. Surely, there would be no shootings in Green Zone bus queues surrounded by guards. In the Yellow Zone, guards themselves were the main source of trouble; armbands constantly searched buses for contraband food in packed lunches or illegitimate electronics that posed security risks. Fortunately for Evelyn, guards mostly left the Green Zone passengers alone.

The bus terminal speakers played YEA news between the standard warnings about unattended luggage. "Two security officers are dead after being shot by an unknown assailant at surprise checkpoint in the Yellow Zone. A spokesperson from Armor Security said they, quote, 'died heroically in the line of duty, protecting all of us from cowardly drug traffickers.' Be on the lookout for a man with sunglasses and a dark coat, who is armed and extremely dangerous.

"And good news from Triage Administration: twelve blocks in midtown are being upgraded from yellow to green. The agency's director gave credit to vigilant triage officers who have rehoused ten thousand residents over six months. Residents carrying infectious diseases were sent for proper treatment."

Evelyn passed the checkpoint without trouble and boarded her bus. It was a new vehicle to her, the well-kept interior a step up from her former bus to the Yellow Zone.

Despite her anxiety, Evelyn's trip went smoothly. She disembarked at Triage Administration, and on the front steps she handed her green ID card to another blue-gloved guard. As he inspected it, she gazed up at the tall smokestack and antenna towers atop the building.

He handed the green tag back to her, pleasantly enough, but as she moved past him she glimpsed the guard eying the back of her coat. Sara had stitched the torn edges together by flashlight after evening power-down, but streaks of red felt were still visible. Evelyn's anxiety spiked, but the guard said nothing, so she entered the building and went to her desk.

Her desktop held a computer terminal, a scanner, and several empty clipboards. She took off her coat and hung it on the back of her chair. Then, realizing that the red scars were visible, she rolled it up and tucked it into an empty desk drawer. She took a seat.

Sitting there, she realized that she had little sense of what her job actually *was*. Stanley had given her a perfunctory tour, but with the rush of the previous afternoon—meeting the director, signing HR forms—she hadn't actually *done* anything. She considered the problem as a thirtysomething woman sat down at the adjacent desk. Evelyn turned to the woman and introduced herself.

"Ah, the new girl! I'm Phyllis," said the woman. Phyllis had a carefully made-up face and meticulously coiffed, dyed blond hair. She wore a classic-looking dress that resembled something Evelyn had once seen in a movie starring Katharine Hepburn.

"Nice to meet you," Evelyn said. Of course, she did not offer to shake hands. Few people here—aside from the director, apparently—would clasp bare hands with a stranger. "I guess we'll be working together?"

"Side by side! You get a full orientation yet?"

Evelyn shook her head. "Yesterday was hectic."

"Don't worry," said Phyllis. "I'll get you up to speed. You've done this kind of work before? Filing, sorting, typing?" Evelyn nodded. "Then you'll have no problem. Lemme explain." Phyllis had a slightly nasal way of speaking, a dialect that Evelyn found familiar but unplaceable.

"Records and hard copies come straight to us from the triage facilities. Doctor's notes, charts, receipts, that sort of thing. Ten years ago, we scanned everything and shredded the paper, but after all those EMPs and blackouts and cyberwarfare, we keep paper copies of everything."

Phyllis stood and gestured at various pieces of equipment. "We scan hard copies and update the computer files, then collate the papers and send them down to the archives."

"Sounds like my old job," Evelyn said, "I worked in Health Care Records Administration."

Phyllis smiled. "You're gonna do great, then. Lemme introduce you to the girls," she added, for the office had filled up around them. "Everyone, this is Evelyn! She's new. Evelyn, meet Betty, Margaret, Dolores, Eleanor, Jacqueline, and Elsie." Phyllis pointed to each woman in turn, and the women greeted Evelyn in response. Each wore a conservative dress or skirt that was classic to the point of being old-fashioned.

"Nice to meet you all," said Evelyn. As they turned back to their desks, Evelyn asked Phyllis, "All women in this department?"

"Oh yeah, the director mostly hires girls for this job," said Phyllis. "Nimble fingers and all!" She laughed brightly and checked her watch. "Ready to start?" Evelyn nodded, and she heard a clattering sound as a young man rolled a cart into the office. "Our nine o'clock delivery," said Phyllis.

The man left the cart in the center of the office. Phyllis pulled on a pair of blue rubber gloves (which stretched to near-white over her long fingernails) and then retrieved a heavy box of files and papers from the cart. "I'll walk you through everything. Put on some gloves, though. They sanitize these, but they *do* come from triage sites, so you never know."

Evelyn found a box of blue gloves in her desk drawer. She pulled on a pair and turned to Phyllis. "Let's get started."

—⚡

In the basement of the safe house, Layth ate a breakfast of cold porridge made from ration powder. X and Felicity had been up all night planning, so Layth ate alone as they slept in. He had three things on his agenda: look for new potential safe houses to replace those they had lost, pay a call for his cover occupation, and distribute new Samizdata coins.

Samizdata tied together the scattered network of anti-YEA dissidents. Layth had risked his life many times to protect the system and extend its reach. The system was based on thousands of nodes, each small enough to hide in a pocket. The basic unit was a sealed module the size of a coin with an integral battery, a solar cell, an ultra-low-wattage processor, a short-range wireless antenna, and a gigabyte of flash memory. A generation earlier, the coins could have been cranked out for cents per unit. But now each one was worth its weight in gold to Layth.

The Authority claimed to have a supercomputer that listened to every phone call, read every electronic message, and analyzed every frame of video surveillance. News reports were regularly published about its enormous size, its astronomical memory, its inconceivable processing speeds. Not only could it understand electronic conversations, it could insert phony information into them to deceive "terrorists." It supposedly parsed more data every microsecond than a human could experience in an entire lifetime.

In contrast, a single Samizdata coin was useless by itself: its processor too anemic for games or video, its wireless range no better than shouting distance, its memory laughably small. Only the battery life was better than mediocre. It had no keyboard, no screen, no mouse, not even a single LED to indicate that it was functioning. It was featureless except for a fingernail switch along the edge. Alone it could do nothing; it was not even heavy enough to be a paperweight.

But once it neared another coin, something amazing was possible. Provided their batteries were charged, one of the coins might emit a brief wireless signal—a chirp. And then another coin nearby—or many other coins—would chirp back, and they would start a conversation. In a burst of encrypted data lasting a millisecond, they would exchange blocks of information: a bulletin about YEA atrocities. A political manifesto. A warning about extra surveillance in a certain block of town. A how-to guide on bypassing ration restrictions. Short histories of historical resistance struggles, which X would type out from memory (which was how she relaxed). Even the occasional book, split into short pieces.

Layth finished his porridge and grabbed a handful of Samizdata coins out of the bag he had salvaged from the cache of the doomed cell. He recognized the handwriting on the bag and tried not to think about the dead man who had written it. Then Layth put on his green alibi tag and walked out the front door.

The system's name, X had explained, came from an old communications network called "samizdat." To defy Soviet authorities, dissidents painstakingly copied banned political materials and shared those copies with others. Copying an entire book by hand took months.

That old system required subtlety and great dedication. But Layth suspected that if an Eastern European dissident from eighty years go were dropped into YEA territory they would not last long. Nowadays, any person could be digitally tracked using the phone in their pocket or contact-traced through the triage card on their jacket. A system that required many people to know each other and physically meet on a regular basis would be easily destroyed.

Someone caught with a library of books in their Red Zone apartment could be arrested and interrogated. Authority agents would inspect the recorded movements of that person for months into the past. They would download the location records from their triage tag and cross-reference that with surveillance video archives, facial recognition databases, checkpoint logbooks—their contact-tracing software did this automatically. They would figure out where that person had been and, unless that person was a careful and well-trained professional, they would find out who they had interacted with, who they might have shared books with. Then they would track *those* people, and find out who *they* met with, until a whole movement was arrested and placed in triage camps, or worse.

Strolling around his neighborhood, Layth casually dropped fresh Samizdata coins in a dozen different places: inside a ventilation grate, in a tiny patch of grass between street and sidewalk, in the menu display box of a long-closed restaurant.

The rise of the surveillance state had restricted truly private communication to small groups of secretive, paranoid, expert dissidents. And so, for years, the Authority's power had grown as resistance withered.

Samizdata had changed everything. No longer did people have to *meet* to exchange books. No longer did a person have to be a trained underground cadre to get hold of dissident literature. You merely needed a Samizdata coin and some other device with short-range wireless functionality—a tablet, or an e-reader, so long as it wasn't entirely locked down. You didn't even have to *do* anything to exchange bulletins. You could put a Samizdata coin in your pocket, or your shoe, or sew one into the hem of your coat, and go out and run your errands.

Somewhere on your travels you might pass near someone else with a Samizdata coin in *their* pocket, or purse, or cap. That person might not be in the same room, or even the same building. You might not see them. Certainly, you would not know who or where they were. But the coins would chirp at each other and then exchange a burst of highly compressed data, updating their bulletins. Maybe you'd pass another coin in a potted plant, and one would pass you on the bus where it was wedged between two seats.

And when you got home, you would connect to the coin and find a whole new selection of underground news stories and manifestos and calls to action.

The flexibility of the coins amazed Layth. They were sealed, waterproof, and weatherproof. They could recharge themselves through solar power or by being placed on an induction mat. They could be disguised as an old quarter or a metal washer. If placed near a source of light they would continue to function independently for months or years. He had hidden them inside of fluorescent light fixtures in offices. He had tossed them into public fountains where they would blend in with other lucky coins. He had slipped them on top of light standards and glued them to the roofs of train cars.

Samizdata was far from perfect. Coins were best turned off when not in use, as an active but stationary coin could eventually be tracked down by a YEA wireless sniffer. The system was difficult to use with large files like images and audio, impossible with video. As an ad hoc system of peer-to-peer data sharing it was optimized for secrecy, not speed; a news story published on one side of the city might take days, or weeks, through various random hops and intermediaries, to get to a person on the other side of the city. It was, in theory, possible for people who knew how to put files onto the coin to send a brief, encrypted message to another person whom they knew was on the system. But it might take a long time to reach that person, if they ever received it at all.

Samizdata, Layth reflected, as he approached his first checkpoint of the morning, was no substitute for proper tradecraft. But it was incredibly useful—or had been, until the Authority had found out about the system and began to spam it with nonsense and propaganda messages. Their technical cell had been trying to solve the problem for weeks without success. But that was a problem for another day.

—⁄

Addy awoke before sunrise. She did her morning chores and ate a breakfast of duck eggs and root-vegetable latkes with Carlos and the rest of her household. Then she and Carlos went down to the dock below the generator shack, and together, they canoed across the flooded quarry toward the opposite corner. En route they passed a few floating chunks of ice and the rusted and partially submerged hulks of long-ruined quarry equipment.

They tied up at a dock and walked the rest of the way to Bill Farnham's house. The whole trip took half an hour, much faster than Sandra's long and indirect route around the outer edge of multiple adjoining quarries.

Addy and Carlos got halfway up Bill Farnham's driveway before Farnham himself came trotting down on horseback to meet them.

"Good morning," he said aloofly from the saddle. "Are you here to pay the overdue rent your people owe me?"

Addy scrutinized Farnham. The straps of his saddle looked hastily tightened, the horse's bridle somewhat askew. Farnham had obviously seen them from a distance and hurriedly jumped on a horse to make an impression of strength.

"You jumped on that horse all of sixty seconds ago," said Addy. "Why not come down and talk to us?"

Farnham frowned and refrained from dismounting. "Come up to the house." Then Farnham turned his horse and cantered back up the driveway, leaving them to walk.

"Glad he's in a friendly mood," said Carlos sarcastically.

"I'll handle him," scowled Addy. "Just stay cool."

A few minutes later they were in the Farnhams' kitchen. Bill's wife, Olivia, offered them cookies with actual—hence very expensive— black tea. While they waited for Bill to reappear, Olivia engaged them in polite but idle chitchat, deferring or deflecting any mention of the interns. The radio played a YEA newscast in the background.

"The Authority's chief economist warned today that household debt is rising to record levels. He suggests a few simple tips to reduce debt, like making sure to pay bills on time and collecting rewards for reporting suspicious activity."

Bill Farnham failed to arrive until they had nearly finished their cups of tea. He entered the kitchen with a loud non-apology: "I had to attend to some things." He did not sit down at the kitchen table until Olivia gave him a pained smile and a look of pointed discomfort. "I hope you're enjoying my wife's fine hospitality," he said.

"The tea and cookies are delicious," said Addy.

"I'm glad," replied Farnham. "It's a shame those young people didn't share your appreciation of our generosity."

"Sandra and the others weren't receiving your 'generosity,'" said Addy. "They weren't even your employees. They were participants in a work-exchange program facilitated by the Thistleroot Institute as part of a binding contract."

"A contract isn't *legally* binding without a court to judge it and police to enforce it," replied Farnham. "You lack legal authority to enforce contracts. And your *commune* is hardly in the position to lecture others about following the law."

Addy resisted the urge to roll her eyes. "Arguing about enforcement is not a road you want to go down, Bill. The Thistleroot Institute has been extremely generous to you over the years. Without us you wouldn't even have electricity."

"It's a shame our electricity only works on sunny or windy days," said Farnham, "barely enough to pump well water—"

"Ground water depletion is a problem everywhere, and climate change—"

"—but we've been magnanimous to the guests you have boarded here."

"Sandra wasn't your 'guest'—" began Addy.

"If she wasn't our guest, it was our prerogative to charge her rent for room and board," snapped Farnham. "If she didn't pay she *was* a guest, and we refuse guests as we please."

"You receive compensation for work placements," said Addy, "in the form of hardware, labor, food, and knowledge. It's *not* your prerogative to unilaterally change that arrangement. We saved your family from disaster after—"

"We handled things just fine," interrupted Farnham. "You people *wish* everyone needed you, but the truth is people of faith can deal with adversity. If you hadn't been there, we'd have gotten help from the Mennonites. Or from the Emergency Authority."

Addy scoffed. "The Authority is a parasite that bullies people with fear of epidemics long past. They gnaw farms to the bone and then move on. They offer nothing of value."

"They can offer fuel," replied Farnham, "and labor. Both of which we need to sow and weed and harvest crops. You send a couple of workers who sap our resources most of the year. The YEA has teams of hundreds of laborers who can plant or harvest an entire farm in days."

Addy frowned. "Says who?"

"Everyone knows!" said Farnham. "My cousin near the city has labor teams brought out three times a year. And he doesn't have to pay for them or board them. The Authority pays *him*! They pay for his crops and bring their own workers to weed and harvest them."

Addy and Carlos exchanged a look of guarded concern. "The Authority coerces those people. They're treated like serfs. Their working conditions—"

"Working conditions!" exclaimed Farnham. "Do you want unions and labor laws now? Those went out with the rest of the socialist bullshit that ran this country into the ground. This is capitalism! It's lean. Efficient."

"You call it capitalism, we call it fas—"

"I don't give a damn what you call it! It's the future!" yelled Farnham, banging on the table. "And I won't be condescended to by a pair of people who, from the looks of you, aren't even from this country!"

Carlos gave Farnham a look of open disgust. Addy considered her rhetorical options—*Oh, so are you Ojibwe or Algonquin?*—but decided to ignore the racist slight and stay on topic.

"I'm not here to talk ideology or ancestry," said Addy, speaking with deliberate slow calmness. "The Authority is a long way distant. *We* are here. We have a deal with you. We have given you support and equipment for more than a decade, and we expect you to fulfill your end of the bargain."

"I don't need you," spat Farnham. "It's winter. The Authority is expanding, and come spring they'll be here. I'll use their work crews, not your insubordinate hippies."

"Are you refusing to honor our contract?" asked Addy.

"We have no contract. That time's past. You get out of my kitchen and off my land. If you have any sense, you'll keep on walking. Maybe when the spring thaw comes, you'll be out of the Authority's reach."

Addy glared. "We'll be back, Bill—with enforcement. If you aren't willing to honor our contract, we'll repossess everything we've given you in the past fifteen years."

Bill Farnham broke eye contact with her and stared at the kitchen floor. "I'd like to see you try," he said, though he spoke without enthusiasm.

Addy pushed back from the table. She gave Bill Farnham a cold, unbreaking stare as she addressed his wife. "Olivia, thank you for the hospitality."

Moments later, Addy and Carlos were on their way down the Farnham driveway.

"Fuck, fuck, fuck," muttered Addy under her breath.

"You made a strong showing," said Carlos, "though the plan *was* to play it cool."

"I shouldn't have focused on what he owed us," said Addy. "It was a challenge to his ego. Made him feel like he had to prove himself. I should have just let him brag about his hospitality."

"No," answered Carlos. "If you acted submissive, he'd have run right over you."

"We don't have time or resources to send militia down here in the middle of winter," said Addy. "Are we going to dig up his root cellar and take it home? Our midwife helped deliver Farnham's daughter. Are we going to confiscate her?"

"You can't win them all." Carlos shrugged. "Other people are grateful, and they'll stick with us. Maybe we should just ignore Farnham. Cut him off."

Addy sighed. "Farnham is the thin edge of the wedge. If the Authority gets here, he'll be a foothold. They'll set up a forward operating base. And faced with gun-wielding armbands, some of our neighbors will fold."

"That may happen someday," said Carlos, "but today I'm mostly worried about getting home in time for a hot meal."

Addy took his hand in hers. "Fair enough. Let's go."

—⚡

That morning, Layth went through three checkpoints and the gate of a twenty-foot-high concrete wall to travel from the restaurant safe house in the Yellow Zone to a stately home in the Green Zone. The house was a large brick building—a mansion really—with eyebrow dormers and flying buttresses and a gold-inlaid gable stone and other fancy architectural features he had learned the names of in order to support his cover profession.

He walked up to the door, rang the bell, and waited. The air in the Green Zone seemed clearer. There was no visible guardhouse, no checkpoint on the street, no machine gun nests anywhere to be seen. Instead of armed sentinels, old oak trees lined the street. The very absence of visible security demonstrated just how far into the heart of YEA territory Layth had travelled, how secure the wealthy elite felt in their homes, and how useful Layth's cover story was.

Layth, according to his YEA employment file, was an "antique and rare items consultant." If someone needed a special component for some old machine, or to replace a leaky faucet that was no longer manufactured, Layth would track down a part. It was a lucrative job in and of itself, since his well-heeled clients would pay handsomely for difficult-to-find items. But as a cover story, it was ideal. Layth could freely travel the length and breadth of the city and beyond without being questioned unduly at checkpoints. He could justifiably carry strange items from place to place. He could loiter in abandoned buildings and even gain legitimate access to quarantined zones. Without raising any suspicion, he could interact with people of many different backgrounds and classes. It was a perfect cover for a resistance organizer and courier.

The door was opened by a man in his late sixties, well dressed in a dark suit, who greeted Layth. The man was the house's majordomo, Quinn. With minimal small talk, Quinn conducted Layth into a large office in the rear of the house, which overlooked a wide garden with fountains and architectural follies. The office itself was spacious and decorated with dark cherry panels and antique lamps.

One of these lamps had been overturned, its stained-glass shade smashed against the hardwood floor. The shards had been collected and laid out on a tray. "This is why we called you," Quinn explained.

"It's ruined," said Layth, surveying the remnants. "You'll have to buy a whole new shade. An art dealer could find a similar piece."

"For a Tiffany lamp, that would be true," said Quinn. "If only we were so fortunate as to have smashed an expensive work of art, which would be easy to replace! But this lamp is a knockoff. Its value is sentimental. It was purchased by my employer's grandfather and is something of a family heirloom."

"Where was it manufactured?" asked Layth.

"In this city, a century ago," replied Quinn. "It's rare, but surely you could find more floating around."

"I can try," said Layth. "I'll need to photograph it thoroughly to guarantee a match. It will take a couple of minutes." Quinn nodded but remained standing in the room. It would not do to leave a contractor unattended in his employer's private office. Layth produced a camera.

A spy less able than Layth would have tried to gather intelligence by framing the photograph so some useful piece of information was in the background. Perhaps they would place the broken lamp on the desk, claiming the light was better. Then they would "accidentally" photograph whatever pages happened to be exposed on the desktop. Later, they would try to piece together something useful.

But Layth was an expert and needed only to stand there, taking photos, as the wireless device in his left boot—a specialized Samizdata module—downloaded data from bugs he had placed in the office on a previous occasion. He simply had to stall until the transfer was complete.

"How was the lamp broken?" Layth asked conversationally as he clicked away with his camera.

"An *accident*," Quinn said stiffly, in a way that meant it was not. An intelligence cell would review the data from the bugs later. Layth expected the audio would reveal something unsavory—a fight between the home's owner and his wife, or mistress, or both. Or a bout of alcohol-induced violence.

"Is there anything else I should look for?" Layth asked, stalling. "A matching set, perhaps?"

"One will suffice," said Quinn.

A moment later, Layth felt a buzz against his big toe. *Transfer complete.* He stowed his camera and prepared to go.

As Layth left, Quinn handed him a small package. "To cover expenses," Quinn said.

Layth peeled back the wrapping to find nearly eight hundred grams of genuine chocolate. "This is too much!" he said. "The lamp won't cost nearly as much as this."

Quinn shrugged. "Keep the difference. They won't notice."

—✦

"So I type in the serial number," said Evelyn, "and number of pages?"

"Exactly," said Phyllis. "And check here"—she turned to the cover of the large manila envelope—"to make sure you have the complete contents."

Evelyn emptied the envelope onto her desk and checked the contents against the list on the envelope. "Patient's name is Manuel Rodriguez," she noted. "There should be seven pieces of documentation in the envelope. Here's an intake form . . . triage officer lists reason for detention as 'possible signs of illness.' That's vague."

Phyllis shrugged. "Oh, I don't even look at the details. Triage station handles that."

Evelyn checked the form off the list. "Okay, next we have a sheet of fingerprints, which is present. Photographs of Mr. Rodriguez at his intake. And a list of symptoms from the medical officer at the triage station."

"You *do* have to enter those on the computer," said Phyllis, "for the epidemiologists. Just read the paper and click the matching checkboxes. So, click 'fever,' 'disorientation,' and 'headache.'"

"There's no box for 'contusions,'" said Evelyn, "even though it's on the paper."

"It's too common to track," said Phyllis. "Their sickness gives them anemia, or they don't eat a balanced diet and it affects their blood so they bruise really easy. A lot of these people just don't take good care of themselves; it's why they get sick."

"I see," said Evelyn. "The last form is an invoice from the security contractor who brought him in. It's marked 'paid.'"

"By us, obviously!" said Phyllis. "User fees will be collected from the patient. Once you finish an envelope—"

"Hold on," interrupted Evelyn, "that's only six items. There should be seven." She checked the list on the envelope. "There should be a list of the patient's personal effects." Evelyn looked in the vicinity of her desk to see if she had dropped it by accident.

But Phyllis waved a dismissive hand. "Happens *all* the time. Patient keeps the list and it doesn't get filed properly. We're just supposed to stamp the file "input complete."

Status: Retained for treatment, read Evelyn, and stamped.

"Okay, done! Then close up the envelope and put it on the archive cart." Phyllis demonstrated as she spoke. "Gets a bit boring after a while, but you can get entertainment from the details. Yesterday I had a file for a guy who was running a secret library out of his Red Zone apartment. Can you imagine *all those people*, sharing filthy books around?" She shuddered visibly. "It's the twenty-first century; get a tablet! Of course, they had to burn everything on the spot."

Phyllis walked Evelyn through the process of handling several more patient envelopes. Evelyn found herself lingering over the photos of each patient, staring blankly into the camera. "It's funny," Evelyn remarked as they leafed through the contents of the seventh envelope. "A lot of these people don't even look sick."

Phyllis shrugged. "Maybe," she said dubiously, then brightened. "Of course, that's why the triage system is so important. You could see these people on the street and never know they were sick. Completely asymptomatic! They'd be out spreading disease right now if they weren't checked."

"Hmmm," acknowledged Evelyn as she flipped through the envelope's contents. "Well, this looks complete. Oh, except . . ." She pointed to the bottom of the list of personal effects. "See?"

Phyllis looked. "What's wrong? It's signed."

Evelyn tapped the signature line. "Yeah, but it says 'signature of patient.' So, it should be signed by . . . Lauren Watanabe. But it's signed by the security officer who did her intake."

Phyllis shrugged again. "Happens sometimes. You know"—and Phyllis lowered her voice—"some of these people are basically illiterate anyway."

"I see," said Evelyn.

"Okay!" said Phyllis cheerfully. "Time to go to the archives." For as the two of them had slowly processed a handful of files, the rest of the women in the sorting pool had sped through the first cart's entire stock and begun sorting a second. One rolling cart, destined for the archives, was entirely full. Phyllis stood and grasped its handle. Evelyn followed her, and together they took the cart into the elevator and descended to the basement.

—⚡—

"What's our progress on rebuilding the network?" asked Layth between bites of rice and beans. He sat across from Felicity in the dim light of the safe-house kitchen. It was a spacious industrial kitchen with stainless steel counters and sinks, but the restaurant had been closed for a decade even before the network had taken it over as their headquarters.

"Slow," said Felicity. "We've recruited new couriers, but they're inexperienced. Losing the drug stockpile makes it hard to support the survivors. To smuggle John's wife, Charlotte, and their son out to the country we had to pay with canned fish and US dollars."

Layth laughed. "I can't believe you got a bunch of hardheaded smugglers to accept paper money. Did you deliver their fee in a wheel-barrow?"

"Charlotte got them to agree to half and half," said Felicity, gesturing with her fork. "To match the value of fifteen kilos of canned fish I had to weigh out near as many kilos in paper bills." They both laughed.

"Well, at least John's family is safely out," said Layth. "They're probably eating steak and eggs right now instead of reconstituted ration powder and moldy beans."

"Hey, I picked *out* the moldy ones," said Felicity with mock indignance. "Besides, a little mold isn't so bad—your poxy ass could use the penicillin." Layth flicked a bean at her.

A few moments later, X walked into the room. She scanned the table and their plates. "Jesus Christ, beans again?" she said. "I survived six years as a vegan, but another week of beans will probably kill me."

"We could always turn to self-cannibalism for extra protein," joked Layth.

"Felicity, maybe," replied X. "You're too damned gristly." She changed the subject. "Did you find a location for another safe house?"

"I mostly made the Samizdata rounds—including a visit to a Homeland executive's house. I have my eye on some quarantined buildings," said Layth. "But they're in rough shape—water damage, mold. And rats, speaking of protein." Waving his fork, he pantomimed chasing something along the table and stabbing it.

"Make a list of the best candidates," said X. "For now, you have another mission." Her faced darkened, and she paused for so long that Layth wondered if she was still breathing. Then she spoke, quietly: "There's a rumor from a triage camp. Just a rumor. But it's possible that some of our comrades from the lost cell survived."

"I thought they were all killed during the shoot-out," said Felicity. "If they're being held captive, if the rumors about nerve clamping—"

X held up a hand. "It may be false. But Layth, you need to find out if there is any chance this could be true. If one is alive, we could arrange rescue, or some other assistance . . ."

Layth nodded and pushed away his plate, leaving the last of the rice and beans. He stood. "I'll ask some sources, whatever it takes."

—⚡

The archives were enormous. Evelyn had assumed that "the basement" was only one floor. But there seemed to be as many stories underground as above, sprawling off in different directions.

"Triage Administration has underground tunnels to other buildings," said Phyllis as she pushed the file cart down a dimly lit corridor. "The basement is way bigger than the footprint of the building above. Don't get lost down here!" Evelyn laughed good-naturedly, but Phyllis didn't smile. "Seriously. Not everything comes into this building sterile. There are medical-only sections. Storage for quarantined items. An incinerator, for old papers and hazardous waste, that heats the building. But if you wander through a biohazard locker by accident, you'll spend the next few weeks—or longer—in solitary quarantine." A door at the end of the corridor was marked **D WING ZONED RED. QUARANTINE. ENTRY FORBIDDEN.**

"I'll be careful," said Evelyn.

"Great!" said Phyllis, back to her usual cheerful self. They pushed through a set of double doors into a new space, and Evelyn saw what Phyllis meant. The room went on for hundreds of feet that she could see, filled from floor to ceiling with large steel file cabinets. Each drawer was four feet wide, and each cabinet six drawers high. "Everything important is kept on paper now, safe from cyberattacks. Here's our stop."

Phyllis grasped one of the drawer handles and pulled. The enormous drawer slid out smoothly on oiled bearings.

"Are the files alphabetical?" Evelyn asked.

"Oh no," said Phyllis. "They were at the start, but now there's just too many. We file by serial number. Take these new intakes"—she grasped a sheaf of envelopes from the cart and deposited them into the file drawer—"and put them in the first empty spot at the end." Evelyn helped to transfer files from the cart to the drawer.

"Just remember," added Phyllis, "there are two sections in the archive. Active files are here, near the front doors. Closed files *are* alphabetical and are *strictly* for archival purposes. It means that those patients have exited the triage system."

"So they've gone home?" ask Evelyn, feeling a twinge of anxiety over the rumors Sara had mentioned.

"Technically anyone who could be a carrier of disease is still in the triage system, even if they go home," answered Phyllis. "But imagine, if you like, someone *has* been permanently cured. Then they become a closed file." Evelyn thought there was a more obvious reason a file would be closed, but said nothing. They finished transferring the files, and Phyllis slid the drawer shut. "Once in a while you have to destroy contaminated files," Phyllis said as they walked back to the elevator. "Just toss them through that hatch there. The chute leads to the incinerator."

When they got back upstairs there was a package waiting on Evelyn's chair. She opened it to find a dark fur coat, soft and warm to the touch.

—⚓

Addy and Carlos pulled the canoe up to their own dock in midafternoon. The dock was hidden from the low winter sun by the quarry cliff opposite, but as they ascended the ladders toward the farmstead they came back into sunlight. Addy's stomach was growling enthusiastically for lunch.

They arrived at the farmhouse expecting to find the kitchen and dining room mostly empty, since it was well past lunchtime. Instead, as they took off their boots, they could hear chatter and hubbub in the kitchen. They entered it to find a dozen familiar people crowded around two strangers. One was a woman with curly red hair, and the other a young boy of eight or ten. The woman was answering a stream of questions, but she seemed distant and clearly exhausted, speaking in barely more than a whisper. Addy couldn't even hear her.

Sridharan, a former computer engineer who lived in one of the cabins down the lane, sidled up to Addy. "How did it go?" he asked quietly. "Any luck?"

Addy shook her head. "We'll need stern measures. Any word from Lieutenant Dumont?"

"LT is still on patrol," said Sridharan. "Meanwhile we have other arrivals—refugees from the city. Got here an hour ago."

Addy thought she knew the red-haired woman from somewhere, but perhaps she was imagining things.

"Sounds like things are getting worse in the city," said Sridharan. Sridharan had left the city years earlier, when things were already getting bad. "Are you hungry?"

Addy nodded. She would eat. And then, later, she would figure out how she knew this refugee.

⚓

At the end of the day, Evelyn tidied her desk and shut off her computer. She followed the lead of her coworkers in wiping down her desk with disinfectant and sanitizing her workstation. Then she put on the fine fur coat, eliciting a chorus of admiring *oohs* and *aahs* from her coworkers.

"You should come out with us after work," said Phyllis. "We're going to a restaurant on the new green block east of here. Maybe some public safety officers will join us!"

"So exciting," said Elsie. "I never would have gone before; you couldn't pay me enough to go into the Yellow Zone."

"It wasn't a restaurant before," said Phyllis. "What do you think, Evelyn?"

Evelyn checked the time. She was excited at the idea of going out, which she hadn't done in years; prohibitions on public assembly made restaurants impractical outside the Green Zone. But if she didn't catch her bus she wouldn't make it back to the Yellow Zone in time for curfew. And the cafeteria's free lunch—half of which she had saved to bring home to Sara and Sid—was already a welcome culinary upgrade. "Sorry, girls, I've got other plans tonight," she said.

On the way toward the front doors, Evelyn passed the director, who looked her coat up and down before flashing her a smile and nodding approvingly.

Her trip home was quick and uneventful. The bus was quiet, but news headlines scrolled on screens visible from each seat.

"Chief Officer of Public Health Todd
Buchanan warns against the dangers of fresh

```
tropical fruit. 'You have no idea where
a pineapple or a banana could have come
from. The people who bring these into the
country carry agricultural pests, fungal
infections, typhoid, even malaria. Stick
to the law: report suspicious produce.'
The chief officer also said canned fruit is
more available now than at any time since
emergency was declared."

    "Radiation cleanup in Fort McMurray is
proceeding well, and oil-sands production
should resume soon. Authority residents can
be proud to have provided important cleanup
labor."
```

Evelyn arrived at her apartment block as the sun was setting. Noise and distant shouting came from a building in the east block. But she could see nothing, so she walked on.

Mrs. Schmidt was waiting in the apartment lobby. Evelyn suddenly realized that she had completely forgotten to visit.

"Hello, Evelyn, did you get my note?" asked Mrs. Schmidt. "I saw it was taken off the bulletin board."

"I'm sorry, Mrs. Schmidt; I got your note last night but I didn't have a chance to come down before power-down."

"That's okay, Evelyn. Maybe you come up now and help with my forms?"

Evelyn checked her watch. "I should go upstairs to say hello and drop off my coat. Then I'll come down and help, all right?"

"New coat?" asked Mrs. Schmidt.

Evelyn turned back and forth to show it off. "What do you think?"

Mrs. Schmidt frowned. "Too fancy. I like mine better," she replied, stroking the fur trim of her own blue corduroy coat, a classic but stylish number that was coming back into vogue with the people who had money to spend on such things. Mrs. Schmidt was not one of those people but had been gifted the coat by Sara, who in turn had received it as barter for a box of preserves.

"Sara does have an eye for fashion," Evelyn said. "I'll come see you soon, Mrs. Schmidt."

Evelyn climbed the twelve flights of stairs to her floor. A few moments later, she was walking through the front door of her apartment.

"Honey, I'm home!" she called. She could hear someone was in the living room, so she strode forward. Then she froze, midstep, at the sight of his deep-set eyes. Her jaw clenched. Her fingers went cold, her stomach turned, and her skin suddenly felt tight.

In her own living room, she was face to face with a murderer.

6

2028

Helen held up the newspaper so Gwendolyn could see the headline: *Attacks on Police in Wake of Terror Arrests.* Helen slammed the paper down on her wobbly kitchen table in frustration. Gwen swiftly lifted her mug so it wouldn't spill.

"Well, how about that?" remarked Gwen, sipping her coffee.

"*How about that?*" echoed Helen with obvious frustration. She paced around, sloshing her mug of tea, and splashed some onto the floor. "You're too relaxed for a coffee drinker."

"Wait until I've had five more." Gwen chuckled. "What's the problem? Some cop cars got damaged in the middle of the night. Probably a bunch of kids. No one was hurt."

"It looks terrible," Helen began, ticking off points on her fingers. "It validates the government line about dangerous radicals. It doesn't help attain our campaign goals. It's unaccountable vigilantism instead of community-based action. It reflects badly on us—"

Gwen raised her palms, placating. "Sure, it would be a terrible idea for *us* to do something like this. But we didn't. It's not our job to police everyone else."

"Most people won't understand that," said Helen. "To them it's just, Oh, leftist kooks are at it again.'"

"For conservatives, maybe," said Gwen, sipping more coffee. "But I think you're underestimating the intelligence of our supporters."

"I think you're *over*estimating the number of *our* supporters," said Helen. "We can't afford to lose people over this high-school crap. This is one more excuse for people to stay home instead of marching."

"People who *want* an excuse for inaction can get it anywhere.

The kids—or whoever did this—saw something *they* felt needed a response. They planned an action and they accomplished it without getting caught—"

"Yet," interjected Helen.

"Just by taking action independently they've done more than ninety-nine percent of people ever will. Heck, most of the people who come to our protests don't even do that."

"So, what? You think they just need better guidance?"

"They probably think *you* need better guidance," said Gwen wryly. Helen frowned at that. "I'm teasing. You know I think you're doing a great job. But your way—our way—isn't the only way. I wish that the people who came to our protests were all as willing to defy authority as these people. The people who smashed those cars saw that their community was under attack, so they counterattacked without hesitation. We can argue over the details, but I admire their directness."

"What are you saying?" asked Helen. "That they counterattacked instead of sitting around holding meetings and collecting signatures for petitions like we do?"

"I'm not trying to make you defensive, kid," said Gwen. "There's room in this struggle for community outreach *and* militant action."

"That kind of talk got Apollo arrested," said Helen pointedly.

"Maybe," said Gwen, "and maybe that's why it's important to *keep* talking that way." She paused. "Are you going to visit him in jail? I know you guys are on again, off again. But even if you're off—"

"I know." Helen resumed pacing. "I'll go later in the week."

"Okay," said Gwen. "He'll be glad to see you."

Helen paused at the window. There was a black SUV across the road, engine idling. "Has that car been there since you arrived?"

Gwen walked over to look out the window. "Hmm," she said.

〜

"So Andy's mom says, 'It's summer, and you've graduated from high school—when are you going to get a job?'" Samantha recounted, dipping a French fry in ketchup. "He looks straight at her and says, 'My job is the revolution.'"

"I wish I'd thought of that," said Taavi, plucking French fries from the middle of the picnic table. "What did she say?"

"She asked if the revolution would pay my rent," Andy replied, shrugging sheepishly.

"Hmmm," said Taavi, adjusting his ball cap. The sun was bright as the three shared a batch of French fries near a food truck. "Thinking about moving out?"

"It's time," said Andy. "I don't want to get hassled constantly; I'm an adult, you know? Hey, these fries are vegan, right?"

"They use vegetable oil," answered Samantha.

"Hey, punks!" came another voice. They greeted Corben as he joined their table. "Did you hear about those cop cars?" He nodded approvingly. "Tough stuff."

The three exchanged glances. "Yeah, really something," said Taavi cautiously.

"Well, kudos to whoever did it," said Corben.

"Yeah," agreed Andy. "Kudos."

"The way I see it," said Corben, gazing at Andy, "this kind of thing needs to happen more often if we're going to win, right?"

"Totally," said Andy. "But what's it going to take?"

Corben glanced around. "This isn't the best place to talk. Meet me at the pub tonight. Back room. Nine o'clock." He abruptly rose and left.

"Huh," said Taavi once Corben had gone. "Do you two want to go?"

"Of course," said Andy, obviously excited. "Why not?"

Taavi turned to Samantha, who had remained silent through the whole encounter. She spoke with hesitation. "I don't know. Isn't he, like, trying too hard?" Andy and Taavi glanced at one another, uncertain.

"What do you mean?" said Andy. "He's hard-core. He's been in jail!"

Samantha shrugged. "Okay. Let's go, I guess."

Taavi nodded. "All right," he said. "Nine o'clock."

❧

Dee sat beneath a shade tree in a sprawling urban park. She often used the park to rendezvous or to drop hidden messages. The day was sunny and pleasantly warm. It was a beautiful day, and Dee was happy.

She was also alert. Dee understood with complete clarity that the life she had chosen required constant attention. She could not allow birdsong or the laughter of children in the park to lull her to sleep. Nor could she drift off into idle daydreams. Perhaps if she had an affinity group for support. But that was not an option for her.

So, she enjoyed the sunshine and she watched. As usual, she had arrived early and was waiting near (but not at) the day's rendezvous spot to watch for warning signs: videographers who loitered too long, strange vans, people with perpetually attached Bluetooth headsets who mostly seemed to listen rather than talk. None of these were concrete signs of surveillance, but only an incompetent crew would leave indisputable signs. And it was not an incompetent surveillance team she was afraid of.

Dee spotted a familiar figure in the distance. She checked her travel alarm clock: right on time. The woman Dee watched was dressed casually in a light-yellow sundress, a diaphanous blue scarf around her neck. A red scarf—or a red handkerchief or even a pair of red knee socks—would have meant danger. *Warning. Run away.* The *absence* of blue clothing was the same. Those signals would have meant that Dee's contact was under duress, being followed, compromised in some way—that Dee should not approach or even acknowledge her. But today everything was according to plan.

Dee stood and lifted her small shoulder bag. She walked casually in a direction parallel to her contact. A few moments later, they both entered a small copse of oak trees and approached each other in a shaded grove where two burbling brooks joined.

"Rebecca!" Dee greeted her contact happily.

"Hello, Dee!" replied Rebecca. As they approached, Dee reached out and hugged Rebecca spontaneously. It was the kind of reaction that Rebecca elicited. Rebecca had a natural attractiveness; she exuded a confident, warm intelligence. This was a major reason that Dee had recruited her. Rebecca had the kind of personality that would allow her to recruit, to win trust and inspire action. Dee knew that she herself didn't have such charisma. But she didn't need it—she had Rebecca.

They exchanged pleasantries—some *Nice to see yous* and *Lovely day, isn't its*, rehearsed phrases that confirmed they felt safe. Then they got down to business.

"I was surprised that you wanted to meet again so soon," said Rebecca. "Is something wrong?"

"Everything's fine," said Dee. "Well—except that the planet is being torn to shreds by authoritarian misogynists. I'm here to relay a message from the council." Rebecca nodded and walked slowly along the edge of the brook. They looked an asymmetric pair. Rebecca, in her thirties, wore her hair in a springy ponytail that made her look younger. Dee had put her hair up in a fancy braid that she hoped would make her look older. Rebecca's sundress was flattering, while Dee's blue T-shirt and shorts were utilitarian and genderless. Rebecca had an olive complexion, while Dee's was comparatively dark.

"The revolutionary council is very happy with your work," Dee said, speaking with the metered, precise diction of a memorized message. "They are impressed with the quality of new recruits you have gathered and with their quick organization into cells. Because of the skill you have shown, they are allocating you new resources."

Rebecca looked pleased. "I'm glad to hear it," she said.

Dee nodded. "New safe houses are being set up for your recruits," she explained, "along with a business—a front—that you'll use to pass messages and resources to other members of the network. Details here." She reached into her bag and passed a disposable plastic water bottle to Rebecca. A tiny memory card was glued to the inside of the bottle's cap under a concealing circle of white plastic. "Encryption passphrase is the same as last time."

Rebecca accepted the bottle, drank from it as though quenching her thirst, then continued nonchalantly to carry it. "When will the next safe house be ready?"

"Soon," said Dee. "The committee wants to know what cell you think best suited."

Rebecca considered. "Cell Seventeen," she said with slow certainty. "They have the most experience. They're reliable, and they're small enough to have room for growth."

"I'll pass that on," said Dee. "They trust your judgement."

"Great! Anything else?"

"The council has asked you to compile assigned readings for new recruits," Dee added, "about underground groups in history. The

Weather Underground. Black Panthers. Anticolonial struggles. Use your best judgement."

"I'll pull something together," Rebecca answered.

Dee paused for a moment. "Tell me a story," she said. "Something that reminds you of what we're talking about."

The *tell me a story* prompt was something Dee encouraged in the network. If there was one thing she knew about infiltrators—and she had read quite a lot—it was that no level of police fakery, no phony backstory could overcome the fact that police infiltrators had a shallow knowledge of movement history. Reading a book or two wouldn't give a police officer the deep knowledge that came from participating in and reading and talking about resistance struggles for years.

Dee wanted to make sure that everyone in the network had that deep knowledge, so they could tell the difference between a true friend and a false one. And so they could learn from and celebrate past movements—but people didn't go to prison for failing to *appreciate* their predecessors.

Rebecca had taken a pause of her own, considering Dee's request, glancing up past verdant leaves toward a patch of blue sky. "I've been thinking a lot about Amílcar Cabral."

"The west African revolutionary from the nineteen-sixties." Dee nodded. She had a photograph of him hidden in her room. "What about him?"

"He was a master recruiter," said Rebecca. "His home country, Cape Verde and Guinea-Bissau, was a colony under military occupation by fascist Portugal. Cabral built a powerful independence movement. But he did it by *listening*...."

Dee gave an encouraging nod, and Rebecca continued.

"Like, when you watch a movie about revolution, it's all speeches and shouting. And sure, Amílcar Cabral could give a good speech, but his strength was that he *listened* to new recruits. He listened to their problems; he helped them understand how the occupation and the liberation struggle affected *them*. He defeated the might of the occupying Portuguese military using gentleness, basically." Rebecca shrugged and then half smiled. "Well, *and* guns."

Dee smiled back, listening carefully. Rebecca's truthfulness shone through, as usual.

"Anything else?" Dee asked. "Something we can learn from?"

"Amílcar would train young revolutionaries," Rebecca said, her eyes bright, "and then send them back to their communities to organize. But when he sent people back to their home villages, their own families, it didn't work. They fell into old patterns. So, he decided to mix people up—to send new organizers to different communities, to break bad habits and make new ones. That seems important, but I'm not sure how to apply it yet."

Dee nodded. "I'm sure that will become clear." She checked her watch. "Remember what the council says. Recruitment is our priority."

"Thanks for carrying these messages," said Rebecca. "Sometimes I worry about you—so young, and already so radical! You are very careful, right? Always?"

Dee smiled. "Very careful."

"Okay," said Rebecca. "Say no to drugs!" she joked. Dee laughed. Rebecca patted Dee on the arm. "Take care of yourself, little sister."

From any other contact, Dee would have found the appellation patronizing. But from Rebecca she accepted it happily. "You too. Meeting with you is the highlight of my week." And with that unscripted and genuine remark, they parted ways.

～

Taavi, Samantha, and Andy arrived at their meeting with Corben five minutes early. And since Corben was twenty minutes late, they spent an awkward time sitting in the back room, drinking water and studying the menu and stalling the server while they tried to avoid drawing attention to the fact that none of them had *quite* reached the legal drinking age.

At 9:21, Corben pushed into the back room carrying a pitcher of beer and a stack of glasses. He greeted them. "Hope you weren't waiting long." He poured them each a glass of beer from the pitcher. "I heard from Apollo. He's doing all right. Staying strong. Prison's not easy—I know it."

Taavi nodded. Corben had spent a year in prison after taking a sledgehammer to the ATMs of a bank tied to clear-cutting of Amazon rainforest. He had been arrested in the process of smashing his fourth ATM of the night. Corben's defense lawyers argued that he was high on cocaine at the time of the incident and that Corben should spend time in rehab rather than prison, but he was sentenced to three years. He was released early through a legal loophole whose details Taavi hadn't followed. Corben's time in jail, and his bold action, had won him adoration from many a young radical.

Corben pulled his phone out of his pocket and turned it off. He gave the others a significant look, and they followed suit. Except Samantha. "I didn't bring my phone," she explained.

Corben took a long sip from his beer and stared at Taavi, Samantha, and Andy, one after the other. "Would you be afraid to do something that could put you in prison?"

Andy responded immediately. "No way. They asked one of the Black Panthers if he was afraid of prison, and he said 'No, I was born in prison.' That's how it is. You have to be free to be afraid of prison, and no one in this society is free."

Corben raised his eyebrows and nodded. "Good answer," he said. "How about you, Samantha?"

She considered for a moment, cleaning her eyeglasses on a napkin, and then said, "The way I see it, they arrest people all the time for doing nothing. Like, Apollo is in jail even though he didn't break the law. Most of the people in prison are people of color, or poor people. I'm a White person, middle-class. For me to be afraid of prison would be, like, just White privilege."

"Smart answer," said Corben. Taavi also thought Samantha was smart, but noticed she didn't really answer the question. Corben turned to Taavi with an expectant look.

"Yes," said Taavi. There was a pause and the others watched him, perplexed. Taavi continued. "Of course prison scares me. Of course I would be afraid to go to prison. Prisons exist to make people afraid, right?" Andy and Samantha watched him evenly. Corben wrinkled his nose slightly. Taavi finished: "But there are worse things than prison. So, I would risk it if I could really accomplish something first."

Corben stared at Taavi for several seconds and then smiled slightly.

"All right. It takes a big man to admit when he's afraid." And he clasped hands with Taavi for a moment. Taavi grinned back.

Corben took another sip of his beer, then glanced around to confirm no strangers were loitering nearby. "I was really excited when those cop cars got trashed. I'm not saying you guys did it, obviously. But you've got the guts to do something *like* that. And I think you've got the guts to do even more. Am I right?"

They nodded, and Andy added, "Damned right."

"Do you think these marches and protests are enough to stop the tank farm?" Corben asked. They shook their heads. "Everyone knows it's not enough, because it's not working. But most people are too afraid to do anything about it."

"So what would it take?" asked Taavi.

"You're smart," said Corben. "What do you think?"

"Paint a message on one of the big tanks," said Taavi. "'We won't take it anymore!'"

"It's a start," said Corben. "Do me one better."

"Trash the developer's office in the middle of the night," said Andy. "Steal files, smash computer monitors, clog sink drains and leave the faucets running."

"I like it." Corben grinned. "Very creative. Samantha?" Samantha looked at him as a server appeared at the door to ask if they needed anything. Corben, whose glass was empty, ordered another pitcher. There was an awkward pause as they waited for the pitcher to arrive. Taavi and Andy finished their glasses of beer. Taavi felt light-headed, invigorated by the prospect of action. The pitcher arrived, and Corben topped off all the pint glasses.

Once the server had left, Corben spoke. "How about this? The tanks are *totally* empty right now. I bet you can think of stuff to do now that would never risk a spill."

"Drill holes in them so they can't be filled," said Taavi.

"Punch holes in the sides with a pickax," added Andy.

"Make holes in the *top*," said Samantha, "where no one can see them, so rainwater will drain in and rust the tanks."

"Wow," said Corben. "Great ideas. And I think we should work on them. I think we should start a group—just the four of us—in secret.

An underground group, to work on our plans and make shit happen. I picked you because you're the bravest in Newbrook, and there's no one else I'd rather work with. I trust you guys, you know?"

"Thanks, man," said Andy. "Same to you."

"I've got a house on the edge of town," said Corben. "My grandparents left it to me. It can be our headquarters. I'm living there, but you can crash whenever you want."

"I can't wait to move out," said Andy. "My parents are driving me crazy."

"Well fuck, move in, then!" said Corben, and they slapped hands. "There are, like, five bedrooms. You can all move in if you want. Don't worry about rent."

"I could use a change of scene," mused Taavi.

"Awesome," said Corben. "Let's do it, punks. Let's do it."

Helen stepped into the tiny visiting booth in the prison. She sat on a metal stool that was bolted to the floor and picked up the telephone handset from a bracket on the concrete wall. Apollo sat smiling on the other side of a thick pane of transparent plastic, the distortion of which made the tiny locked room on his side seem out of perspective, like the view into a fish tank.

Apollo lifted his handset. "Hello!" he said.

Helen returned the greeting and grinned widely. "How are you doing?"

Apollo shrugged, "I'm doing fine, it's just that . . ." Helen was distracted by a hissing sound that grew in volume. Apollo continued to speak, but his voice became inaudible. He began to cough and gasp. The hissing grew louder.

Helen lowered her handset. "Apollo? What's happening?" As she spoke the pane between them stretched and buckled toward Apollo's side of the booth. Apollo gaped at her in horror, unable to breathe as the air in the room was sucked out. "Help!" called Helen, banging on the door behind her, calling for guards. The negative pressure warped the pane over Apollo's body and face, sealing him with his back against the door. Apollo stared at Helen, looking like a dead fish in the supermarket, vacuum-packed in plastic wrap.

The phone in her hand began to ring.

Helen woke gasping, damp with sweat. She was lying on the couch, her cell phone ringing. She sat up, glanced at her phone, and answered it.

"Are you okay?" asked Gwen over the phone. "You sound strange."

"I'm just waking up from a weird dream," replied Helen. "I try not to nap, but I'm dead tired today."

"Did you go to visit Apollo this morning? How was it?"

"Oh," said Helen. "It was fine. Lots of security and waiting. The visiting booths are claustrophobic. Apollo seems to be holding up well."

"Good," said Gwen. "Look, we should meet soon about the tank farm. I know everyone's worked up about the arrests, but we're close to a win on this campaign. We've got to push it over the finish line."

"You're right," said Helen. "Let's bring everyone to my apartment tomorrow."

"I'll check in about schedules," said Gwen, "but that sounds like a plan. I've got some ideas I'm pretty excited about."

"Can't wait to hear them," said Helen. She said good-bye and hung up. Then she rubbed her face, took a deep breath, and stood up. It was time to go to her office and get back to work.

Corben's house was on a cul-de-sac near the edge of town. It backed on to what had, until recently, been a golf course. After economic troubles—and a pesticide ban won by Friends of the Watershed—the golf course had defaulted on its taxes and shut down. The land was in legal limbo, slowly being taken over by weeds and small trees.

Taavi knocked on the front door. Corben answered almost immediately. "Hey, T!" he greeted. "Come in. Did you bring your stuff?"

Taavi gestured to the backpack he carried. "Just this."

"Cool, cool. Let me show you around." Corben led him through the house's various rooms. "Living room, dining room, office." The décor was old fashioned. The faded wallpaper showed dark rectangles where photographs or paintings had once hung; the house was now rather bare. "There used to be more decorations, but it was all old-people stuff," explained Corben.

The kitchen was spartan, with a few plates and utensils on one counter and several cases of beer stacked in a corner. The fridge, at least, was stocked with vegetarian faux-meat products, one bag of carrots, another of potatoes, and an entire case of beer.

"Bedrooms are upstairs," said Corben. "But first you've *got* to see the basement." They went downstairs, and Corben flicked on the lights.

"Holy shit," said Taavi. The entire basement was one large rectangular space, interrupted only by metal posts supporting the stories above. In one corner was a recreation area with a pool table, several couches, and an enormous television mounted on the wall. There was a small bar, well stocked with various kinds of liquor, against the wall near the pool table. "Grampa liked to party," explained Corben.

Another corner held a large workbench with a pegboard of tools above it. Shelves held nails, screws, hardware, and a variety of antiquated power tools. In the third corner were a furnace, a hot water tank, and other utility fixtures. On a concrete wall was a cork bull's-eye with an air rifle hanging underneath.

Taavi found the final corner most impressive. Maps of the city and surrounding area were taped to the wall: topographic maps, infrastructure maps of various pipelines, zoning areas. A street map was affixed to the top of a large table, a set of ceiling lights illuminating it brightly. A whiteboard on one wall held a list of addresses in Corben's handwriting, under the heading *Targets*.

"It's our war room," said Corben, striding into the space and spreading his hands wide. "It's got everything we need to plan right."

Taavi looked around and grinned. "Awesome," he said.

When Dee got home from the park—via a circuitous route peppered with countersurveillance maneuvers—her father was already asleep. He had left her a note in the kitchen: "You seemed distracted this morning," he had scrawled. "When you are driven, when you have high standards, it's easy to stress yourself out. A bookstore is not the only thing in the world. Don't worry about everything being perfect. Just do your best."

Dee ran her fingers over the scribbled ink. Her father's handwriting had gotten worse over time, but his words still touched her heart.

She ate takeout from the fridge and then went to her bedroom. She sat on her bed, closed her eyes, and visualized her circuits.

Dee was responsible for specialized resistance circuits with different jobs, the details of which she memorized. She could be anywhere—sitting on the bus, going for a run, lying on her bed—and review her action plans. But when she needed to prompt herself without having to encrypt anything, she would write innocuous notes in a simple code.

If she needed someone to investigate possible actions and targets, to perform background checks on friends or foes, she might write "eyeglasses" to remind her of the intelligence circuit. The counterintelligence circuit, "screwdriver," maintained security and watched for leaks or infiltrators. The logistical support circuit, "wrench," performed R&D on new equipment, built special devices, and funnelled supplies to the action cells. The fundraising circuit, "wallet," brought in money from sources that Dee kept secret from the other circuits. And then there was the action circuit, "hammer," and its many cells. Dee had personal staff, like the hacker Simón, who had no interactions with the others.

Hammer, under Rebecca's guidance, had become the largest circuit. But wallet had been the first, and it funded the rest of the operation.

She opened her eyes, went to her desk, and scribbled a few notes. "Check prescription," she wrote, "get new frames"—*consult with the intelligence circuit and add a new cell.* "Get box of nails," she wrote—*new recruits for the action circuit.* "Get cash for wallet"—*allocate more cash to the fundraising cell.*

Dee's father had left several printouts on her desk about different nonprofits: Friends of the Watershed. A disaster relief organization for climate refugees. Doctors Without Borders. She looked through them briefly. This was Dee's gig for her father; she assessed charities to which he might donate. Her father's retirement income was large. He reduced his taxes by donating generously and felt it gave Dee valuable experience to handle money.

Dee realized early on that through these donations she could launder money and route it back to the nascent network. That seed money allowed her to hire people to perform other, more illegal fund-raising activities. She wasn't stealing, exactly. Much of the money still went to the charities, eventually—or would, once she finished making back her seed money.

In the top drawer of Dee's desk was a stack of black-and-white photographs. Not photos of family—there were a handful of those in the living room, and many more in her father's room—but photos of historical figures important to Dee: Nelson Mandela. Bhagat Singh. Harriet Tubman. Subhas Chandra Bose. Angela Davis. Sophie Scholl. There were nearly a hundred, all prominent members of movements for freedom around the world, in India, South Africa, the United States, Nazi-occupied Europe. Dee had collected them when she first studied social movements, using the photos as a mnemonic aid; she would stare at each face in turn as she committed their deeds and strategies to memory. Later she could pull them out in a moment of uncertainty: *What would Amílcar Cabral do?*

It was bending security culture to keep them in her house. But she didn't have the heart to throw them out. Besides, a person was allowed to own photographs, and if things got to the point that police were searching her desk it would be too late to matter.

Outside her window, the sun was low in the sky. She pulled out her travel alarm clock and checked the time. Eight o'clock. Then she pressed several buttons on the clock, and a countdown appeared. Ten months, four days, seven hours, twenty-two minutes, and fifteen seconds. The seconds ticked down as she watched. She set her jaw and snapped the clock shut.

The Friends of the Watershed offices were in a building next to the river that crossed downtown Newbrook. Helen couldn't actually *see* the river from the office—their nonprofit was not so well funded as to afford good views—but she could go and sit by it during lunch, or use it as a backdrop for interviews or photographs.

This evening she had no such engagements. She looked forward to some solitary time to handle the growing backlog of tank-farm correspondence, especially the perpetually growing number of unanswered e-mails. She had stacks of paper on her desk comprised of petitions, handwritten notes, pamphlets and flyers, and feedback sheets from the town hall meeting; community members were encouraged to write down thoughts about the petroleum depot approval process and how the campaign against it had been organized. She dreaded sorting through those. Feedback at big public events was usually a mixed bag, and losing a panelist over terrorism charges wouldn't help.

As she worked, someone unlocked the main door and entered. "Burning the midnight oil?" asked a man's voice.

"Hello, Leon," she replied. Leon was the chair of the Friends of the Watershed board of directors. "Just catching up. It's been a hectic month."

"That's why I wanted to talk," he said. "Have you prepared our submission for the Lakes Conference? It's due Monday."

The annual Lakes Conference had been a cornerstone of FotW's work since the nonprofit was founded. Every year, academics, researchers, and grassroots organizers got together to discuss the state of freshwater lakes. Helen had attended the conference and given seminars for the past several years, but she increasingly found the whole affair to be dry and lifeless, a meek gathering in the face of converging ecological crises. "The package is almost ready," Helen replied. "It'll be in on time."

"Don't forget that the conference is part of your contract," Leon said. "We need to maintain a solid profile to ensure funding. Some new grants coming out this year—could be a game changer."

"I understand," said Helen. "No problem." She glanced out the window behind Leon. Across the street she could see an idling blue sedan with tinted windows. She frowned, an expression which Leon misinterpreted.

"You don't seem sure," he said. "Are you working on it now? Tonight?"

Helen measured her response carefully. She was paid a little over minimum wage to work thirty hours a week. In actuality she worked twice as many hours and regularly purchased supplies for the nonprofit out of pocket. This would have been bad enough with one boss.

But with six directors on the board—and various funders wanting regular updates—it often felt like she had ten. So she kept her tone even when she said: "I'm getting my job done, Leon. You don't have to worry."

"It seems like you're doing a lot *more* than your job," he said, nodding at the stacks of paper on her desk. "Look, everyone loves a feel-good campaign. But if things get messy, it's not good for us. Funders don't like political controversy. It's very bad for our prospects if our name shows up in national papers next to criminal charges."

"What exactly do you expect me to do about it?" she asked.

"Tidy this up," he said. "Get some video of local politicians promising they'll do their best to keep the tank farm closed. Edit that together with some footage of protest marches and speeches, throw it up on the website, and call it a victory. Everyone feels good about it, we still get funded, and you can get on with your actual job."

"My job is to protect the watershed," Helen replied.

"Your job—and mine—is to maintain the viability of this organization," Leon said. "Not to run it into the ground with a campaign that drags on for years. And not to take on federal government initiatives, as I've heard talk of. We're a small organization. Focus on small victories."

"Small victories aren't enough. We can't solve global problems piecemeal. What about the future?"

"The future is what I'm worried about," said Leon. "The future of this nonprofit. Are we clear?"

The sedan was still idling across the street. "Was that car idling when you arrived?" Helen asked.

Leon furrowed his brow at the change in subject but looked out the window. "Oh, my wife's waiting to give me a ride," he said. He shrugged sheepishly. "In the summer she likes the air-conditioning. Anyway, do you understand me?"

Helen nodded.

"And take that down," Leon added, pointing to a *Free the Newbrook Four* poster on the door. "We don't want to be associated with that." Leon said good-bye and left. She watched him get into the car and drive away.

Helen sat down, feeling increasingly overwhelmed. Apollo had been invaluable in addressing correspondence because he didn't care what people thought of him. He could empty an inbox in forty-five minutes, while she felt obliged to compose a thoughtful and tactful response to each message, even when the sender was basically ignorant or offering unnecessary advice.

She added two items to her to-do list: *Find more organizing volunteers for campaign. Talk with sympathetic board members in private.*

Well, she thought to herself, *no use delaying.* She pulled up her contacts and started dialling.

～

Taavi and Corben spent the evening in Corben's basement watching a 1999 DVD of riot footage from European protests. "A fine vintage," joked Corben. Around eight o'clock, Andy and Samantha arrived to join the viewing. Corben shared his stockpile of beer generously and encouraged them to practice with the air rifle and cork target in the corner while the TV blared.

"Why do they always smash windows right in front of the riot cops?" asked Samantha.

"To show the pigs they aren't in charge," said Corben.

"But a bunch of them are getting arrested right after," said Samantha. "Why didn't they just smash those bank windows the night before?"

Taavi's phone rang. He answered it as he walked to the other side of the room.

"Hi Taavi; this is Helen," said the voice on the phone. "I'm the coordinator at Friends of the Watershed?"

"Oh, yeah, I know who you are," said Taavi.

"Great. Apollo worked with me on the campaign against the tank depot. Since he's been in jail, I've needed extra organizing help," said Helen. "Apollo mentioned you're good with technical stuff; he thought you might be willing to lend a hand."

"Apollo suggested you call me?"

"He said you had the makings of a sharp organizer," said Helen.

Taavi pondered this. "I've got a really busy schedule most days," he lied.

"I understand," she said. "But if you ever want to drop by, I'm in the office most afternoons and evenings. Every bit counts, right?"

"Sure," he said. "Maybe I'll come by."

"I look forward to it," she said. "Your friends are welcome, too."

They hung up. When Taavi returned to the couch, Corben turned to him.

"Who was that?" Corben asked over an enormous crowd chanting *Ya basta!* Taavi told him, and Corben frowned. "I don't know, man. You've got to be careful who you're seen with, after all these police raids and stuff. Surveillance and all."

"I don't think Helen is a cop," said Andy. "She's been around a long time. I know her."

"But, you know, security culture," said Corben. "We've got to keep to ourselves now, if we're going to be doing serious shit. We can't go talking to liberal activists."

Samantha took off her glasses and squinted at him. "I'm not sure that's how security culture works," she said.

"Well, I'm not gonna argue with you," said Corben casually. "I've been to jail; I kinda know how this stuff works."

"It's no big deal." Taavi shrugged, trying to head off an argument. "I wasn't going to call her back, anyway." He hadn't been entirely sure, before. But now he certainly would not.

7

2051

Evelyn stared. A murderer stood in her living room, only feet from Sara. Evelyn recognized him instantly, even without his sunglasses. His face, its eye sockets like deep pits, was stamped into her mind. Sara seemed cheerfully oblivious to the danger.

Evelyn backed into the kitchen. "Sara, get away from him!" she said, seizing a chef's knife from the counter. Sara raised her hands in a calming gesture as the man stepped back fearfully. Evelyn pointed the knife at him: "Get the fuck away from her!"

"Evelyn," Sara began, "this man is a friend."

"This man is dangerous!" Evelyn barked back.

"I don't think we've met," said the man in a friendly tone. "I'm—"

"I know who you are!" Evelyn said, brandishing her knife. "Sara, he's here to finish me off! I'm a witness!"

Sara stepped *between* Evelyn and the man. "I know this man well. He's no threat to us. Who do you think he is?"

Evelyn's throat was tight. Nearly weeping from anger and fear, she choked out: "He shot the guards at the checkpoint!" The man looked shocked.

Sara stepped closer and gently put her hands on Evelyn's. "He's a good friend from a long time ago, part of a movement against the Authority. He's saved many lives." Sara pushed Evelyn's hands so the knife pointed toward the floor. "Who do you think brings me antibiotics?"

Evelyn was confused and shaking slightly as Sara disarmed her. The man stayed where he was, his hands clearly visible. He spoke: "You were at the checkpoint yesterday?"

He didn't even recognize her, hadn't given her a thought. This enraged her. "I was knocked over! You almost shot the guard next to me."

"Ahhh," he said gravely. "I'm sorry you saw that. And sorry to surprise you; I didn't mean to upset you."

"Of course I'm upset!" retorted Evelyn. "It's not every day I'm in a room with a murderer!"

His eyes narrowed slightly. "Respectfully," he said," if you work at Triage Administration, you spend every day in a *building* full of murderers."

"What the *fuck* are you saying!" said Evelyn, truly shouting now. "How dare you come to *my home* and accuse me of—"

"Evelyn. Evelyn!" said Sara in a hushed voice. "The guards on the roof—we don't need attention."

"Where's Sid?" Evelyn asked quietly.

"Playing downstairs with the other kids," said Sara. "He's fine."

Evelyn took several deep breaths to calm herself, exhaling raggedly and keeping her eyes locked on the man.

"I'm sorry for this upset," he said. "Let me start again. My name is Layth. I work with a movement that helps people get medication and avoid imprisonment in the work camps. We *have* to smuggle things. A backpack of antibiotics can save hundreds of lives. If I had been captured yesterday, my supplies confiscated, it would have been a disaster for the people who depend on us. And I would have been tortured and killed."

Evelyn shook her head in disbelief. She looked at Sara, who nodded. "He's telling the truth," she said.

Evelyn sighed. "Is that why you came here? To deliver antibiotics?"

"No," said Layth. "I could leave items in a dead drop. I took the considerable risk of coming in person to ask a very important favor."

Evelyn glanced between Sara and Layth with narrowed eyes. "I see. And exactly *what* dangerous task do you want the love of my life to undertake?"

Layth raised his eyebrows. "I'm afraid there's a misunderstanding," he said. "I'm not here to ask a favor of Sara.

"I'm here because I need a favor from *you*."

—⚡

Twice a week, everyone at the Thistle got together for dinner at the common hall, converging from nearby houses and cabins. This day the rotating duty of making dinner fell to the men's bunkhouse, who had cooked up an enormous beef-and-vegetable stew. The stew was served with a generous side of steamed beets, cooked (like the stew) on a wood-burning stove. The warmth of the hall made Addy doff her sweater, the long scar on her abdomen itching from the heat.

Addy filled her bowl, surveyed the long tables, and found a place next to her neighbor Gretchen, sitting across from the woman and boy who had arrived that afternoon.

"No, we're not here to run away," the red-haired woman was explaining. "We're looking for aid. The movement in the city is strong, but we need help to win."

"We have our hands full here, too," said Gretchen, a shepherd. "We used to trade with people near the city, but now everything they produce is taken by the Authority."

"That's *why* we have to work together," said the red-headed woman, "to support struggles in Authority territory. They can't spread outward if they're overwhelmed from the inside."

Addy inspected the woman's face carefully, trying to remember why she looked familiar. The woman's intelligent eyes were deeply sad. The boy beside her was bowed over his bowl, his eyes in shadow as he devoured spoonful after slow spoonful of the stew and beets. He probably hadn't eaten fresh vegetables in months.

"But how can you fight totalitarians?" asked Gretchen. "I don't want to be insensitive, but why would you and your husband take such a risk? Why not just move here, where it's safer?"

"Fighting back is difficult," the red-haired woman agreed. "My husband knew the risks. He lost a sister to the triage camps. Even though"—the woman paused to swallow wetly before continuing—"even though he died, he wanted to die fighting. He didn't regret joining Kraken." Addy flinched slightly; no one noticed.

Carlos came and sat next to Addy. The young boy looked up and stared at his bushy beard; Carlos winked back.

"What help do you need?" asked Gretchen.

"We need safe houses, areas for rest and training," said the woman.

"We had rural retreats close to the city, but they've been overrun. We need supplies. Ammunition. Medicines, if you can get them. And, of course, food." She ruffled her boy's hair. "Getting enough nutritious food for the children is a challenge most winters. My son has never seen so many beets in his life."

The boy leaned in to his mother and whispered something. She listened and then asked, "He's still hungry; is there . . ."

"There's plenty left," said Gretchen. "Eat your fill, both of you."

The boy slid off the bench and took his bowl to refill it.

"I heard your husband's entire cell was obliterated," said Addy, her eyes following the boy. "Is that true?" Addy looked at the woman, who nodded slightly. "Isn't it irresponsible to have a child if you're going to do something so dangerous?" Addy asked.

Everyone at the table went abruptly silent, some freezing with spoons halfway from bowl to mouth.

The red-haired women flushed and gave Addy a fierce look. "I love my son. I fight to make a better world *for* him. I take care of him."

Addy returned her stare. "It looks like you want *us* to take care of him."

"Okay!" said Carlos, standing up. "We're on dish duty tonight, Adelaide; we'd better go." He picked up his bowl, stood, and tugged on Addy's sleeve.

A few moments later they were alone in the kitchen. Carlos looked confused and upset. "Addy, what was that?"

"I realized that woman has been here before," said Addy. "Years ago. Remember? She asked us to be a safe house. We voted no. Too dangerous."

"Our farm wouldn't exist if people were afraid to break the law," said Carlos. "If it weren't for Helen's bulldozer, this would all be part of the hole."

"That's different," replied Addy. "We made a group decision about Charlotte, and now she's back anyway. Using us. Drawing attention. Forcing our participation."

"We invited her for dinner!" said Carlos. "We're having a conversation! She's not forcing anything. Why were you so rude to her? You're always polite to newcomers and refugees."

"She's not a refugee," replied Addy. "She's here because of her own actions. If she had spent more time fighting and less time having children she couldn't support, maybe her husband would still be alive."

"What?" said Carlos, astonished. He slapped his forehead, ran his hand through his hair. "That's ridiculous. That's victim blaming. What's gotten into you? You're always the one talking about how people need to stick together, build alliances, stay strong. You should be all over this!"

"They're reckless," said Addy, almost shouting. "They'll get people needlessly killed. They've done it already!" She grabbed him by his bearded cheeks and stared fiercely into his eyes.

"Addy," he began softly, "I don't understand what's—"

But she released him, turned away, and rushed out the kitchen door into the night.

—✗

Layth placed a page on the kitchen table and backed slowly away to sit on the couch, hands clearly visible on his knees.

Evelyn advanced a few steps and picked up the sheet. It was a list. Names, with birthdates beside most of them. Evelyn looked at Layth. "What do you want me to do?"

"It's simple," said Layth, his body language relaxed and nonconfrontational. "Members of my network were attacked and killed. I need to know if any are still alive, in the triage system."

Evelyn looked at Sara. Sara took her hand. "If you could do this, I'd appreciate it greatly," said Sara. "I knew some of these people."

Evelyn reviewed the list. "Paper forms come a week after intake," she said. "I'll keep my eyes open."

"I'll give you a camera to photograph anything you find," said Layth. "And a Samizdata coin for reading underground messages."

"We can't bring outside electronics into the building," said Evelyn. "One wing holds the cyberwarfare unit; they're very picky."

That wouldn't be a problem, it turned out; the camera Layth produced was disguised as a pocket-sized bottle of disinfectant spray. The spray aperture contained a pinhole-sized digital sensor.

"You said a week," Layth began. "Is there a computer system you can check sooner? It's a matter of life and death."

"I can try," said Evelyn. "But some of these don't even have birth dates or full names." She read from the list. "Like these at the bottom." *M. Ruiz, possibly Medea Ruiz, born 1981. Jad, surname unknown, born circa 1979.* She looked up quizzically. "Are many of your guerillas senior citizens?"

"Please," he asked. "Find what you can. It's important to me. The names at the top are most urgent."

"If the others aren't urgent, who are they?" asked Evelyn.

"For security reasons," apologized Layth, "I can't say."

"I could get fired for poking around," said Evelyn. "If we can't pay rent, we lose this apartment, lose everything."

"If you can't find them," said Layth, "my friends may suffer a fate much worse than death."

—✻

Addy lay on her bed in the dark. Outside her closed window, she could hear faint good-byes as diners dispersed. Then the bedroom door squeaked as Carlos entered. He shut the door, sat down on the side of the bed, and began to speak.

"When you arrived, I didn't ask a lot of questions," he said. "Some of the people who make it here have terrible, traumatizing experiences. You know that; you've interviewed plenty of them. Even lately, as we've gotten closer, I've tried not to be nosy. And you don't volunteer much."

He paused for several long moments, silent in the dark. "I care about you. I don't know your history, but I care. I'm sorry that something about this woman has upset you. If you want to talk, I'll listen."

Carlos waited a minute, then two. Addy said nothing. Carlos spoke again. "I'm not sure what I can say. Is there something you want me to ask you?" Silence, again. He waited thirty seconds. "Well, a lot of people stayed to talk with Charlotte after you left. That's her name— Charlotte. And people want to help her. The youngsters admire her; she reminds them of LT."

He paused and sighed. "I think we should help her, too. It might be dangerous. But the Authority keeps growing, keeps gobbling up more land. We've got to fight them eventually, right? It's just a matter of when and where. The longer we wait, the fewer allies we'll have left when the time comes." More silence. "Are you listening?"

Addy's mind churned with things she wanted to say, stories to tell, things she had sacrificed. But she felt frozen. All she could say was: "I just want to sleep."

"Oh, okay," said Carlos. He shifted his weight to leave. But she turned toward him and pulled him down gently beside her. They held each other. Soon Carlos began to snore. It was much later when Addy finally slept.

—⚡

"How long have you been doing this?" Evelyn asked as she lay in bed with Sara after evening power-down. "Resistance stuff."

"Since before we met," said Sara. "When Sid was a baby, he got sick. Deathly ill. I went to a nurse I knew. She said if I took him to an Authority doctor they'd decide he was too sick; it would be a 'poor allocation of limited resources' to give expensive drugs to a yellow-tagged infant. In the worst case we would get red tagged. She got me medicine—not just herbs but pharmaceuticals. They saved Sid's life. Without the resistance, he'd be dead, and I'd be in a triage camp."

Evelyn knew Sid had been sick but had not known the full story. "Why didn't you tell me?"

"When we met, I didn't know you well enough. Later, when I came to care for you, I didn't want to put you at risk. You aren't a good liar, and you worry." Evelyn frowned, and Sara reached out to caress her hair. "Besides, the network operates on secrecy. Need to know."

"What do you do for them?"

"Pass messages back and forth with Samizdata. Look for promising recruits. Give medicine to people who need it on our block. If we keep people from getting visibly sick, we can protect the whole block from triage."

"If you give people unprescribed antibiotics, their effectiveness will decrease for everyone."

"But not everyone can access antibiotics. That's the problem. Plus, the people who get sick in the triage camps are a reservoir of contagion. The system doesn't make any sense from a medical perspective. It only makes sense if you really want to keep things as they are."

Evelyn sighed and thought for a long while. Then she said, "Is this why you didn't argue with me about staying in the closet? When we moved in together, and I said I didn't want to come out, you barely argued. Is this why?"

"You made some good points," said Sara. "That 'homosexuality' is an official contagion risk factor, the superintendent wants to kick us out already, your career—"

"I remember what I said," Evelyn interrupted. "But is this why you didn't argue?"

Sara looked away. "I have to keep a low profile if I want to work with the underground. Thirty years ago, it wouldn't have been a problem. Everyone and their mother was out and proud. But the way things have backslid—well, you've got to pick your battles, right?"

Evelyn started to cry. Not sobbing, just a steady stream of noiseless tears. "This sucks," she said, with a vague gesture that seemed to encompass the entire city.

Sara pulled her close. "I know, hon," she said. "I know."

Evelyn slept in fits, waking over and over with a gnawing feeling in her stomach. She to tried rest, pressing herself against Sara's warm, sleeping body. But at five in the morning, she got up and went into the dark living room. Normally she had tea before breakfast, but power-up was still an hour away. So, she looked out the window.

There was an unusual amount of YEA traffic below, trucks passing behind her building to a different high-rise she couldn't see from her window. She slid the balcony door open for a moment and heard distant shouts and banging.

While she waited for the power, she used a flashlight to read and reread Layth's list of names, memorizing them.

Then Evelyn picked up the Samizdata coin; through her e-reader she found the contents as an external drive. She browsed the headlines.

Fascist armbands crack down but the people
fight back
Please we need help in Yellow 5 (old town)
FOOD RATIONS ON THE INCREASE
Fanon wanted: please post anticolonial
literature
How to survive a triage camp #3
Homeland diesel stockpile sabotaged!
Suggestions for filtering dirty water?
HOW THE YEA RESTORES PROSPERITY
The Protectorate welcomes all skilled
workers!
Re: Suggestions for filtering dirty water?
Getting rid of spam?
EROTIC EXPLOITS OF THE RED ZONE SLUTS (3/9)
overwhelmed by yea spam
AMNESTY FOR TIPSTERS (DETAILS INSIDE)
Cake recipes with ration powders?
Drone shot down west of city!
Nerve clamping more than a rumor
FIVE BEST RATION RECIPES
Tips for dealing with spam
VICTORIES AGAINST BANDITS MEAN MORE CHARCOAL
FOR ALL

There were pages and pages like this. Evelyn chose "Tips for dealing with spam."

Unfortunately, YEA capture of Samizdata coins
has allowed them to inject spam into our
network—propaganda, obscenities, calls for
informers, gibberish to clog our bandwidth.
    We're working on a technical solution.
Meanwhile, please promptly delete any spam
your coin downloads so you don't pass it on
to others.

```
Remember, not all spam LOOKS like spam.
For years, the YEA has run software designed
to manipulate social networks and public
opinion in favor of fascism. We encourage
you to read stories of resistance defeats,
and news in general, with a critical eye.
```

She browsed the bulletins. Some were factual reports, first-person news updates from parts of the city that couldn't normally exchange messages. Many were requests for information, often practical. Others were short manifestos and rants against the Authority. And then there was a large amount of spam, ranging from appeals for informers to X-rated fiction.

Evelyn tapped "How to survive a triage camp #3."

```
My family managed to stay together for three
days in the camps.
    I wrote last time how they puled our truck
over at a checkpoint and found contrband
food inside. My mom wanted to bring extr
food to our relativs in the city, but
the soldiers found it. They confscated
everything and sent us to the triage camp.
    Where did you get the food from, they
askd? I said I didnt know. They swabbed
my mouth with a long q-tip and put it in a
plastic container.
    Where was the food going? Why did it have
to be hidden? Its just for our family, I
told them. They listened to my breathing
with a cold stethescope and they squeezed my
arm with a blood pressure cuff.
    Where are the rebels hiding? I don't know
what you're talking about. They checked my
temperature with a plastic thermeter that
tasted terrible. I hate them.
```

They searched me three times but never
fuond the coin.

They asked me about skills. Could I sew?
Could I shovel? Use machines? Could I cook?
Garden?

They told me I was sick, a carier of
contagious diseases. I asked which ones.
They said it didn't matter. I asked which
of them was a doctor, and they just sent me
into the camp.

We sleep in "dormitories," but they're
just old apartment buildings with the
valuble stuff ripped out. There are separate
buildings for men, and women, and juveniles.
Anyone who is really sick gets transferred
to "quarantine." I got put in juveniles
building with my little brother.

I asked him about the interveiw. He
said they made him answer questions for
even longer than me. While they asked him
questions they put him in cold room in his
underwear, until he was almost too cold to
shver. They checked his temperature after
and said it was too high, he had a fever!
That's why he got sent into the camp, too.

Some people in this dormitory cant sleep
because they cough so bad. I asked a guard
why no heat, he said it was treatment
for tuberculosis. I said I didn't have
tuberculosis. He laughed. Not yet, he said.

My battery is almost gone so I have to stop
until I can charge phone. If you have tips
for surviving in a triage camp, post them.

At sunrise, Evelyn stared out the window at the small slice of harbor
she could see, where an abandoned container ship rusted offshore.

When Sara and Sid got up, Evelyn had a distracted breakfast with them. Sid kept trying to tell her something he read in a book, but she couldn't maintain her focus on his rambling monologue.

Evelyn knew she couldn't bring her e-reader to work—it wouldn't be allowed in, and it was foolish to bring in anything with illegal Samizdata messages. So, she stole a moment in the bathroom to read the next bulletin while she brushed her teeth with rusty water. She skipped to "How to survive a triage camp #5," unable to find all the bulletins sequentially.

```
After they took my parents away it was just
me and my brother left in the camp. I askd
bunch of times where they went but the
guards won't tell me.
    She said she would stick with us and I
guess she did her best.
    Weve been at Triage West for two weeks,
so most people from our dormitory have been
send somewhere else. This place is just for
sorting people. No one stays long.
    A boy on our floor lent me this phone and
solar charger. I gave him extra biscuit for
rent. He didn't come back after the work
detail so I guess it's mine now. Too bad the
phone part doesnt connect. Frequencies are
jammed to "prevent cyber-terrorism" and I
have to leave it in airplane mode.
    I try to make sure my brther is in same
work detail as me. Work details in the
kitchen are nice because it's warm but we
havent gotten any yet. We did sanitation
duty which means digging latrines. A few
months ago there was a fight and people used
shovels to fight guards but they got stopped
and sent to a mining camp where people never
come above ground. Now they give us shovels
```

with short litle handles so we can't fight
and it makes digging very hard.

Another work detail was materials sorting.
Trucks with rubble come and dump them in a
big pit. We sort out the good stuff, metal
and rebar. If rebar is in concrete we smash
it out with a hammer. And if there are
blocks of concrete we braek it into little
pieces and put it into a wheelbarrow and
they use it to make more concrete. They let
us have the hammers in the pit, but they
make us put the hammers down before we climb
back out so we can't fight with them.

My brother says it's not so bad to do
work because we get paid. They scan our red
triage tags before and after work detail,
and they pay us by the hour. But they also
charge us room and board. My little brother
said it's not so bad because you have to pay
rent on the outside and lots of people there
are unemployed. I don't know if the guards
said that to him or the other patients. The
guards say if we work hard, they send us to
a higher level of triage that is nicer.

Evelyn kissed Sara and Sid good-bye, took the stairs, and passed
through her building's lobby. Additional YEA guards congregated
around the entrance of the building, and one of them demanded to
check her ID card as she left the lobby. She asked if something was
wrong.

"Disturbance in E Block yesterday," he said. "It's sealed off while we
check things out. You can go about your business."

She proceeded to her bus stop and then to Triage Administration.
Once Evelyn arrived at work, she went to her desk and took her fur
coat off. But before she could sit down, she heard a man's voice behind
her: "Ahem—Evelyn Park?"

Evelyn turned, startled. A public safety officer in a clean and pressed uniform was standing a few feet away from her, staring at her. "Yes?" she asked in surprise.

"I just wanted to introduce myself," he said. "I'm Constable Johnson. Call me Jim. And I, err, just want to say, ahh, welcome to TA, and let me know if there's anything you need." He handed her a small packet wrapped in tissue paper and left abruptly.

Evelyn looked in confusion over at Phyllis, who was grinning and waggling her eyebrows. "Well, it looks like *someone* is popular."

Evelyn unfolded the tissue paper. There was a chocolate bar inside. She looked at Phyllis again. "I don't get it. Why did he give me chocolate?"

Phyllis rolled her eyes cheerfully. "*Why?* Because you're new, and you're cute, and you're not married. He wants you to know he's a man of means."

Evelyn frowned slightly. "How does he know I'm not married?"

Phyllis dropped her smile. "Anyone can find out if they work here. It's in your ATLAS file." Evelyn looked even more confused, so Phyllis pointed to Evelyn's computer. "Officially, only triage officers are supposed to use it. But everyone can. Just go to the main screen and press Control-F12."

Evelyn did this. A new, unfamiliar interface appeared on her screen. At the same time, a cart full of new files arrived. "I'll show you later," said Phyllis.

Evelyn took a stack of envelopes from the cart and began to input them. But after twenty minutes, she checked over her shoulder to make sure no one was watching and switched to the ATLAS interface. She typed in her own name. An enormous amount of information came up: her past addresses, the fact that Sara was her roommate of two years, a copy of her proof-of-health card. A record of every checkpoint she had passed through going back years. Copies of performance assessments from previous jobs, even records from before the Authority existed.

She typed the first letters of a name she had memorized. But as she did this, she had a sudden burst of paranoia. Given how much information was being collected about her—about everyone—was even this computer being monitored? If she simply typed names from Layth's list, would she trigger a warning system and alert security? Rumor was that every message in the city was read by an artificial intelligence, a supercomputer run by the Authority to scan for terrorist activity.

She opted for an oblique approach. Surely there was a list of recent intakes. She started clicking through promising links. *Metadata. Statistics. Input. Revenues.*

None yielded anything comprehensible. But a list called "Outcome Tables" showed all triage sites, numbers of people admitted, severities of illness, numbers released. She skimmed the numbers. Surely there was something useful. If only she could—

"Evelyn!" came a man's deep voice behind her. She jumped involuntarily and spun in her chair to see the person behind her.

It was the director. She stood and leaned back on her desk slightly, to try to cover the screen without *looking* as though she was covering the screen. "Good morning!" she said, trying to mimic Phyllis's bland cheerfulness. "What can I do for you, sir?"

"Nothing at all," said the director. "I was passing by, thought I'd see how your first few days have been, if you had questions."

"Well, actually," she said, desperate for a distraction, "I was wondering if you could explain"—she grasped a page at random from her desk—"how this form works."

The Director frowned slightly but took the form. "Recent Associations," he read. "Well, Evelyn, this is straightforward—it's contact tracing. Anyone who is triaged must give a detailed list of people they've seen, places they've visited. Anyone who might have shared an infection with them, or vice versa. Simple epidemiology: track down sources of infection and seal them off before they spread." He made a chopping gesture and handed the page back to her. "Does that answer your question?"

Evelyn nodded and tried to smile. "Simple epidemiology!" she repeated.

"Anything else I can help you with?"

"Nope, nothing," she replied, smiling more broadly.

"All right, then," he said smoothly, turning as if to leave. Then he looked back: "Learn anything from those outcome tables?" He gestured to her screen.

A chill went through her. "I must have pressed the wrong button."

"Now, Evelyn, no need to be coy," he grinned. "Everyone pokes around a little bit! It's part of the fun. Now tell me, what do you see here?" The director stepped forward, grasped her by one elbow, and turned her to face the screen. "You were studying these figures intently. What do you see?"

She picked a line at random. "Well, in this triage camp it looks like more people are sick each month than the month before. These ones, too. Maybe you should take a closer look at those camps, in case they're making people sick." She stopped. She had spoken carelessly. The easy smile faded from the director's face.

"Evelyn, Evelyn, you misunderstand," he said. "Triage camps can't *make* people sick. That's a contradiction in terms." He squeezed her elbow for emphasis. "Like saying prison makes people criminal, or school makes them stupid.

"No, Evelyn, what you see here is a simple by-product of statistics. Statistics is a very complicated field, you understand, very mathematical. Things that *look* like patterns can appear for many reasons. Perhaps, in this case, people who have recently been infected are showing symptoms *after* they've been triaged, and so it *looks* like they're getting sicker." His regular smile returned. "It's all very hard to follow, even for me! You should probably stick to your regular work from now on."

She nodded slowly and tapped her keyboard to close the outcome tables.

The director released her elbow. "All right then," he said, giving her a big wink as he backed away, "I'll be seeing you!"

—⁄⁄—

Everyone did chores before breakfast at the Thistle. For some this meant filling buckets of water and carrying them to sheep or goats or horses or chickens. For some it meant bringing firewood into the house and cooking breakfast on the woodstove. For Addy, it meant shredding roots for animal feed, something she did with the help of a farm apprentice.

Thirty years earlier, the animals would have been fed with grain; corn, soy, and wheat had been cheap and plentiful. Those days were past. The farm's terrain was unsuitable for grain, the climate had worsened, they lacked fuel for combines and tractors, and demand for grain as food made it too expensive to use as animal feed.

So, they fed their animals hay, alongside shredded root vegetables, which were easy to grow and store. Each fall they buried caches of turnips and beets and carrots and wurzel for use through the winter. The best roots were eaten by humans (and stored in a proper root cellar). But those less prized—wurzel, for example—or those that had softened were shredded for animals.

There was a large shredding machine in the barn; Addy arrived there while the air was still cool and frosty. An enthusiastic apprentice by the name of Nathan brought a bin of root vegetables. They greeted each other, and Nathan dumped the bin into the shredding machine's hopper.

"Are we using the motor this morning?" asked Nathan. If enough water flowed in the stream, the batteries would be fully charged each morning and ready to run pumps and motors and lights and even the coffeemaker (though the beverage it produced did not technically include any coffee).

"Not today," replied Addy. With minimal flow in the stream, she didn't want to risk running out of power again. They needed the batteries for luxuries like music players, but also for their comm equipment and to run a water pump in case of fire.

"I'll go first, then," said Nathan, hopping onto the bicycle mounted next to the machine. He strained to get the cold machine spinning smoothly, but soon he had it purring along, dropping a slow but steady stream of shredded vegetables into a bucket.

Once the bucket filled, Addy swapped it for a new one, and she kept the hopper topped off with vegetables. After a few minutes, she offered to spell Nathan off on the bicycle.

"But you're . . ." he began.

"Not too old to ride a bicycle," Addy finished for him. Barely middle-aged, perhaps she seemed older to twenty-year-old Nathan. He looked healthy, and she would have been glad to let him continue except for the fact that he was so skinny. A recent arrival from a village that wasn't thriving, Nathan had slowly gained weight at the Thistle. Addy wanted to let him put on a bit more, so she took over the pedaling and sent him to get another bin of root vegetables. Soon she had taken off her coat, sweating in the early morning cold, the scar on her abdomen itching from the warmth.

As she rode the machine, Addy sunk into a rhythm of rumination. She tried to think of what to say to Carlos, how to make him understand the danger of mixing the secretive work of Charlotte's cells with the public community organizing of the Thistle. In another life, she had studied this—how the Black Panthers had mixed community food programs with armed underground groups, and in the end both kinds of work had been overwhelmed by police repression. How some radical environmentalists in the early 2000s had protested deforestation by day and burned logging equipment by night, until the lack of separation led to their capture and imprisonment. How guerrillas from India to Vietnam to the Philippines had stayed *away* from friendly villages—hiding out in deep forest or rugged mountains—to keep both militants and civilians safe from state reprisals.

Every example, every discussion topic she could think of would veer too quickly into dangerous territory. Still, the thoughts turned over and over in her head, spinning like the gears in the machine.

Once they had shredded the day's vegetables, they dumped them in various feeding troughs and went back to the farmhouse for breakfast.

Most others had finished their chores and were eating. Breakfast was a mix of vegetables and scrambled eggs—today's mixture contained mostly kale—with a side of oatmeal. Addy poured herself a mug from the carafe of the electric coffeemaker. She decided to peek into the filter holder of the coffeemaker, which was lined with a piece of reusable silk and contained roasted dandelion roots (crushed), dried mint, and a few herbs she couldn't identify. She added milk and honey to her mug of "coffee."

She found a seat across from Carlos and smiled at him. But before they could chat, the redheaded woman came downstairs. She looked bedraggled and red-eyed, one hand pressed against her cheek.

"Is there a doctor here?" she asked.

"We can send down the road for one," said Carlos. "But is there some way we can help? Addy and I have medic training, and we've a midwife and herbalist next door."

"It's my son." She sniffled. "Something's wrong with his . . . stool. In the toilet—it's bloody. I'm worried about dysentery. That was common in our neighborhood, in the city, with young kids."

Carlos stood immediately and put one arm around the woman. "Let's take a look rather than rush to conclusions," he said. He gave Addy a *don't be rude now* glance and gestured for her to follow. They went upstairs. Addy reviewed the symptoms of dysentery in her mind: diarrhea, blood in the stool, severe abdominal pain. There had been cases among refugees arriving at the Thistle. They'd treated it successfully with rehydration therapy and beef broth. But early in her time on the farm, two young children had arrived severely dehydrated and unconscious and had not survived.

The boy sat on the edge of the empty bathtub next to the composting toilet. He had a fearful, guilty look. Carlos opened the lid of the toilet and looked inside. He gave Addy a worried glance, and she stepped forward. Atop the bed of dried leaves and wood chips there was a fresh deposit: a mass of loose stool the reddish-purple color of partially digested blood. Addy's stomach lurched for a moment. Then a second look: the color was not quite right; it was *too* purple.

She smiled and began to chuckle softly. Carlos looked at her in horror.

"It's the beets." She laughed. "The kid barely ate on the trip to the farm. Once he got here, he ate his weight in beets. Of course he has red poop!"

The red-haired woman sighed with enormous relief and hugged her son. Carlos shook his head and said, "Phew!" Charlotte stood and gave Addy an unexpected hug. After a moment's surprise, Addy hugged her back.

"Thank you," Charlotte said.

—⊁

"So, she'll do it?" Felicity asked Layth, as they waited for X to arrive in the old dining room of the safe house.

"She'll try," Layth replied, staring at the pattern of golden lions on the peeling wallpaper. "She's not exactly an experienced operative."

"She'll have to do," said Felicity, shrugging. "She has the full list?"

"The five, yes," said Layth. "Plus two . . . old names."

Felicity gave Layth a sad, sympathetic look. "Layth, that was a *long* time ago. The Triage Administration database is only ten years old."

"The Authority has databases from before," said Layth. "Police records. Medical files. Social-network analysis. There could be leads."

Felicity gave him a slow, dubious nod before X entered the room and greeted them. "Any trouble getting out of the apartment block?" X asked.

"A lot of security in the area, and more moving in. But I got through with a green alibi," answered Layth.

"Use the dead drop from now on," said X. "There's more radio chatter on that block than I'm comfortable with. Which reminds me, we got a signal from the underground railroad this morning: Charlotte and the boy made it to the Thistle. I think Charlotte can persuade them to join our cause."

"It's far," said Layth. "Any nearer possibilities?"

"I'm open to suggestions," said X, "but we've had contact with the Thistle before."

"Didn't they snub us a few years back?" asked Layth.

"I was thinking a couple *decades* back," said X. "You'd have been a small child. Actually, you passed through that farm with your parents."

Layth straightened. "What? You've never mentioned that."

X shrugged. "Your parents visited a lot of places. I believe that they visited the Thistle during the uproar after the stock exchange was shut down. It's been a long time, memory is foggy."

"If I'd known that I'd have escorted Charlotte and the boy myself," said Layth.

"There's nothing to learn there," said X. "They've had thousands of guests since, and your parents were circumspect. Deliberately forgettable."

"All the same—" began Layth.

"As you said," interrupted X, "it's far, and you have plenty of work here." Layth nodded reluctantly. X continued: "I need you to make contact with the priest. He's had time to look around. I want to mobilize offshore support ASAP."

"You want me inside the triage camp?"

"Use your regular cover and alibi card," X said. "You've done it before."

"Fine," said Layth. "But if we need another person to visit the Thistle . . ."

"I'll send you personally," X promised, only mildly exasperated.

—✐

"It's the Thistle's policy," said Adelaide, "to interview every new arrival about their skills and needs—and a bit of their history."

"Of course," said Charlotte, sitting opposite Adelaide on a couch in the library.

"But our aim isn't to pry," Addy said, adjusting the notebook she held in one hand. "Many people have been through traumatic experiences before making it here. If you'd rather not talk about it, or you'd rather talk to a therapist, that's fine."

"Addy. Unusual name," Charlotte observed.

"It's short for Adelaide; my father liked Australia. Do you understand what I'm saying?"

"I'm here to tell my story, Adelaide, even when it's uncomfortable. That's the only way to get the help we need from people outside the city." Charlotte stared at Addy unblinkingly as she spoke. Perhaps, Addy wondered, a symptom of PTSD? She had seen many refugees with post-traumatic stress who seemed distant or detached but would jump into fight-or-flight mode in response to seemingly tiny triggers.

"Can you tell me a bit about the circumstances that led to your becoming, err—"

"A refugee?"

"Yes." Adelaide put her pencil to paper.

Charlotte inhaled deeply. "I was a student in my second year of university when the Authority came to power. I had no family except my parents out west. I couldn't go home because of travel restrictions over Paraflu-41."

"It's usually more recent events that we—" began Adelaide.

Charlotte plowed on. "After the federal government declared bankruptcy, the authority took control in the city and banned public gatherings that could 'spread contagion.' The university was shut down; students who lived nearby went home. I was part of a movement that challenged the Authority's legitimacy. We had rallies, marches, all that."

"Let me guess: you were triaged."

"Yup. Detained by actual police—not armbands, who were just then being organized—charged with breach of the Third Pandemic Act, and red-tagged."

"Red-tagged?" said Adelaide with surprise.

"They still do that for people new to the system—assume you're a rotting sack of cholera and MRSA until you prove otherwise. Of course, they didn't have electronic tags back then." Charlotte rolled up her sleeve to show a faded red rectangle tattooed on her forearm. "Intimidation worked against most people. No one wanted to associate with disease-carrying radicals, especially once we'd literally been labelled reds."

"Your movement was crushed."

"Overnight. Sent us to an early triage camp, a recycling plant in the countryside. We sorted whatever they sent us. Cans, old electronics, clothing. Soon we realized that they were sending us the personal property of people who'd died in the epidemics."

"Or people who had been forcibly triaged."

"Exactly," answered Charlotte. "And Triage Administration had the gall to charge us for room, board, and medicine. They paid us for sorting, a few cents per pound. In a month everyone was in debt."

"The Authority doesn't believe in free government services."

"No, they'd call that 'charity.' It was 'a hand up, not a handout'; that's what they said. We could have fought it, maybe—if the camp had been just the politicals. But they flooded the camp with new red tags. Most were apathetic, afraid to rock the boat. Some were genuinely sick. You know what happens in those camps."

"Poor food, lack of water, inadequate shelter . . ."

"Within three months, the camp population had grown tenfold, but half the people I had arrived with were dead or disappeared. The Authority proclaimed us sick to justify arresting us, but they made us sick for real." Charlotte stared into the distance blankly. "I was there for two years. I lost . . . a lot of friends."

Adelaide didn't say anything. Just listened.

"Finally, someone came looking for us—for politicals who had survived. He was basically a teenager, but he was part of a network. Layth."

"He was your child's father?" asked Addy.

Charlotte stared at her a moment, then laughed. "Layth? No, no. He was too young for me. And I'm not his type. But Layth got me out of the camp. Got me a new triage card, an alibi tag."

Addy looked confused. "Alibi tag?"

"Hacked ID card. Stuck in a red zone? Make the card turn green. Need to run a secret delivery across town and cover your tracks? Use a card with a different bar code from your cover identity, so it looks like you never left. Trade secret."

"I won't write it down," said Adelaide.

"Through Layth I met others in the network. Moved to the Yellow Zone, got an apartment with John. Got pregnant, and all that follows."

"But something happened to John," Adelaide prompted.

"The network's been getting desperate," said Charlotte. "The Authority is cracking down—plugging holes in their security systems, disrupting our comm networks. Restricting movement more tightly. Cutting rations. People are getting sick across the city. They need meds."

"Antibiotics," guessed Adelaide.

"The Authority won't give antibiotics to people outside the Green Zone," said Charlotte. "Barely any of the antibiotics still work against TB or staph. YEA doesn't want to 'waste' them, doesn't want to risk more strains becoming resistant to antibiotics. John and his cell were trying to liberate a YEA pharmaceutical hoard. It—it didn't work. The whole cell was lost."

"I'm sorry," said Adelaide.

"The Authority knew where we lived, so we were smuggled out to find refuge and assistance," said Charlotte. "Anyway, I'm here to get help."

"I understand that," answered Addy. "And we'll see what we can do. The Thistle works collectively, so we'd need consensus to intervene. The town of Newbrook, nearby, has more resources. They might be willing to assign militia. We'll call to get a place on the next town council agenda."

"You have a phone?"

"A landline. We can't use our radio transmitter, obviously—we aren't reckless. But really, you should talk to Lieutenant Dumont."

"What about you?" asked Charlotte. "I'm sure you personally could do something to help, if you wanted."

Addy closed her notebook and looked away. "I'm not sure what I could do."

—✒

For the rest of the afternoon, Evelyn was too nervous to poke around the computer system. She felt as though everyone was watching her.

"The director seems to give you a lot of attention," said Phyllis, perhaps a little jealously.

"Mmm-hm," said Evelyn, not looking away from her work.

"A great man, the director," added Phyllis. "They say he could become CEO of the entire Authority one day."

In the late afternoon, Evelyn seized a chance to bring the cart of processed files down to the basement alone. When she arrived, she unloaded the files into the active section of the archives according to serial number. And then she left her cart and went to the section of the archive that held the alphabetically organized "closed files." That area was larger than expected, but after a few minutes she found a bank of files marked *RUA-RUZ.*

In one pocket she had the digital camera that Layth had given her. It looked indistinguishable from a common bottle of personal disinfectant, except that pressing the top would take a photo through the pinhole opening instead of releasing a squirt of isopropyl alcohol and bactericide. Layth had showed her how she could view the last photos she had taken by twisting the cap a particular way and holding the bottle up to one eye at a set distance; the photo would appear in the transparent fluid, shimmering and holographic, before disappearing into the encrypted memory of the camera. A public safety officer who inspected the device would think it was a disinfectant bottle with a broken pump—hardly unusual.

Evelyn found a drawer containing files with last name Ruiz. Many had first initials beginning with M. She flipped through, and found three people who were born in the early 1980s. She photographed the first page of each file with the tiny camera; from a distance it would look like she was disinfecting them. She was about to take a closer look when she heard footfalls in an adjacent aisle. She carefully replaced the files, and then slid the drawer shut as quietly as she could.

In the next aisle, a drawer was slid open. She could hear papers being rifled through, and then the drawer was slammed shut decisively. Then more footfalls, and another drawer ten feet down was slid open, then slammed shut a moment later.

Evelyn decided it was probably one of her coworkers, so she walked to the end of the aisle and stepped around the corner to greet them.

It was Stanley, the director's lieutenant.

"Ms. Park," he said.

She froze at the end of the aisle, and tried to cover. "Can I help you find anything?"

"I was about to ask you the same question," he replied, moving to another drawer and pulling out a file without pausing to look at her. "I wasn't aware you were working with the closed files." He had a stack of fifteen or twenty files accumulated under one arm.

"Just looking for the powder room," she said. She realized she was still holding the concealed camera in one hand. She tried to shift it nonchalantly into her pocket.

"No powder rooms down here," replied Stanley. "In fact, it's just about quitting time, don't you think? You don't want to miss your bus and get stuck out after curfew."

He walked to the end of the aisle and brushed past her. As he did, on a whim, she clicked the shutter button on her camera. It silently captured an image. Stanley continued on down the main corridor and was soon out of sight with his files.

Evelyn retrieved her cart and took it to the elevator. Once she was alone, she checked the screen on the camera, holding the bottle up to one eye, twisting the cap to zoom in. The photo was blurry, but she could just barely make out a few of the names on the files Stanley was carrying. One of them was similar to an old name Layth had given her: Jad something.

Evelyn went back to her desk. Her coworkers were putting their coats on. If she was to catch her bus and make it home before curfew, she would have to go. But tomorrow, Evelyn decided, she would get to the bottom of things.

As she walked past the director's office, she glanced in. He smiled at her and slowly waved.

8

2028

"You must be the new recruit," said Helen.

"Potential recruit." The young man at her door smiled. He was tall, with angular cheekbones and thick black hair. "Tom said my skills and connections would be useful."

"You're early for the meeting," said Helen, "but come in 'til everyone arrives. I'm Helen."

"Philip," he replied. "Philip Justinian."

She knew the family name. Philip's father, a prominent lawyer, had been in the news after winning a series of free-speech cases; his family was affluent, well connected, and vaguely liberal. She brought Philip upstairs and offered him a glass of water. He accepted, taking a seat at her kitchen table.

"Could you bring me up to speed on the campaign?" said Philip, sipping his water. "I've read news stories and watched some of Gwen's videos. But to help you I need the whole picture."

"The executive summary?"

"Exactly," said Philip, producing a small laptop. "Mind if I take notes?"

"Go for it," she said. She poured herself a glass of water from the tap. "A year ago, we heard, from someone in the pipe fitters' union, talk of reopening the tank farm as a depot for oil from the Alberta tar sands. Same time as the diesel shortages?"

"I remember," said Philip, tapping his keyboard.

"The organization I work for, Friends of the Watershed, was founded twenty years ago to deal with groundwater pollution from those leaky tanks. You know there are still people with chronic illnesses from that?"

"Doesn't surprise me," answered Philip.

"That's how the story broke back then: mystery illnesses. People in a few older houses still had their own wells, and they started getting sick. Then a school."

"This is more historical than—"

"I'm getting there," said Helen. "The tank farm was sued into oblivion; the owners went bankrupt. The oil companies that supplied them denied responsibility and refused to pay damages, but stayed clear of that tank farm ever since.

"Last year, my board at FotW asked me to research the reopening rumors, renew some public education work, just in case. I gathered a few people together. Teresa, whose father is still coping with illness from the leak and ended up in a wheelchair at thirty-nine. Tom, the labor organizer you know. Elijah, a grad student in environmental remediation over at the university."

"I met him at a party. I'm working on my master's in public health."

"This should be right up your alley, then. And we have—well, had—Apollo, an experienced activist. And Gwen, a farmer and veterinarian and one of the hardest-working people I know. Her farm is a kilometer from the groundwater plume. If there's another spill . . ."

"It's kaput," inferred Philip.

"Exactly," said Helen. "So we started making inquiries and doing public education. The city government refused to give us answers, and bureaucrats in the county weren't talking either. We put their feet to the fire. 'What are they hiding?' That was our first slogan."

"I saw that slogan on a poster of the tanks," recollected Philip, "with a monster skulking behind them that looked like the mayor."

Helen laughed. "Apollo's idea. 'You've got to personalize it,' he said. 'It's the only way to make them feel the heat.' Then the newspapers got on it, and soon an there was an anonymous leak from the mayor's office that he and a couple of city councillors had had private meetings with the tank farm developers! They wanted to skip environmental permits, claimed it was an active site."

There was a knock on the door below. Helen called down: "It's unlocked!" The door opened, and someone clomped up the stairs. "Teresa! Welcome." Helen hugged the woman.

Teresa stepped into the room, saw Philip, and introduced herself.
"Philip Justinian," he replied.

"Joining the party?" Teresa asked.

"I'm getting him up to speed," said Helen. "Glass of water?"

"Brought my own," answered Teresa, showing a steel canteen with a sticker reading *Homeland Security!* and an image of an Apache warrior.

"Once we found out about the secret meetings," Helen continued, "we showed up to city council. The council chambers were packed; must have been two hundred more standing outside. We had a chance to make a statement."

"Oh, don't forget!" said Teresa. "We found out just before—"

"I'm getting to that!" said Helen. "We found out the mayor's *brother* had bought a bunch of land next to the tank farm, so if it expanded—"

"Big bucks," said Teresa. "Gwen changed her speech, just tore strips off the mayor for five straight minutes."

"The mayor wanted her ejected for 'libel,'" said Helen, "but their only security guard was too scared to do it." They laughed, and Helen continued. "Then things really got going. We created a coalition, and the last three months have been constant organizing, giving talks and slideshow presentations to whoever will host us. Showing up at city council and committee meetings to push our case. Door-to-door canvassing."

"And wildcat protests," added Teresa.

"Right," said Helen. "Apollo loves those. Get a bunch of people to rendezvous at a certain time and place. At the last minute, the real target is announced and they head to a bank or a construction site run by a backer of the tank farm redevelopment and make so much noise that everything shuts down for an hour or two."

"We hand out leaflets to passersby," said Teresa, "and some actually join the protest. A lot of families in town are still affected by the old plume."

There was another knock at the door. Tom arrived, followed by Elijah. Tom thanked Philip at length for coming. Elijah looked surprised and not entirely pleased that Philip was there, but after a moment he hid his expression and kept things moving.

"Do we have markers and a flip chart?" asked Elijah. "We should start with a brainstorm."

"I must have left them at the office," said Helen. "I'll call Gwen so she can get some on the way."

There were many things Dee adored about the old Greek Orthodox church a few subway stops from her house. The architecture was archaic and Byzantine, with nooks and crannies and alcoves and a dozen different entrances. The old building had no security cameras or surveillance. The church hosted a choir that sometimes sang prolonged chants and polyphonic pieces that Dee found trance inducing, that allowed her to sink into her work, to focus completely. The church had small meditation rooms that could be rented for an afternoon for a small cash donation.

One of those rooms was just *barely* in range of the wireless internet network of the university across the street. With help from Simón, she had accumulated a long list of passwords for the wireless network.

Dee sat down after lunch in her favorite meditation room and flipped open her computer. She propped the laptop beside a narrow window. The computer ran a clean Linux install using full disk encryption; it was virtually impossible for anyone else to access it. She fastidiously avoided using the computer for idle browsing or anything that could link it to her.

She logged on to the university network, along with ten thousand other users. From there she connected to the Tor network so that every message her computer sent would be encrypted and bounced around the planet before emerging from a random outlet node in Amsterdam or Rio de Janeiro or Pretoria. It was not an unbreakable security system, but it was close enough for her purposes.

Dee checked her travel alarm clock. She had a few minutes until her appointment, so she reviewed upcoming action plans for the cells in her circuits. She studied maps of a petroleum depot and examined drawings of an explosive robot crawler. Soon the meeting time arrived, and she opened her encrypted chat client. Simón was waiting there, as planned.

HEllo, he typed immediately.

Hi, she typed back. *How is your dog?*

Happy as a turnip in July, he responded, an exchange they had prearranged in person. *Got friends to drop off drives. P/u 4/15*. Simón had dropped off flash drives containing malicious software in the parking lots of several of the companies and agencies she wanted computer access to. Four of the fifteen drives had been picked up and plugged into computers, silently installing Simón's backdoor software.

Didn't think we would get Sec5, Simón added, *but someone in IT picked it up. They had bypassed firewall to browse pron at work. haha.*

pwned, typed Dee encouragingly, hoping that was something hackers actually said.

Put zip of e-mails at dd, Simón said. Dee and Simón shared the login for an e-mail account in Singapore they used as a dead drop. Dee would log in later and find a zip file he had saved as an attachment to a draft message there.

n e thing interesting? Dee asked.

BIG TIME, Simón replied. *Guy in Sec5 e-mailing cops about surveillance counterintelligence ops re: IRI. Lots going on, hinted about tank farm stuff.*

A chill went down Dee's spine. *Who is running it?*

Joint intel body. Who knows.

Can you find more inside? Dee asked.

Need $$$, he replied.

Dee sighed. *Will send more soon*, she typed. *Get me list of people surveilled, agent names, etc.*

Sounds tough. Will try.

Dee ended the chat. She was beginning to suspect that somewhere in the tank farm movement—and maybe in her own network—there was a spy.

Helen picked up her phone and dialled Gwen, who answered after two rings. "Gwen, can you pick up markers on the—" Helen stopped and stared out her front window. A black SUV with tinted windows was idling across the street. "Surveillance is back."

"Do you have your good video camera?" asked Gwen. "Get it. Talk soon."

Helen hung up and retrieved her video camera (which had a better zoom lens than her phone). She had just turned on the camera and walked to the window when a rusty red pickup truck squealed to a stop in front of the black SUV, blocking it in. Gwen kicked her door open and jumped out. Helen raised her camera. "Come look!" Helen called to the others.

They rushed to the window as Gwen strode around the front of her truck, grabbed the passenger door of the SUV, and yanked it open. She started yelling something that was muffled by the window. Helen grinned widely as she zoomed in. Gwen reached into the SUV and pulled out a handful of file folders, which she waved in the air.

A bald man in a white shirt and tie stepped out of the driver's side of the SUV and spoke angrily, beckoning with one hand. Meanwhile, Gwen was flipping through the file folders and holding documents up in the air toward Helen's apartment, then tossing each casually onto the ground. The man in the tie rushed around the back of his vehicle to confront Gwen directly. As he approached, she raised an accusatory finger that stopped him in his tracks.

The man tried to grab a folder out of her hand. Papers scattered. He stooped to grasp at them as they slid along the pavement in a light breeze. By this point, everyone in the apartment was laughing uproariously. They could hear Gwen's muffled shouts through the window: "Want to intimidate us? You'll have to do better than that!"

The man had a phone in one hand as he tried to grab papers with the other. He seemed to be threatening to call the police. Gwen berated him for several moments, then got in her truck and drove off, scattering more pages as she left.

In the apartment, everyone laughed and talked animatedly. "Unbelievable!" said Elijah. Helen filmed the man as he collected his folders and then drove off.

They heard a clanking on the rear fire escape as Gwen let herself in through the back door. They cheered. Gwen's tanned cheeks were ruddy, her green eyes blazing with excitement. "He looked like he was going to shit a brick," she said. "Could you videotape the documents?"

Helen checked. She had tried to zoom in on the papers that Gwen had held out. But at a distance and fluttering in the wind, any text was an illegible blur. Helen shook her head, disappointed.

"Don't worry about it, kid." Gwen shrugged. She reached into her jacket, and pulled out a crumpled handful of pages to thrust triumphantly forward. "Let's turn the tables on those bastards."

～

"Let's start with something easy," said Taavi. "We don't need big risks on our first try."

"Some practice would be a good idea," said Samantha. Taavi and Samantha, along with Corben and Andy, were standing in the basement "war room" around the map table. An aerial photo of the tank farm showed on the big screen next to them.

"Come on," said Corben. "You already *have* practice." The other three were silent, but Corben persisted. "Sure, security culture, keep your mouths shut if you want. But we all know."

"Corben's right," said Andy. "Why wait around? Liberals will never do anything. It's up to us to escalate."

"We talked about this over beers, remember?" said Corben. "Smash up the tank farm a little, break some shit. Nothing dangerous. Why are you backing down now?"

"I'm not backing down," said Taavi. "I want to think this through."

"It's simple," said Corben. "Sunday night, we cut the tank farm fence here, where it meets the brush at the end of this road." He pointed on the screen.

"No streetlights," added Samantha. "No one to watch us go in."

"We run across here," Corben pointed, "and split into pairs. One pair goes to the main office, here, and smashes the windows. The other pair takes this chisel"—he held up an enormous, pointed chisel—"and a hammer, punches a few nice big holes in the nearest tank. Then we rendezvous where we came in and leave. Whole thing takes five minutes. We're gone before police can respond."

"How do you know you can punch through the tanks with that thing?" asked Samantha.

"It's a cold chisel," replied Andy, obviously excited. "Tempered steel. Made to cut through metal."

"It will take a lot of muscle," said Corben, "so Andy and I will do that. You two can take the windows."

"What about security cameras?" asked Taavi. "Guards?"

"There are cameras, probably not connected," said Andy. "We can mask up."

"I did four nights of recon last week," said Corben. "Never saw a guard or cop go near the place."

"What do you think?" asked Andy.

"It looks like a good plan," said Samantha. "But I feel like you should have consulted us before coming up with it." Taavi nodded, and Corben's face showed a flicker of uncertainty, replaced a moment later by a conciliatory smile that was almost smug.

"Hey, I don't mean to offend," said Corben. "We got pretty pumped about this. And we need to get it done before city council meets on Monday, you know? Next time, how about you two take the lead?"

Samantha and Taavi glanced at each other and agreed, with muted enthusiasm.

"Better get some rest," said Andy. "Before the big night tomorrow."

The crumpled pages that Gwen had taken were not as informative as the coalition had hoped. One was simply a printout of the FotW website. Another was a list of links to videos featuring Gwen, which Elijah had produced and uploaded. Another sheet showed headshots of members of the coalition. Helen recognized hers as the photo on her driver's license. Another page held strings of numbers, some of which were highlighted, but which meant nothing to any of them and returned no useful results after a Google search.

"We should research in more detail," said Elijah. "Do some freedom-of-information stuff."

"If you have time, go for it," said Helen. "But we need to plan the action we wanted to have before the city council meeting Monday night."

"How about another protest march?" said Tom. "Start downtown, circle around, show up at city hall."

"Everyone's tired of marches," said Teresa. "We've had, what, four so far? Turnout at the fourth march was less than the third."

"The mayor has said they won't let the public speak at the council vote," said Helen.

"That's why we have to set up outside," said Tom. "If they won't let us speak, we have to make our voices heard there. Invite the media." He glanced at Philip. "Maybe we could convince a well-known free-speech lawyer to make an appearance." Philip smiled tightly and noncommittally.

"Local media is bored with this story," said Gwen. "They only want to talk terrorism charges and anarchist conspiracies. National media can make the mayor worried, but they aren't paying attention."

"We should get *their* attention," said Helen. "Take it up a level."

"Is there time to organize anything big for tomorrow?" asked Philip. "The council meeting is forty-eight hours away. You should focus on preparing a legal challenge after the vote." Elijah gave Philip a flash of side-eye.

"We have time if we start small," said Gwen. "A last-minute march would be a lot of work, but we *can* do something with a dozen people."

Helen looked at Gwen, who had the hint of a smile in her eyes. "Why do I get the feeling you have something specific in mind?"

Gwen's hidden smile bloomed. "It's something Apollo and I talked about before he was arrested. The mayor has said if the proposal passes he wants construction crews in as soon as possible, cleaning up and getting work underway. If we wait until work starts, it will be hard to stop. I say we go into the depot and set up camp—chain the gates shut, take over the main building. Don't let trucks in, don't let work start."

Helen loved the idea immediately. "So if the proposal passes we rally people to take the site the next day? On Tuesday?"

Gwen shook her head. "If the proposal has passed, people will feel defeated. Like it's a lost cause. Obviously we're being watched," she said, gesturing to the crumpled papers. "If we wait, we lose the element of surprise. I say we go in Monday at dawn."

Everyone looked surprised at this.

"Only one day to prepare?" said Teresa in shock. But after a moment, she warmed to the idea. "We'd call people in after we arrived? Have a rally there?"

"And call national media," said Tom. "This would finally get their attention."

"If something like this gets out of hand," said Philip, "you risk losing the respect of the community." There was a pause, and a distinctly raised eyebrow from Elijah, but the momentum of the group pushed forward.

"How many people would we need?" asked Teresa.

"I think fifteen or twenty at the beginning," said Gwen. "Enough to keep local cops from just arresting everyone. They might call in off-duty officers or cops from out of town. But we'll get more people, too."

"My dad will come," said Teresa. "He already jokes about locking his wheelchair to a pipeline valve."

"I know a lot of students who would come," said Elijah.

"My union won't like it if I get arrested," said Tom, "but I'll come at least until the cops threaten to arrest people."

"I bet those young anarchists would come, too," said Gwen. "They're bored of marches; they'd love this."

"Let's invite them. But if we want to do this, we have to get ready," said Helen, checking her watch. "It's three thirty p.m., which gives us less than forty hours to contact people, get supplies, write a press release—"

"Oh, and sleep," said Teresa.

"Let's divide and conquer," said Tom. "If we each take on some tasks we can get done in time. I'll call my union buddies to come picket."

"That's a great idea," said Helen, "but are we all committed to doing this?"

There was a brief pause as the organizers paused to look at each other. And while Philip looked skeptical, there was a chorus of affirmation from the majority.

"Okay." Helen smiled. "Let's do it!"

⁓

Taavi lay on a futon mattress in his unadorned bedroom at Corben's house. He tried to get to bed early on Saturday night so he could stay up late the next. But streetlights, which had never had bothered Taavi in his basement apartment, shone in on his face. Taavi was restless, uncomfortable, vaguely anxious about the upcoming action.

At ten in the evening, his phone began to ring. He looked at the screen. It was Helen again. He sighed and silenced the phone. Then, unable to rest, he got up and began to lay out black clothing for the following night's events.

⁓

Dee spent the evening in the church, carefully studying the files Simón had sent her. The corporate security e-mails were vague and nonspecific. But the implications were clear: private security officers were being given detailed information about activists in Newbrook, and those activists were closely watched.

There would be a spy within the tank farm movement. Though she had no clear evidence, she knew this for certain. But would that spy try to disrupt the campaign at its heart? Or worm their way to the militant arm of the movement? Was the spy, at this moment, wriggling into Dee's own network?

Rebecca, Dee knew, had recruits and contacts in and around Newbrook who might be at risk. She had pushed Rebecca to recruit more, to make it her priority. But was that reckless? She debated calling Rebecca directly to arrange a meeting. But this risked drawing attention, and there was nothing in the e-mails Simón had sent her—admittedly dated a week earlier—suggesting anyone was in urgent danger.

She opened her own encrypted files on infiltrators, a hodgepodge of book and article excerpts that someone in the intelligence circuit had pasted together to share.

Some infiltrators were actual police officers posing as activists. She had a bio in her files on Mark Kennedy, a British police officer who had posed as an environmentalist for seven years, taking part in demonstrations and sleeping his way through activist circles until he was finally found out. That creep had stayed undiscovered for years because he was so committed to his cover identity; after he was exposed, he quit the police and even apologized for what he had done. Few police infiltrators could fake their identity to that degree—hence the "tell me a story" prompt that Dee encouraged.

The other kind of infiltrator was much more insidious: the former activist turned collaborator. This type was someone with a legitimate backstory who had run afoul of the police and agreed to cooperate—out of fear of prison, or in exchange for bribes, or simply to fluff their ego.

Dee clicked to another infiltrator bio. In the 1960s, when Nelson Mandela and other antiapartheid leaders were working in secret against the South African government, police offered huge payments for activists to turn traitor. The cops finally found a volunteer in Bruno Mtolo, an established member of the movement who cooperated willingly with police and who gave authorities the location of the farm that was the hidden headquarters of the African National Congress. Mtolo wasn't *forced* to give up information to the police—it just made him feel important.

Mandela and the others were arrested and very nearly put to death, until the state offered to show them "mercy" with lifelong prison sentences.

That was the kind of infiltrator Dee was afraid of—someone who looked superficially trustworthy but who meant devastation for the network.

She typed a terse message to apprise Rebecca of the situation in Newbrook and encrypted it. Then she checked the small travel alarm clock she carried and uploaded the message to the appropriate place for Rebecca to see it.

It was getting late. The church would close to visitors soon, and she should go home to see her father.

Before she left, she checked one more clue Simón had dredged up: copies of electronic money transfers from a pipeline company. The files showed that the mayor and several councillors in Newbrook were receiving substantial "campaign donations" from the company, even though no election was imminent.

She ensured the banking-record files were free of personal metadata that could lead back to her or Simón's computer and then uploaded them to a file-sharing site that was mostly used for GIFs of cats and pony cartoons. Then, with an anonymous remailer, she forwarded the banking records to several investigative journalists whose work she had seen in recent newspapers.

She shut down her computer, checking her clock again as she did. It was Saturday night. People in the city were getting ready to go out. Dee couldn't wait to get home.

~

Taavi did his best to rest on Sunday, finally falling asleep around dinnertime. His phone alarm woke him up just before midnight. He got up and flipped on his bedroom light. He donned his black outfit and left the phone where it lay beside his bed. It would be a liability on this mission.

He went down to the living room and woke Samantha, who had been sleeping on the couch. Taavi turned on the coffeemaker and waited for it to brew. Andy came downstairs a few minutes later and helped himself to a cup of black coffee from the carafe before the pot was finished.

"Where's Corben?" Andy asked. "I knocked on his door, but he didn't answer."

"The basement?" Taavi suggested. Before anyone could check, the front door creaked open, and Corben entered the kitchen.

"Hey punks," he said, pulling on a red cap. "Had to grab cigarettes. You ready?"

"Almost," said Taavi, gesturing to the coffee pot.

Taavi and Andy drank their coffee in nervous silence, while Corben rambled about how excited he was. Taavi's coffee was too hot and too bitter, so he splashed a generous quantity of rice milk into it. This cooled it but didn't improve the flavor. He gulped the coffee down and retrieved from the living room a black backpack he had prepared earlier. It contained black gloves, a black balaclava, a hammer, and a blue hoodie. He planned to switch into the hoodie after the action.

At 1:05 a.m., they went into the garage and got their bicycles. Soon all four were riding along empty and silent suburban streets. Taavi, in layers of black clothing, found himself sweating on the warm summer night.

They followed a back route through a trail in the woods. The moonlight was enough to keep Taavi on the path. In ten minutes, they reached the back corner of the tank farm.

They hid their bikes in the woods and approached the fence. Razor wire atop the fence gleamed menacingly in the moonlight. Corben donned gloves and pulled out a set of bolt cutters. "Mask up, everyone," he said.

Taavi pulled on his gloves and balaclava. As Corben snipped the wires of the chain-link fence, Taavi stared up at the full moon in the cloudless sky. It seemed especially crisp and sharp as it hung above the tanks.

"Go, go, go!" hissed Corben, and he held the flap of fence open. Samantha went through first, then Taavi, then Andy, who held the fence for Corben. They were in. "Time to split up," said Corben. "Meet back here in five minutes."

Things happened very quickly after that. Samantha and Taavi ran flat out to the office building. A few flickering floodlights illuminated the building's facade, but the interior was dark. The unused front office was lined with floor-to-ceiling plate-glass windows. Taavi pulled the hammer out of his bag, his heart thumping. He looked over to Samantha as she pulled a pipe wrench from her bag. She glanced at him as she raised her wrench high. Then she smashed her wrench through the nearest window.

There was a *thunk*—deeper and duller than Taavi expected—and then the high sound of shattered glass falling on pavement. Taavi raised his hammer and smashed the nearest window, jumping back from the shower of shards that came down on his boots.

Samantha was working her way down the length of the building, methodically shattering each window she passed. Over the sound of breaking glass, he could hear another noise, the metallic *clang* of a sledgehammer striking a chisel. He raised his own hammer and smashed the next window, and then the next, working his way down the building in the opposite direction from Samantha.

His arm began to tire after a dozen windows, so he paused to look at Sam, who had almost made it to the corner of the building. In the distance behind her, he saw a white vehicle at the main gate. The gate slid aside, and suddenly the vehicle was roaring down the driveway toward them. Samantha didn't seem to notice and was still smashing her way along.

Taavi ran toward her. "Hey!" he yelled. "Hey, Sam! Look out! Run!" She stopped her work and stared. The vehicle, a white SUV, screeched to a halt thirty feet away. Taavi grabbed Samantha's sleeve, and they sprinted behind the building to a cluster of rusted metal piping.

Taavi wasn't sure if Andy and Corben had seen the vehicle. He kept yelling, "Hey! Hey! Run!" until Sam hissed at him to shut up. She grabbed his arm and pulled him around the curve of one of the smaller tanks.

"Is he following us?" huffed Taavi.

"Shhhh," she said. They could see a figure with a flashlight walking along the path where they had run, about a hundred feet behind them. His vehicle was idling, headlights bright, in the parking lot by the building. The shield logo of a private security company was visible on the open driver's door. Sam pulled Taavi by the cuff of his sweater all the way around the back curve of the tank so they could watch the figure from the other side.

"We're cornered," whispered Taavi. "We've got to go around him to get back to the cut in the fence."

"If we run for it," said Sam, "we could—"

Before she could finish, a black-clad figure sprinted across the parking lot to the white vehicle. The figure jumped into the SUV and slammed the door shut. The security guard immediately turned the flashlight back toward his vehicle and started running toward it.

He was far too slow. The vehicle began to accelerate across the parking lot. For a moment it was on the opposite side of the office building, hidden from sight. And then it appeared again, moving with great speed across the asphalt. A moment later it smashed through a cluster of rusted pipes, cracking several in half.

"Holy fuck," whispered Sam.

The dark figure opened the driver's door, giving them a glimpse of still-inflated airbag. The figure tumbled out and began running with a slight limp. The security guard sped after the figure in black and seemed to be catching up with him.

"They're going toward the cut in the fence," said Taavi. "We'll never get around the guard; he'll be there before us." As he spoke, there came a siren in the distance, and then flashing lights speeding down the main road toward the gate.

"We can't get out that way," said Samantha. "So it's over the fence!"

She grabbed his arm and hauled him toward the nearest section of fence. As they approached, she pulled a spare piece of clothing out of her own bag and, when they reached the fence, tossed it over the razor wire. He produced his own blue sweater and threw it over the same spot.

Sam deftly climbed the chain-link fence and swung herself up and over the barbed wire. A moment later she descended. Taavi climbed the inside of the fence and tried to imitate Samantha's graceful vaulting maneuver.

He failed. Halfway over he slipped, lost his footing, and began to tumble toward the ground. He flung his arms out, and one of them caught the sharpened wire. As he fell, razor teeth cut deep into his flesh, tearing away strips of skin. He hit the ground and cried out involuntarily.

Sam helped him to stand. "Can you walk?" she asked, and he nodded. They stumbled into the edge of the forest nearby, and then Taavi sat down for a moment. He was trembling uncontrollably. Samantha winced at the sight of his arm. It was bleeding profusely. Sam reached into her backpack and pulled out a menstrual pad, still in the wrapper. She opened it and pressed it to the largest gashes.

"We need to get out of here. We'll have to leave the sweaters. I threw my wrench into the tall grass while we ran," Sam said. "Where's your hammer?"

"I don't know," said Taavi. "I must have dropped it at the building."

"Well, you were wearing gloves." She shrugged. "And you wiped it for fingerprints before you put it in your bag, anyway."

"Err, wiped it?" said Taavi, his expression doubly pained.

"Jesus, Taavi," said Samantha. "We can't go back now. We've got to fix your arm; it looks bad." They found their hidden bikes; Andy and Corben's bikes were gone. The other two had left.

"We can't go to the hospital," said Taavi. "If the police tell the ER to watch for razor-wire cuts . . ."

Samantha frowned and thought a moment. "I know where to go," she said. "It's not far."

It was Monday predawn, and Helen hadn't slept in two days. Their hasty preparation for the tank farm sit-in had been exhausting and exhilarating. The group painted banners in her hallway, made long lists of supplies, and phoned activists to invite them (while swearing them to secrecy). It went smoothly, aside from a few moments of tension due to Philip's tendency to offer unsolicited advice.

At sunrise, Tom picked up Helen so they could rendezvous with their trusted friends at a coffee shop near the tank farm. The plan was to drive from there to the tank farm and meet Gwen, who had gone home to her farm late Sunday night to get a tractor and a wagon full of hay bales for improvised barricades.

On the way to the coffee shop, they passed the tank farm. Helen could see immediately that something was awry. There were police cars and even a fire truck in the parking lot. Helen cursed.

"What's happened?" asked Tom.

"I don't know," said Helen. "But I don't think this is going to be as easy as we thought."

9

2051

By the time Evelyn reached her apartment complex, an hour before power-down, she was thoroughly exhausted. The stressful week had left her physically and emotionally drained, wanting only to go to bed. But the new checkpoint in front of her building told her something was very wrong.

"What happened?" she asked the masked guard who inspected her papers.

"A murder in one of the buildings," he said. "And a riot. It's quarantined."

"What building?" she asked, her stomach gripped with fear.

"Building G," he replied, to her relief. "Proceed to your home building."

"Who died?" she asked.

"Go directly to your building," he insisted, turning to the next person in line.

In Evelyn's lobby, armband-wearing soldiers sat on folding chairs— not waiting for a shift change but stationed there. The community bulletin board had been stripped and replaced with posters on quarantine and the Third Pandemic Act. Evelyn didn't look at the masked soldiers whose eyes followed her to the stairwell.

As she passed the second floor, she heard Sara's voice through the hallway. Evelyn followed Sara's voice to the open door of Mrs. Schmidt's apartment.

"Try not to move, Mrs. Schmidt," she was saying. "The ice is cold, but it'll reduce the swelling."

Evelyn entered Mrs. Schmidt's apartment. Sid and two young girls were at the kitchen table, quietly coloring on scraps of paper. Sid ran to Evelyn, and they hugged.

"What happened, Sid?" she asked.

"Mrs. Schmidt tried to visit her friend in the other building because she was worried but the soldiers didn't let her and they were mean to her," Sid replied in a single breath, fidgeting anxiously in her arms.

"Keep drawing; I'll talk to Mom." Evelyn walked into Mrs. Schmidt's bedroom. The walls bore yellowing photos of Mrs. Schmidt's grandchildren. Mrs. Schmidt lay in bed in obvious distress, shifting her legs restlessly, waving her arms to try to dislodge the bag of ice Sara held to her face. Evelyn caught a glimpse of a swollen eye, of bruised skin flecked with blood. Sara turned to look at Evelyn.

"Thank goodness you're here," Sara said, giving Evelyn a one-armed hug. Sara looked as exhausted as Evelyn felt. "It's been a hell of a day."

"Someone was killed?"

Sara nodded. "YEA guard fell off the top of Building G last night." Evelyn's eyes widened. She knew only one person willing to kill a guard; he had been in her apartment the night before. Evelyn opened her mouth to speak, but Sara cut her off with a sharp shake of the head.

"They sent inspectors to search Building G this morning. But residents kicked out the inspectors, barricaded the doors. YEA put the building under quarantine with everyone inside. Shut off power, water, heat, everything."

"Oh my god," said Evelyn.

"Mrs. Schmidt tried to bring a pot of soup over to a friend of hers. The guards wouldn't let her in. They got into an argument. And then. . ." She gestured to Mrs. Schmidt.

"Can I do anything?" asked Evelyn. "She's shivering."

"She says she's cold," said Sara. "Won't take off her coat, even under the covers. She's in shock." Sara paused. "Look, I need you to take the kids for a bit. They're upset. Distract them."

"I'll take them to the games room to—"

"Not the games room," said Sara. "The armbands commandeered it."

Evelyn guided the children upstairs to her own apartment and found them a box of scuffed plastic trucks, bulldozers, and excavators. She sat on the couch while the kids played "gentrification," demolishing and rebuilding imaginary neighborhoods with the toy equipment.

Evelyn closed her eyes and leaned back into the couch, exhausted. Over the soft noise of the children's play, she could hear more sounds of distant trouble at the other building. Though tired, she was restless, in need of distraction.

She pulled out her e-reader, connected to the Samizdata coin, and opened an article at random:

They called it the Pipeline: a series of
concentration camps build by the British in
Kenya to crush the Kenyan liberation movement.

In the 1950s, Kenya was under occupation by
the British Empire. Kenya was a rich source
of tea and tobacco for the empire. But a
homegrown independence movement was gaining
steam, and the British Empire, already
wracked by WWII and the loss of India, didn't
want to give up another colony.

The British were desperate to control the
country, but the liberation movement called
the Mau Mau was getting too popular.

In 1962, the empire cracked down. The
British forced hundreds of thousands of
Kenyans into concentration camps; many more
were herded onto reserves, stripped of their
lands and the cattle they relied on. The
British Empire split revolutionaries from
their people, and split the people from the
land that sustained them.

The British built three levels of camp:
black, gray, and white.

If they suspected you of sympathizing
with the movement, you would be ruthlessly
interrogated and sorted based on the results.
If you were labelled "gray," the state was
unsure of your loyalties; you would endure
"reeducation," propaganda, and forced labor.

If, after some years of this, the British
deemed you to have been "cleansed," you

might be lucky enough to move to a "white" camp. That's why they called it the Pipeline; prisoners were supposed to move through it as they were "cleansed."

Many, however, were deemed "incurable" and send to the "black" camps.

If only the appalling White supremacy—apparent in even the naming of the camps—were the worst part. Tens of thousands of men, women, and children were worked to death building roads, airports, and other colonial infrastructure. Thousands more were tortured and executed.

According to the official British figures, ninety thousand people were killed, many of them children who starved to death in the camps. Unofficially, the number of people disappeared is closer to three hundred thousand.

Think of the numbers of collaborators required to administrate such an enormous operation.

We must remember the brutality of the British, their crimes against humanity. But we must also remember that their worst efforts delayed independence by only a decade; in 1963, Kenya finally broke free.

Know this: the YEA is holding on by their fingertips. Their brutality is the result of their weakness.

Stay strong, my friends. We will outlast them.

In solidarity,
X

Evelyn sighed and clicked off the e-reader. The story was horrifying but impersonal. How could a person conceive of atrocities on this scale—hundreds of thousands of lives destroyed? There wasn't room in her mind for the scope of it; just trying to think about that story, to process such numbers, was like trying to push an elephant through a keyhole.

She gazed at the children playing, still thinking of the British in Kenya. She tried to imagine the life of one child who had survived those camps. She pictured a boy, his parents taken from him by the colonizers, his family's land and possessions stripped away from him. His family shattered.

What would that do to a child? How would that trauma echo down through the generations? How would a child, and their children, and their children's children, cope with that?

And what would be worth sacrificing to keep that trauma from happening in the first place?

—✐

Charlotte insisted on attending the Newbrook town meeting, and Addy agreed to take her. Newbrook was an hour away by bicycle. En route, Addy and Charlotte cycled past small vegetable plots. In town, Charlotte observed aloud that at least half the green space in Newbrook—parks, lawns, sports fields—was under cultivation, though much of it was mulched for winter.

"All these gardens . . ." said Charlotte, amazed. "In the city, food gardens require special permission. The Authority claims they attract rodents that carry disease."

"That's profoundly stupid," Addy replied.

"It keeps the people under their thumb, keeps them dependent. Even when the Authority deigns to grant people permission to grow food it can be revoked at any time."

"Newbrook was more forward-thinking," said Addy. "Forty years ago, they were encouraging people to install rain barrels and cisterns. Thirty years ago, they were paying high school students to grow vegetables in the summer. Twenty years ago, they started turning old parking garages into cold storage. Ten years ago, by the time the economy really fell apart, they were able to switch to local food almost seamlessly. Changed the sports stadium into a year-round farmers' market."

They passed an open, grassy field. In the middle were several enormous and rusting cylindrical tanks, one of which was ruptured and sagging.

"No gardens here," Charlotte observed.

"The soil is contaminated with hydrocarbons," Addy answered. "Town uses the tanks as waste receptacles. Old, brittle plastic gets dumped in the hatches up top. Supposedly someday they'll be able to harvest it all, turn the plastic into fuel—*thermal depolymerisation*, blah blah blah. I'm skeptical. But it's better than burning the stuff."

They rode past Newbrook's bustling farmers' market and arrived at the town hall. Addy would ask the town to intervene in the conflict with Bill Farnham. Ultimately, she wanted them to assign militia to compel Farnham's cooperation, but that was the last link in a chain of events beginning with a mediator and then an arbitrator. Addy was certain Newbrook would vote in her favor; the Thistleroot Institute had helped draft the town's Unity Charter, and everyone had benefited from the Thistle's training and support programs in the years of economic collapse and depression that gave rise to the Authority.

Charlotte had her own reasons for attending. Having planted some ideological seeds at the Thistle, she hoped to turn the entire town into an area of redoubt for resisters. This was an ambitious goal, but Addy didn't want to discourage her. Not after what Charlotte had been through.

In the town hall they joined 200 people who would be attending that meeting. Tens of thousands lived in the area, but it was impractical for more than a few hundred people to discuss and vote on any issue. Instead, a random sample of 150 people were given voting rights at each biweekly meeting. This number provided a diversity of opinions and allowed the town to make quick decisions on uncontroversial issues.

Charlotte's proposal would be polarizing, but a favorable vote would advance her request to the larger monthly assembly. Charlotte had not, as far as Addy could tell, prepared any written statement in advance (aside from the one-sentence resolution Carlos had helped her to draft) but rather would address the group extemporaneously. For herself, Addy had written a careful, short statement and posted it on one wall of the auditorium along with the text of other motions to be voted on.

The auditorium was quite full when the evening's proceedings began. The weather was good, so almost everyone who had been assigned voting rights for the evening had chosen to attend. Addy and Charlotte found seats near an aisle. The first hour was mundane. There were reports from various committees on fuel stockpiles, freshwater reserves, food supplies, and so on. Small decisions accompanied each report, such as whether to release more apples from the cold cellars on the assumption that there would be an early spring. *Be it resolved that, given the continued shortage of nutritious fruits in winter and the decreasing length of the winter period, each resident shall be issued an additional two apples per week,* et cetera, et cetera.

Each voter had two numbered paddles (as at an auction), a green paddle for "yea" and a red paddle for "nay." To vote, they simply held the desired paddle in the air so it faced the stage. The secretary of the meeting used a high-resolution camera to record a photo of each vote and automatically count the numbers of green and red paddles. The motion to increase apple rations passed by a significant margin.

"Is this what meetings are like?" asked Charlotte in a whisper.

"It's mostly minor stuff," Addy whispered back.

"People just make a decision?" said Charlotte. "Just, whoever happens to be here tonight? What if other people don't like their decision?"

Addy shrugged. "The next meeting can put a hold on the motion. But there's no back-and-forthing. If a third meeting wants to approve it again, they'll have to put it forward at the monthly gathering—that might have a thousand voters and last all weekend." Addy checked her watch. "It's almost your time to speak. You should wait by the stage."

And indeed, a few minutes later Charlotte was called to speak and briefly introduced by the secretary as "speaking for a motion to assist resistance groups opposed to the York Emergency Authority." This elicited a rumble of chatter.

Charlotte made her way to the front of the stage. The noise faded to a polite, expectant silence. Charlotte paused, collected her thoughts, and began.

"I come to you with a request, humbly and as an outsider. I've spent my life in the city, and my adult life under the rule of the York Emergency Authority. I don't know about farming, or cutting wood, or all the difficult things you've done to keep body and soul together these last years. I don't know the risks you're taken to build and keep what you have. I don't know how I must appear to you. A rabble-rouser? A lunatic? A dangerous revolutionary from the bad old days?"

Charlotte continued. "Let me tell you some things I do know: The York Emergency Authority is an abomination. They claim to have saved a million lives; I think they've ended as many. And how, you might ask? They aren't Nazis with gas chambers. They aren't Rwandan mass murders with machetes. Their weapon of death is the triage system.

"Triage is the key to their power and the shameful truth behind their myth of 'prosperity restored.' Perhaps there was a time when the system protected people from disease, but it has become a way to steal from those who won't cooperate with the Authority. Want a return to democracy? Better not make a fuss, or you'll end up in a triage camp. Do you have a workshop full of tools, a stocked pantry? Unless you're rich, you might end up thrown onto a triage bus, your possessions confiscated. I've seen people sent to the camps so a triage officer could steal the bag of groceries they were carrying. Maybe you've heard these rumors before. I'm here to tell you that they are the cruel truth."

Charlotte took a deep, sighing breath, and continued. "And what happens in the camps? Simple: people are enslaved. Indentured. They are charged outrageous fees for their 'treatment' and cannot leave until they pay them back—which means they must work. If they cooperate, if they are skilled, they 'graduate' to a better camp. Perhaps they'll do horticulture, manufacturing, even office work and cleaning. If they don't cooperate, if they are unskilled, they are shunted into demolition work, waste disposal, remote logging camps, or mining. Those camps have worse conditions. If you weren't sick before, the Authority can make sure you get *sick*. Antibiotic-resistant tuberculosis, dysentery, typhus—pick an epidemic of the eighteen hundreds and you'll find it thriving in the triage camps."

To one side, the meeting secretary raised a sign indicating that Charlotte had two minutes left. She showed a flicker of annoyance and plowed on.

"The Authority has coopted the language of public health to neutralize opposition. But make no mistake, this system is a slow-motion massacre. It maintains the illusion of progress and prosperity through the degradation of countless human beings. It provides luxury and comfort to elites and collaborators at the expense of everyone else. It supplies the resources the Authority needs to expand and conquer new territory. Understand: if you do not resist, it will soon be on your doorstep.

"My husband died fighting that system. Many comrades died. I risked my life many times, even the life of my son, and nearly lost both. But I was helped by people like you. Given shelter and aid.

"I don't ask you to march into combat with the Authority, to risk your lives the way I have. But understand that people in occupied territory are fighting and dying every day in many different ways. They need your help. They need resources and supplies to fight. They need shelter and places to safely retreat and recuperate.

"Some of you might think if you stay out of the fight, the Authority will leave you alone. You would be dead wrong. The Authority is looting and robbery; it must expand to survive. If you stand aside, my people will lose their fight, one by one, until when it is your turn, you will have no one left to help you. But if you are willing to take a small step, to help us, then we all have a chance at a future."

There was tepid applause. But the motion passed, which was enough to get things moving, and certainly enough to get people talking in Newbrook and the nearby villages. In that way, the speech was a success.

It was a speech Addy found both affecting and uncomfortable. She was moved by Charlotte's obvious passion and truthfulness; the speech reminded her of the sort of pep talk she would have given a generation earlier. And that thought gave Addy a painful sensation deep in her abdomen.

When Evelyn arrived at work the next day, there was another package on her desk. She opened it. It was a red silk dress from the same officer who had given her chocolate the day before. It was embroidered with yellow dragons. She put a hand to her forehead and groaned in audible disgust, then stuffed it into a bottom drawer before Phyllis could make any comments.

That morning, as she typed, she considered how to gain access to the files Layth wanted. Surely she could return to the archives without seeing Stanley every time. Or during lunch, when everyone else was in the cafeteria, she could use a different computer to find the files without drawing attention to herself.

She was turning these options over in her mind when a woman behind her began to cry. The sound was soft at first, but soon the woman was wracked with sobs.

Evelyn pivoted in her chair to look. One of the other women was standing at her desk, her hands over her mouth, her eyes full of tears. She had dropped the stack of files she was processing, and their contents had spilled out onto the floor. Evelyn picked one up and shuddered.

The photograph she held was the most gruesome thing she had ever seen. It showed a young man, naked, dead or close to death. He had been partially disembowelled, with blood and gore covering his lower abdomen. There were deep lacerations on his hands and face and thighs. She was looking at a man who had been tortured to death.

As Phyllis comforted the upset typist, Evelyn collected the scattered files. She recognized the name on the file—one of Layth's. They were all there, the five she was to look for. And all dead. Evelyn struggled to keep her composure as she placed the files back on the desk.

"What happened?" asked the director. The sobs must have attracted him.

"Just an unexpected sight, Director," said Phyllis, nodding at the files.

The director opened the top file and looked. The skin around his eyes went white, and his lips twitched. He closed the file and collected himself.

"All that blood," he said, shaking his head. He looked at the woman Phyllis was comforting. "Clearly a case of hemorrhagic fever. Terrible bleeding, a horrible disease. I'm sorry you had to see that. But"—and he raised his voice to make sure that everyone could hear him—"it has been *contained* by the triage system. The system has done exactly what it is supposed to do, sparing others this terrible fate. You can be proud to do your part. Carry on."

There was a smattering of perfunctory applause. Evelyn returned to her desk and sat down, feeling the perspiration over her body.

"Evelyn, how are you?" asked the director from behind her. "Stanley tells me you looked out of sorts in the archives yesterday." He put a hand on her shoulder.

Evelyn didn't trust herself to look at him directly, so she stared at her computer screen. "I'm fine," she lied, searching for a change of subject. "It's just that"—she reached for the drawer that contained the silk dress—"there's an officer, Jim something, who has been, ahh, pursuing me, and . . ."

"And you're not interested in this particular fellow," guessed the director.

"Exactly," replied Evelyn.

The hand on her shoulder squeezed gently. "I'll call him into my office and set him straight. He won't bother you anymore."

"Thank you," Evelyn replied. The hand was withdrawn from her shoulder, and she heard the director walk away.

The length of that day was agonizing. She expected something grisly in every file. But the rest were mundane. She went through the hours in a daze, her eyes just sliding across each sight until it was time to leave.

At her apartment block there were more soldiers; another building had been quarantined. A public safety officer at the checkpoint claimed its residents had thrown objects from their balconies onto the soldiers below.

When she went into her apartment, Sid was lying on the couch, sniffling. She picked him up gently, asked what was wrong, but he only cried harder. Sara came out of the bathroom. Her own eyes looked red.

"Sara, are you okay?"

"They took Mrs. Schmidt today," Sara said. "Took her on that fucking bus to a triage station. It's freezing out there!"

"My god," said Evelyn. She almost said *at least she has that warm coat you got her,* but that was little consolation. "What happened?"

"The guards found out she used to visit her friend in Building G every day. They dragged her out of the apartment, claiming she carried 'contagion' from the other building. *Contagion,* Evelyn!"

Evelyn shook her head slowly, in shock. "'Simple epidemiology.'"

———

Layth tried to imagine how many mobile phones, laser printers, and laptop computers had been built in the decades before the fall. One billion? Ten billion? A hundred billion? Some large fraction of that number was piled in heaps in front of him, electronic refuse stacked in hills thirty feet high.

Layth was in deep in the Red Zone, searching for the priest. If he were blindfolded, the smell would tell him exactly where he was—the smell of the mine.

The land where Layth stood had a long and ugly history in the hands of the city. It had spent millennia as a temperate forest, crisscrossed with little streams, cared for by overlapping Indigenous nations, home to forest creatures like white-tailed deer and pileated woodpeckers. When the land was colonized, the city's builders cut the trees, drove out the deer and the woodpeckers, scraped away the soil, and dug a rectangular hole a hundred feet deep to quarry for stone. Eventually they stopped building with stone, but they needed somewhere to put their ever-growing stream of garbage: old used-up furniture, cracked televisions, broken refrigerators. The pit became a landfill.

The city kept sprawling, kept producing more garbage. The hole in the ground filled up, and soon developers were drooling over that location, location, location. They covered the landfill in sod, and on top they built a high school with a fine, grassy sports field. For many years, you could look over that field and have no idea what was underneath.

Layth knew. Layth knew because he was standing in the parking lot of what had been that high school, a parking lot piled thirty feet deep in electronic waste. The fine, grassy sports field had been eviscerated, turned into an open pit mine—a vast, open sore filled with ramps and wheelbarrows and deep trenches.

When international trade had collapsed into a morass of piracy and protectionism, imports were reduced to a trickle. But there were still rich people, and they still wanted *things*. There was a lifestyle to which they had become accustomed. Yet gadolinium does not grow on trees. You can't fill a bushel basket with coltan from the back garden. You couldn't go to the fishing hole and reel in hexavalent chromium—or maybe, Layth reflected, you could, depending on where you fished.

Many people in the Green Zone had never heard of the minerals that undergirded their way of life. But without reliable imports, with the best mines in North America long emptied, there was an obvious place to turn: the very place they had thrown all the gadgets that they had previously bought and used up or gotten tired of—the landfill.

The sports field became the stinking mine that Layth stared over, and the high school became the operations center for that mine. Mrs. MacArthur's geography classroom was where they stacked lithium batteries for processing. Mr. Smith's chemistry lab was where they extracted gold from the circuit boards. There were still stacks of quizzes in his office, which the workers used to mop up droplets of spilled acid. The gymnasium was where they burned insulation from copper wire—they had knocked holes in the outside wall for ventilation.

As for the students, well, plenty of them were still there, working. The city's garbage went to the Red Zone for sorting, along with dead electronics pulled from office buildings and e-waste from wealthier places that didn't want to recycle their own junk.

Working in the old school building, desoldering capacitors from circuit boards and prying open dead iPhones, was bad—but not as bad as the mine. Guards there wore gas masks that still couldn't keep out the stench. None of the workers had gas masks. They barely had footwear.

They coped with the sharp edges of broken glass, rashes, endless shovelling. They never knew when a trench might simply collapse. Fetid groundwater constantly seeped into the pit; it had to be pumped up out of the mine to a lagoon in the old baseball diamond, from which it flowed down a concrete culvert, through the ghetto wall, and directly into the harbor.

Layth had many contacts in this part of the Red Zone. His cover as a procurer of antique items and spare parts allowed him to enter these camps as he needed. Many times, he had entered this zone to find some obscure type of computer memory, or replacement parts for a faucet from the old days.

His excuse for entering the Red Zone today was that he was looking for a particular type of Bible for a wealthy evangelist and collector. This would not lead directly to the priest, who had of course concealed his identity. But word would spread quickly that someone was willing to pay a lot for a particular Bible. That rumor would reach the priest, and he would know that Layth was trying to find him. Hopefully the priest would make himself easy to find.

But Layth searched for hours without success. He searched the aluminum conveyers, the lithium stacks, the brickworks, and the ash sifters. And he grew concerned. The priest was not young, but he was healthy and reasonably fit and planned to cooperate. He should have been placed on a favorable work team after his capture. But Layth did not see him.

He finally got a hint from a contact in the metal-sorting district when he asked about a Bible. "You're the second person to ask for a Bible in twenty-four hours," his contact said. "The last guy had a fever, seemed delirious, speaking Spanish."

"Where did you see him?" asked Layth.

"Camp infirmary," said the man. "He had gotten in a fight; he was in rough shape."

Layth thanked him and began walking—almost running—toward the camp infirmary, his fears growing with every step.

—⚹

Evelyn waited up late as Sara made her 'rounds,' checking on other residents of the apartment building to make sure they were coping. When Sara finally returned, well after midnight, the couple spent hours arguing over what to do. Evelyn wanted to leave immediately, to use Evelyn's higher salary from Triage Administration to move to a neighborhood in the Green Zone. Sara refused point-blank, arguing she was needed where they were; the block was full of old and retired people. If young people left, the Authority would be ruthless with the "unproductive" people who remained. Evelyn promised to try to convince the director to intervene in Mrs. Schmidt's case the next day.

When Evelyn arrived at work, she nearly ran up the stairs and went straight to the director's office, without bothering to shed her coat. He was there, early as always, his suit crisp and his black hair coiffed, the streaks of gray at his temples almost luminous in the lamplight.

"Evelyn." He smiled tightly as he looked up from a stack of files. "What can I do for you?"

"There's a problem at my building," she said, out of breath. "A woman has been taken wrongfully. She's not sick. Just . . . obstinate."

"This woman," asked the director, "is a friend of yours?"

"A neighbor," she replied. "A senior citizen, and frail. Normally I wouldn't ask, but the triage camps can be so cold in winter. Her health—"

"Will be just fine," the director finished. "I can see how upset you are, rushing in like this. But *trust* me, your neighbor is in good hands. I visit all of our triage facilities regularly, and I can promise you they are in *perfect* working order."

As he spoke, he stepped around his desk, took one of her gloved hands in his bare one, conducted her to a chair, and sat her down. Without releasing her hand, he leaned back against his desk slightly so that he was looking down at her.

"I know it's our desire to . . . adjust the workings of the system when it affects someone we know. But we can't use our positions to make personal interventions in the triage system. Believe me, this is *exactly* the kind of situation the triage system was designed for. It is designed to sort the healthy from the sick, to assess need so we can assign our finite resources.

"We can't know what her health situation is until she has been examined by a *trained professional.* Does she have a fever? Crackles in the lungs? Inflamed lymph nodes or skin lesions? Well, you and I can't tell, because we aren't qualified."

He leaned slightly closer, her hand still held in his. She pulled back reflexively, which had the effect of loosening her glove where he held it. He chose to interpret this as an attempt on her part to remove the glove, and so he slid it the rest of the way off and then grasped her bare, cool hand in his. His skin was warm, soft, and scented with cologne.

"If she is in good health, she will be home in a jiffy. And if she is, god forbid, in some way ill, she will get precisely the medical care she needs."

His eyes were locked on Evelyn's, a caring smile fixed to his face. He would have radiated compassion if not for the fact, Evelyn realized, that the director very rarely blinked.

Evelyn felt sick to her stomach. Despite having concluded his pep talk, the director failed to release her hand so that she could leave.

"Maybe we should do something to take your mind off this," said the director. He smiled his most charming smile. "Come over to my place for drinks tomorrow night. I won't take no for an answer."

She was so surprised she couldn't rally her wits to decline. By the time she extricated herself from his grasp, she had silently accepted the date, and the rest of her coworkers had begun to arrive.

Near her desk there was a circle of women chatting and cooing admiringly at something. From the center of the circle she heard a voice say, "Oh, my boyfriend gave it to me."

As she neared the circle, it broke, and she could see the object of attention. A young woman, Elsie, was wearing a new coat: blue corduroy with a fur fringe.

Evelyn recognized it immediately as Mrs. Schmidt's. Her heart thumped. She broke out in sweat under her own fur coat, overwhelmed by confusion and horror.

She walked to her desk and, knees weak, she sat for a moment to recover. She bowed her head to her desk for a few heartbeats, then raised it with a sense of conviction. She stood and let the fur coat slide from her shoulders. It pooled on the floor, where she left it.

Tucked in the bottom drawer of her desk, beneath the unsolicited silk dress, was her old coat. She pulled it out; the tears in the back, which Sara had so hurriedly mended, showed hints of red felt. She donned the coat and went for the exit.

—✎

"Silvio," said Layth. "Silvio, can you hear me?"

Silvio moaned slightly. The priest was handcuffed to the bed where he lay in the infirmary. This was standard practice, to discourage people 'faking' illness to get out of work—as if the rancid stench of the infirmary were not dissuasive enough.

"Silvio, it's me, Layth. Wake up."

Silvio stirred, then raised his head to look at Layth. Silvio was obviously feverish. Layth mopped his forehead with a damp cloth from a bucket next to the bed. Silvio managed to focus on Layth and to speak, but Layth could not understand him. For a moment he thought that Silvio was mumbling in Spanish, or maybe Latin. But then he realized, from the inflammation on the left side of Silvio's face, that the priest's jaw had been broken.

"Who did this to you?" asked Layth. "Was it the guards?" Silvio shook his head no. "Was it other people in the camp?" A nod. "Did you tell them you were a Catholic priest?" Silvio nodded, and Layth sighed. Layth had warned him about the evangelicals. "We need to get you out of here," said Layth.

"No," moaned Silvio. "I am not finished. But you must take this." He reached into the folds of his sweater and pulled out a tiny notebook filled with cramped handwriting in what seemed to be Latin. "My report. Bring it to them." This effort was too much for Silvio, who leaned back on his thin pillow and closed his eyes in silence.

Layth put the book in a hidden pocket in his bag. "Silvio, I'll try to find help for you. Is there something you need?" But the priest was finished talking and simply squeezed his eyes in pain.

On his way out, Layth bribed the doctor on duty to give Silvio pain medication and white-market antibiotics. He needed to get the report safely back to headquarters and on to their contacts abroad. What it contained could win the resistance real support from outside. The future of their movement depended on it.

He rushed toward the exit of the triage camp, doing his best to look as though he were *not* rushing. As he passed through the checkpoint, he had to step aside for a convoy of buses entering the camp with fresh prisoners. As he watched, he caught a glimpse through a bus window of a woman he recognized, a young child sitting on her lap.

"Oh, fuck," he said.

Because commuter buses were available only at the beginning and end of the working day, and because it was still only nine in the morning, Evelyn had to walk all the way back to her apartment building. This took two hours and required her to pass through four different checkpoints, but her green tag sped her passage.

When she turned the corner and saw her apartment block, she stumbled and nearly fell in the middle of the street. She clutched her stomach as nausea overwhelmed her.

Smoke filtered out of smashed windows in her apartment building. It was obvious from a distance: the entire block had been quarantined. Soldiers were everywhere. Work crews erected tall new fences around the block, fences marked with fluttering red cloth to make it clear the area was now part of the Red Zone.

Her thoughts leapt to the worst things that might have happened to Sara and Sid. She tried to push these thoughts from her mind. She tired focus long enough to guess whether she could use her Triage Administration credentials to get in to her building and retrieve her family without being pulled into quarantine. She doubted it, but she would have to try. She began to shuffle forward to the new fence as if on autopilot.

"Evelyn!" a voice called softly. "Evelyn! Here!" She looked around for the man's voice and spotted Layth in an alley to her left. She walked into the alley and directly toward him.

"*You*," she said coldly. She was no longer afraid of this man but rather filled with anger. She wanted to strangle him in the street. "This is your fault. You pushed that guard off the roof. You started all of this."

Layth backed away, but she kept approaching him. Layth raised his hands as he backpedalled. "No, I didn't. That guard must have gotten drunk, stumbled off the edge. It happens a lot."

"Why should I trust you?" she asked, still walking.

Layth backed into the chain-link fence that bisected the alley and stopped there. "You need to trust me because I can help you. I know where your family is. I saw them being bussed into a triage camp."

The thought of this filled Evelyn with terrible despair. She stopped walking and lost her urge to throttle the man.

"I'm sorry," said Layth. "If I'd known this was going to happen I'd have smuggled Sara and the child out before the quarantine."

"You'd never have convinced her to leave," replied Evelyn, not looking at him. "She wouldn't have abandoned our neighbors."

"I can get her out of the triage camp," said Layth suddenly. "I can reunite your family and get you to a safe place outside of the Authority's reach. But I need your help."

"What do you want me to do?" Evelyn asked, turning toward him.

Layth looked her straight in the eye. "I need you to assassinate the director of the Triage Administration."

Evelyn's eyes widened. "What?"

"You heard me," said Layth. "I'll save your family. But first, you must kill Director Justinian."

10

2028

"Was there a leak?" asked Helen, peering through the windshield at the petroleum depot. "Did the cops get warned?" She wondered about Philip—she knew very little about him.

"Who had time to leak the plan?" asked Teresa.

"They've been watching us," said Tom, "following people. Maybe this is a bad idea."

The three sat in Tom's car just around the corner from the tank farm. Four other vehicles were parked nearby, all filled with willing participants for the early morning blockade.

"Maybe it's unrelated," said Helen, squinting. "I see a car accident in the yard."

"Where's Gwen?" Teresa asked, sipping coffee from her travel mug.

"She went to her farm to check her animals and get supplies during the night," said Helen.

"We can't go ahead with police there," said Tom. "It's walking into a trap."

"We have to act *before* the council meeting," said Helen. "Maybe it's the perfect time. Think how dangerous the accident would've been if some drunk driver had crashed into those pipes when they were full of fuel. The whole thing could have caught fire, exploded."

"It's the safety argument," agreed Teresa. "We can film a video with that wreck in the background and post it by lunch."

"But the site's swarming with cops," replied Tom. "If we charge in they'll stop us cold. We need to step back and think about—"

As he spoke, they heard the growing rumble of a diesel engine. Helen looked. Approaching on the road was a red tractor with Gwen in the driver's seat. She pumped her fist in the air as she passed. Then she waved her arm in a *let's go* gesture before accelerating down the road, towing a wagon of hay bales behind her.

"I don't think she knows about the cops," said Teresa, wide-eyed.

Helen watched the tractor roar around the corner toward the tank farm gate.

"Well," she said, "I guess we're on."

~

"What the hell happened back there?" Taavi asked. He and Samantha stood in the basement of Corben's house, staring at Corben and Andy. "Were you trying to get someone killed?"

"Sorry, man," said Corben. "We had trouble with the hammer and chisel. Tanks were thicker than we thought. Couldn't puncture them. When that guard showed up, I decided to turn a problem into a solution."

"So, you hijacked his car and drove it through a bunch of pipes?" demanded Samantha.

"It worked!" said Corben, the sallow skin of his face already bruising where it had collided with the airbag. "Those pipes are trashed, along with his SUV. And I distracted the guard from chasing you."

"We'd have gotten around him," replied Samantha. "You drew him to the gap in the fence."

"Why are you complaining?" asked Andy. "Did you *see* how fucking *epic* that was? He stole a security truck and trashed the target by smashing them together! On a moment's notice!" He slapped Corben on the back. "Awesome, man. Awesome."

"Is it awesome that Taavi nearly got his *arm* torn off when we had to jump the fence to escape?" said Samantha. Taavi pulled up his sleeve, exposing a white dressing that covered his forearm from wrist to elbow. Brownish-red spots of blood had oozed to the surface.

Andy stepped forward with obvious concern and gently touched Taavi's arm. "Are you okay?"

Taavi shrugged. "It hurts a lot. It's deep. I'm woozy, maybe from blood loss."

"Wow," said Corben. "You went to the hospital?"

"No," said Taavi, "Sam had the clever idea of going—"

"To my house!" interrupted Samantha. "I took a wilderness first aid course last year and still have supplies. I patched him up."

Andy admired the tidy dressing. "You did a professional job."

"You'll have to be our medic," said Corben, "you're good at that."

"I shouldn't *need* to be good at it," said Samantha. "We've got to plan more carefully. How did security show up so fast? They must have been watching. You said that . . ."

As Samantha spoke, Taavi lost track of her words; her voice dissolved into the rushing sound of a waterfall. Her face faded to a black field of shimmering stars. His skin felt warm and flushed, as though he had stepped into a hot tub.

". . . aavi? Taavi, can you hear me?" Samantha was calling his name, patting his face. Her hand felt cool against his hot, damp cheek.

"What happened?" he asked. He realized he was on the floor.

"You fell over," she said. "You need rest and fluids."

A few blurry minutes later, he was upstairs on his futon, Samantha pushing a bottle of sports drink into his hand. They were alone in his room. He felt hot and dizzy and exhausted.

"We need to watch for signs of infection," she said. "There are some nasty antibiotic-resistant bacteria floating around." She peeled back the blood-spotted dressing to look at his wounds, the deepest of which had been closed with a few neat stitches. Samantha laid down a clean dressing.

"Why didn't you tell the truth," he asked her, "about who fixed my arm?"

"Security culture," she replied. "I don't trust Corben enough for him to know. Don't show him the stitches. Even he could probably figure out those are beyond me."

"Are you sure we can trust her?" Taavi asked. "I'm still worried about the hammer."

"She said she'd take care of it," said Samantha. "She helped us once. But this isn't the time. You need sleep."

He drank thirstily from the bottle of blue sports drink. Once it was empty, he put it down and rolled over so his uninjured arm was beneath him. Sam got into the bed behind him and, gently avoiding his injury, cuddled up to spoon him. "Do you want this?" she asked. He nodded. A few minutes later, he was asleep.

Led by Gwen on her tractor, the convoy rolled through the tank-farm gate just after seven o'clock. They parked near the main building, and within thirty seconds everyone hopped out of their vehicles and began their assigned tasks.

Philip and Teresa stretched a banner across a fence by the building. It read: "Enough! No tank farm!" Helen pointed a video camera at Gwen, who stood in front of the banner.

"Hi, y'all. My name is Gwen," she said. "It's seven o'clock on Monday morning, and I'm here at the abandoned tank farm on Third Line. This tank farm has poisoned and sickened so many people in our community. Now the mayor and his greedy business buddies want to reopen the tanks, to make a profit while poisoning us more. They want to bring in oil from the toxic tar sands that are destroying the land out west. We aren't going to let them. We've taken over this farm, and we won't leave until the mayor and his cronies promise to keep this tank farm closed for good. Come and join us! People and company are much needed. Click below for details."

Helen panned across the banner and finished recording. "That was great!" she said.

Near the banner, Tom was in a heated conversation with a police officer who had gotten out of his cruiser when they drove up. She walked over to them. "Is there a problem?" she asked the officer as sweetly as she could.

"A problem?" he said. "This is private property. And a crime scene! Are you the leader here?"

"No," she replied, "just a concerned citizen."

"You need to get all your friends here to move on," said the cop. "You can't be here."

"The landowner defaulted on his property tax," said Tom. "Technically this land belongs to the city, which means it's actually not private prop—"

"Doesn't matter," said the cop. "You're contaminating an active crime scene; a forensic team is en route."

"We'll stay out of your way," said Helen. "We don't need to go near the car crash."

"Lady, this whole *area* is a crime scene," he replied. "Look!" He pointed at the tank-farm office. Helen noticed, for the first time, that all the windows were smashed. The pavement nearby sparkled with broken glass in the light of a sunrise that was already heating the asphalt.

"Huh," said Helen. Tom looked at the glass, too, confusion on his face.

"Yeah, 'huh'!" said the cop. "You need to move it, now."

"What happened?" asked Helen.

The police officer slapped his forehead. "Vandalism. Destruction of property. Car theft. Do you want to be an accessory?" Helen struggled to compute the implications, but the cop wasn't tolerating delays. "Look, are you going to leave or are you going to give me trouble?" He rested a hand on his utility belt, loaded with pepper spray, handcuffs, and a pistol.

"You're damned right we're gonna be trouble," called Gwen. She was pulling square hay bales off of her wagon to set up a sitting area beneath an overhanging roof. "We'll be a whole lot of trouble, and in twenty minutes there's gonna be a lot more of us. So you better go call for backup or whatever it is you think you'll need, because we aren't going anywhere. Elijah, you send out those tweets?"

Elijah was standing at the tailgate of a truck, where he and his boyfriend had two laptops and a tablet. "Tweets are out. So are e-mails and mass text messages. Your video already has a hundred likes. People are on the way."

The cop grumbled something threatening and retreated to his cruiser, where he began speaking loudly into his radio.

Helen walked to Gwen. "Do you need a hand unloading bales? Or should I help with the literature table?"

"These bales are nearly done," replied Gwen.

"What's with the hammer?" asked Helen. Gwen casually held a hammer at her side.

"Oh, this?" said Gwen. "I forgot I was holding that." She tossed it into the cab of her tractor and turned back to her wagon without another word.

~

When Taavi woke, Samantha had gone. He felt better, though his headache and wooziness felt like a hangover. He drained the glass of water Samantha had left for him and headed downstairs. No one was in the kitchen, but he could hear the television on in the basement, so he made himself some toast with peanut butter and went down.

"Hey, man," said Corben from a couch in front of the TV, which was showing a mixed martial arts fight. "How are you feeling?"

"Not bad," said Taavi.

"Have a seat," said Corben. "I don't want you fainting on me again."

Taavi sat on the other couch. "Where's Sam?"

"She went home to get some sleep." Corben watched the fight for a moment, then turned to Taavi. "Look, man, I'm proud of you. You did a great job last night, in a tough situation. You're almost ready for the next level."

"The next level?"

"I talked to Andy about it this morning. He feels the same way. Last night was great, but it's still kindergarten stuff. It'll slow them down, but not by much."

"Sam and I talked about that, too," said Taavi. "Maybe the damage is superficial for the level of risk we took." He waved his injured arm.

"Sam is great," said Corben. "But I don't know if she's ready like you are. To take things up."

"I thought we already took it up."

"Hey," said Corben, "there's more than one level to insurrection."

"What do you mean?" asked Taavi.

"I'll tell you," said Corben. "When you're ready."

~

The influx of supporters at the fuel depot was not instantaneous. A dozen early birds brought their numbers up to thirty within an hour. That was enough to keep the police from doing more than *threaten* to arrest people. The cops restricted themselves to videotaping the arrivals. Philip Justinian spent an hour talking to police at the gate, apparently trying to win them over.

During the midmorning hours, few people arrived. Those present tidied up litter on the lawn and swept broken glass from the pavement in front of the office building. The cop who originally argued with them had left, and the remaining police seemed resigned to the fact that their "crime scene" was hopelessly contaminated by newcomers.

Helen spent the morning setting up the logistics of the sit-in. She received delivery of a portable toilet and jugs of water. She placed several large tents, including a kitchen tent with a propane burner for tea and coffee. One visitor brought a solar hot water heater.

She began to worry, around eleven in the morning, that no one else would show up. But at lunch there was an influx of new people. She recognized most of them from meetings and marches past. Teresa's father, zipping up and down the access road in his power wheelchair, greeted people and showed them around. The newcomers brought coolers and picnic baskets, and they opened up their containers and shared food and drink with everyone. By midafternoon, Helen estimated that more than eighty people were present. That was when the media started to show up: a woman from the radio and a man from television. The group had designated Helen as their media rep for the day; while she gave her interview, Philip Justinian waited just out of frame, as though he expected she would forget her lines and need him to step in.

"Why are you here?" asked the man from television.

"We're tired of our community being harmed," Helen answered, "by outside profiteers. We're here to stop them from making money by making our neighbors sick."

"Can you comment on the corruption charges?" asked the woman from radio.

"Corruption charges?" asked Helen.

"The documents leaked online," the television man explained, "alleging the mayor received payments from the pipeline company—bribes."

"It's disgusting," Helen ad-libbed. "It's disappointing to us, as community members, but not surprising. The mayor has displayed poor judgement from the beginning. This project is a threat to public safety and the environment."

"What do you think ought to happen to the mayor?" asked the woman from radio.

"At this point, he must resign," improvised Helen. "This conflict of interest—this fundamental breach of ethics—is not something citizens will tolerate."

Helen joined the picnic. And as the day wore on, their numbers grew slowly. By dinner, there were more than a hundred. Someone ordered a dozen pizzas. Another brought venison stew to share. Yet another brought firewood and set up a hearth.

"This is amazing," Helen told Gwen as they sat by the campfire, eating in the light of the setting sun. "I never imagined so many people would show."

"It's good, kid," said Gwen. "But remember, people are always excited by new things. Fresh stories about document leaks and vandalism will get attention today. But *staying power* is the challenge with occupations. People get tired after days or weeks in a strange, uncomfortable place."

"Maybe we'll win by then," said Helen.

"Maybe," Gwen chuckled, with good-natured skepticism. There was a pause.

"Hey," Helen said in a hushed voice, leaning toward Gwen, "what do you know about the new guy?"

"Justinian?" said Gwen.

"Yeah, Philip. Who knows him?"

Elijah sidled over. "Are we talking about Philip?" he whispered. "He has quite the reputation on campus."

"Because his dad is famous?" asked Helen.

"Because he loves hearing himself talk," said Elijah. "He shows up at all kinds of political meetings to give his opinion. Acts like he's the smartest guy in the room. Doesn't like listening to women. Loves consensus-based decision making because he can just blather on about whatever he wants until the group gives in out of exhaustion. Never does dishes after a meeting, but the first guy in front of the cameras if media show up."

Gwen frowned. "Would he tip off police?"

"He talks to cops at protests," Elijah answered, raising his eyebrows to project contemptuous disbelief, "like he's going to convince them to switch sides." Then someone came over to offer a plate of cookies, and their private conversation ended. As they chatted with others and snacked on shared food, night slowly fell.

⌇—

Dee sat beside her father as he slept on the couch. His health was getting worse. As a young man, before moving to London and earning a degree, he had worked in a textile factory in Bangladesh. He was exposed to countless hazardous chemicals and dyes, from nonylphenol ethoxylates to p-Phenylenediamine and formaldehyde.

Only in his late forties did obvious symptoms surface—anomalous headaches and nausea, at first. But he wouldn't go to the doctor until his first seizure. There were tests: MRIs, blood assays, and spinal taps. The doctors threw around potential diagnoses like toxic encephalopathy and chemical neuropathy. A drug cocktail prevented more seizures, but Dee's father still slept much of the day.

The evening news came on. With her father still asleep beside her, Dee watched the news, buoyed by the coverage of the tank-farm sabotage and subsequent sit-in. For her it had been a gamble to leak the documents about mayoral corruption. She'd had some advance notice of the occupation, but the SUV crash was a complete surprise to her. Not a bad surprise. The campaign against the petroleum depot had become a multipronged attack; the mayor couldn't endure an assault on several fronts—from the media, respected citizens, and nighttime saboteurs—for very long. Cell Seventeen, which was preparing for a major action at the petroleum depot, might have to hold off.

But Dee could not afford to dwell on her sense of success. Two things nagged at her. First, she knew that any success would bring a backlash, retaliation. She didn't know what form that would take.

Second, she was troubled by the surveillance Simón had warned of. She knew it in her bones: there was a spy in Newbrook. And perhaps that spy was after her network.

The strength of underground organizing—why it appealed to Dee in the first place—was that she could think and plan and watch her opponents, but they could not watch her or know her plans. Dee didn't intend to be put in the opposite position.

She considered the coalition against the tank farm. It was open, public. So, it had already suffered an attack in the form of the arrest of a key organizer. But it had also proven itself resilient. The group had responded to the loss of a member by rallying, calling in new volunteers, and counterattacking. Its openness allowed that.

Dee, in contrast, gave none of her subordinates a full strategic picture. She had five circuits with different tasks. She was the only thing that connected those circuits to each other and to the larger strategy. If she were captured and compromised, each of those circuits could be penetrated, their members apprehended. Or they would be cut loose from each other, neutralized. This was a problem. But she didn't yet trust the circuit heads to work directly with each other.

Dee didn't think that *she* was being surveilled. But she had read about a resistance network in Holland called North Pole that had been taken over by Nazis in World War Two. The network kept sending phony wireless messages to allies in the United Kingdom; it kept recruiting new people, and all those new recruits were captured by the Nazis. She couldn't afford to have the recruitment machine she had assembled used to destroy or capture good people.

She turned down the TV and tucked a blanket over her father on the couch. Then she went to her room and drafted a short memo to each circuit. "This is a period of high alert. I will contact you at least once every forty-eight hours. If I fail to contact you for forty-eight hours straight, assume I have been captured and compromised. Abort pending operations, move to new safe houses, assume all electronic communication suspect. Be alert, reconstruct your circuits, and continue the struggle."

She encrypted the memo and checked her travel alarm clock. There wasn't a proper communication window for all circuits until the morning. Dee would put the hidden memo on one of the digital dead drops then.

She shut off her computer and went to bed.

Helen had planned to stay up as late as possible, so she could be ready if police raided the camp. But by midnight, Helen felt exhausted, nauseous, and achy. Three nights in a row without sleep just wouldn't do. So she crawled into her tent and fell asleep to the sound of people chatting and the dim crackling of a small campfire.

Helen woke at sunrise. She felt stiff, but better than the night before. She unzipped her tent and stepped out into the early-morning light. A few other activists were awake, drinking coffee or smoking cigarettes. Others were out in the open on mats or bales of straw, needing no blankets on account of the hot weather.

Helen headed to the cooking tent, which was generously stocked with donations. Bags of food and coolers were lined up on the ground. Someone had put a stack of *Free the Newbrook Four* flyers on a table, weighted down by a bunch of bananas. She ate a banana, then went to the toilet.

As she sat, she pulled out her phone and typed "Philip Justinian" into the search engine. But before she could read the results, she heard shouting outside. She pulled up her pants and kicked the door open. Was it the police raid she had anticipated?

Elijah was whooping, still at the back of the truck with his electronics. She ran over. "Are you okay?" she asked. "What's wrong?"

He was grinning broadly, holding a tablet out to her. On the screen was a short press release from the mayor's office, issued with so much haste that it was full of typos: "The mayor rejects the incorrect and libellious allegations made against him by irresponsible media outlets. However, after an all-night meeting he and his fellow councillers have elected to withdraw their application for the reactivation of the South City Petroleum Depot. This will cause an unfortunate lose of employment for our city."

Gwen, hearing shouts, had appeared at Helen's elbow. "What happened?"

Helen turned to her with a broad grin. "We won."

11

2051

"Have you ever killed a man?"

Evelyn stared into the eyes of the gray -haired woman who asked the question. X's prominent eyebrows—what kind of name was "X" anyway?—cast her eyes into shadow in the dim light of the safe house basement. Evelyn noticed that X had an old but intimidating scar over one eyebrow.

"Of course not," replied Evelyn, wrinkling her nose and flicking her gaze briefly toward Layth.

X shrugged. "It's not as hard as you might think. Mechanically, I mean—a man's vital organs are quite soft. The psychological part, well, that's up to you. We'll train you as best we can in the time we have."

"And you'll rescue my family?"

"Once you do the job," replied X.

"Why not rescue them before?" asked Evelyn. "Then I could focus." X and Layth exchanged a glance. "What, you don't think I'll do it?" asked Evelyn. "That I won't follow through if you aren't holding my family hostage?"

"*We* aren't holding your family," replied Layth. "Justinian is. Think about that when you kill him."

"Evelyn, it's an operational requirement," said X. She raised her eyebrows earnestly, her left brow furrowing asymmetrically over the old scar. "They're deep in the Red Zone, surrounded by armbands and barbed wire. If we send a team now, it'll be obvious they had help to escape. Security will realize you're roommates with a member of the resistance, they'll alert Justinian, and you'll never get near him."

"What if they realize my block was quarantined? It's no secret," said Evelyn.

X shrugged. "Bureaucratic trappings aside, the authority rules by intimidation, not organization. Maybe Justinian already knows where you live. Men like that want *power*—the power to help you, or the power to send you to a triage camp."

Evelyn grimaced.

"I'm telling it like it is," X said. "This is a harsh business. Avoid harsh truths and you get killed. Or worse, you lose the war."

—✗—

Lieutenant Dumont arrived at the Thistle in the late afternoon on a cold and blustery day. She looked weatherworn, her tanned cheeks reddened by frosty gusts. A crowd gathered as she ate a bowl of lamb stew in the kitchen, her well-oiled rifle leaning against the wall in the corner nearby. Everyone wanted to hear updates from the Authority's frontier.

"You'll have to update your maps, Adelaide," she said. "The front has moved thirty kilometers."

There were gasps in the room. "Is it bad, LT?" asked Sridharan.

Dumont chewed and swallowed. "It's way beyond raiding. Authority scouts aren't stealing chickens; they're sending whole companies into the field. One village stood up for themselves, said they wouldn't feed or quarter Authority troops. Blocked a road, stopped some charcoal trucks. They were unarmed, but YEA arrested the whole village. Called them 'bandits.' Hanged the leaders, threw their bodies in the river."

There were horrified noises from the listeners.

Dumont took another bite of stew. "Authority sent the survivors to triage in the city. Then sent red tags *from* the city to cut charcoal."

"That doesn't make sense," said Carlos. "What do city folk know about cutting wood? They have no country skills."

"Exactly," said Adelaide. "So, they don't know enough to try to escape."

"They know better than to try," said Lieutenant Dumont. "They've seen the bodies in the river. In any case, they cleared the forest behind the front. Chopped it up, heaped it in piles, covered it with dirt, and set it to smolder. Turned all the woods into charcoal. There's a haze that hangs in the air all around the front. Soil's already washing away."

An hour later, Addy was in the common hall shouting at a roomful of people with quarterstaffs. "Raise! And strike!" she called as she swung her staff. Two dozen people followed her motions, swinging their staves through the air at imaginary targets. "Left. Right. Left. Right. Strike! Strike!"

Addy led self-defense classes twice a week; a good way to keep warm on winter nights. She taught stick fighting, a useful art on a farm where some long-handled implement—a hoe, a shepherd's crook, a walking stick, a length of pipe—was always at hand. Between kickboxing on Tuesdays and Thursdays, wrestling Fridays and Sundays, and thrice-weekly target practice with pump-action pellet guns, a person could practice some form of combat every day of the week. It was a tradition that emerged from a women's self-defense collective and that—outside of the militia—few of them had needed in real life. Addy attributed this to their tendency to practice often and publicly. Lieutenant Dumont had agreed to help teach this evening's class, though she was surely exhausted from travel.

Addy was pleased to see that Charlotte had decided to join them. Charlotte had no experience in stick fighting, but she was strong, quick, and unafraid. She had turned down the padded gauntlets that most wore to protect their knuckles during sparring, suggesting—to Addy's chagrin—that she would develop bad habits for real combat if she weren't worried about hurting her fingers.

"Okay, partner drills! Pair up!" shouted Addy, beckoning Lieutenant Dumont to demonstrate with her. Dumont faced off against Addy and raised her own quarterstaff. "Watch this!" said Addy. "One partner starts, the other defends. Ready, LT? Overhead strike! Thrust! Right! Right! Left!" Dumont blocked and parried her blows. "Then switch!" They demonstrated.

As the partners practiced, Addy and Dumont walked amongst them, occasionally offering advice. Addy enjoyed the rhythmic clacking of wood on wood, the mingled cadence of each sparring pair. Carlos was practicing with Sandra, the woman who had been driven out by Farnham. Addy visited about half of the pairs before there was a loud yelp and everyone froze.

"Damn it!" yelled a man's voice. Addy turned. Sridharan had dropped his staff and was pressing a hand against the left side of his head. His sparring partner, Charlotte, had lowered her staff and looked concerned.

Addy hustled over. "Let me see, Sridharan," she said. He grimaced and removed his hand. His ear was turning an angry red, but there was no blood. Sridharan's brain, which the Thistle relied on for clever technical fixes, would be fine. "It's superficial," she said, patting his shoulder. "Take a water break." Sridharan found a seat in the corner, still wincing.

Addy pulled Charlotte aside into the kitchen, gesturing for Lieutenant Dumont to continue with the class. "Charlotte, we try to be careful in practice," said Addy, "not to hurt anyone by accident."

"I'm sorry," said Charlotte. "But it was a gentle whack. He was slow on his parry. He'll be faster next time."

"We like to give people time to practice the drill and warm up before we go to free sparring," said Addy. "You weren't supposed to actually hit him."

Charlotte frowned. "He should be able to handle it. That guy has fifty pounds of muscle on me. It's my first night, and he's been training for how long?"

"I appreciate your enthusiasm for the combat arts," said Addy, blood rushing to her cheeks, "but this is just practice."

"No!" replied Charlotte. "Nothing is 'just practice' anymore! Maybe it was practice thirty years ago, when everything started going to shit. But now it's real, and you better start acting like it."

Addy scowled. "You weren't even born thirty years ago."

"So what?" said Charlotte. "What were *you* doing? Same thing you're doing now? 'Practice'—bullshit! People are dying out there! When are you people going to wake up?" Addy said nothing. "It's the same crap with Farnham. 'Oh, he breaks his word, oh, he takes our supplies. Gee, we'd better apply to a committee for permission to ask him to be nicer.' The more slack you give him, the bolder he gets. You should take these people right now, march down to Farnham, and beat the crap out of him! Then you'll see results."

"Is that how you do it in the city?" asked Addy angrily. "Is that what you do to people who don't go along with what you want?"

"No, that's what the fucking YEA does to us," said Charlotte. "That's what the whole system does. You comply, or you get beaten up, or you go to a triage camp, or you just get shot. Farnham wants to get in on that system. He doesn't want to negotiate with a *woman*; he wants to call the shots, and the YEA will let him. When they arrive, he's going to lead them right over here, and together they'll finish stripping this place down to the bedrock."

"The Authority won't get this far," said Addy. "People will fight them."

"Oh yeah? When will they start?" asked Charlotte. "Because I see a bunch of people who have gotten soft. You talk about hard work, and sure, you do your chores and carry your buckets of water and feed your sheep. But you've got it better than ninety percent of the people out there, do you realize that? People in the city don't spend the winter doing *tai chi* and studying *nonviolent communication*. We try to keep our toes from freezing off and hope we don't get triaged!"

"You've got to give these people time," said Addy. "You can't rush them."

Charlotte narrowed her eyes and spoke softly. "How much time do *you* need?"

Addy was taken aback by her change of tone. "Excuse me?"

"She said you would help me," said Charlotte. "But I'm just getting more bullshit from you." Addy looked confused. Charlotte stepped forward and leaned in so her face was only inches from Addy's. Charlotte looked her in the eye and whispered: "*I know.*" Addy jerked back, her body stiff.

Then Charlotte turned and stalked out of the kitchen.

—⚡

"Do you think she'll pull it off?" Felicity asked Layth as they sat in the kitchen of the restaurant safe house. "Actually kill him?"

"I don't know," said Layth. "I hope so. She needs to."

"And that will help us, in the long run?"

"Help us do what?" asked Layth. "That man deserves death. The Authority and their goons have killed countless thousands. It will give us justice. It will show people we can accomplish things, instead of just being whittled away."

"Will it stop the Triage Administration?" asked Felicity.

"It will slow them," said Layth. "His replacement will think twice about how they treat people in the camps. I hope you aren't about to say, 'This won't bring your parents back to life.'"

Felicity shook her head slowly. "Of course not." A long silence passed. Layth checked his watch. "Are you going back out?" Felicity asked. "It's after curfew."

"Evelyn took photos of some old files," said Layth. "My relatives, maybe. There were addresses. Most of the buildings don't exist anymore. But one of them is still standing, under quarantine."

"You're exhausted," said Felicity. "And you're escorting Evelyn tomorrow night. Just get some sleep."

"After the assassination, the streets will be filled with soldiers; they'll be on alert for weeks," said Layth. "Tonight is my chance." He didn't mention that Evelyn had found Justinian's right-hand man retrieving the files in question. Nor did he speculate about what Justinian would want from the long-closed files of Layth's family.

—⟋—

Evelyn followed X to a room in the basement. There was a punching bag in one corner. A mannequin stood in the middle of the room, illuminated by the room's single, bare compact fluorescent bulb. A table to the side held sparring gloves and several different hand weapons.

"What do you want me to do with this mannequin?" asked Evelyn. "Stab it in the heart? Beat it to death?"

"Don't be ridiculous," said X. "This mannequin represents Director Justinian. He's what, six foot two? He's a foot taller than you and weighs half again as much. Do you have some Krav Maga skills you haven't mentioned?"

Evelyn narrowed her eyes. "No. Which is why you should send someone as big as Justinian to do the job."

"Most of my assassins are women, Evelyn," said X. "Years ago, I used men who looked like football players, as you suggest. I sent one to kill the warden of a triage camp who had been sexually abusing prisoners. My guy's gun jammed, and instead of bugging out he tried to beat the warden to death with his bare hands. Do you how long that takes? The warden called for help, and my guy got caught. The rest of his cell was on the run for months after that. They barely escaped with their lives."

"Did your assassin survive?" Evelyn asked.

X just cocked her head and gave Evelyn a pitying look. "I still use men for some assassinations," said X. "Long-distance stuff. Snipers. But for close-up work I stick to women. Mostly petite women, like you. They draw less suspicion. They never fuck things up by starting a fist fight. They understand that they'll succeed by careful planning, surprise, and lightning speed—not by a goddamned boxing match.

"Besides," added X, "Justinian is well guarded. But you can get close to him."

"So, you want me to be sneaky?" asked Evelyn. "Poison him?"

"Poison takes too much time," said X, "and too much subtlety. No, you're going to use this." X picked up a device from the table that seemed to be made from plumber's discards, a length of pipe with a cap on one end.

Evelyn held it in her hand. It was cold. "It's heavy," she said.

"It has to be," said X, "to minimize recoil."

"It's a gun?" Evelyn turned it over in her hand. While one end was capped, within the opposite end she could see a second, smaller diameter of pipe, which protruded about half an inch from the outside piece.

"Zip gun," said X. "Simple, improvised firearm. You put a round in the inner pipe and then slide it into the receiver pipe, the larger one. It has a firing pin on the inside and a spring from a staple gun. Go ahead, press it against the mannequin."

Evelyn placed the open end of the pipe against the shoulder of the mannequin.

"The heart," said X. "Always aim for the heart, the center of the chest. If you miss, at least you'll hit the spine, a major artery, or a lung."

Evelyn corrected her aim. She pressed, and the projecting tube slid into the receiver with growing resistance until there was a sudden, mechanical *snap*. Evelyn jumped in spite of herself. "It's not *that* loud," she said.

"Well, it's not loaded," replied X. "But it is suppressed. The actual noise will only be as loud as someone slamming a door."

"Why not give me a real gun?" Evelyn asked.

"Supply problems," replied X. "We have capable shooters who lack guns. We manufacture *these* so people can shoot a YEA soldier and take *their* gun."

"But why not make it with a real trigger? Why do I have to press it right against him?"

"It doesn't have a trigger because it's difficult to make something with lots of moving parts. This is an insurgency weapon. Easy to make, hard to break," replied X. "And you have to press it against him because you only have one shot, and you have to be close enough that you won't miss. Now let's try with a bullet." She showed Evelyn how to slide out the inner tube and put a cartridge into it. Then she showed Evelyn the "safety," a piece of bent wire that slid through two holes to lock the sliding tube in place.

"I want you to stand behind it," said X, "and shoot it in the heart." Evelyn looked hesitant. "The dummy is full of sand," X said. "The bullet won't go through."

Evelyn pressed the muzzle of the zip gun against the mannequin's back. And then she pressed harder, and then jiggled the gun around a bit. Nothing happened.

"Is the safety off?" X asked. Evelyn checked and pulled out the piece of wire. Then she jammed the zip gun against the mannequin as hard as she could. The gun fired. The sudden jerk stung her hand and she almost dropped it. But X seemed satisfied. "A good start," said X. "Now you practice. You practice what you'll say to the guards in Justinian's neighborhood. You memorize your arrival route and the escape route to Layth. You practice pulling the gun out of your bag and shooting Justinian, just as you'll do for real tomorrow night."

The long-empty, now-quarantined apartment building was inky black inside, but the air was thick with the smell of mold and rot. Layth, wearing a respirator, entered through the basement from a subway maintenance tunnel that had been incompletely walled off. As he breathed, the respirator's one-way valve clicked loudly in the silence, wet with the moisture condensed from each exhalation.

Periodically he stopped to listen for other noises. There were sometimes people living in quarantined buildings, off the radar, who survived by slowly stripping leftover material to barter for food, medicine, and fuel. He passed an old fuse box in the basement which had been methodically dismantled for its copper. The wiring's plastic insulation had been stripped on site; there were coils of it in a dark corner, covered with years of damp dust.

Layth held a tiny flashlight with a red filter. He was careful not to shine it toward exterior windows as he ascended the concrete stairs of the basement. He checked the mail room on the ground floor. The door was ajar; there were footprints on the floor, but it was hard to guess how old. The address on the file Evelyn had photographed was Unit 604. There were locking cabinets in the room that once held mail for the residents of each floor. If there had ever been one for the sixth floor it was gone.

He climbed the stairs quietly to the sixth floor. The stairwell was filled with garbage that scavengers had left behind. When he exited the stairwell at floor six, the air seemed worse. He coughed involuntarily. Had there been a fire here at some point? The underlying odor of mold was present, but entering the floor was like sticking his face in an old ash tray. The air seemed thicker, hazy in the beam of his flashlight. He paused to pull a pair of goggles from his bag; the air was making his eyes burn.

The door to Apartment 604 was propped open—not simply ajar but propped—which struck him as strange. He entered it slowly, panning his flashlight back and forth, as his sense of anticipation faded. The apartment had been emptied long ago. There were a few large splinters on the peeling linoleum floor among dust and bits of drywall; he suspected that someone had, years ago, broken up the furniture for firewood. There were ragged tears in the drywall where wiring had been pulled out. He surveyed the other rooms but found nothing except garbage and some old plastic utensils in the tiny kitchen.

He sighed, a long, slow exhalation that produced a wet, guttering sound from the valve in his mask. Another wasted trip. He had been in a dozen buildings like this before, sorting through garbage for clues that were never found, probing crumbling drywall in a pointless search for hidden compartments. Soon these buildings would be dismantled wholesale and he could stop wasting his time.

In the distance, someone coughed.

His eyes widened, and he pivoted to shine the flashlight toward the apartment entry. Nothing. In the silence that followed, he wondered if he were imagining things. Then the coughing came again. A muffled sound through the floor.

His breathing became rapid and deep. His ears were filled with the sputtering rasp of his mask. Someone else was in the building. A YEA scout, following him? The only way out was through the stairwell. He crept toward it and, seeing no one, descended one flight of stairs to the fifth-floor door.

Crouching slightly on the landing, he reached into his coat. He clicked off the safety on his pistol, advanced a round into the chamber, keeping the gun holstered but ready. With his right hand, he lifted his mask so he could exhale in silence. With his left, he grasped the doorknob and pushed.

Nothing happened. The door was locked or bolted shut. For a strange moment, he considered knocking. Then a small voice came from behind him.

"Do you have a coin?"

He spun, reached reflexively toward his pistol. A little boy was standing on the stairs a flight above. No mask. Shoes with big, dirty socks pulled over them—good for sneaking around. No wonder he hadn't heard the child approach. Layth showed both of his hands in a friendly gesture.

"You need money?" asked Layth through the muffle of his mask.

"A data coin," said the boy. "Samizdata."

"Ahhh," nodded Layth. He reached into a deep pocket and pulled out a couple of coins, both switched on.

"I thought so," said the boy. "We got new files when you arrived. Do you want to come in?"

"Sure," Layth said, the mask turning his response into a sibilant buzz.

The boy approached cautiously. Layth stepped back from the door to let him unlock it, but instead the child slipped behind a piece of garbage leaning against the wall and disappeared. A hidden hatch, Layth realized. A moment later, there were sounds of sliding bolts, and the door into the stairwell opened up. A burst of warm, humid air fogged Layth's goggles, and he stepped forward.

—✒

"Don't do anything rash," X told Evelyn. "Nothing brave or unexpected. Stick exactly to the plan. Do you know it by heart?"

"Knock on the front door of his house," said Evelyn. "If he offers to take my coat, keep my handbag. 'I might need it to freshen up.'"

"If he asks why you missed work?"

"I needed the day off to prepare for our date," Evelyn said. "I asked Phyllis to tell him; maybe she forgot."

"After that?"

"Ask for a glass of water," said Evelyn, inhaling deeply. "When he turns to go to the kitchen, approach him and shoot him in the back."

"Then what?"

"Out the back door," Evelyn said. "Leave my coat. Layth will meet me with a new coat and hat. I'll change. We'll meet the private ambulance and leave for the rendezvous."

"Excellent," said X. "Follow the plan, and everything will be fine. Two days from now, you'll be with your family, out of the city, on your way to a new life." She checked her watch. "For now, get some sleep. We'll rehearse again tomorrow."

X handed Evelyn off to Felicity, who led Evelyn to a small room deep in the basement. Felicity showed Evelyn the bathroom and a jug of drinking water, then left her. The room reminded Evelyn of a prison cell. There was a firm yet lumpy futon in one corner. Evelyn lay down on it. She thought of Sara and Sid and tried to sleep. Two restless hours later, she pulled out her reader and checked Samizdata. Thinking of Sid, she scrolled to the posts written by the young boy in the triage camp with his brother.

How to Survive a triage Camp #7

They finally moved us out of Triage West. I got to see my account balance on the transfer clipboard. My baalance is way negative because we got charged for police services when they stopped the truck and we got a public safety fine, too.

At least my brother and I got to stay together. The new place is mostly better. We work inside taking aprt computers. They bring in big loads of old broken computers and put them on work benches. We get paid to take them apart, put everything in little trays.

Our bunks are in a building with no windows. So even though I still have this phone and charger I'm almost out of bateries.

How to survive a triage camp #11

Awesome! Someone wrote a buletin on how to charge my phone!

There are little batteries in the old computers the same size data coins. A lot still a charge. I connected them together to make a bigger battery that could charge my phone. Thanks TriageStar88!

Network is in bad shape today. A lot of Authority spam.

My little brother asked when we would see our parents.

A lot of coughing in the bunkroom. They try to hide it but I think people are getting sick. Hopefully it will be spring soon and they move us to agriculture camp. Fresh air.

TriageStar88 do you know how to get rid of propaganda spam its blocking the real posts.

The post, she realized as she finished, was several months old. It was the last of the series she could find. She switched off her reader, lay back, and tried again to sleep.

—✂

I know. Lying in bed, Addy fumed over what Charlotte had said. Was it a gesture of solidarity or a warning? It didn't matter; Charlotte had gone from an annoyance to a threat.

Carlos rolled over in his sleep, put an arm across her abdomen. The tiny hairs on his forearm tickled the scar across her hip. She turned away slightly so he wasn't touching her scar. She reached out and silently slid open the drawer of her bedside table. She reached inside and pulled out the little plastic alarm clock she kept there, its battery long dead. Addy ran her finger slowly over its contours as Carlos slept.

—✂

Layth raised his foggy goggles as the door was closed behind him.

"You won't need that mask," said a man's voice in lightly accented English. "The air here is as clean as anywhere in the city. Which," he admitted dryly, "is not saying much."

Layth looked around. The fifth floor was surprisingly clean, dimly illuminated with strings of LED Christmas lights. Layth saw the entrances to several apartments were open. A tall man was standing before him in the dim light; several other figures were visible nearby.

"Welcome," said the man. "I'm Habib. My son tells me you're looking for something. Not scrap, obviously, since this place was stripped even before we got here."

"I wasn't sure what I'd find," said Layth. "But I think it's long gone."

"Let us offer you a cup of tea, at least," said Habib. Layth was about to refuse, on account of the late hour and the failure of his mission, but Habib added: "While your Samizdata downloads. The children said you have good, new stuff on there. You must be well travelled."

So that was why they invited a stranger into their home so late at night. It was true; Layth's contact with all parts of the Samizdata network gave him an impressive collection of recent additions. This was a risk that Felicity and X warned him of often; if he were arrested with the coins he would be a high-value detainee, condemned to weeks of "special interrogation." But with continuous spam attacks on the network, he felt it was his duty to share good material. So he accepted the offer of tea.

"I do get around," Layth said. "I grew up in places like this."

The occupants of the long-quarantined building had set up a kind of warming room in one of the apartments. The windows were insulated and blocked off (since light coming from a quarantined building would doom anyone inside). The periphery of the dim room was lined with triple bunk beds, and Layth could see a few small figures—children—and a few with gray or white hair. In an adjacent room someone coughed loudly, the familiar sound that had given them away.

In the center of the room was a tiny homemade stove, with a chimney pipe that went up into the ceiling. "The smoke vents to the upper floors through the air ducts," explained Habib. "Nothing on infrared, no plume of smoke. It just dissipates into the rest of the haze." He opened the stove and threw in several handfuls of broken-up furniture. Then he put a kettle on top of the stove. "What is it you seek?" he asked, gesturing at an old couch cushion on the floor. Layth rested on it. Other adults sat quietly nearby.

"I'm trying to find someone who lived on the sixth floor," said Layth. "A long time before the quarantine. Did any of you . . ."

Habib shook his head. "We lived in another neighborhood until six months ago. Everyone was getting triaged—separated from their families, children being taken, elders sent to charcoal camps up north. We snuck away and hid here."

"Ahhh," said Layth. It was dangerous to hide so many people in one spot for so long. Even though the apartments had been stripped of copper wiring and pipe, eventually there would be demand for steel or glass or something else embedded in the structure itself. But that was another conversation. "When you moved in, was there anything leftover upstairs?"

Habib gave him a regretful look. "Some furniture. A few papers." He left unspoken the obvious fact that they'd burned everything for heat.

"I checked the mail room. Some cabinets had been removed."

"That was us," replied Habib. He gestured through the door to the hallway, where a mail cabinet was standing with some doors open, little toys and knickknacks visible within. "But any paper is gone. I'm sorry, we didn't expect that after all this time anyone who had lived here would still be—that anyone would come back."

Layth nodded. His eyes were stinging; perhaps the improvised chimney wasn't as good as they thought.

A little girl appeared beside Habib, whispered something into his ear. She must have been lying on one of the bunks. She had a tablet in one of her hands—one of the ultra-low-wattage types with a display based on squid skin that lasted weeks on a charge. "She wants to know why none of your files are rated," Habib asked. "She says you have a lot of good ones, but they'll get lost in the spam."

Layth was perplexed. "My files should have highest priority," he said. "They're official releases."

The girl whispered more. "She says all the spam is marked 'official,' too," said Habib, "until you downgrade it."

Layth grew even more confused. "You can only change ratings with admin access," which only the original developers had.

"I don't know." Habib shrugged. "The kids do it all the time."

Layth held his hand out for the tablet. The screen had the list of bulletins he was familiar with, but also extra options he had never seen before. A developer menu appeared at the top in Hindi. "Show me how you use this," Layth said. The girl showed him how to rank bulletins and how to mark them as spam using the hidden menu. Her fingers moved so quickly he had to get her to stop and show him several times, while he tried to memorize the commands. "You read Hindi?" he asked.

The girl shook her head shyly. "She taught herself how to access developer options in another language," said Habib. "We often have to lie still and be quiet. There is a lot of time for these things."

194 🖋 Kraken Calling

Layth had the girl demonstrate several more times what she could do. Felicity would be ecstatic when he passed these skills on. But it was well after midnight. "I have to go," said Layth. "What you've shown me will help many people. Let me give you something in return." He drew out a vial of antibiotics and handed it to Habib. "If your friend has tuberculosis, or a bacterial lung infection . . ."

Habib's eyes filled with tears, and he hugged Layth spontaneously. Layth hugged him back.

On his way out, Layth passed the mail cabinet. The number 604 was marked on one of the doors, which was slightly ajar. He flipped it open to look. It contained a napkin, several pencils, a single AA battery, and a Buddha figurine. He realized that there was something stuck to the back of the door, a few strips of white cloth tape that had endured the years. Perhaps his search was not over, after all. He peered closer. In scrawled handwriting it read, *Forward mail to*—and then a blurry address he couldn't read. Totally illegible.

Layth sighed. Another dead end.

—✒

Evelyn spent the day rehearsing. There was a large underground space that Felicity had marked out with charcoal lines to approximate the floor plan of Justinian's house. Evelyn navigated it all day, practicing different escape routes that would lead her out the back into a little ravine, where she would meet Layth.

She ate sparingly and thought of her family. Soon enough, it was time to go. X had arranged a taxi to deliver her. Costly, but someone riding in a taxi was less likely to have trouble at a checkpoint than a person on foot. Shortly after dark, she was delivered in front of Justinian's house. It was large and obviously expensive, but not as enormous as she had expected—a tasteful expression of power. A guard station was located nearby, but X had told her there was no private security inside the house. Not even security cameras, since Justinian saw no need to compromise his own privacy. The privilege and comfort of wealth.

She knocked on the front door, and in the pause that followed, she mentally rehearsed her steps. Justinian would offer to take her coat. As he turned away, coat in hand, she would reach into her purse, draw out the zip gun, and slam it against his back. Turn, draw, slam. Turn, draw, slam.

Then the door swung open. To her great surprise, it was Stanley who greeted her, his shaven head gleaming, a faint smile on his face.

"Dr. Justinian is expecting you, Evelyn," he said. "Please come in."

Evelyn walked through the open door.

12

2028

Dee and Rebecca sat on the back step of the café safe house. A circular saw buzzed inside; contractors were completing final renovations needed to open the bookstore-slash-coffee shop.

"Have you found the spy?" Dee asked. She had become obsessed with identifying the spy Simón's intelligence showed was active in Newbrook.

Rebecca shook her head, took a draw on her cigarette. "We're running countersurveillance, following our contacts in the area to see if anyone meets a handler. It's not easy—there's a lot of private-security and police activity." Her computer screen held thousands of photos from her countersurveillance team. Dee swept through the highlights as they spoke, seeking signs of duplicity, a familiar face in the wrong place. She found nothing.

"Keep trying. We'll need to act fast once we know," replied Dee. "Do your cells understand what must happen if someone is compromised? If we lose contact or receive a silent alarm?" Silent alarms were the subtle, prearranged cues a person would use to indicate they were under duress. Like answering the phone with *Everything is fine here,* which meant exactly the opposite.

"If someone is compromised before the operation, everything goes dark," Rebecca said. "Warning message goes out. All pending actions are aborted. Everyone retreats to backup safe houses, and in six months we use backup channels to rebuild."

"Good," said Dee.

"It's pretty drastic," said Rebecca, exhaling smoke.

"It's necessary," Dee replied, "for security. Are we ready to go on the petroleum depot?"

"Cell Seventeen is set," said Rebecca. "Crawlers are prepped. Teams have rehearsed. We're just waiting for the go-ahead. But people are wondering: should we proceed after the occupation at the tank farm? Maybe what they've done is enough."

Dee nodded. The same question had been on her mind. With the sit-in and the sudden cancellation of development plans, she had wondered if they should focus their efforts elsewhere. But no. "The committee has been clear," Dee said. "We need to consolidate our gains. That occupation was a good sign, but when public sentiment cools, the developers will try again. We need to make sure they can't. And what better time to get public support for"—she lowered her voice—"large-scale property destruction than now?"

Rebecca nodded.

"Remember," said Dee, "we're focused on one target, but the depot is part of a network. Taking out one node doesn't bring down a network. We need to destabilize the whole thing. This action will help do that."

Rebecca nodded with more conviction. She checked her watch and butted out her cigarette. "I'd better get back to Newbrook. After the action, we'll move my main team to the new safe house. But this is getting expensive. All the apartments we're renting, backup safe houses, multiple vehicles, cash expenditures for surveillance teams—it adds up. My branch has five action cells, and the support cell is getting run off their feet. "

"There's more money coming in," said Dee. "Just do your best."

~

"Well, punks, our plan worked," said Corben. He sat on the leather couch in the basement, Taavi and Andy across from him. "The mayor gave up." They high-fived.

Taavi leaned back in his chair. His forearm throbbed continuously, and his head ached. But he felt elated.

"What's next?" asked Andy.

Taavi though it was an open question for brainstorming, but Corben responded immediately.

"I'm glad you asked," he said. "I know you're ready to take things up—new targets, new tactics. Time to make things personal for the capitalist bastards who started this fight."

"Shouldn't Samantha be here for this?" asked Taavi.

"Nah, this is a special present from me to you," said Corben. "Ready for the real guerrilla shit?" He pulled out a large black duffel bag, which he lifted onto the coffee table with obvious difficulty, knocking several empty beer cans onto the floor. "Merry fucking Christmas."

Taavi leaned forward and unzipped the duffel. Metal glinted from inside. Taavi's stomach turned slightly as he pulled the bag open with both hands. The bag was full of guns and boxes of ammunition.

Andy laughed, and cursed, and laughed some more.

⭢

By noon, the petroleum depot was nearly abandoned again. The dozens of people who had stayed overnight departed in twos and threes until only a handful remained, along with a surprisingly large amount of debris and detritus. Helen and Gwen cleaned up and loaded straw bales onto Gwen's wagon under the hot midday sun. Even the cops had mostly gone; only two cruisers remained at the front gate.

"Is it just me," asked Helen, "or was that almost too easy?" She stuffed a few empty food wrappers into a garbage bag near the ashes of the small campfire.

Gwen picked up a straw bale with each hand. "It did go quick," she agreed. "But can't things go well, once in a while? Besides, the bosses don't expect much real pushback." She tossed the bales up onto the bed of the wagon. "Sometimes a little bit of fight is all it takes to get them to back down."

"It was more than a *little* bit of fight," said Helen. "How many months have we been protesting? Plus years of organizing." She paused her work for a coughing fit.

"Exactly. It wasn't *that* easy." said Gwen, picking up another two bales. "Did you get any rest last night? You look rough."

"I'm behind on my sleep," said Helen, stretching her sore joints. "And stiff from sleeping on the ground. I'll nap this afternoon."

"Well, you deserve it, kid," said Gwen.

Helen's phone rang. She pulled it out and looked: Leon. She swore under her breath.

"More journalists?" asked Gwen.

"My boss," said Helen, muting the ringer. "He wasn't happy about the direction of the campaign. Wanted me to tone things down."

"Ha!" Gwen laughed. "Well, you can't always get what you want. Invite him to the victory party tonight! He'll see all those happy faces and change his mind."

"Maybe," said Helen dubiously. She grabbed the last piece of loose garbage she could see. The site was strewn with bits of loose straw, and the pavement near the tank farm office still sparkled with bits of glass too small to be swept up.

"Looks tidier than before," said Gwen, throwing the final bale onto the wagon.

Helen laughed. She found it grimly comical to collect litter above a kilometers-long plume of toxified groundwater. But her laugh turned into another coughing fit.

Gwen frowned and put an arm over Helen's shoulders. "Go home, put your feet up for a few hours before the victory celebration." She released Helen and hopped up to the door of her tractor. "I don't know about you, but I plan to party all night!"

~

The choir was chanting something in Greek as Dee opened her laptop in the small church cell. A lamentation, she suspected.

As she logged on, she was surprised to see Simón already online and waiting, though their appointment wasn't for another hour. He messaged:

Thank fuck you're online.

That was not on the list of prearranged greetings. She tried a legitimate option. *Good morning from Taipei,* she typed.

Fuck that, he responded. *You've got big trouble. Police about to make a bust in Newbrook. Sending photo of their spy.*

She opened the photo, her eyes widening in recognition.

They've got press releases ready to go, dated tomorrow. More transfers appeared. Simón was sending files faster than she could read. *Probably planning to arrest ppl today. WARN THEM!!1!!*

Dee turned on her disposable phone and dialled the number of Rebecca's burner. The phone rang once, and then the call was dropped. The old stone church had terrible cell reception.

Dee hastily forwarded some documents to Rebecca, then stood and shouldered her bag. She grabbed her laptop in her left hand, holding the phone in her right. She ran for the door; if she went straight home she could take her father's car and drive to Newbrook herself. She might have only hours—or minutes—to warn people.

Out on the sidewalk she dialled again. It went to voice mail immediately. "Rebecca, it's me," she said. "It's an emergency. I'm sending you a photo." The sidewalks were crowded with lunch-hour foot traffic. She bumped into several people as she jogged down the street, ignoring the dirty looks they gave her.

Dee stopped at a traffic light where others were waiting and opened the laptop. With the phone, she snapped a picture of the photo on the screen and sent it to Rebecca. "This is the infiltrator. You need to deal with it immediately. You have hours. Maybe less."

The walk signal began to beep. She rushed forward without lifting her eyes, staring at her laptop, raising her voice over the traffic noise. "I'm on my way. It's very important to—"

She did not even see the truck that slammed into her body and sent her flying, her laptop and phone flung into empty space. She flailed midair before her head crunched loudly against the pavement and everything stopped.

~

Samantha met Taavi and Andy downtown. "It feels like I haven't seen you in a while," she said.

Taavi laughed. "It's been, like, two days." The downtown street was awash in pink light from the setting sun, illuminating a *Free the Newbrook Four* poster wheat-pasted to a nearby newspaper box.

"Well, it's been a busy week," said Samantha.

"You're telling me!" said Andy.

"What do you want to do tonight?" asked Taavi.

"Let's go out!" said Andy.

"Don't you guys have to hang with Corben?" asked Samantha.

Andy missed the edge in her question. "Nah, he's gone away to visit his aunt for a few days."

"I'd go to the victory party," said Taavi.

"Corben said—" began Andy.

"Fuck Corben," said Samantha. "He doesn't know shit about security culture."

"—it's suspicious we show up," said Andy, "with all those people . . ."

"We've been to lots of their events," pointed out Taavi. "It's suspicious if we *don't* go."

"We did our part," said Samantha. "Let's drop by and enjoy our share of the victory nachos, yeah?"

"I guess," said Andy, "if it's just for a couple of minutes."

Helen napped longer than she intended. By the time she got to the pub, the victory party was in full swing. The place was packed with cheerful supporters, each wanting to shake her hand and share some anecdote about the campaign. "When I arrived at the petrol depot that morning and you had a whole *encampment* set up," said one smiling woman, gesturing with both hands, "*that's* when I knew we were going to win."

"I knew months ago, at the city council meeting," said a man, "when they cut off our testimony and the whole crowd started chanting and stomping their feet. That's when I knew."

Everyone wanted to recount a tiny victory or share some moment from a protest march. They had all known, all along, that they would win. Many of them crowded around a table with Teresa's father, who was having the time of his life. She was glad; these shared experiences would fuse them into a stronger community of resistance. She was also exhausted, headachy, slightly nauseated—in need of a soft chair and a cold drink.

She made her way to the back of the pub and found her fellow organizers bivouacked in a booth. Tom, Elijah, and Elijah's boyfriend were splitting their second pitcher, faces flushed and grins wide. Teresa and Gwen were talking animatedly about something, but when they saw Helen, Gwen stood up and hugged her. They made room for her on the bench.

"The whole town is here!" said Gwen.

"Yeah!" said Helen. "Even Apollo's younger friends."

"Don't think I've met them," said Gwen. "Can I buy you a drink?"

"Something cold and bubbly," replied Helen, and Gwen returned a moment later with a glass. Their entire table raised their glasses, yelled "Cheers!" and drank. The joy of the environment was contagious, and Helen felt her previous fatigue begin to melt away. "Where's Philip?" she asked.

Tom shrugged. "He probably slept late. Like you!" Tom drained his glass, while Elijah rolled his eyes.

They laughed and chatted and drank and ate pub food for the better part of an hour. It was just after nine when Leon, the Friends of the Watershed director, appeared from the crowd and zeroed in on the organizers' table. Helen felt her stomach tighten. She couldn't ignore him any longer, so she decided to take a friendly tack. She had, after all, succeeded.

"Leon!" she said with a smile and a wave. "Can I buy you a—" But his lethal expression froze her.

"We've been served," he said, slamming a manila folder onto the table.

"What are you talking about?" she asked. Elijah flipped open the folder and began reading the legal-sized pages within.

Leon scowled. "Friends of the Watershed, me, you, Tom's union, pretty much everyone sitting at this table. We're all getting sued, by name. According to this affidavit, you're conspiring to cause damage to reputation, interfering with the legal use of property, and so on, and so on. The mayor, the petroleum company—they're seeking damages of fifty million."

There was a brief silence, and then Gwen laughed once, sharply. "Come *on*. Fifty million dollars? That's ridiculous."

"It's a SLAPP suit," said Elijah. "It's meant to scare us into silence. Classic corporate bully move."

"It's not a scare tactic if it works," said Leon. "Any of you got fifty million to spare? Tom, does your union's insurance cover criminal conspiracy? Gwen, how much does a part-time veterinarian make?"

"SLAPPs are actually civil suits," said Elijah, "so technically it's not a *criminal* conspiracy so much as—"

"Shut up," said Leon. He turned to Helen. "Did you file our papers for the Lakes Conference?"

Helen blanched. She had meant to finish the papers over the weekend, but the idea for the sit-in had come up suddenly and taken over every day since. "I'm sure the conference will accept them," she began.

"It doesn't matter," said Leon. "FotW is shutting down for the duration. We can't afford to do anything to make this worse. The office will be closed indefinitely."

"Wait, wait!" said Helen. "There's still a lot of work to do. I need to—"

"*You* don't need to do anything," Leon replied, "except clean out your desk. You're fired. Get your things, return your keys, and find yourself a good lawyer, because we sure aren't paying for your screwup."

"Whoa, whoa, slow down," said Gwen. "Let's not rush into anything. Think about it: why are they doing this now? It doesn't make any sense. We won."

"Haven't you seen the news?" Leon asked. "The mayor gave a press conference twenty minutes ago with the head of economic development of whatever. Apparently, the tank farm is 'critical infrastructure' needed to 'protect the national economic interest.' They're folding the whole thing into the Industrial Revitalization Initiative."

Most of the pub nearby had gone silent to watch the argument. Someone started flipping channels on a wall-mounted TV, trying to find the news.

"It's over," said Leon. "Just by sitting at this table right now you're giving them more evidence for their conspiracy case. Give up and go do something useful with your lives." Then he turned on his heel and strode out through the crowd.

"Jesus Christ," said Tom. "My union can't handle this," he said, putting a palm on his forehead. "We barely have any money after the last strike. Jesus, what have you pushed us into? We've gone way too far."

"Just calm down," said Gwen.

"It's you, too!" said Tom. "You've both been pushing these illegal actions. What did you expect?"

"My father has huge medical bills every month!" said Teresa, "We don't have money for lawyers!"

Helen slumped forward on the table, pressing her face into her hands. She suddenly felt so tired, her limbs like lead, her joints stiffening. Everything was falling apart.

Around her, the table erupted into argument.

~

"That was fucking terrible," said Taavi as he walked home with Samantha and Andy. The sidewalk radiated the leftover heat of the day.

"What a meltdown," said Andy. "That Leon guy is a real asshole."

"The whole thing is a clusterfuck," said Taavi. "But it shows we were right all along."

"Like protest was going to work," agreed Andy, "if they can just change the law whenever it's convenient."

Samantha was oddly quiet. Taavi reached out with his uninjured arm and grasped her hand. "Everything okay?" he said.

She squeezed his hand, then whispered, "I think we're being followed."

"What?" he said, craning his neck around.

"Don't look!" she hissed. "Act natural. There's a car I've seen several times behind us. Let's get back to your place, quickly."

When they got to the front door of Corben's house, Taavi couldn't fit his key into the lock.

"What are you waiting for?" asked Samantha.

"It won't fit!" said Taavi. He looked more closely. There was a plastic sheen over the opening of the lock. "I think it's been superglued."

"Maybe Corben's pranking us?" suggested Andy.

"We'll go in through the garage," said Samantha, and they hustled around to the side of the house.

They entered the garage and flipped on the light. A dark-haired woman was sitting on a chair in the middle of the garage, a lit cigarette in one hand. "You're late," she said. "Your visit to the pub cost us precious time."

The three of them stopped partway through the door. "You'd better come all the way in so we can talk," she said. "We only have"—she checked her watch—"six minutes."

"Who the hell are you?" asked Samantha.

"Your only hope," replied the woman.

"Did you superglue our front lock?" asked Taavi.

"It's better that we talk in here," the woman replied, taking a drag from her cigarette. "Nearly every room in your house is bugged. Except this one," she added, gesturing to the unfinished stud walls of the garage. "Let's get to the point. Do you know where your 'friend' Corben is right now?"

"Visiting his aunt?" replied Andy in a querulous tone.

"Only if his aunt works for a joint police and federal intelligence venture," said the woman. "You've been duped. That man is a paid police informant who has been leading you into a trap. After you go to sleep tonight, you'll be dragged out of your beds by a SWAT team. Your faces will be plastered on front pages across the nation with the headline 'terrorists.' The bag of guns downstairs will ensure that."

"Guns?" asked Samantha.

"You don't know about the guns?" the woman asked. "Quite a boys club he's got going."

"This is bullshit," said Andy. "Corben isn't a cop."

"No, not a cop," agreed the woman. She drew a folded sheet out of her pocket and handed it to him. It bore a mug shot of a younger, gaunter-looking Corben. "A former cocaine dealer who got high on his own stash, tried to rob some ATMs, and nearly beat one of his customers to death. The police cut him a deal—work for them to avoid jail time." She took another pull from her cigarette.

"Let me lay it out for you: I work for an underground network of revolutionaries. We're going to bring capitalism to a grinding halt and make room for a sane society. If you want, you can come with me and join your fellow revolutionaries underground. Anarchists, queers, radicals of every flavor—you'll find solid comrades. We'll give you the resources and training you need to take real direct action.

"Or," she said, "you can stay here and be woken up by a SWAT team in a few hours. Or you could go on the run alone." She looked at Taavi and shrugged. "Eke out a living somehow despite your faces on every TV channel. Maybe get shot trying, who knows." She checked her watch. "You have three minutes to decide."

Taavi began to feel woozy and felt around for a chair with numb fingers. Finding nothing, he sat down heavily on the concrete floor and put his head between his knees. "This is your chance," said the woman, "if you're serious. Of course, if you want to keep screwing around, slashing your arms open and playing with guns until you end up dead or in jail, I'll leave right now, and you can take your chances. But if you genuinely want to save the future of this planet, then come with us."

"How do you know about my arm?" asked Taavi.

"Like I said, we're professionals," the woman replied.

"Were you following us tonight?" asked Samantha.

"I had *a* team following," answered the woman. "The other surveillance team was, well, *theirs*." Taavi felt as though he was going to vomit.

"What will happen if we go with you?" asked Samantha.

"You'll be sent to safe locations until things cool down," the woman replied. "Then you'll be trained, assigned jobs and new teams. You'll be given orders, sometimes, and be expected to follow them. This is a war, after all."

"We'll be in the same cell?" asked Andy.

"Certainly not," she replied.

"You've left us little choice," said Samantha.

"I've given you a lifesaving warning and offered you a new home, training, and equipment. If that's not enough, I'm not sure what I can say in the next"—she glanced at her wrist again—"two minutes to convince you."

Taavi raised his head from his knees. "Who *are* you?" he asked.

"Rebecca," she said. "You can call me Rebecca."

13

2051

Evelyn's brief training had not prepared her for contingencies. Implicit in her training was the assumption Justinian would be alone.

So when Stanley opened Justinian's door, the plan simply went out of her head. When he invited her in, she proceeded on autopilot, relying more on polite social habits than her brief assassin training. She removed her boots and put them on a mat in the large foyer. Stanley took her coat. It was a dark alpaca-wool coat, and not the fur coat Stanley had arranged for her, but he didn't notice. Or so she hoped.

With both hands, she grasped the large purse Layth had given her.

As Stanley carried her coat to a wardrobe in another room, Justinian appeared, dressed down slightly in a shirt and tie with a white chef's apron. "Evelyn!" he said. "How lovely to see you. I was worried when I didn't see you at work today."

"I took the day to get ready for our date," Evelyn began. "Didn't Phyllis tell you—"

Before she could finish, he put his hands on both her shoulders and leaned forward to kiss her on the cheek. She smiled, suppressing an urge to shiver. "Dinner is almost ready; I just need to finish some business with Stanley. I've decanted some wine in the dining room."

He guided her, one hand unnecessarily on her back, to the dining room, where he poured her a glass of wine. Then Justinian strode off to follow Stanley toward the back of the house.

Her mind flickered through possibilities faster than she could consider them. Should she wait until Stanley left before attempting the assassination? Was he going to leave? Was he the only additional person in the house? Was Layth really waiting to meet her, or did X secretly want the assassination to be a suicide mission? Would she be captured moments after doing her job, a disposable instrument no different to X than an empty shell casing? Did she really know anything about the underground at all?

Seeing no other choice than to play along, Evelyn took a sip of Justinian's wine. It was an expensive vintage; in that moment it tasted to her no better than dishwater. She sipped more to moisten her uncomfortably dry mouth. Holding her wineglass in one hand, she stepped back into the foyer, which was decorated with paintings and a few sculptures. Justinian had a taste for Renaissance art depicting ancient Rome.

With her wineglass in one hand and her purse in the other, she walked deeper into the house on silent stocking feet, listening. She heard men speaking in low tones from behind a closed door near the rear of the house.

She stepped close to the door and listened. Her heart jumped at the words "murderer" and then "targeted assassination."

Abruptly, the door swung open; she found herself staring into Stanley's face for the second time that night. But she focused on him for only a moment. Over his shoulder she saw a large screen displaying a blurry surveillance photo from a day she remembered well. She saw herself on the ground at a surprise checkpoint, hands raised above her face. Standing above her, gun in hand, was a masked man she now recognized well.

—◢

Layth crouched by the ravine behind Director Justinian's house, checking his watch for the third time. The taxi driver had delivered Evelyn to the house eleven minutes ago. According to plan, she should already have killed Justinian and exited through the back door.

He raised his binoculars, but he could see little of the house from his low vantage point by the ravine. Above was a grassy hillside, and farther still a garden with high limestone walls that blocked Layth's view of the house's lower stories. He could see only the third story, with its dark bedroom windows.

He checked that his pistol was fully loaded with a round in the chamber. He would wait five more minutes. Then he would have two choices: abandon Evelyn and retreat, or draw his pistol, break into the house, and do the job himself.

All this was assuming that Evelyn had not decided to collaborate, to broker her own deal with Justinian. If that was the case, another underground team—the one sent to rescue Sara and Sid from the triage camp—was walking into a trap. How well, after all, did he really know Evelyn?

—≥

Addy was lounging on a couch in the library, half dozing with a biography of Che Guevara on her lap, when the hubbub began. It started slowly, with the opening and closing of the kitchen door downstairs. Soon it escalated: footfalls on the stairs, a knock at a door across the hall—Charlotte's door—and a hushed conversation with a growing number of people. Then bustle at the boot rack below, opening and closing of the wardrobe as people grabbed their coats. The kitchen door opened and slammed shut several times, then there was silence.

Addy came totally awake. She left her book and went downstairs. There was no one there. She donned her boots and coat and walked outside. There was a heavy frost on the ground. The lights of the common hall were off, but three people stood at the entrance to the root cellar. "What's going on?" Addy asked them.

"Patrol captured a YEA spy!" said Sridharan. "Charlotte just went down to interrogate him for the resistance!"

Addy frowned, opened the root-cellar door, and descended the concrete stairs that led to the main storage chamber. People crowded at the foot of the stairs, conversing intensely.

". . . but once they got back to the car, we had already taken it," reported Lieutenant Dumont, the militiawoman who helped Addy teach her combat class. "Farnharm ran, but the agent hesitated, and we captured him." Addy looked around but couldn't see any prisoner. He must have been put in the deep chamber where they kept crops that needed high humidity.

"Excellent job," said Charlotte. "Where is the vehicle now?"

"We didn't bring it back here, in case the Authority had a tracker on it," Dumont replied. "We drove it to the old underground parking garage and took the battery out, to shut off transmitters and keep people from moving it."

"Good thinking, LT," said Charlotte. "Were you able to salvage anything from the vehicle?"

"His computer, a phone, a few handheld radios, a briefcase full of papers," she said. "Oh, and this." Addy stepped forward to see that Dumont was holding a shotgun. "We didn't know if he had an implanted GPS transmitter, so we blindfolded him, bound his wrists, and put him in the root cellar, where the earth would block radio signals."

"Clever," said Charlotte. "You brought him to the right place. I'll learn what we need to know from him."

Addy cleared her throat loudly; everyone in the small space turned to look at her. She realized Carlos was there, too, and scowled inwardly. "It's my responsibility to interview new people at the Thistle. I'm surprised I wasn't brought here immediately."

Carlos looked abashed. "I thought you were asleep, and I know you don't really want to get involved in militant stuff, so . . ."

Charlotte lay a hand on his arm to silence him, which irritated Addy more. "I appreciate that it's your job to interview new members. But this man isn't a guest. He's a prisoner of war, and I think it's necessary that someone with resistance experience question him to gain the most intelligence. Don't you agree?"

Charlotte stared unblinkingly at Addy, awaiting her answer, and Addy stared back evenly, in silence.

"Adelaide," began Carlos, "no one thinks that you—"

"Fine," said Addy. "We'll both do it."

Charlotte arched one eyebrow, smiling almost imperceptibly. "So be it."

⌁

"Looking for the bathroom, again?" Stanley asked Evelyn.

Evelyn listened to her heart beat several times, slow and leaden, as she mentally searched for an excuse. She debated reaching into her purse and shooting Stanley that in moment, but the zip gun took twenty seconds to reload. There wouldn't be enough time to—

"Stanley," said Justinian, "We're done. You may go."

Stanley didn't break eye contact with Evelyn. "All right then," he said, shouldering past her. She heard him clomp down the hall in his boots.

Justinian gave her a faux-sheepish grin from across the room and beckoned her in. "I wasn't going to tell you until afterward," he said, "but I've been working on a little surprise for you." Evelyn gave him an attentive look, not trusting herself to put any other expression on her face. "I'm sure you remember this day," he said, gesturing at the photo on the screen.

She nodded in response.

"This terrorist," said Justinian, "killed two men in cold blood. He also shot the head-mounted camera on a security officer, depriving us of a high-quality image of his face." He gestured at the desaturated and blurry image, taken from a high angle. Evelyn was clearly visible on the ground, but Layth's face was almost entirely concealed by the hat, sunglasses, and high collar he wore. "Permanent checkpoints have fixed security cameras, but for this surprise checkpoint we could retrieve only a handful of images, after the fact, from a high-altitude drone."

He clicked a button, and the image sprang into choppy motion, the blurry Layth lowering his gun and sprinting forward. There were a few frames of video before the angle changed—probably from the forward flight of the drone—and a rooftop cut off the view of Layth. "We had only thirty frames of video. Not usually enough for gait analysis, especially since he's running and not walking."

He stepped closer, smiling down at her. "Stanley was here to tell me that he's finally isolated the man's gait. It's someone who often enters quarantined areas, and in recent months has often been seen near a shuttered Chinese restaurant in the Yellow Zone." He stepped even closer, reaching down to take the wineglass from her hand and put it on a table; she squeezed the handles of her purse reflexively. He grasped her free hand with both of his, and his face turned serious.

"I don't want to frighten you, Evelyn," he said, "but Stanley told me that this man has been sighted near Triage Administration. It's possible that he's been stalking you. That he wants to"—his voice hushed—"eliminate all witnesses to his heinous act. Stanley is right now rendezvousing with a special team that will raid the block where this terrorist sleeps and eliminate his entire group."

He leaned close and stroked her arm gently. He smelled of a cologne that Evelyn now found repugnant. "There's no need to thank me, Evelyn. I know this has been weighing on you. But tonight, we can drink wine and . . . enjoy ourselves." He bent his face down toward hers and raised one hand to her cheek.

She stared at his lips in a moment of paralysis. "Wait!" she said, and he stopped, eyes wide and slightly displeased. "There's something I have to give to you. A present."

His eyelids drooped. "I do love . . . surprises."

"Turn around and cover your eyes," she said. He grinned cockily and obeyed.

Carefully, Evelyn reached into her purse.

Layth had allocated five minutes to decide whether to leave or approach the house. Eight minutes had passed.

His inclination had been to leave, to return to the safety of headquarters, tell the others Evelyn didn't have the guts to do the job. But he had already stayed three minutes past his self-imposed deadline.

"Fuck it," he muttered to himself, standing up. He held a pistol in his right hand, a short crowbar in his left. From the brush he sprinted up the grassy hillside. He reached the limestone garden wall and pressed himself against it, waiting to see if he had triggered any alarms. Nothing obvious happened, so he went to the tall oak door in the garden wall.

He hooked the crowbar onto his belt and reached for the gate handle, then jerked back when he heard the gunshot. It was quiet—suppressed—but unmistakably close.

The time for subtlety was gone. He jerked the garden door's handle.

When it didn't work, he grasped his crowbar and smashed the latch into cooperation. He ran into the garden. Half a dozen motion-activated lights switched on. He ignored them.

One room at the back of the house was fully lit, but the view through the windows was obscured by white curtains. Suddenly something slammed against the curtains and window, then pulled away. It left a red stain the size of a dinner plate on the curtains.

Layth struck the glass once with his crowbar. The surface layer of the bulletproof glass cracked but did not shatter. He ran to the solid metal back door and tried it—locked. He went to work on the lock with his crowbar. An alarm sounded. The door shuddered from an interior impact and he backed up, raising his pistol.

The handle swivelled, and the door swung open to release Evelyn, wild-eyed and covered in blood.

—⚡

Addy pulled open the door to the rear chamber of the root cellar. The room was cold and cramped. Crates were piled high with potatoes and beets and carrots. A man was tied to a chair in the middle of the small space, blindfolded and temporarily deafened by a scuffed pair of yellow ear protectors. He wore a thin jacket and a suit. He didn't move when the door creaked open, but he jumped a little when Charlotte pushed his chair backward to make room. Then he scowled behind his blindfold.

Addy didn't want him to see their faces, but she needed to see his entire face to judge whether he was telling the truth. She had asked Lieutenant Dumont to retrieve a spotlight they used for performances in the common hall, had her bring it down and point it directly at the man's face. Once they closed the door of the moist storage area, Addy, Charlotte, and Lieutenant Dumont were literally rubbing shoulders in the tight environs.

With, everything in place, Charlotte pulled off the ear protectors and blindfold, leaving the man's hands tied behind the chair. He winced and squinted in the brilliant light.

"Hello," he said, sounding as friendly as one could under the circumstances. "I think there's been a bit of a misunderstanding. I'm a licensed agent of the Authority, carrying out my lawful duties. I'm going to have to ask you to untie me right away."

"What is your name?" asked Charlotte.

"Kenneth Woodborough, YEA development contractor. And with whom am I speaking?" Addy watched his eye movements carefully. Nothing indicated a lie, but it seemed unlikely that Woodborough would try to lie about his name when he had a pocket full of business cards.

"What is the purpose of your visit?" asked Charlotte.

Woodborough tried to smile, but in the glaring light it looked like a grimace. "Well, it's quite simple. The Authority is aware there has been hunger and deprivation in this area since the economic downturn. We're here to restore basic services—reliable power, monetary confidence. Get capitalism back on track, you know? 'Prosperity Restored!'" There was a pause as the three women watched him in silence. "I understand you're still using barter systems in this area, Miss . . . ?" He trailed off, then tried again. "Or is it Mrs. . . . ?"

Charlotte's face flashed with momentary rage, and she clenched her fists as though she were about to strike him. Addy stepped in.

"Why were you visiting Farnham?" she asked.

"Oh, we're visiting plenty of people during the redevelopment process," Woodborough responded, turning his head toward Addy. "To get the lay of the land, you know, the products and services in most demand, promising sites for investment."

"Are you aware the Newbrook town council has banned YEA agents from this area?" Addy asked.

Woodborough chuckled. "Yes, well, the 'town council'"—he said the phrase with exaggerated skepticism—"isn't really a *legitimate governing body*, now is it? And if *they* don't want to talk with us, well, plenty of people do, you understand? May I ask, when was the last time you had canned tuna? Or a delicious beef steak? Or maybe medicine is what you've been lacking? The YEA has an ample supply of food and other supplies for people who cooperate. I'm sorry, I didn't catch your name earlier."

"How many times have you visited Farnham?" Addy asked.

"It's hard to say exactly; I travel a great deal," said Woodborough evasively. "Gasoline car, you may have noticed. Good range. Not many of those around today. If its petroleum you're after, the Authority has the largest supply on this side of the continent. Heating oil, lubricants. Even tractor fuel—under the right circumstances."

There was a soft knock on the door, and Lieutenant Dumont opened it to reveal Carlos, who was holding a few sheets of paper. Back at the farmhouse, he was coordinating the examination of Woodborough's briefcase. He handed the sheets to Charlotte, who had recovered her composure. She examined the pages briefly.

"You offered all these things to Bill Farnham, didn't you?" Charlotte asked. She passed the sheets to Addy. Farnham had signed a contract of cooperation with the YEA that offered him payment in exchange for a very long list of services that extended from information through to quartering contractors on his farm and providing truck storage and maintenance. Which meant, Addy inferred, scouts and probably troops. No wonder he had kicked out the interns.

"We have *many* ongoing negotiations," said Woodborough, his smile increasingly forced. "If you would kindly untie me so we can have a real conversation, I'd be happy to offer you the same terms as Mr. Farnham. Maybe better?"

"Why do you think we'd accept that?" asked Addy.

"It's important to stick together in tough times, you know," said Woodborough. "I bet your family has been farming here a long time. Hardworking people. It's not your fault that our country's social safety net was overrun by immigrants, bringing disease and economic ruin. This land belongs to *North Americans,* not to foreigners."

There was an icy silence. Addy and Lieutenant Dumont exchanged looks. Addy raised her eyebrows and mouthed, *Immigrants.* Lieutenant Dumont pointed at her chest and mouthed, *North American.*

Woodborough seemed to realize that he had misstepped, though he didn't acknowledge the possibility that his interrogators might not all be White. Nonetheless, he changed his tack. "It's terribly cold in here," he said. "Could I please have a warmer coat? Something hot to drink?"

"You can have something when you cooperate," said Charlotte.

"I'm cooperating!" the man insisted. "I'm giving you information.

You don't even need me, really. You should just let me go. All of the information is in the papers you have, from my car. I'm more trouble than I'm worth."

"We know," said Charlotte, "the purpose of your visit is to prepare for a military deployment."

Woodborough twitched visibly. "Not at all," he said. His eyes were already squinting in the bright light, but to Addy the lie was clear. A strained contraction of the orbital muscles, a barely perceptible tic at the corners of his mouth. These were his tells. She realized, then, that he'd been lying about giving them the same terms as Farnharm.

"You came up this road," Addy said, "to inspect our farm, because Farnham told you we'd be an obstacle to the Authority."

"Oh no," replied Woodborough. "Please, just give me a hat. I'm not a young man! It's terribly cold down here."

Charlotte jumped in. "When will the first military units arrive?"

"This paranoia doesn't help anyone," protested Woodborough. "Just untie me so we can have a reasonable conversation."

"Are they coming next year?" asked Addy. Woodborough was stone-faced. "Six months?" She watched him carefully. "One month?" A lip twitch. "Two weeks?" Addy saw an infinitesimally brief smile. Woodborough was happy they would be coming—triumphant. "One week?" Nothing. A chill went down Addy's spine. How could they prepare for an armed invasion in a matter of weeks?

"Soon," whispered Charlotte to herself. Then louder: "Give us the troop deployment information. How many units are coming?" Before Addy could react, Charlotte reached out and struck the man viciously across the face.

Woodborough began to shake in his chair. Addy's mind flashed back to old spy novels she had read as a child; the captured spy would swallow a cyanide tablet hidden in a false tooth. They would seize and foam at the mouth and die without giving anything away. But Woodborough was not dying. He was twitching with desperate laughter.

"When they come, it's going to be like Detroit all over again!" He laughed, a tiny stream of blood trickling from the corner of his mouth. "They're going to burn you bitches alive!" There was a moment of complete silence, and then Woodborough began to shake and convulse in the chair with all his strength. "Let me go!"

"We're done here," said Addy.

"I'm an official of the most powerful government in this hemisphere!" he shouted. "You can't just leave me down here!"

"You are a spy and part of a government of occupation," replied Charlotte. "And you're going to be put on trial for your crimes."

—⁄—

For Layth, the escape from Justinian's neighborhood was a blur. In the first few minutes he was sharp, professional, methodical. Against the blaring of the alarm, he asked if Evelyn was injured. She shook her head. "I shot him in the chest!" she exclaimed, and they sprinted down the hill to the edge of the forest where he had left his bag. They donned reflective antidrone cloaks and rushed through the darkness to a private ambulance where a resistance driver waited, leaping aboard so the ambulance could speed into the night.

But as soon as Evelyn gasped out what she had seen—the surveillance on him, the likely identification of their headquarters, an imminent raid—Layth's mind was overwhelmed. Just keeping track of one escape plan took his full attention. To imagine that he could be on a drone camera at that very moment, that X and Felicity—the heart of his network and his only family—could be dead within hours or minutes: such thoughts paralyzed him for several moments as he struggled to push down panic. The terror was a physical sensation, an icy waterfall that drowned out his senses as he—

"Layth!" called Evelyn, not for the first time. "Layth, what should I do?"

He breathed out slowly and deeply, as though by doing so he could slow the rush of time itself. "Get changed," he said, thrusting a backpack toward her. "Wash the blood off your face as best you can; we'll reach a checkpoint soon."

"A checkpoint? There's blood all over me," said Evelyn.

"They shouldn't look in the back of the ambulance," he said. "They protect the dignity of the elite." Besides, a bloody person wasn't unusual in an ambulance.

"Is my family safe yet?" Evelyn asked as she struggled to change in the tight space.

"I haven't heard the report," said Layth, checking his watch.

"Can't you call them?" Evelyn asked.

"Radio silence," Layth replied. "But the mission should be underway right now. They'll be smuggled out the opposite side of the city. You'll rendezvous later."

Layth muttered a few instructions to the driver, who nodded. They pulled up to a Green Zone checkpoint, and there was a long moment of silent anxiety in the back as the driver spoke with the guards. But the guards did not look in the vehicle. The ambulance sped away from the checkpoint and toward the waterfront.

Ten minutes later, Layth turned to Evelyn. "I've got to go warn them. Good luck."

Evelyn looked anguished. "What do I do?"

"The driver will drop you at the docks," he said. "You'll be passed off from there." And, not knowing what gesture would be appropriate, he squeezed Evelyn on the shoulder. "It's going to be okay," he said. Then the ambulance slowed, and he jumped out onto the street a hundred feet from the block where the Chinese restaurant was located.

He was tempted to run directly there but knew that somewhere above a drone was watching for his gait. It was also after curfew, so every moment on the street meant danger. Layth adopted a limping, lopsided jog to hamper gait analysis. Once he got to the cover of an abandoned building, he began to sprint.

He burst into headquarters four minutes later to find X talking into an encrypted phone. "I don't care how many extra guards are at the perimeter fence," she was saying loudly. "This is a time-sensitive operation. Proceed at once if you—stand by." She turned to Layth, staring at his panicked expression and sweat-drenched clothing. "What's happened?"

"We need to evacuate," he said. "Now."

—✐

"That's a good idea," Carlos said after the interrogation, "but we don't really have a court system. How are we going to put him on trial?"

Addy rubbed the scars over her knees as they sat together on her bed. The time spent in the cold, cramped root cellar had left her slightly stiff. "I don't know," she said. "But for now, I'm more worried about the deal he's made with Farnham. For all we know, they're planning a full military invasion."

"Maybe arresting their agent will make them postpone their plan."

"Maybe they'll *accelerate* their plan," said Addy. "Either way, we need our own strategy, and a really good one, soon."

Carlos nodded, then paused. "It sounds like you did a good job questioning Woodborough. I'm proud of you."

"Thanks," Addy said, patting his knee.

"Even though," he added, "you don't really have any experience with this cloak-and-dagger stuff." Addy's lip twitched slightly, but he didn't seem to notice. "We're going to have to rely a lot on Charlotte in the coming weeks," he said. "She's the only one with the resistance connections and knowledge we need to handle this." Addy said nothing, and Carlos continued after a moment. "Look, Addy, I know you don't like Charlotte, but we *need* her to—"

She cut him off. "Carlos," she said, "there's something I have to tell you."

—⟋

The driver dropped Evelyn off near a quarantined warehouse at the waterfront. He didn't get out of the ambulance or even make eye contact. "Walk one hundred meters south," he said. "The boat will meet you there in five minutes. Don't dawdle. They won't wait." Once she got out, he drove off without another word.

She followed his instructions and walked out to an old dock that was barely visible in the light of a distant street lamp. The dock was in such disrepair that much of it had crumbled away. Parts of it were coated in a thick rime of ice from waves that splashed up onto the structure. The shallow water around the dock was filled with hunks of ruined concrete, debris, and slush. It seemed an unlikely place for a boat to dock. She began to sweat slightly in the icy breeze that blew off the water. Could she be at the wrong dock? Was there any other dock?

She squatted where she was, trying to conserve heat and not wanting to sit on the frigid concrete. And for a few minutes, perhaps longer, she went into a daze. She pictured Sara and Sid in her mind: pictured them as they were rushed out of the triage camp by black-clad resistance operatives, pictured a sunny grove outside of the city where she would soon see them again. Her anxiety had not disappeared, but the feeling of overwhelming panic that had gripped her for more than twenty-four hours began to wane.

She persisted in this reverie, shivering occasionally, until she was roused by a rhythmic splashing sound. She looked up. She could resolve nothing in the darkness. And then, a moment later, she saw it—a canoe, pulling up to the very end of the dock.

She walked forward as quickly as she could without slipping on the ice. Two men sat in the canoe, bodies hidden under reflective cloaks. One of them pulled his cowl back for a moment, exposing a grizzled face and a shock of gray hair. "Evelyn?" he asked. She nodded. "I'm Archie. Come aboard," he said, and raised his hand.

Five minutes later, the dock was out of sight off the stern. Over the point of the bow, Evelyn could see the harbor's most recognizable landmark: the enormous, derelict container ship that had run aground years earlier. She shivered and pulled her cloak tighter around herself as the boat moved forward into the icy blackness.

14

2028

In darkness, Dee struggled. Her head was agony. Her legs were pinned against the pavement; she couldn't move them. She reached down to pull her legs free, but her fingers found only asphalt.

She gasped and opened her eyes. It took a moment for them to clear. She apprehended that she was no longer on asphalt but on a bed in a dimly lit room. A hospital. She could remember a few snippets of the terrible hours after the truck struck her, but only vaguely, and she preferred not to dwell on them.

Dee did a head-to-toe assessment of herself. She had the worst headache of her life. Her skull felt detached, like a balloon. When she turned her head, the world lagged slightly behind. She had been given a lot of drugs.

She reached up to touch the epicenter of pain on the right side of her head. A large dressing was taped there; she was missing a lot of hair. A plastic mask across her nose and mouth hissed softly. As she explored her head for injuries, there was a slight tug on her arm. She looked down to find an intravenous line, looped back and forth several times where it entered her skin.

Dee checked her torso and arms and found a large number of swollen bruises, though to her surprise they didn't hurt much when she pressed them gently. There were sticky pads glued to several places on her chest and wires running from them. A large dressing covered a painful would across her abdomen. And yet another tube ran across her hip to her—*ugh,* she thought, *a catheter.*

Both legs were confined in plastic splints that prevented her knees from moving, though she could feel and move her toes. So that was something.

There was a call button on a cable hooked over the bedrail to her right. She pressed it and waited. A few seconds later a nurse appeared, a woman in her fifties. "How are you feeling?" she asked.

"What . . . time?" croaked Dee. Her throat felt dry and inflamed; simply speaking made her want to cough.

"It's quarter after nine," said the nurse. With warm hands, she grasped Dee's wrist to check her pulse.

"Wednesday?" asked Dee.

"No, Thursday," said the nurse. "You came in Wednesday." She frowned. "Do you know where you are? What your name is?"

But Dee was gripped by a sense of dread. It took her mind several moments to push through the fog of sedatives and painkillers to remember why: She had to check in every forty-eight hours with her cells. She had not had time to do so on Wednesday, when she had gotten the sudden message from Simón. Which meant that she needed to find a computer—or something—within the next few hours. If she didn't, they would assume that she had been captured or compromised, and the entire network would collapse as each cell fled, going deeper underground.

She moaned aloud.

"Are you in a lot of pain?" asked the nurse, walking around to check the IV bag and line. "The fentanyl should help."

"I need a phone," said Dee, her own voice so rough that she barely recognized it.

"Do you want me to call someone for you, honey? There's a phone at the nurse's station."

Dee swallowed painfully several times in an attempt to moisten her throat. "Where's my father?" she asked.

"He's just down the hall," the nurse replied. "Don't worry about him; you need to take care of yourself."

"Can you tell him I'm awake?" Dee said. "Tell him to come visit me."

The nurse gave her a puzzled look. "Visit you? Didn't they tell you about . . ." The nurse trailed off, then clamped her lips together and furrowed her brow.

"Tell me . . . what?" asked Dee.

"You rest," said the nurse. "I'll have your doctor come and visit you soon. Try to sleep, if you can."

～

Just after ten o'clock on Thursday night, Rebecca sealed Taavi in a seedy motel room with terse instructions: "Don't leave this room for *any reason*. Don't answer the door. Don't make loud noises. There are sandwiches in the minifridge. If you have to pass the time, read this training booklet. And for god's sake, don't use the telephone." She handed him a booklet, photocopied zine-style, with a blank cover.

On the drive out of Newbrook, Rebecca had taken and destroyed his mobile phone and his debit card. At a rural rest stop she had made him change clothing, trading his black hoodie for an uncomfortable blue polo shirt blazoned with the logo of a bankrupt video-rental franchise.

"Any questions?" she asked.

"Why do we have to stay in such a shitty motel?"

"*We* aren't staying in this shitty motel," she answered. "*You* are. I have other things to do. But shitty motels like this one let you pay cash and don't have cameras." She put one hand on the doorknob. "I'll be back within forty-eight hours. Keep your head down." And then she was gone.

Once she left, the motel room was shockingly quiet after hours of frantic activity.

Taavi was dazed but decided to take care of himself. He removed the dressing on his forearm—the stitches the veterinarian had given him looked neat and even—and put on the fresh dressing Rebecca had left him. He slipped off the uncomfortable shoes he wore (no doubt bought in cash from some small-town thrift shop) and switched off the light. He removed his jeans and jacket and uncomfortable polo shirt and slid into the bed. Its sheets were threadbare.

Exhausted though he was, he could not fall asleep. He missed Samantha and Andy already. Were they also in cheap motel rooms, headed in different directions? And what of Corben? How much of Corben was fake, and how much real? Had Corben's handlers orchestrated everything, down to the security guard's appearance during the tank-farm sabotage? Taavi's head swam and spun drunkenly even as it remained in place on his lumpy pillow. Outside his window, a four-lane highway buzzed. The panes rattled whenever transport trucks shifted gears.

He slowly drifted off. Some hours later, he was woken by angry screaming. Someone banged on his wall. He sat bolt upright.

"Fuck you, you fuckin' bitch!" A man's voice came through the wall. A female voice responded more quietly, but angrily. Then a stream of curses. Then more rattling and thumping next door.

He got out of bed and walked halfway to the room's door before he recalled that a) he was naked and b) he was a fugitive, and getting involved in strange disputes at sketchy motels was probably the quickest way to get caught.

Leaving his room—or interacting with anyone—was also against the express instructions of the woman who had just saved him from years in prison, who still held his fate in her hands.

The yelling and banging continued, and in his exhausted state Taavi wondered if this was a test. Rebecca had criticized their failure to keep to good security rules. Had she put some actors in the next room to have a fake argument, to entice him into breaking her orders? Or was it a moral test that *required* him to act? If he failed the test, would Rebecca simply abandon him at this motel, dooming him to a brief life on the run?

His answer came in the form of flashing red and blue lights visible around the edges of his curtains. He peeked out the window. A police car sat in the parking lot below, light bar strobing silently.

He ducked, cursing quietly. Were they already on their way up? Had the front seats of the police car been occupied or empty?

There was a sharp banging on his door. He looked through the peephole and broke into a cold sweat. Two policemen stood there, hands resting on their guns. "Open up!" one called, knocking loudly.

～

Sometime later, Dee woke again. The noises outside seemed muted, and the room was darker, so she reasoned it was night. She felt a sudden skin-crawling sensation as she remembered that she needed to get to a computer, or at least a phone, immediately.

She shifted herself up onto her pillow. Her head felt clearer than before. She threw back the sheets. The warmth of the room was stifling—no wonder she had felt groggy beneath the blankets.

On a chair beside her bed, she could see a full plastic bag; visible in its opening was the shirt she had been wearing when she was struck. Her personal effects.

Dee reached for the bag. She pulled out her bloodied shirt and threw it aside. Pants, socks, everything went onto the floor. There was something heavy at the bottom. She pulled out her computer; the screen was shattered. When she pressed the power button, nothing happened.

"Fuck," she said. Her throat was clearer, but she felt rising panic. She searched the bag for her phone but found nothing. She had been holding the phone when she was struck. It had likely been flung into traffic and smashed.

She found the call button beside her, pressed it, and waited several minutes. No one came. She pressed it again. No response. She guessed, from the darkness outside, that she had only hours before Cell Seventeen's carefully planned action at the petroleum depot was aborted and her entire network disappeared.

Hospitals had plenty of phones and computers, Dee reasoned fuzzily. She began the process of unhooking herself from all the tubes and wires. The oxygen mask came off easily enough, but the catheter was unpleasant to remove. The IV she pulled straight out; the wires on her chest popped off easily.

She pivoted her splinted legs off the bed. She couldn't bend them, but they didn't hurt as much as she expected. She slid forward so her feet touched the ground. She tried to bear a little weight with them. It was painful, but not impossible. She took two shuffling steps before growing so light-headed that she nearly fell. Shuffling back to the chair to rest, she perched awkwardly on the edge of the seat.

She would use the chair, she decided. Standing slowly, she pulled the chair away from the wall and pushed it in front of her, like a child learning to ice-skate. By putting weight on the chair, she was able to shuffle to the door of her room.

The dim hallway was empty, but she heard agitated voices and alarms coming from the opposite end of the ward. She heard, "Code blue!" Someone was in trouble. Perhaps that had woken her. Dee shuffled toward the nurses' station, occasionally peeking into other patients' rooms to see if any of *them* had phones. The nurses' station seemed a terribly long way.

She stopped to rest again, leaning on her chair in the middle of the hallway and looking around. The rooms around her were partially illuminated. She could see at least the general shapes of patients in most of the beds. The hospital seemed crowded, but at least—

Dee froze and turned her head slowly to the left. The patient in the room she was passing seemed terribly familiar, in a way that her addled brain could not process. She stood and leaned over to look through the window into the room. As she leaned she grew suddenly dizzy, and she grasped for her chair as she fell to the ground. The chair clattered loudly, and surprised voices echoed down the hall.

Dee could not hear them. She lay on the floor, horrified, reaching out her arms. "Dad?" she called. "Dad!"

✒

The police banged on Taavi's motel room door again. He stayed silent, eyeing the back window as an escape route. Suddenly there was another burst of shouting through the wall. "Hey," said one of the cops, "it's the next room." They moved on. Taavi slumped against the wall in relief, his sweaty skin sliding against the peeling paint.

He got a drink of water from the bathroom, then got back into bed and listened as his shouting neighbors were arrested.

✒

The morning after the victory party turned into a fight, Helen could not get out of bed. She hadn't drunk a single glass of beer, but she had the worst hangover of her life. Every sound was a hammer blow to her aching brain. The shafts of sunlight coming in around her bedroom drapes were needles through her eyeballs. Each time she shifted her body she was overcome by waves of nausea. Her phone rang, and she let it ring on and on until it went to voice mail.

Sometime around noon, she literally dragged herself out of bed and staggered down the hallway toward the bathroom, sliding one shoulder along the wall for balance, her eyes barely open.

In the bathroom she managed to turn on the tap and fill a plastic cup with water, but before she could drink, she was overcome by another wave of nausea. She dropped her cup and stumbled to the toilet. She retched dryly into it. She felt feverish and dizzy. Folding her arms across her forehead, she rested against the cool porcelain of the toilet until her head partially cleared. Then she managed to fill her cup from the sink and gulp down the water. She felt better for a moment, then began to shiver uncontrollably.

She filled the bathtub with water so hot it almost scalded her. With trembling hands, she removed her pajamas and lowered herself into the tub. The water was painfully hot on her skin. She lay with her ears submerged, floating with her face just above the water, breathing slowly and shallowly.

Lying there, she did not think; she reverberated. The previous day's events echoed through her brain. Over and over she heard Leon firing her. The news footage of the government overruling the tank-farm cancellation. The lawsuit slapped onto the table. And the arguments, the terrible arguments. Memories echoed through her mind like over-amplified music in a tiny nightclub, a screeching feedback loop of anxiety and despair.

Sometime later, the bathtub water had grown cold; sunlight came in red through the window. She got up, wrapped herself in a towel, and drank another cup of water. She went to the kitchen, opened a can of tuna, and ate half of it from the can with a spoon. Then, still clad in her damp towel, she shuffled back to her bedroom and sat on her bed.

Her phone rang again. She turned it off. Then she lay down and stared at the ceiling and fell into a fugue that was something like sleep and something like a nightmare.

At dawn the next day, Taavi woke, showered briefly, and ate a cheese sandwich from the minifridge. Then he opened the little booklet Rebecca had left for him. It was not, as he half expected, a manual of improvised explosives or instructions on field-stripping Soviet military rifles. Rather, it was an eclectic assortment of activities and exercises. Some were what one might expect in the daily routine of the modern urban guerrilla. There were pages of bodyweight exercises; he did some push-ups and sit-ups but avoided the jumping jacks and burpees—too loud. These pages were followed by illustrations of yoga postures, which he decided to save for later.

The middle section of the booklet contained tips for avoiding tails in urban areas—passing through malls, wearing cloth face masks to foil facial-recognition software, getting onto and jumping off of trains at the last minute, and so on.

After that were mental exercises: memory drills, drawing exercises that promised to "strengthen one's powers of observation and hand-eye coordination." Finally, there was a section on encryption; a few simple ciphers were suggested, along with primers on one-time pads and dead drops and other means of passing messages.

He spent an hour encrypting and decrypting passages from the room's Gideon Bible by hand. As a mental break, he flipped to an earlier section and did some yoga. Then he tried the memory exercises, using the only other volume of text in the room: an old phone book. He found he could memorize strings of ten names quickly and reliably, but retaining blocks of telephone numbers evaded him.

Taavi welcomed the challenge; it helped him to cope with the tedium and anxiety he felt in the stale motel room. He took a deep breath and flipped to a new page in the phone book.

<hr />

"Your father suffered a seizure," the doctor explained to Dee. The doctor was a young man, clean-shaven, dark-haired. "We phoned him when you were admitted, but when he was told what had happened, he ceased speaking."

Dee said nothing. Morning sun came through the window of her room. After she'd discovered her father, she had been carried back to her bed and reattached to the tubes and wires. A nurse checked her every fifteen minutes for the rest of the night to make sure she wasn't trying to escape.

"We thought there was a problem with the phone connection. We didn't realize he was having a seizure. Once he was discovered by your neighbor and an ambulance dispatched, some time had passed. He wasn't breathing fully on his own. His brain was deprived of oxygen. He hasn't regained consciousness." The doctor flipped through sheets of paper on his clipboard. "Your father has a . . . complicated medical history. We've run CT scans; the results are inconclusive. He likely struck his head during the seizure and suffered some bleeding in his brain."

"Are you saying he's had a stroke?" asked Dee.

"Possibly," the doctor replied. "Any bleeding in the brain is serious in a man your father's age."

"He's not that old," said Dee.

"Hmmm," said the doctor gently, "he's not young, either."

"He was over forty when I was born," said Dee, staring out the window.

The doctor cleared his throat, awkwardly. "Anyway, *your* X-rays are looking good. Knee damage is not as bad as we had worried."

"I need a phone," said Dee. "I need to . . . contact my family."

"I have good news, then," said the doctor. "Your cousin is waiting down the hall."

Dee tried to mask her confusion. They had reduced her drug dosage, but this made no sense. Had some distant relative flown all the way from Bangladesh? "My cousin," she repeated.

The doctor went to the doorway, beckoned someone—"I'll give you two a moment"—then left the room.

A moment later, Rebecca walked in. She stood beside Dee's bed and took Dee's hands in her own. Her eyes looked deeply concerned, but there was a smile on her face. "Hi cousin," she said softly, squeezing Dee's hand.

Dee squeezed back. "The network?" she asked.

Rebecca looked away. "When we didn't hear from you, we almost ran. But we were so close to something momentous, that I—" She paused and looked back at Dee. "I hoped that the communications breakdown was just an accident. I told the others to go ahead with the plan. It happened last night."

Dee nodded. "And?"

"It was amazing," said Rebecca, and they both smiled.

Dee's smile faded quickly. "My father," she began.

"I know," said Rebecca, her soft eyes full of sympathy and understanding. She leaned over and hugged Dee tightly.

In spite of herself, Dee began to cry. But only for a moment. Then she swallowed her tears, patted her eyes on her bed sheet. "We'd better get back to work," she said.

~

Helen awoke to banging at the door. Someone entered, calling her name. She recognized Gwen's voice. "I'm here!" she croaked. She heard Gwen clomping down the hall in her work boots. Gwen opened the bedroom door and flicked on the light. Helen shielded her face with once hand.

"Jesus, I thought you'd shot yourself," said Gwen. "You look like shit, hon."

"I feel sick," Helen said hoarsely. Gwen knelt beside the bed and lay a hand on her forehead, asked her to open her mouth, felt under her jawbone and down Helen's neck. "I'm not a cow."

Gwen ignored that. "Does this hurt?" she asked. Helen shook her head. "Your lymph nodes are a bit swollen, but they aren't sore, and you don't have a fever. When did you last eat?"

Helen considered. "Yesterday?" she suggested. "Wednesday?"

Gwen's eyes widened. "It's *Friday*, hon. Do you mean to tell me you haven't eaten in two days?" Helen shrugged noncommittally. Gwen frowned, stood, and retrieved a full glass of water. Helen sat up and drained the glass quickly. Gwen refilled it. "You drink that, too, and I'll go and make you a sandwich. I need you on your feet. A lot has been happening."

Gwen went to the kitchen. Helen sipped her water and stretched slowly, rolling her neck from side to side. Gwen returned a few moments later. "All your bread is moldy. Get dressed. We're eating out."

Helen complied only reluctantly and with repeated prompting and encouragement from Gwen. She felt light-headed and slightly wobbly standing up, but Gwen insisted on getting her out of the house. As they exited the back door, Helen asked, "How did you get in? Was the door ajar?"

Gwen snorted. "I picked the lock, kid," she said, and left it at that.

The greasy spoon around the corner was in the middle of its brunch rush, but Gwen and Helen managed to find a table. To her surprise, Helen felt hungry as she smelled the toast and frying eggs, and her stomach began to growl as she sipped orange juice.

"I'm worried about you, Helen," Gwen said. "What's going on in that head of yours? How are you handling all this?"

Helen shrugged and avoided eye contact. "How are *you* handling things?"

Gwen replied: "I'm mad as hell. But you're avoiding the question. What have you been doing? Getting drunk? Smoking pot?"

"What? No! Of course not!"

"I've done worse things over smaller disappointments, Helen. Everyone has their own way of coping—or not coping—with these things."

Helen shrugged again. "Social change is a long-term project," she said flatly. "We have to accept that sometimes there are setbacks. What's important is the process."

"See, your mouth says that, but I've seen happier eyes on a dead fish." Helen gave a single snort of laughter, and Gwen continued more softly. "Helen, I've always admired your strength. You are one of the most committed, most capable people I know."

Helen looked Gwen in the eyes. "That means a lot coming from you."

"You've done amazing things. But don't downplay what you're feeling right now. You've got to deal with it. You've got to grab that bull by the horns, or it will gore you. Gore your guts out."

Helen rolled her eyes. "Delightful imagery, Gwen."

"Helen, the work you've done on this campaign is different from what you've done in the past. Giving workshops to little kids is great. The same for handing out pamphlets and doing radio interviews. But that will only get you so far. Sometimes to win you need to get out on the front lines, right?

"I know this, Gwen."

"Sure, in your *mind* you know it. But there are things you've got to understand in your *bones*, Helen. The more you have to win, the more you have to lose. You got real close this week. You took big risks." Helen opened her mouth to protest, but Gwen plowed on. "When you organize a campaign, you risk your heart and soul. It's like any other gamble; you wager your soul, and if you lose the bet, it tears something out of you, deep. If you don't tend to the wound you won't recover for a long time. Maybe never. Do you know how many people I've seen get into activism over the years and then leave out of disappointment and heartbreak? Who got worn down to the nub and threw in the towel? I can't even count."

Helen reached out and laid her hand on Gwen's. "I appreciate your concern. But there will be other campaigns." Helen sighed deeply. "I'll get another job, and . . ." She trailed off.

Gwen gripped Helen's hand firmly. "Look, sweetheart, I know you're brave. But you've stepped on a landmine here. You've been wounded in action. If you'd had a leg blown off in a war, well, then it would be obvious you need a medic. But most people around you won't understand what's going on, because they can't see it. I just want you to know that I care about you, and I understand what you're going through, and I'm here whenever you need me."

Tears began to flow down Helen's cheeks. Her hand trembled in Gwen's, from both feeling and hypoglycemia. At that moment, a teen-aged boy in an apron appeared beside their table and cleared his throat awkwardly. "Uhh, two breakfast specials?"

They released hands and made room for the plates. As they ate, Helen began to feel gradually, if only slightly, better. After a few moments, she asked, "Isn't this affecting you, too? I mean, can I do anything for you?"

"I'm actually doing all right, for now," said Gwen. "Besides, I've been through plenty worse."

"Like what?"

Gwen looked sad. "That's a story for another time." Then she brightened and said, "But there is some good news!" Helen devoured most of an egg in one bite and nodded expectantly. "The campaign isn't dead yet." Gwen pulled a newspaper from her shoulder bag and showed the front page to Helen. The photo showed a cluster of pipes blown into twisted fragments, a ruptured tank visible in the background.

Helen gaped at the newspaper in surprise. "Holy fuck!"

And then she grinned.

15

2051

Evelyn stared up in awe. The ship was a rusting hulk the size of several city blocks. White Chinese characters showing the ship's name and owner had flaked and peeled off in patches.

The deck was heaped high with shipping containers. The ship leaned dangerously toward the port side, and many containers from that edge were missing or tilting precariously. As the canoe slowly rounded the ship, Evelyn could see an enormous gash near the bow on the port side. The stacks of containers—there must have been over a thousand rusting on the deck—looked as if they could slide off at any moment.

"Don't worry," said her guide, paddling as he spoke. "It's totally safe. It's been like this for a decade." Evelyn nodded, dubiously.

She had heard many versions of the ship's story. After the dollar had crashed—or maybe it was after the two-week blackout—foreign ships in the harbor had waited at anchor instead of unloading their cargo, their owners concerned that no one in the port could afford to pay for their contents. Eventually, vessels started to leave, and the coast guard was ordered to blockade the harbor to prevent the departure of precious food and supplies. After a Pacific skirmish between Chinese stealth planes and an American carrier group, this ship tried to make a run for it.

But the vessel never made it out of the harbor. It had rammed—or been rammed by—a coast guard ship and veered out of the shipping channel. It ran aground on a sandbar at full speed. Rents in the bow let in water, and the ship settled in the spot where it was currently rusting. The fuel was pumped out, and authorities abandoned the vessel.

The canoe was almost at the ship, headed directly for the gash. They slowed, and the paddler at the bow of the canoe probed the dark water. "Submerged shipping containers," Archie explained from the stern. "Some are piled on the bottom; others float below the surface. Major navigational hazard. Patrol boats give this a wide berth."

"How long has this been a resistance base?" she asked in a hushed voice.

Archie smiled slightly in the starlight. "It's a *smugglers* base. After official salvage was abandoned, people came out at night to open the containers and unload them by hand. Electronics fetched a good price on the black market. A container full of food was worth more than a *house* back then." He paused in thought as they navigated around a submerged obstacle. "Still is, I 'spose.

"We had to burrow in, cut through the walls of the containers to get deeper. When we could get fuel, we cut with torches. Otherwise, we used cold chisels and hacksaws." Archie shook his head and sighed. "Took weeks to cut a door through two layers of steel. And it was dangerous." He held up his left hand; she could see his ring finger was only a stub.

"But it fed our family," he sighed. "Cargo is gone now, but it's a warren in there. Hidden tunnels and doors connecting all the containers inside. A smugglers paradise!"

They reached the bow of the vessel. She looked up at the bulk of the ship as they passed silently through the enormous rent in the hull. It was completely dark inside—no starlight. But she could hear the sounds of water rippling against metal, soft overlapping echoes in a long empty space.

It was so quiet that she jumped when their boat scraped against something on her left. Archie switched on a tiny red-filtered flashlight, clipped to his cloak by a lanyard. There was yet another container floating to their left, this one protruding two feet above the water. It seemed to serve as an improvised dock.

"You'll have to sit tight here," Archie said, tying up to the dock, "until we find someone to smuggle *you*."

—⁓

"Say something."

Carlos stared at Addy in silence for a long while. Then he said: "You're serious." She nodded. "You were a teenaged revolutionary? When did you start?"

Addy considered. "I started with research and careful outreach. Maybe sixteen?"

"Sixteen! That's too young."

"Young people can do difficult things. How many Olympic gymnasts or figure skaters broke records when they were sixteen, or even younger? Lots of teenagers formed resistance cells to fight the Nazis when their countries were invaded. Or what about Khudiram Bose?"

"Who?" asked Carlos.

"Indian independence fighter. Born in eighteen eighty-nine, in the aftermath of famine. In the eighteen-seventies, the British had stolen so much food from India that *eight million people* starved to death. Khudiram Bose was already part of the struggle against the British when he was fourteen. By the time he was sixteen, he was planting bombs," explained Addy.

"That sounds dangerous for a sixteen-year-old."

"It was. Bose was captured and hanged," said Addy. "Plenty of anti-fascist fighters ended up dead. It's *always* dangerous, whether you're eighteen or thirty-eight or eighty. But young people have that reckless courage to take action."

"So, you did what, exactly?"

"The first phase was preparatory. We built networks and secret methods of communication. We recruited people. Trained them. Organized them into cells. We gave them useful tasks to build experience: Intelligence gathering and mapping. Establishing safe houses and supply caches. Building cover stories. Raising funds. Sabotage and light arson."

Carlos laughed. "First time I've heard the phrase 'light arson.'"

Addy smiled wryly. "It had to feel like we were accomplishing something, making progress, without provoking repression we couldn't handle. That was key early on—to be subtle and small-scale, to avoid patterns that would suggest coordination. It had to *look* spontaneous, scattered, and disorganized so we could fly beneath the radar."

"Makes sense," said Carlos. "But subtlety only gets you so far."

"If you always avoid repression then you aren't accomplishing anything," agreed Addy. "And we were on a tight timeline. So, we escalated. We would look for some small-scale fight—against fracking, say, or suburban sprawl—that had a lot of popular support but that was maybe on the verge of losing. And we'd send in a cell. They'd do some sabotage—set an unoccupied construction site on fire or destroy industrial equipment—and leave before they got caught. They were careful not to hurt anyone, to avoid a backlash from locals we wanted to help."

Carlos nodded. "That's admirable. I don't know why you waited so long to tell me. Compared to what partisans do these days, it's tame."

"But that was practice, too," said Addy. "We weren't only saboteurs. We were revolutionaries. We didn't just want to smash things. We wanted to bring the powerful low. We wanted to collapse capitalism before it destroyed the planet. Before it destroyed every noncapitalist culture. We wanted to let a million other cultures blossom in its place. So, we set our sights higher."

"Like what? The blackout in 'thirty-seven, was that you?" asked Carlos.

"No, that was solar flares," said Addy. "Saboteurs were blamed for political reasons."

"What about the nuclear detonations in the tar sands?"

"What?" said Addy. "Where would we get nukes? No, the official story about the rogue US general is true."

Carlos got a strange look on his face and asked his next question with obvious hesitation. "There were rumors a long time ago that undergrounders might work on a virus. A disease to reduce the population—"

"Jesus fucking Christ!" exclaimed Addy. "We would never do anything like that! I told you, we were careful to avoid hurting humans, or any living creature. We would never use biological warfare."

"But there are so many diseases now. Who did it?"

"Thirty years ago, there were already five billion people living in cities," said Addy. "When food and sanitation systems broke down, the old diseases of poverty returned. Billions of hosts crowded together in slums. No one needed to create disease on purpose. There were new strains mutating every day."

"Okay," said Carlos with obvious relief. "But what about—"

"Would you stop interrupting and let me tell you something we actually *did*?" said Addy. Carlos obligingly fell silent. Addy asked, "Do you remember K-Day?"

"You're shitting me. That was you?"

"That was us," she replied, pleased she had elicited a curse from him.

"If you've got those skills," he said, "you need to tell the others. We'll get your crew back together, fight the Authority before tanks are coming up our driveway."

A look of despair and pain spread across Addy's face. "I have a cache with comm equipment," she said. "But I don't have a crew anymore. I wasn't ready. I was too young. I fucked it up, and they . . . they got killed, or went to jail, or both. That's why I came here."

And Addy began to weep more freely than she had in decades.

—✦—

At sunrise, the morning after evacuation, Layth was in an abandoned suburban garage, burning his own clothes in a metal bucket. He had brought virtually nothing with him during the frantic escape. Long in advance they had prepared a careful evacuation plan, with safe houses, go bags, alibi tags, and all the rest. But that plan called for Layth to stick with X and Felicity, which he refused to do. He had been singled out for surveillance, and he would only draw attention to them. He needed to get out of the city.

But Layth wasn't going to some pastoral retreat to hide and wait out the end of the world. He wanted to track down his family, find help, and return. And he had a single lead. In the thirty seconds he had to speak with X before they fled the underground safe house, he had told her his intent. And she gave him one real name and one alias. The alias—"Gladys McGivens"—was who he needed to track down.

Layth threw his identification into the smoldering fire. His plastic proof-of-health card produced a cloud of foul black smoke. The three different triage cards took longer to burn, and he used a stick to crumble the layers of foil and circuitry inside their plastic housings. Back at the safe house he could have reflashed the cards, hacked them to display whatever he wanted, but now he lacked the necessary tools.

From a blue backpack he pulled a clean set of travelling clothes and an envelope of identification. It was an old, emergency-only cover he had almost forgotten about. He flipped through it. Driver's license, triage tag, and press credentials—so he was a journalist. "Percival Lagrange." He frowned. There was no proof-of-health card enclosed, since the ongoing checkpoint and doctor's records needed to maintain a plausible history were too hard to maintain for a mere backup cover. He would have to avoid large cities where he might encounter a YEA checkpoint.

He tucked the identification into his pocket, shouldered his backpack, and stepped outside. Down the street a shepherd was at work, herding a small flock of goats and sheep across overgrown suburban lawns.

Percival Lagrange began walking down the road. He waved to the shepherd, and she waved back. He felt invigorated. His charge, Evelyn, was safely out of the city. His colleagues had escaped a raid that would have led to their terrible deaths. And the air was fresh and clear, without the pervasive smell of burning charcoal. The grip of the Authority was not so tight out here, where patrols were few, checkpoints far apart. He picked up his step. He was looking forward to his next mission.

—❧

A week into Evelyn's stay on the rusting container ship, Archie summoned her to the cavernous space where the canoe was tied up. "Do you have much scuba diving experience?" Archie asked Evelyn as he opened a large orange equipment case on the improvised dock inside the ship.

"'Much'?" Evelyn asked in surprise. She was groggy from waiting a week to continue her journey, sleeping on a futon in an empty shipping container. "I've never scuba dived."

"Just breathe normally," he encouraged, "and pop your ears if you feel discomfort. You won't be going too deep." He pulled a plastic bulb on a cable from the equipment case and tossed it into the water. "Cold's the worst part. Put on a wet suit and get your clothing into this dry bag." He tossed her a rubber sack.

She stared at him. "Right now?"

Archie pulled a phone handset from the case and flipped several switches. "Of course! Didn't they explain the procedure?"

"My departure was rushed," said Evelyn. "There wasn't time to—"

He held up a wrinkled hand to silence her and then spoke into the handset in halting Spanish. "Tiburón, Tiburón, responda. La ballena . . . está lista." He listened carefully, and then Evelyn heard three distinct beeps come through the handset. "They're here. You'd best change."

Evelyn looked out through the rent in the ship's hull. "I don't see any boats."

"They can't surface in broad daylight," the old man replied. "A drone would spot them. We can't even use radio; we have to use the Gertrude," he said, gesturing to the machine in the orange case.

Evelyn was perplexed. "But you paddled here in your canoe."

"The Authority *expects* scavengers. Even smugglers. Armbands take their share. That's the economy. But they don't much like foreign, uhh, subversives." He chuckled to himself. "And subversives don't like waiting, so get changed. Use the green wet suit."

Evelyn went to a changing room near the dock. Donning the wet suit was a challenge. Removing her clothes left her shivering in the cold air, and the suit was incredibly difficult to get onto her body. The cold rubber felt damp, clinging to her feet and ankles as she put her legs into it. She tried to force in both feet at the same time, but when she had the legs halfway on she was seized by a sudden claustrophobic feeling that she would not be able to get the suit off again. She had to pause, still trembling from the cold, and breathe deeply to prevent the feeling from overtaking her.

Eventually she managed to pull the suit's legs on one at a time. The arms slipped on more easily. She donned the little booties and gloves and a balaclava, then stuffed her own clothes into the dry bag.

As she walked to the dock she saw streams of bubbles appear at the water's surface just inside the tear in the hull. And then she saw a pair of divers, wearing suits more substantial than her own.

One of them removed his mouthpiece. "¿Usted lista?" he asked. He was looking at her.

"Are you ready?" the old man asked.

The diver switched to accented English. "If you have your things, jump in. We can't stay long." The other diver passed a heavy-looking bag to the old man, who accepted it gratefully, giving Evelyn's dry bag in return.

Evelyn sat down, putting her feet into the water. She wasn't sure which felt more chilling, the water on her ankles or the freezing metal of the dock under her buttocks. She took several deep breaths.

"It's better to get in all at once," Archie said.

Evelyn braced herself and slid in. She started treading water, but it splashed against her exposed face. She gasped and fought the almost irresistible urge to jump back out.

"It gets better," said the diver, "after a minute."

"Don't I need an air tank?" Evelyn asked through chattering teeth.

He produced a second regulator from his belt. "You'll breathe from my tank," he said. "It's a short trip." He passed the regulator to her and she put it in her mouth. She breathed. It wasn't as hard as she expected. "Okay, let's go," he said. The second diver joined her on the other side. And together, they descended.

—⁄

It took Layth less than a week to find her. She had a low profile, but she wasn't hiding; the trail led him straight to one of the upscale company towns.

When he actually saw the place—cruising by in one of the electric cars the Authority used out there—he couldn't believe his eyes. From the name—the Willamot Institute—he was expecting a medium-security prison or a decrepit psychiatric institution. But the place looked like something designed by Frank Lloyd Wright, with modern angles and bright, clean lines. The lawn was perfectly manicured, actively maintained by a crew of landscapers in white coveralls (no red tags here) who trimmed it precisely and perpetually. The little shrubs dotting the grounds were eerily similar, as though they had been copied and pasted from a single master version.

It's a goddamned retirement village, he realized. *An old folks' home for the postapocalyptic uber-rich.* An hour north, being "affluent" meant you could afford a fence to keep wild boars out of your vegetable garden.

Layth reflected bitterly. The retirees in this complex lived on a planet that was ecologically ruined, that they had stripped to the bone. But the view out their windows was green and harmonious. Layth's stomach pained him as he drove; he tried to stifle a wish that these people should suffer for their privilege. And he tried to figure out why the hell Gladys McGivens, a resister, had ended up there instead of in a camp.

As he pulled around a traffic-calming curve designed to optimize pedestrian safety, he could see there was actually a *waterfall* built into the structure of the building. Some enormous aqueduct had been built to carry water to the complex for the sole purpose of dumping it over the side of the building and into a pond that drained back into the larger river.

It took him two more days to get inside. He used the cover of Percival Lagrange, a roving journalist for the Authority. Or rather, "the company," as everyone living nearby called it.

Lagrange told the PR manager of the Willamot Institute that he was writing a story about how civilized cultures treat their elderly. He wanted to emphasize how well the company treated elders compared to the barbarous, retrograde peasants and tribespeople who made their old folks work all day when they weren't abandoning them to freeze on ice floes. The PR guy ate it up.

Soon Lagrange had the run of the facility, albeit with the uncomfortably close escort of a PR flunky. He got tours of recreation facilities, clinics, and spas. The dining halls had enormous glass walls with spectacular views of the grounds. From some tables you could actually look out *through* the waterfall.

Lagrange interviewed the staff, scrawling illegible chicken scratches on a notepad while he gathered intel. He got a tour of one kitchen—all stainless steel and gleaming tile—just before dessert was served. A bank of monitors displayed individual nutritional plans for each resident. He scanned for Gladys's name while verbally gushing over the display of technology.

He didn't see her name, but he did see a recipe for the dessert about to be served: fresh pudding, dusted with cinnamon. The puddings were lined up on a counter, sans cinnamon. He distracted the flunky with a complicated question about convection ovens, and when the flunky left the kitchen to find an answer, Lagrange went to the spice rack and dumped a generous amount of ground cayenne pepper into the cinnamon jar. He finished screwing the lids back on just as a server came to prepare the puddings.

The flunky returned, and Lagrange commented on how impressed he was with the displays, how they tracked all that resident info. The flunky took him to a file room around the corner. It was full of actual *paper* files and clipboards and charts. A nurse was there, writing notes.

Lagrange introduced himself to the nurse and asked a few questions. But before she answered, there was an uproar back in the dining room. People sounded very upset.

The flunky and the nurse both ran out of the room. Lagrange stayed to snoop, flipping through charts as fast as he could. There was no file for Gladys—she must be in a different wing—but he found a file that gave him an alternative plan. It contained information on one Joseph Marcus, male, eighty-six years old, diagnosis: Alzheimer's. There was a photograph, a bio, and a blank family contact form.

The flunky and the nurse were back a moment later. The flunky was intensely apologetic about the disruption, some sort of confusion with the pudding recipe, and wanted to make sure Lagrange knew for his story that this sort of thing never happened and that there would be a full investigation. Lagrange told the guy not to worry about it, but that he would like to chat with some of the residents next.

He carried out perfunctory, phony interviews of a few residents before he zeroed in on his target, a white-haired man with a cane sitting in front of a television. *Well, how about that! It's Uncle Joe, from Toronto! We got separated from his branch of the family during the unrest;*

I didn't know he was even alive! What's that? Uncle Joe has dementia? He couldn't even recognize his own family? What a shame.

The stage was set for the final task. With "Uncle" Joe as the final element of his cover, Lagrange could make repeated visits to the residence without arousing suspicion or requiring an escort. With any luck, he could even take his uncle for walks around the facility until he found what he was looking for. Until he found *her.*

—✎—

"He's said nothing at all?" asked Carlos, pitchfork in hand.

"Clammed up completely," Addy replied, tossing hay into the goat pen with her own pitchfork. "Total silence after the first interview."

Carlos shrugged. "We've got enough evidence in his papers. That should convince Newbrook's town council that we're in serious trouble."

"Charlotte and LT went to call on them to raise the militia," said Addy.

"That won't be nearly enough," said Carlos. "We're peasants. They've got drones and tanks. We need professionals. We need to find your old network."

Addy sighed and leaned on her pitchfork. "We can go to my cache," she said. "But it's hours of driving from here, on bad roads. We'd need a truck. And even if my equipment still works, I doubt there's anyone to answer."

"We've got to try," said Carlos. "We can use the old farm truck. It needs a tune-up, and it will take me a few days to scrounge enough diesel to fill the tank. But let's go as soon as we can."

Addy shrugged, and sighed again. "We can try."

—✎—

Evelyn had never been on a submarine before. She spent the first two hours aboard just shivering, recovering from the extreme cold of the brief trip between the container ship and the submarine's underwater air lock. The divers wrapped her in blankets and put her on a firm bunk while they went about their duties. After she was warm enough, she got up to look around. The boat was tiny, she realized. She had thought of submarines as behemoths carrying hundreds of crew and dozens of missiles. But this submarine was barely as large as the bus she rode to work. Well, *had* ridden.

The majority of the vessel was a single corridor with an engine room at the stern and an air lock and diving equipment room near the front. The middle section of the corridor was lined with bunks, storage cabinets, a command area, a sink and stove, a ladder and hatch to exit the boat when it surfaced, and a tiny closet containing a toilet. There was no real privacy and little human comfort on the boat. They could heat meals on a tiny stove, but there was no table to eat at. The six crew members simply ate at their stations or their bunks.

The crew was not unfriendly, but they rarely spoke to her. They barely communicated with each other, limiting themselves to hushed exchanges in terse Spanish. The diver claimed they didn't speak much English, though she suspected they were trying to maintain some kind of operational security. The diver, Juan, would not even say which country they were from. Evelyn guessed Cuba, or another one of the Latin American countries that had flourished during the slow collapse of global capitalism. Venezuela, maybe, or even Colombia?

She had no chance to find out. The crew became agitated whenever she left her bunk and would not let her go into the engine room or the command area. She felt grateful that claustrophobia was not among her many sources of anxiety.

"When do we depart?" she asked Juan. He gave her a quizzical look. "When do we get"—she made a thrusting gesture with one hand—"underway?"

"Ahh," he said, "we are already moving. The engines are electric. *Silencioso.*"

"How long till we get to the farm?" she asked.

Juan looked confused. "We are not bringing you to a farm. Your network instructed us to bring you to a freelancer south of here. He'll take you by land. Long way around. But safer." He smiled and nodded encouragingly.

"Will I meet my family soon?" she asked.

Juan looked apologetic. "I'm sorry, I don't know about your family. We make landfall tomorrow. You'll find out then, maybe?"

—✦—

Percival Lagrange took his uncle Joe for three different walks around the Willamot Institute on three different days. The walks were confusing for Joe and nerve-wracking for Layth. His thrown-together identity was imperfect; he could only make so many visits before people started to wonder how long it took to write a single magazine article.

Joseph had strange moments of lucidity between long periods of disorientation. These moments were frightening; one instant Joe would be asking when he could have more ice cream, the next he'd complain about bodies floating down the river. Joe mentioned the bodies so many times that Lagrange actually asked a staff member about it. The staffer explained that, unfortunately, there had been an outbreak of terrorism up in the hills that was put down by the company. "Sometimes bodies would float down the river where the residents could see them. People complained. It doesn't happen much anymore." But the staffer added in a whisper: "If you see one, just ignore it. Drawing attention will upset the residents."

His breakthrough came on the third day. He was looking at a trophy case in one of the hallways while trying to keep Joe from wandering off. Her photograph was right there in the case. The caption read: "Gladys McGivens, Simmons Wing Backgammon Champion, 2048." In the photo she was smiling and holding a certificate. Green eyes, gray hair, her cheeks deeply creased with smile lines. He shook his head in bewilderment.

Thirteen minutes later, he had ditched Joe and made his way to the Simmons Wing. He walked through the wing as calmly as he could. Some of the staff smiled and waved. Why not? After all, he was a kind visitor who spent hours and hours with an uncle who didn't even recognize him. His presence was welcome.

He walked along a residential corridor, scanning nameplates on doors. He ran into an older nurse who asked what he was doing.

Lagrange smiled. "I heard someone here could give me a challenging game of backgammon!"

The nurse gave him a suspicious look. "Gladys is in the spa. You'll have to come back later." He thanked her and walked around the corner before heading toward the spa. The wings all had identical floor plans, and he knew exactly where to go after his walks with Joseph.

He opened the door of the spa and walked in. And there Gladys was, wearing a pink bathing suit and floating in a huge soaking tub in the middle of the room, her eyes closed. He walked over to the edge of the tub and spoke. "Hello, Gwendolyn."

She opened her eyes, inspected his face carefully, and then smiled. "I was wondering when you would come."

—⟋

"You didn't tell us she was Chinese," sneered the man in the cowboy hat.

Evelyn frowned back at him. "My family is Korean."

"Her ethnicity doesn't matter," said Juan, crossing his arms over his blue overalls. They were standing in a shack a few kilometers inland from a secret submarine dock and a hundred kilometers south of YEA territory. "You're paid to move her. That's your job."

"I'm not in the habit," said the man, "of associating with people whose true loyalty might be to a Chinese army."

"I just want to get to my family. Besides," she offered, "Korea fought several Chinese invasions in its history, and was sometimes occupied. Koreans resisted."

"Well, *thanks* for the history lesson," the man said sarcastically. "You ever heard of *North Korea?*"

"None of this matters," said Juan. "Either take her and get paid or stop wasting our time and we'll find someone else."

"Fine." The man snorted. "Be ready in five minutes." He walked out of the shack to a short school bus nearby. It had been repainted with patchwork camouflage, green and brown, and several passengers were already visible through its windows.

Evelyn turned to Juan. "I'd rather go with someone else," she said.

"There *is* no one else," he replied. "Not on this route. Sorry. Everyone fights despotism for their own reasons. That man, unfortunately, is a nationalist and a profiteer." He handed her a bag. "Your travel payment is in here. I've already paid him half in advance." He reached out to shake her hand and locked eyes with her sternly. "Whatever you do, don't get separated from the rest." Then he smiled and bade her farewell. "Buena suerte."

—⤳

The trip to Addy's cache took five hours. Three hours were spent travelling; the other two were spent freeing the truck from a mud pit that had been hidden by fallen leaves on the back road. It was late afternoon when they finally neared the gravel pits that were their destination.

"Where exactly is it?" asked Carlos from the driver's seat. Addy was reading an old road map of the area. Now that they had reached the abandoned gravel pits, the map was useless.

"We're getting close," she said, lowering the map and scanning their surroundings through the windshield. The gravel pits were sprawling and loosely connected, with multiple lobes. Brush had overgrown the edges of the pits, and erosion had changed the terrain. It looked very different from what she had remembered.

"So . . ." said Carlos, "I'm getting the feeling you don't know where it is."

"It's been more than a decade," she said. "But we're close. Look for a wrecked car." There were a number of ruined vehicles in the gravel pits, and they inspected each as they passed.

"I guess Adelaide isn't the name you were born with," said Carlos, as casually as he could.

"Adita," she answered. "I was born Adita." They passed a burned-out Volkswagen Beetle. "There it is!" she pointed. "That's it."

They pulled up and stepped out of the truck. Addy shouldered her rifle. "When I decided to go to the Thistle, I needed a place to stow my equipment. I buried everything except my clothes and a bicycle in the gravel and parked my car on top of the cache."

"And then you set the car on fire?" Carlos asked.

Addy shrugged. "I didn't want anyone to drive it away and expose my cache."

"Why didn't you just drive the car to the farm and sell it, or salvage it?" he asked.

"I was worried about being tracked," Addy replied, "so I didn't want my cache too close to my safe house." Carlos accepted this, staring forlornly at the charred and ancient battery packs in the remnants of the electric vehicle.

He sighed. "Well, I guess we'd better move this." It took twenty minutes to set up a chain and use the truck to drag the wreckage of the car off to the side. Then they took turns digging for another thirty minutes before Carlos's shovel struck hard plastic. "Here we are." They pulled three hard-sided cases out of the ground.

Addy opened them and examined their contents. They contained two sets of business clothes, a handgun with an extra box of ammunition, a makeup kit (long since hardened and discolored), a wilderness survival kit, an extensive first aid kit, a down sleeping bag, a watch, four walkie-talkies, two mobile phones, a satellite phone, a laptop computer, numerous spare batteries, and a solar-powered charger. In the same waterproof bag as a stack of black-and-white photographs, she found sixty thousand dollars in a mixture of US dollars, Canadian dollars, euros, Quebec francs, expired Ontario ration stamps, and gold coins.

"Holy shit," said Carlos. "That's a lot of money."

"It was before hyperinflation, anyway," she answered, tossing it aside. "I hope the electronics still work."

"The corrosion is pretty bad," he said. He held up a ziplock bag of batteries covered in green fuzz.

"I'd have packed more carefully if I'd known how long it would be. My idea was just to lay low for a year or so," Addy said. "I was planning to go back and rejoin my network."

"Why didn't you?" asked Carlos.

Addy took a long time to respond. "A lot of reasons, I guess. Nothing rational. I was tired. Burned out. I just couldn't handle the idea of going back. I was a coward."

"Survivor's guilt," suggested Carlos. "Depression. PTSD."

Addy shrugged. "Maybe. But here I am, finally."

She flipped up the antenna on the satellite phone and pressed the On button.

⟋

Gladys got out of the tub and put on a bathrobe and slippers as she spoke. "I assume Kraken sent you?" He nodded. "So, what's the plan? Am I being called back into action, or are you just here to get the data?"

"The data?" he asked. He might have assumed too much from his parting exchange with X. Gladys squinted at him, reevaluating. He continued haltingly: "Actually I'm—well, I came here looking for my family. My—my parents."

Gladys—Gwendolyn—gave him a long, sad look. She put a hand on his cheek. There were tears in her eyes. For a moment, Layth thought she was going to say *she* was his mother. "You look just like them, you know. I haven't seen you since you were a baby, but I recognized you. You have your father's eyes."

"You knew them?"

"I spent a great deal of time with them. But let's talk more after we deal with this. Come along." Layth followed her to her room, which was decorated with unframed ink drawings. In the corner was an easel that held a canvas bearing a partially finished watercolor. There were several potted plants by the window. Gwendolyn reached underneath one and pulled out a memory card.

"Here it is," she said. "Everything I've gathered from correspondence in and out. We have a complete picture of the Authority's upper ranks."

He frowned. "Wait, are you saying that—" He stopped. Out the window he could see a large black van pulling up in front of the institute. Black-clad officers swarmed out, assault rifles in hand.

Gladys turned and followed his gaze out the window. Then she pivoted back sharply. "They surveilled you." Perhaps, he thought. Perhaps the suspicious nurse raised questions. Perhaps the PR schmuck e-mailed the company magazine and got a confused e-mail back asking who the hell was Percival Lagrange. He had taken major risks. How he was exposed didn't matter—only escape mattered.

"Is there a back exit?" he asked her.

"Follow me," she replied. She guided them toward a back door, but a glance through the nearby window showed security officers already converging—they were cut off.

She pushed him to a stairwell that led to the roof. He was shocked at how spry she was as they climbed a ladder through the roof hatch. She led him to a rooftop garden nestled between some ventilation stacks and a little shed. There was a large pond adjacent to them, some kind of ecologically friendly cooling system for the building.

Gwendolyn popped the cover off a nearby vent, then removed her bathrobe and stuffed it into the air intake. She was still holding the memory card, so she popped it into her mouth, tucking it inside of one cheek. She pulled a flame weeder—a little butane-powered wand that burned up unwanted plants—from the garden shed, lit it, and threw it into the duct after her bathrobe. Then she hopped into the pond. "Hurry up!" she hissed. He jumped in after her, fully clothed. The smell of smoke reached his nostrils.

She grabbed several handfuls of dirt from the nearest garden bed and smeared them into her hair, over her face. She efficiently covered half of her pink bathing suit in soil until she looked half mad, half corpse. Then she grabbed a double handful of wet dirt, raised her arms, and smacked him over the head with it. She rubbed it into his hair and down his neck, over one shoulder of his shirt.

"Follow me!" she said, and started swimming across the pond. At the far end a current began to sweep them along. "Play dead!" she said.

In the complex below he could hear fire alarms, announcements blaring, and nearby a roaring sound that grew louder. Suddenly he realized why there was such a swift current. And before he could think, he was flung over the waterfall into spray and weightlessness.

16

2028

Helen had expected to awaken the next morning feeling great—that her meeting with Gwen would reconnect her with the world. She had caught up on lost sleep, and then some. She had expected the underground attacks on the petroleum depot—which made her campaign a success after the fact—would reawaken her sense of purpose. That she would feel reinvigorated. Alive.

She felt like shit.

The fourth day after she lost her job—or was it the fifth?—she woke up feeling as terrible as ever. She managed to drag herself to the kitchen to make breakfast from some duck eggs that Gwen had left her the day before. But her joints ached, her head hurt, she felt nauseous, and all she wanted to do after breakfast was lie down. She plunked herself on the couch and watched *Thelma and Louise* for perhaps the twentieth time in her life.

After that, she forced herself to get some work done. She checked her mailbox, finding her final paycheck from Friends of the Watershed along with a terse reminder to get her things from the office. She read several newspapers, feasting on the details of the tank-farm explosions. Forensic investigators found that robotic crawlers had been inserted into the underground pipelines, carrying explosive payloads deep into the branching pipes.

When the crawlers finally exploded, they had damaged one of the tanks and cracked the underground pipelines in a dozen places. The infrastructure was damaged beyond repair. The tank farm was finished, for good. An anonymous communiqué online had expressed solidarity with the sit-in, declaring admiration for the community mobilization. They had won. But Helen felt in some way that she'd had nothing to do with the victory, that all her work had contributed nothing.

She checked her voice mail to find three dozen messages: concerned check-ins from Gwen and a few friends, journalists requesting immediate comment on the tank-farm bombing. More than five hundred texts, including a dozen from Philip Justinian offering his dad's help with the lawsuit. She deleted the voice mails but sent a short reply to Philip with genuine thanks for the offer.

Before she put down the phone, Gwen called. "I'm coming to pick you up," she said. "We're going to have a nice day at the farm. Eat good food. Visit friends."

"I'm not feeling great," said Helen hesitantly.

"Fresh air and company will do you good," replied Gwen. "I'll be there in ten."

Helen found some clothes and washed her face, then waited on the front step. Someone had stenciled *Free the Newbrook Four* on the sidewalk. The morning sun was warm—too warm, she thought. Even at an early hour, the sunlight made her feel hot, feverish. She went inside to find a hat, and when she came back out, she could see Gwen's truck coming down the road toward her.

And then, crossing the street at a distant intersection, she caught a glimpse of a black SUV.

⟡

Taavi felt great relief when he and Rebecca pulled out of the motel parking lot. The tedium of the tight quarters had begun to wear on him, along with anxiety exacerbated by the late-night police visit.

"Sorry for the delay," said Rebecca. "There was an emergency."

"Everything okay?" asked Taavi.

"If it were," she replied, "we wouldn't be doing this."

"Hmmm," he said. "Well, it feels good to be on the move." She nodded silently in response. "What's next?" he asked.

She smiled slightly. "Field trip." There was a quiet moment as they took a ramp onto the highway. Rebecca drove no faster than five above the limit.

"So, how long have you been doing this?" he asked.

She glanced at him sidelong. "Is that the most pressing question you have?"

Taavi considered this. "How many people in your organization? Who runs it?"

"There are dozens of cells, hundreds of people," Rebecca answered. "Most cells are semiautonomous, but there's a coordinating body—a council of experienced revolutionaries, mostly women. Veterans of the Weather Underground. Tacticians from the Zapatistas. For technical expertise, former members of Wikileaks and Anonymous. Some exiles from the old Soviet bloc. A US special forces guy who saw the light and came over to our side. They guide us. And we combine their experience with our people—people who would be in trouble without their wisdom. People like you."

"How did you know that we were in trouble? Heck, how did you know we even existed?"

"We watch closely for allies and infiltrators," she replied, "and we have an interest in IRI. You weren't subtle, either. You were easy to find, for people who know the community. And we received warning of the sting operation Corben was spearheading."

"Sting?" asked Taavi.

"The FBI, RCMP—various police agencies do it a lot. Most of the time, when they take credit for 'preventing a terrorist attack,' they're the ones who set the cell up in the first place," said Rebecca. "We thought people who'd do radical work under poor leadership might also be willing to work in a genuine organization."

"When you say 'we'. . ."

"The underground network," she answered. "Compartmentalized. Meticulously screened membership. Rigorous operational security."

"Better security than us?"

Rebecca snorted. "Yeeeah," she said.

Taavi reddened slightly with embarrassment. Then he asked, "If our security was so bad, why do you want us?"

"Common goals. Solidarity. You have a passion to fight power; you're willing to take risks to save this planet from obliteration. We can train your skills. But you can't train passion." She paused, and then added, "Besides, the bad security wasn't entirely your fault. You had bad leadership."

Taavi furrowed his brow in anger. "We're anarchists. We didn't *have* leadership."

She gave him a skeptical sideways glance. "In this organization we pride ourselves on honesty. So, you might want to think on that."

"Are you an anarchist?" he asked her.

"I'm a resistance cadre," she replied. "A revolutionary with a mission. We don't care if you think of yourself a Marxist or a socialist or a communist or an anarchist or a libertarian or whatever, as long as you do your job—as long as you are, first and foremost, a member of a serious group with ironclad solidarity for your comrades."

"I don't want to work with a bunch of commies and redneck libertarians."

She wrinkled her nose. "I'm going to let that pass, since you barely look old enough to drink and you've had a rough couple of days. But if that's honestly the way you think, I can pull over at the next police station and you can turn yourself in." Taavi's eyes widened slightly, and she continued. "You're already working with those people. They've been busting their butts to keep *your* ass out of prison. You'd be in jail right now if not for them."

Taavi was taken aback and turned to glare out the passenger's-side window. He scratched at his forearm, which itched as it healed.

Rebecca softened her tone. "That's what solidarity is. Little differences don't matter much, because our enemy is so big and so powerful. We don't sweat the small stuff. We welcome radicals and revolutionaries with many backgrounds, as long as they're also willing to welcome others. Not working with people you've never even met because of what you think you know about them? That sounds like crap Corben would say. That won't fly with us. Neither will sexism, racism, homophobia, transphobia, or any other form of ignorant, prejudiced, hateful bullshit. Can you work with that?"

Taavi, not seeing much room for argument, allowed that he could.

"Good," Rebecca said with finality. "Then we'll get along." There were a few moments of silence. "You know, Taavi, I think you'll thrive in this network. You're smart, willing to learn and adapt. You've shown you have the mettle to get through a crisis."

Taavi smiled slightly and turned toward Rebecca. "Does this network have a name?"

She took her eyes off the road for a moment to stare directly at him. "Kraken."

When Dee was officially discharged from the hospital, she was told to stay off her feet as long as possible. She would need weeks of physiotherapy. The damage to her knees shouldn't be permanent, they said, though there would be scarring across her knees and abdomen. Pain that would last for months. Or years, if she didn't take care of herself.

They brought a wheelchair to her room, and she wheeled it directly into her father's room down the hall. He was still unconscious. She sat by his bedside for several hours, holding his hand. She told him she would be back soon. His only answer was the sound of hoarse breathing.

Dee bought a newspaper and read it in the taxi on the way home. The initial burst of coverage about the petroleum-depot bombing had passed. An article on the fourth page detailed what the police had learned: virtually nothing. "Forensics teams have been unsuccessful, according to an inside source. A large protest on the site of the tank farm last week left forensics traces from hundreds of people at the site, and fear of unexploded ordnance in the pipes has slowed examination of the aftermath." The article added, "Officially, police have refused to comment on details of the ongoing investigation. But there is widespread speculation about the technical abilities needed to deliver powerful explosives to multiple pipelines buried underground."

Dee smiled, glad to see that her action cells had been so successful. For her, it was a proof of concept. The cells involved had existed for less than a year. She knew now that they could be trained quickly and act effectively, under the right circumstances.

She checked her travel alarm clock. This success meant it was time to escalate—to increase the size of the network and the ambition of their actions. She would revive contact with different branches of the network and she would move forward.

But part of her mind was left behind, in the hospital, with her father.

Midmorning, Rebecca and Taavi pulled off the highway and followed a series of logging roads that decreased in size and quality until they reached a barely passable dirt track.

Rebecca parked by a dense copse of cedar trees. They stepped out, and Rebecca pulled two backpacks from the trunk. Taavi stood beside the car and stretched his back. He inhaled deeply. The air was sweet, redolent of cedar and pine and humus. Very different from a cheap hotel room, or a jail cell.

He helped Rebecca cover the vehicle in a well-used green tarp, and then they shouldered their packs and set off into the woods, Rebecca in the lead.

As the shade of the forest enveloped them, Rebecca glanced over her shoulder and said, "Tell me a story."

"A . . . story?" asked Taavi uncertainly, watching his step on the rough path.

"Yeah, a story about struggle," she said, without looking back.

He strained to think of something that would impress Rebecca. Sam would have some exciting story, or a dozen, at her fingertips. But Taavi's overtired brain wasn't helping. "Well," he began, "back in Newbrook there was this march against the tank farm—"

"No," she said with a touch of laugher, "tell me something I can't read about in the newspaper. Something meaningful for *you*. You've taken big risks; you must have at least one story that motivates you."

He walked in silence for a moment and then began anew: "Well, as an anarchist—"

"Taavi, I don't want a story about ideologies," she interrupted again. "I want a story about *people*." He wondered if she was putting him off balance deliberately. "Your name, Taavi, is Finnish, right? Your ancestors must have stories."

And Taavi, to his surprise, actually knew what to say.

"At the beginning of the nineteen hundreds," Taavi said, recalling a story told at many a family reunion, "Finland was invaded by the Russian Empire. Not, like, *Soviet* Russia, but earlier, tsarist Russia, aristocrats who occupied the country and enforced Russification."

"What's that?" asked Rebecca, genuinely listening.

"They wanted to make Finland the same as Russia," he explained, "to wipe out the language and the culture and extract resources for the tsar. To make Finland a colony. So, people started organizing, secretly, to form a movement. It was called the Kaagali. My grandmother's grandmother Eevi was part of it."

"What did Eevi do?"

"She spread underground literature, at first," he said. "Talked to her neighbors, helped them to organize."

"That must have been scary," Rebecca said.

"It was," Taavi answered. "When I was a kid, I interviewed *my* grandmother about it, for a school report. She told me that at the start of the Kaagali, Grandma Eevi slept with her boots on. Every night, she worried the tsar's men would knock down her front door and she'd have to jump out her window and run through the snow to the mountains."

"Oof," Rebecca said.

"Yeah," Taavi answered. "After she married Grandpa Kaarle, the tsar proclaimed a military draft. Kaarle—all the young men—were to report for duty, to be shipped across the continent to fight the tsar's war against Japan. My great-great-grandparents, and the rest of the Kaagali, organized in secret against the draft."

"What did they do?"

"They built trust with their neighbors, solidarity, and quietly organized a draft strike. When the day of the draft came, no one showed up! So, the tsar cancelled the military draft."

"Impressive!" Rebecca said.

Taavi nodded as they moved into a dense stand of cedar. "The tsar was angry. His men tracked down movement leaders, exiled them. Still, the Kaagali didn't give up. They began a campaign of sabotage. They created an armed wing. They reached out to allies like the socialist movement in Russia, even got funding from Japan.

"When World War One began, the Russian government was

overwhelmed by a war abroad and by a revolution within. So, when Finland declared independence, no one could stop us."

Rebecca waited a few moments to see if he was finished. "What can we take away from that story?"

Taavi adjusted one of his shoulder straps to tighten it. "I guess, when I was a kid, I was told that story as an example of persistence. Like, when things get tough, you don't quit," he said, "you tighten your boots. And that's true for resistance. It's like . . . persistence *is* resistance. When we win, it's because we kept going, and when those in power try to slap us down, we push even harder."

"Exactly," said Rebecca encouragingly.

"And that injustice can last a long time," Taavi said, "but not forever. If you keep up the struggle, eventually a moment will come when those in power stumble, and you can make room for something different."

"Uh-huh," agreed Rebecca.

"There's another thing," he added, "that wasn't part of the story the way my family told it: What the Russians tried to do in Finland, well, that's what the colonial powers did to Indigenous people here. Take their land, their languages, their resources. Ban their culture. The way I see it, the United States and Canada, all the colonizers, they're governments of occupation. Just like Russia was for my ancestors. The only difference is that Indigenous people here couldn't get rid of those governments."

Rebecca stopped in the middle of the trail and turned back with a sly grin on her face.

"At least," she said, "not yet."

***

Helen arrived at Gwen's front porch to see familiar faces. Elijah and Teresa were pouring lemonade from a pitcher as Helen and Gwen walked up.

"Can I pour you a glass?" asked Elijah. He and Teresa stood to give Helen hugs.

"I hear you had a rough week," said Teresa.

"It wasn't easy for any of us," said Helen, hugging them back.

"At least people are paying attention," said Elijah. Helen gave him a curious look. "We got a huge traffic bump online, after the bombing," he said. "Gwen had a million views this week."

"Apparently that's pretty good," said Gwen. "More than Philip, that's for sure."

"Do we have to talk about that opportunistic motherfucker again?" asked Teresa.

"What do you mean?" asked Helen, accepting a glass of lemonade from Elijah.

"Philip has been calling us over and over," said Elijah. "He leaves voice mails implying his rich lawyer dad can help us with the lawsuit. If you actually pick up the phone, Philip just *talks* and *talks* about everything he thinks went wrong with the left in general and our campaign in particular."

"He's just mad we won't let him do interviews on behalf of the campaign," said Teresa. "That jerk can't stand a woman getting attention instead of him."

"Now, come on; it's a team effort," said Gwen.

"He wants us to do a press conference calling for a 'bilateral solution' on the tank farm and IRI," said Elijah. "Thinks we should let them reopen the tank farm with a promise of tighter regulations, in exchange for the company dropping the lawsuit and giving Friends of the Watershed a generous donation. He's got a goddamned PR firm, some company his father works with. We declined, but he keeps sending unsolicited advice. He's used to talking until everyone gets worn down and goes along with what he wants."

"If he wants to collaborate, why all this complaining about the left?" asked Teresa.

"Apparently he got ejected from lefty campus groups for taking up too much space," said Elijah. "Sounds like he's holding a grudge."

Helen sighed and turned to Teresa. "How's your dad?"

"He took it badly when the mayor's promise was reversed, like you," she said. "But he was ecstatic about the bombing. It's all he talks about. 'They should have blown that up thirty years ago.'"

"You don't seem as excited," said Helen.

Teresa shrugged slightly. "Is bombing really what it's come to? We can't solve problems productively?"

"*We* can," said Gwen. "It's people in charge who can't."

There was a pause.

"I'm so sorry you got fired that way, Helen," said Elijah. "It was brutal to watch. That Leon guy is a complete asshole."

"Thanks," said Helen.

"You could get a job at the university," said Elijah. "I know some people who really respect what you've done. It's obvious to anyone who reads the newspapers you're hardworking."

"I'll give it some thought," Helen said.

"Have you been to the quarry yet, Helen?" asked Teresa. Helen gave her a blank look. "Another IRI site, west of Newbrook. Some rabble-rousers took it over yesterday. Surprise action."

"People are copying our successes already!" said Elijah.

"Hopefully they won't copy our failures," sighed Helen. The others exchanged concerned glances.

"I'm proud of our campaign," said Gwen. "We won important victories."

"And suffered important defeats," replied Helen. "We lost our non-profit, and we're each being sued for a hundred times our net worth."

"We can't lie down and die, Helen," said Elijah. "Exciting things are happening. The government wants to expand a bunch of those old quarries into a new megaquarry, and some old farmers invited in a direct-action crew. It's amazing; you should go see it!"

Helen bent over and covered her face with her hands. Teresa lay a gentle hand on her back.

"Give her a few days," said Gwen quietly to Elijah, "to get back in the swing of things. Let's just enjoy our lemonade for a while."

They sat there quietly for a few minutes, until a car started driving up Gwen's long driveway. Gwen stood and walked to her door. Looking past her, Helen saw a shotgun leaning against the inside doorframe. "What is *that?*" Helen asked, staring at the firearm.

"Most of the comments on Gwen's videos were positive," said Elijah, "but there have been a few, err, dozen death threats." Helen looked startled.

"Nothing to worry about," said Gwen, watching the approaching car through a pair of binoculars. "It's Apollo."

"Apollo!" said Helen incredulously.

"Got out on bail this morning," said Teresa. "I tried to leave you a message, but your voice mail was full."

When darkness approached, Rebecca and Taavi made camp. Rebecca erected a tarp and asked Taavi to make a campfire, surely a test of his wilderness acumen. To prove himself, he gathered a generous quantity of dead leaves, twigs, larger branches, and a few hunks of resinous wood from a tall stump.

He piled this fuel in a convenient rocky depression, with the smallest and driest material on the bottom. Soon he had a conical pile three feet across and almost two feet high. He gazed with pride at what would soon be a roaring bonfire and asked Rebecca if she had a lighter.

Rebecca inspected his pile of kindling and laughed.

"What is it?" he asked, slightly hurt.

She shook her head and smiled. "Rules for survival underground: Always be subtle. Always conserve resources." She had him remove most of the material and stack it nearby. Then they built a core of fluffy tinder small enough to fit in a coffee cup.

"Building an underground movement is tricky," she said, as she helped him lay twigs and bark around the core. "You don't have a lot of material to work with." She drew a matchbook from her pocket and handed it to him. "And you don't have a lot of chances."

He opened the book. It contained only two matches; the rest had been torn out. The striker strip looked worn. He contemplated the matchbook as his stomach rumbled.

"If you can't light it"—she grinned—"we can't cook our dinner."

He nodded thoughtfully. Then he tore out both matches, held their heads together, and struck them. They flared into life. Rebecca laughed. "Oh, all in. Very bold. I like that." He cupped the matches and held them so the flame would crawl up the cardboard matchsticks and then deposited them into the pile of tinder. He blew gently; the pile began to smoke, then to burn brightly. This earned a golf clap from Rebecca. He added larger sticks and helped the fire grow as she began to assemble dinner.

The sun passed below the horizon, and the sky went red.

The evening air on Gwen's farm was warm and dry. Helen and Apollo walked side by side past the barn and into the moonlit pasture. They spoke in quiet tones, passing a grazing horse and a few sheep.

"It was hard for the prosecution to convince the judge to deny me bail," Apollo explained. "Crimes around here all happened *after* I got put away." Helen laughed. "I still have conditions, but it's nice to be out of prison."

"I'm sorry I only visited once," said Helen.

"It's fine," said Apollo. "I know you were busy out here. You did a great job on the campaign."

"It wasn't only that I was busy," said Helen. "I *hated* just being *in* that prison, even as a visitor. I had nightmares about it."

Apollo reached over and squeezed her shoulder. "It's not the worst thing in the world," he said. "I mean, it sucks. It's a big shock, especially for the first few days. But I adapted—not enjoying it, but coping. And I wasn't in there very long. The exciting events out here kept me going, made me stronger."

"What's it like being free?" she asked.

He laughed dryly. "Are we *really* free when we can be arrested anytime we become an obstacle to those in power? Put away for weeks without real evidence?"

"You know what I mean," she said. "Being out of jail."

"I see things with new eyes," he said. "You look different over a few weeks. You look tired. And you've lost weight. You're too skinny."

"You sure know how to flatter a gal," laughed Helen.

"And there are people I haven't been able to reach. Have you talked to Taavi, lately? Or Samantha or Andy?" Helen shook her head. "Strange."

"Do you think they had something to do with the—"

"It's best not to speculate," interrupted Apollo. "We never know who's listening. But if you see them, I'd love to know."

Helen nodded.

"Actually," said Apollo, "the person I missed most was you."

"*Me?*" said Helen, surprised.

"I know we haven't always seen eye to eye, tactically," said Apollo. "But inside, I thought a lot about good times we've had together."

They stopped walking and Helen looked into Apollo's eyes. He averted his, shyly. "You seem sad right now. Maybe we could make each other feel better."

Helen leaned forward in the pale moonlight and kissed him firmly on the lips. It wasn't the first time, but things had been more casual in the past. Now Helen felt as though she needed something. Apollo kissed her back. Ran one hand down her cheek and along the edge of her jaw. Another up her side, under her arm, alongside her breast. She kissed him again and again, deeply.

"Hold on," he said, his hands pressed against her.

"I think you've got that covered," she joked. But he wasn't smiling.

"I don't mean to spoil the moment," he said, "but have you been sick lately?"

"I've been tired," she said. "Overworked."

"But have you had, like, an *infection*?" he persisted. "Your lymph nodes feel really swollen. In your armpit"—he checked—"*both* armpits, and under your jaw. I can almost see the ones on your neck."

She paused. "I'm worn out. I'll be fine in a week or two."

"Hasn't anyone said anything?" he asked. "I saw a file photo from a few months ago in the newspaper. You look different. Your neck is puffy, but otherwise you're skinnier."

Helen stepped back, disentangled herself from his arms, feeling a sudden chill in the summer air. "Well," she said, "I think we've lost the moment."

Dinner, cooked in a single pot on the campfire, was chili. Rebecca burned it slightly—"I'm a revolutionary, not a chef"—but Taavi found it sumptuous and satisfying after the trail mix that had sustained them on the hike.

Taavi felt relaxed, almost entirely free of the anxiety that had clung to him. The fire warmed his face, and he bathed in the hypnotically flickering firelight.

He and Rebecca talked lightly over dinner, laughing. Rebecca smoked a cigarette and offered him one, which he accepted. Rebecca had a talent for establishing rapport—when she wasn't lecturing him—and this allowed him to imagine that, rather than being an underground fugitive, he was simply on a very strange first date with a charming older woman. Well, not *old* old, but she must have been at least thirty.

While they sat in the firelight after dinner, he gazed at her luminous face across the flames. Her face was angular, with high cheek bones. He could not guess her ethnicity. He began to imagine what life would be like moving forward.

Would he and Rebecca travel this way across the country, side by side, through safe houses and forest trails, passing invisibly along rural roads and truck stops? Would they carry out dramatic, high-stakes sabotage against an arms factory in the dead of night and then escape to a cheap motel by sunrise? Would they, perhaps, become lovers, drawn together by the excitement of their lifestyle and the common secrets? One night, after a close call, she might reach out and touch his cheek and say—

"Taavi," Rebecca said. He realized he had been staring and looked away. "There's something I want to show you." She reached into her pack with both hands and then held them out so he could see.

He squinted in the dim light and recognized the objects.

In one hand she held a palmful of ammunition. In the other, a pistol.

✦

When Dee got home, she hobbled into the living room to find a mess left behind by whoever had found her father. The carpet was marked by boot prints, and there was a scattering of medical debris: little paper wrappers that had been torn off in haste, a few disposable plastic caps. She cleaned up as best she could, given that she could barely bend her knees. Then she lay on the couch and made a list of all the things she had to do.

She had to replace her resistance laptop and her burner phone. Normally she would have done that herself—walked into a random store and bought something with cash—but she felt overwhelmed, so she would outsource that to the logistics circuit. That was their purpose, after all.

She needed to regain contact with all circuits and cells. In retrospect, her cautious plan to make everyone depend on her seemed reckless. They needed to be able to function without her. She had no extra capacity and would only get busier.

Dee stared at the empty place on the couch where her father liked to sit, then turned on the TV.

The news was the usual dire stuff. The United Nations was making "historically unprecedented" warnings of food shortages over record heat and drought. Warning shots had been fired between Chinese and American warships near the Philippines. There was an "exposé" on "Third World slums" providing a reservoir for influenza, tuberculosis, and cholera. Gruesome discussion of an alleged organ-harvesting scandal in Chinese prisons. A legal challenge to the use of autonomous military drones for domestic purposes, which had been thrown out of court.

There was a brief interview with Gwendolyn Gibson about damage to the petroleum depot; Dee watched with intense interest. Gibson was vocally supportive. But the interview was short, cut off so that the anchor could segue to "the three cutest endangered species you just have to see before they're gone."

She switched from the news to a nature documentary and ruminated. Dee's brush with mortality gave her a strong urge to accelerate her strategic timetable. If anything, the successful destruction of the tank-farm infrastructure proved that the right people could be trained quickly. Most involved had been trained for less than a year, some for less than six months.

She needed many more cells, and soon. It would take as much time as she gave it, so why draw things out? It would be dangerous, she knew. But in war, sacrifices must be made.

Taavi stared at the pistol in surprise. Despite the fact that Corben had talked about the need for insurrection and brought a stockpile of guns, Taavi had never actually fired one. He said so.

"This isn't firearms training," Rebecca answered. "I have another point. Stoke the fire." He stirred the coals and added wood.

She lay down the pistol and grasped an empty tin of tomato sauce left over from supper, one of a row of cans lined up by the fire. There was a small, triangular puncture in the top of the can, which she located as she spoke.

"Your cell was a group of combatants," she said, holding up a round of ammunition between thumb and forefinger. "You wanted to fight." One by one, she poked cartridges into the hole in the can; they plinked softly. Then she placed the can into the coals.

"Holy shit!" said Taavi, standing to back away.

Rebecca was unconcerned. "But you had a serious problem. Not the infiltrator. Your problem was this fact: movements don't win by combat alone."

The tomato can's label flamed and burned away. The bottom glowed red. "Rebecca, I don't think—"

She cut him off. "Even armed movements don't win that way. They use perhaps two percent of their people as combatants. Those combatants need something pushing behind them. Otherwise, their energy dissipates uselessly—"

There was a sudden pop, and Taavi threw himself flat on the ground. Rebecca sat calmly and watched the glowing can rattle as ammunition exploded inside.

"Noise and fury, signifying nothing," Rebecca said. "Exciting, perhaps. But ineffective."

Then she picked up her pistol, producing an ammunition magazine. "A gun works like so," she said, sliding the magazine into the gun's grip. "When gunpowder explodes, expanding gas accelerates the bullet down the barrel." She cocked the pistol. "Grooves in the barrel spin the bullet, giving it stability, yielding a fast-moving, accurate projectile."

She raised the pistol and fired at one of the empty cans, knocking it into the flames. Then she fired twice more in quick succession, knocking the remaining cans over. A shower of hot embers splashed outward, and the crack of the shots echoed off the trees.

"You could put a bucket of ammunition onto that fire, but you'll only get noise unless you can focus that energy. Get it?"

Taavi got up sheepishly, brushed the dirt from his clothing. "I get it," he said, "it's just that—" A twig snapped sharply behind him.

He pivoted where he stood. He was face to face with an enormous man in military camouflage, wearing a black balaclava and staring directly at him.

Eyes fixed on the camouflaged man in the balaclava, Taavi froze for a split second. Then he stepped back into a boxer's stance, fists raised.

"Are ye ready?" the man rumbled in a Scottish accent. Taavi squinted, his heart pounding, his mouth dry. It was Rebecca who answered.

"Taavi, it's time for the next phase of your initiation. This man is one of us." Taavi lowered his fists slowly.

"Folla me," said the man. He turned and walked into the night. Taavi glanced at Rebecca; she motioned him forward. Taavi began to walk, with Rebecca close behind.

The man and Rebecca clicked on small flashlights to illuminate the ground. The three of them walked for several minutes before coming to a large tent. The man frisked Taavi thoroughly.

Then the man held the door flap open, and Rebecca guided Taavi into the interior. In the nearest corner there was a small folding chair. It was brightly lit by several spotlights from deeper in the tent. Rebecca sat Taavi down in the chair, and the camouflaged man closed the flap, remaining outside.

The spotlights overwhelmed Taavi's night-adapted vision. From his place on the chair he could see only the lights themselves, a video camera on a tripod, and a few dark figures in the shadows, one of whom was Rebecca. She spoke.

"Taavi, we're going to do a job interview," she said, "to confirm you're a match for certain roles in our organization. We'll videotape so cell members can analyze your body language and responses, but the recording will be encrypted and later destroyed. Do you understand?"

Taavi nodded, trembling slightly despite the evening's warm air. He took several deep breaths and clasped his hands in his lap to calm them.

"We'll ask a series of prerecorded questions. My comrades must conceal their identities, but I'll be sitting right here. Okay?"

He nodded. In the darkness, the blue light of a screen glowed, and a new voice spoke. "What is your name?"

He was taken aback by the synthetic timbre of the voice.

But he answered: "Taavi Thorvaldson."

There were soft keyboard taps. "Where were you born?"

He answered a series of boring background questions the inquisitors surely knew the answers to: schools, family, places he had lived and visited. He assumed they were establishing a baseline, and was getting bored when the line of questioning changed.

"How long have you been a police officer?"

"What?" He jerked upright in the chair, eyes wide. He tried to stare past the lights to find Rebecca. His mouth went dry. "This is a mistake. I'm not a cop!"

"Who is your superior officer?" demanded the ersatz voice.

He stammered, keenly aware he was deep in the woods with strangers he knew to be armed. "I don't have a superior officer. I'm not a cop or a snitch or whatever."

"How often do you meet with your handlers?"

"I don't have handlers. I'm an activist, a revolutionary, like you."

A few sharp keyboard taps, and then: "How do you contact your handlers?"

Taavi wanted to slap his palm on his forehead, but he gritted his teeth and grunted: "I am not a cop."

During a lengthy pause, Taavi heard soft whispers.

And then, as suddenly as before, the voice changed tack. "What are the characteristics of your ideal comrade?"

Taavi laughed, quietly, in relief.

Apollo dropped Helen off at her apartment late that night. He offered to come up to keep her company, but she wasn't in the mood. Before he left, he extracted a promise from her to make a doctor's appointment in the morning.

Helen went upstairs and opened her computer. She read some independent news. There were a smattering of surprise occupations at IRI sites. Photos of a rally at the quarry. Promising, she supposed. Rationally, she knew she should be excited. But she wasn't. She couldn't picture visiting them. The prospect filled her with a sense of shame.

Her computer's clock showed it was well after midnight. She scrawled a note for herself—"call doctor"—and rubbed the swollen nodes under her arms. She opened Google, typed in "swollen lymph nodes weight loss fever fatigue symptoms." Then, as the page began to load, she snapped her computer shut. It could wait until morning, she supposed.

But she no longer procrastinated because she thought everything was fine. She procrastinated because she knew it was not.

17

2051

Addy pressed the satellite phone's On button. Then pressed it and held it. Nothing happened.

"Batteries are dead," she told Carlos.

"After only ten years in a hole in the ground?" he asked. "Boy, they don't make things like they used to."

"It's rechargeable," Addy said. "We can plug it into the truck."

"Don't get your hopes up," said Carlos. "Have you paid your sat phone bill recently? What about Kessler syndrome?"

"Diseases don't affect satellites," replied Addy. It was, indeed, a long shot. Satellites that survived the solar flares of '37 had probably fallen out of orbit or been reassigned to military use.

She pulled out the walkie-talkies. They were short-range radios; none of her old comrades would be so close. The cell phones were useless. There were still commercial towers in the city, but cell towers outside the city were repurposed for drone control—many such towers had been destroyed by rebels of various stripes.

"It doesn't look promising," said Addy.

"Come on," said Carlos. "You planned for a million contingencies. Backups to backups. What was the plan to regain contact if everyone were separated?"

Addy sighed. She reached into her pocket, pulled out the travel alarm clock she had carried for decades. The screen was blank.

Carlos looked skeptical. "What, is that your emergency beacon?"

"I forgot my Dick Tracy shoe phone," she replied.

"Who's Dick Tracy? One of your comrades?"

Addy sighed in mock frustration. "Young people today! No, this is what it looks like, more or less: a clock." She popped the back off and looked through one of the suitcases to find a pair of AAA batteries, still in their package. She put them into the clock and put the cover back on. The screen blinked 12:00:00.

"What time is it?" she asked.

"Two forty-seven," he answered.

She entered the correct time and date, then clicked a few buttons.

"Shit," said Carlos. "It's broken." The clock counted *down*, instead of up, and displayed a nonsensical time and date. The year and month both read "00", while the day read "4" and the time was "13:03:42" and descending.

"It's supposed to do that," answered Addy. "That's our next window to make contact. We're lucky it's not weeks. It's random."

"That doesn't make sense," said Carlos. "How can you connect with someone else if it's random?"

"Well, *pseudo*random," Addy corrected. "Synchronized with other clocks."

"What do we *do* in four days?"

"Originally, we'd do something on the internet," she said. "Which won't work now, obviously. I need a ham radio. With the biggest antenna possible."

Carlos frowned. "That's dangerous."

"We're out of options."

⚞

As Evelyn rode the bus toward the Thistle and her family, she could not help but compare the trip to her morning commute. Compared to "business casual," the outfits around her were older and worn, though neatly patched. The passengers did not wear tags of any color. When they passed through a little town, strangers outside would wave.

Evelyn was used to looking at an orderly urban landscape during her commute. The city was stark and undecorated, aside from propaganda posters and advertising, and pedestrians were rare.

Here, south of Authority territory, she could almost always see *someone* out the window. The view was mostly rural, with open fields and gardens and patches of forest. As a child she had ridden through the country and mostly seen cows and cornfields, rather than people. But here, people were everywhere. They rambled around without checkpoints or fear of contagion.

Evelyn rode in silence. She had a pair of seats to herself, and she didn't know who she could trust—she was a fugitive assassin, after all. But she stole glances at the other six passengers. Were they also trying to reunite with family? Did they hope they could work their way up through the triage system to prosperous livelihoods?

Near sunset, they pulled off the main road and into an old barn that had been converted to a machine shop. The man in the cowboy hat stepped up to the front of the bus. "Congratulations," he said dryly. "You are now inside the territory claimed by the York Emergency Authority. We can't go further by road, because of new checkpoints. We're going off-road!"

Evelyn sighed. She had lost her own well-fitting shoes during a costume change. This situation demanded proper hiking boots; her shoes were floppy and oversized.

"You expect us to walk?" one of the other passengers asked. "I paid a lot of money for this."

"You won't walk all the way," said the man in the hat. "We've got electric ATVs. But if we go up a steep hill you might have to get off for a bit."

The bus passengers were loaded onto three vehicles that looked barely sturdier than golf carts. As night began to fall, the vehicles drove—almost silently—out of the barn and into a gloomy forest.

—⚡

"I thought I was done running from cops in the dark," said Gwendolyn through chattering teeth. She pulled a blanket tightly around her shoulders. "I'm too old for this."

"You'll feel better when you warm up," said Layth. He and Gwendolyn had crawled out of the river—soaking wet and chilled though—without being spotted. Layth managed to hotwire one of the company cars and drive a short distance from town to an abandoned gas station where he had previously hidden a cache of food and warm clothing. He guessed they could recuperate until morning. "Will you be ready to travel by sunrise?"

Gwendolyn sighed. "I should be warm by then, if that's what you mean. But in general, I'm going to get worse."

"We'll get a warm meal tomorrow, and maybe even a bed," said Layth.

"That's not what I mean," said Gwendolyn. "You think I was there for warm baths and backgammon?"

"Are you sick?" asked Layth.

"It's not contagious," said Gwendolyn, "but without treatment, I'll get worse."

"We have access to pharmaceuticals," Layth said. Well, they *had*, anyway.

Gwendolyn laughed, but her green eyes were joyless. "Aspirin ain't gonna cut it, kid. They've got fancy treatments up there. Every two months, they burn out diseased cells with custom viruses, then grow me a new immune system from scratch. You got a bag of pluripotent stem cells?"

Layth said nothing.

Gwendolyn shrugged spasmodically—or perhaps it was a violent shiver. "I've had a longer run than I expected," she said. "Longer than a lot of people in this business. You just get me to headquarters, and I'll show them the intel. Now *that* will save lives."

"What intel?" Layth asked.

Gwendolyn grinned. "Where to start? I've scraped correspondence at that place for years. Put keystroke loggers on most of the computers."

Layth was skeptical. "What can you learn from a bunch of old people's birthday cards?"

"Old people!" Gwendolyn exclaimed. "Kid, those 'old people' are the most elite retirees on the continent. Former CEOs. State officials. Their children run the Authority, and those old folks aren't really retired. They give their kids advice all the time. Pry for details they don't need to know. Some still access surveillance databases. Put it all together and you've got lists of personnel deployments and passwords. Order of battle, disposition, all the rest."

"That could be useful," Layth agreed, though he doubted it was recent enough to be actionable.

"It's more than that," she added. "It's unguarded personal correspondence you'd never see in official communication. It's a window into the psychology of the Authority's highest levels—their thoughts and fears and weaknesses. Let me tell you, they aren't as confident as they appear. Some are terrified the regime is about to come crashing down. Some want to use the triage camps to liquidate opposition while they can. But not all of them agree with the camps. There are internal weaknesses, fracture lines. If we can isolate parts of the administration and turn them against each other . . ." She trailed off, a burst of shivers overtaking her body.

She had Layth's full attention. "That's really possible?" he asked.

"Oh yes, oh yes," she said. "YEA expands geographically while their resource base shrinks. They're cannibalizing their own cities, gutting old infrastructure and selling the scrap overseas. The triage system basically cannibalizes the population, right? Takes people on the margins, steals their homes and property, and then works them to the bone, works them to death, just to keep the system running. People at the top know it's a dead end. But they still want a piece of that shrinking pie."

"So, what, they're plotting against each other?"

"The companies are fiefdoms," Gwendolyn said, "competing for dwindling resources. Right now, security contractors are the dominant force. But they don't *produce* anything. They're professional looters. The economics look great—every time an apartment building gets quarantined, the assets get auctioned off, and the GDP goes up. Every time a community barter ring gets broken up or a farm on the fringe is annexed and sold, the Authority's GDP is increased. Heck, every time a mortar gets fired into a noncompliant village—"

"It's good for the economy, because they have to buy a new mortar shell; I get it," said Layth.

"Anyway, the elites aren't stupid. They're a crowd on a melting iceberg; *someone* has to get pushed off the edge to make room. So far it's been regular folks, poor people, people of color, the usual scapegoats. But if you read the correspondence, you can see they're starting to wonder: Is it getting crowded enough that some other bosses have to get pushed off? And if so, who?"

"You've given this a lot of thought," Layth observed.

"I've had a lot of time," Gwendolyn replied, her teeth chattering slightly.

Layth leaned forward. "How did you get into this? When did you join Kraken? How did you know my parents?"

Gwendolyn sighed. "Those are big questions, and I'm exhausted. But get me to headquarters and we'll have plenty of time to discuss."

Layth had not explained to Gwendolyn the network's dire circumstances; they didn't technically *have* a headquarters. But he knew a place he could bring Gwendolyn where they would be safe, where they could plan their counterstrike.

—✞

The dark woods were eerie. Evelyn heard only the soft whine of electric motors and the muffled crunching of leaves and twigs under tires. The sole illumination came from dim purple headlamps on the electric ATVs; Evelyn overheard a driver explain that these were less visible on the Authority's infrared cameras. Though if the convoy were spotted by drones, she hardly imagined purple headlights would do much good.

They travelled slowly. Speed drained the batteries—or fuel cells, or whatever the ATVs ran on—and since they could only see ten feet ahead, driving at full speed was a quick way to get killed. As the time approached two in the morning, Evelyn worried she might doze off, fall from the small seat she was perched on, and be left there, in the woods, alone.

Around three in the morning, the convoy halted. The man in the cowboy hat—who had failed to switch into more suitable headwear despite the biting wind on his exposed ears—addressed the passengers in a hushed tone. "We walk from here," he said. "ATVs have to be back in the barn at dawn, and Authority patrols are near our usual route. So, we walk the rest of the way to Newbrook. Twenty kilometers. Should be there by evening."

There were no sighs or complaints this time; the group was exhausted. They began to trudge forward stoically. Eventually a crescent moon rose, casting long, faint shadows in front of them. Evelyn was so drained that she was practically sleepwalking. That was probably why she fell.

Navigating a steep and icy hillside path before dawn, Evelyn slipped and tumbled downwards before throwing out both feet to stop her descent. Her left foot struck a tree trunk; she heard the ankle crunch. She cried out before she could stop herself.

The man in the hat scrambled down the slope to check on her, shaking his head in disappointment. "Can you walk?" he asked.

She tried and failed. When she put her full weight on the ankle, the pain was almost dizzying.

"There's an old cabin not far from here," he said. "We'll take you there and leave some provisions." He added, "We'll get you on the way back."

Evelyn knew from the look on his face that he was lying.

—⚡

It took three days for Carlos to locate a suitable ham-radio transmitter. It needed to be large, powerful, *and* some distance from the Thistle. Addy planned to use an encrypted data connection over the radio, but even that could draw unwanted attention.

Sniffer drones were a common way of finding wireless transmitters even before the YEA. Illegal transmissions were potential carriers of foreign cyberwarfare activity, according to the official line, one reason that mobile phones (for those who could afford them) connected only to the YEA network.

Sniffer drones were the reason resistance movements in YEA territory remained so isolated from the outside world. Very small transmitters could not reach far enough to be useful, and powerful, long-range transmitters were easy to track down. Anyone with radios strong enough to break through the Authority's jamming would find their position easily triangulated and photographed by high-altitude drones. Soon the police—or worse—would be kicking in their door.

Addy hadn't heard anything about sniffer drones in years, but neither had she heard of anyone attempting international transmission. In any case, she wasn't willing to create unnecessary risk for the Thistle or Newbrook.

Carlos found an intact but abandoned antenna at an overgrown airstrip an hour's drive from the Thistle. Once they arrived, it took the rest of the day to install ham radio equipment (courtesy of Sridharan), to coax Addy's old laptop into communicating with it, and to set up the farm's diesel truck to function as a generator for the transmitter. They tried to make themselves comfortable in the old air traffic control station—a leaky shed two hundred feet from the antenna tower.

The communications window provided by Addy's clock fell in the middle of the night. Addy had worried for days that a thunderstorm would blow through, that some windstorm would take down the tower at the last moment. But the weather was calm and the temperature only a little below freezing when the night finally came.

Carlos parked the truck at the base of the antenna. He left it idling—an incredible expenditure of the fuel they'd borrowed from Newbrook's emergency reserve—then jogged to the shack where Addy had set up her computer. "Ready to go?" he asked.

She nodded. "But this isn't going to work," she said. "It's been years. No one is listening."

"We've got to try," he replied. "What have we got to lose?"

"Let's see what frequencies are actually available to transmit on," said Addy. She spent about five minutes scanning through the shortwave spectrum, listening on her headphones as her computer automatically progressed through the frequencies. She shook her head. "A lot of the stations are just YEA propaganda broadcasts. Some Chinese stations I can't understand, probably coming in from the west coast. Most of the space between is jammed. Only a few open frequencies."

"Okay," said Carlos, "let's try one."

Addy switched to an open frequency. She tapped a few buttons on her keyboard and pressed Enter. The words she typed appeared on her screen:

```
> FOR SALE: ONE STUFFED SQUID.
```

Over the speakers they could hear a binary grinding sound, followed by soft static. They waited ten seconds, and then Addy pressed transmit again, and there was another burst of binary. "It sounds like an antique modem," whispered Carlos, eyeing Addy's strange message.

"Shhh," said Addy, listening. She pressed the button again, and they heard the grinding of binary. Then more silence. She checked her clock, which was ticking down from six seconds. "I'll try another frequency," she said. But as she reached for her equipment, they heard a burst of binary in response.

"Did you do that?" asked Carlos with excitement. A new line appeared on the screen:

> **ENCRYPT OCTOPUS**

"That's them," said Addy. "They want to use encryption. It's prearranged." Several lines of text appeared as they watched, accompanied by the buzzing of data transmission.

> **GWBTS ZYIXW ZHUBR PGYJU JCTHK UIAWC FOGMG**
> **QRGBX EXZHL MKHHY PBGLA NRWLB JCZST GFFMQ**
> **HPRRO QHHSQ UMKEY QCMXH PZBFP DPWGM**

"I'll turn on decryption," said Addy. The line of gibberish resolved into:

> **AUTHENTICATE FOR DIRECT COMMUNICATION.**
> **CHALLENGE: AMETHYST/AMETHYST.**

"Awesome," said Carlos. "What's the secret response?" Addy stared at the text. She didn't remember anything about authentication or challenges. Had she simply forgotten after the decades? Or had the policy changed in her absence? "Addy, don't you—"

"Let me concentrate!" said Addy. She stared at the screen. Then she typed:

> THIS IS D. WHO ARE YOU?

She encrypted and sent the message. The response was rapid.

> **CHALLENGE: AMETHYST/AMETHYST.**

"I don't think that worked," said Carlos.
Addy ignored him and decided to lay things on the table.

> THIS IS D OF KRAKEN. LOST CONTACT WITH
NETWORK. NEED EMERGENCY ASSISTANCE.

She sent the message and waited thirty seconds. Then she added:

> HAVE VALUABLE INTELLIGENCE.

This, too, yielded only silence. Adelaide began to panic. She added:

> I NEED TO REACH SIMON

She waited another ten seconds, and a terse message appeared from
the other side.

> **STAND BY.**

Addy and Carlos waited a nerve-wracking ten minutes. Then the
channel buzzed with binary.

> **WHAT DID I ORDER THE FIRST TIME WE MET**

Addy knew immediately it was the hacker. It was both her blessing
and her curse that she could remember those early years with great
clarity.

> GREEN TEA. PEANUT BUTTER COOKIE.
> **HOLY FUCK, D. I THOUGHT YOU DIED A LONG TIME AGO.**

—✞

Evelyn's ankle was ominously swollen on her first day in the cabin; she iced it continuously with a small plastic bag of snow. On the second day, she ate cold rations and lay on the ancient, musty couch. She opened the bag Juan had given her containing the second half of her travel payment—several vials of pills and half a case of canned alba- core tuna—but was afraid to eat the fish and be unable to pay the rest of her fare when the smugglers returned. By the third day, the swelling had diminished. She snooped around the cabin and found three mys- tery novels on a bookshelf. She read them all in a single day.

The shelf also held a few bird guides; she spent the fourth day mem- orizing all the birds of prey. It took her mind off the lack of food. After four days, all she had left from the smugglers was some flour—which tasted obviously rancid—and a bag of very old dried beans she found in the kitchen cupboard. The beans looked edible, though the bottom corners of the bag were full of dead weevils. She mixed the flour with snow and made little noodles.

She left the beans to soak and spent the afternoon foraging for edible plants with the help of a nature book she found next to the bird guides.

Limping slowly around a nearby clearing, she found some frosted leaves she thought were common plantain. Sara would have known all these herbs. Evelyn couldn't wait to see her and Sid—the idea kept her moving.

That night, with help from an ancient lighter, she started a little fire of twigs in a rusty bucket. She put the bucket on the cabin's damp and moss-covered porch so the overhanging roof would keep her tiny flames out of sight of overhead drones.

She boiled first the beans and then the noodles and plantain. Mixed together they formed a dish that, even back in the city, she would have thrown in the composter rather than eat. The beans were under- cooked and hard on her teeth, the noodles disintegrated in the hot water, and the foraged leaves were stringy as she chewed them slowly in the fading light of her twig fire.

Still, it gave her something to do and filled her stomach.

The next morning, she continued to explore the cabin. On the backside of a closet door she found a series of short notes scratched in with pencil—a growth chart marked for half a dozen different children. A long list of years, and beside them the number of deer successfully hunted. The last three years scratched into the door all said "zero," and then the list just ended.

She hadn't seen so much as a squirrel the whole time she'd been in the cabin.

With hopes of finding more food, she searched on her hands and knees in closets and under furniture. She found mostly dust and mouse droppings, but under one old cabinet was a little packet of coffee, one of the freeze-dried instant-mix types campers used. It was probably thirty years old, but it was honest-to-goodness coffee all the same. She lit the stub of candle and boiled a tiny amount of water over an empty can—just enough for an espresso-sized cup. She mixed in the instant coffee and sipped it. No cream. No sugar. Just the antique packet of instant coffee.

It was the best thing she'd ever tasted.

—✦

"Who *is* this guy?" asked Carlos.

```
> I'M ALIVE. WHERE ARE YOU?
> NOT FAR OUTSIDE YEA BORDERS. DANGEROUS TO
GIVE LOCATION. MAY NOT BE ABLE TO TALK LONG. YEA
JAMMING EXTENSIVE. WHAT IS EMERGENCY? DO YOU
NEED EXTRACTION?
```

Addy didn't even know where to start. Did she need extraction? She typed:

```
> NEED TO REVIVE OLD NETWORK. EMERGENCY
AUTHORITY EXPANDING, NEED HELP TO STOP WAR
MACHINE.
> HOW CLOSE ARE YOU TO YEA TERRITORY NOW?
> TECHNICALLY, WE ARE INSIDE YEA-CLAIMED
BORDERS.
```

> ARE YOU IN BUNKER?

"Why would we be in a bunker?" said Carlos.

> NEGATIVE. IMPROVISED TRANSMITTING STATION.

The response was immediate.

> FUCK. WE MAY NOT HAVE LONG. WE HAVE ACCESS
INTO AREA VIA WATER ROUTE. WILL SEE IF WE CAN GET
AUTHORIZATION TO HELP.

"What does he mean that we may not have long?" asked Carlos.

> WILL SEND MORE INFORMATION AND ASSISTANCE VIA
GERTRUDE IN CITY. YOU MUST GET IN CONTACT WITH
THEM. USE SAMIZDATA OVERRIDE CODE 8D13 A8C3 B7CF
011D 10D2 D572 B242 BEDB.

"What is he talking about?" asked Carlos.
"Write that down!" Addy replied, typing back:

> HAVE NOT MET GERTRUDE. PLEASE ELABORATE.
> BE ADVISED THERE IS EXTRA COMMUNICATIONS
CHATTER ON YEA TELEMETRY BANDS IN YOUR AREA. THEY
MAY HAVE TRIANGULATED YOUR POSITION.

"Adelaide, we need to shut off the transmitter," said Carlos, frantically scribbling down the list of seemingly random characters.
"Just one more minute," said Addy.

> CAN YOU DELIVER WEAPONS? WE NEED TRAINED
FIGHTERS AND ORDNANCE.

Addy pressed enter. She wasn't even sure if the message actually transmitted before the explosion.

There was a flash of light and a concussive boom as the idling truck exploded. The overgrown airfield was illuminated for a moment as a fireball of burning diesel consumed itself. The two windows in the little shack shattered. The flash of the explosion and burst of debris momentarily blinded Addy.

"Drone strike!" yelled Carlos. "Run!" He seized her by the arm and pulled her toward the door. With a cacophony of metallic screeches and pops, the transmitter tower collapsed downward, disintegrating as rusted bolts sheared and ancient welds failed.

"Get to the trees!" said Dee as they ran across the field. Moments later, the control shack exploded behind them. They fell to the ground as a burst of grit and debris struck their backs. They scrambled back up and ran for the cover of the trees.

18

2028

After hours of interrogation, the synthesized inquisitor finally fell silent. Taavi was ushered out of the tent to sit on a tree stump. A nearly full moon was rising through a gap in the trees. Taavi guessed that it was well after midnight.

After several minutes, Rebecca emerged from the tent. She was smiling slightly, which Taavi took as a good omen. "I know you're tired," she said, looking drawn herself. "But there's one more operation tonight."

Strangely, Taavi didn't feel tired. The interview had been exhausting mentally, but coming into the cool night air had reinvigorated him. He felt he would be moving forward into a new phase of his life. Even his forearm wasn't bothering him.

He followed Rebecca along a moonlit trail, the Scottish camo man taking up the rear. It was a clear night after moonrise; they needed no flashlights. They walked in silence for thirty minutes, then forty, then nearly an hour. Without a narrow flashlight beam to look at, Taavi expanded his attention to take in all the sounds and scents of the forest around him.

Soon they walked downhill over rocky ground. Rebecca gestured for Taavi to be silent as they approached a clearing. The three knelt at the edge of the forest cover. In the moonlight, Taavi made out a tracked yellow machine squatting among fresh stumps. It had a high knuckled arm with a shovel on the end. Some kind of excavator, he reckoned.

Rebecca whispered: "This machine is destined for an IRI project. Its job is to scrape away living soil, to replace it with dead gravel and factory foundations and parking lots."

"Is this an IRI site?" Taavi whispered back.

"No, but this machine is owned by an IRI contractor. We need to shut them down here. Send a message that we won't tolerate their involvement in IRI. Your job, Taavi, is to stop this machine. How will you do it?"

Taavi's heart thudded loudly in his ears. He stared at the machine. Gleaming hydraulic pipes ran the length of the knuckled arm. At the joints, rigid hydraulic lines were joined by flexible rubber hoses. He guessed he could cut through the hoses with something sharp, but they would be easily replaced. He remembered having read in an old book, *Ecodefense*, about putting sand into engine oil. He suggested that.

"Do you have any abrasives, Taavi?" asked Rebecca. Taavi shook his head. "It's a good idea. But the engine compartment is locked. Can you pick a lock?" Taavi shook his head again, flushing in embarrassment at his lack of skills. "That's fine," Rebecca told him. "The important thing is to fight, to fight with whatever you have. If you can pick locks, great. If you can put grit in the engine oil, perfect. If you don't have those, then you use what you can get. Slash the tires, or smash the windows. Be careful and sneaky, yes. But if you know you can hurt the enemy even a bit, and you can escape afterward, it's your duty as a revolutionary to act."

Taavi nodded, thinking. "I could break open the engine or the cab and set it on fire." He smiled wryly. "But I used my last two matches."

Camo Man pulled a backpack off his shoulders, reached into it, and pulled out a pair of gloves, passing them to Taavi. Taavi stared at them. "Put them on," the man prompted.

Taavi slowly pulled on the gloves but turned to Rebecca. "Aren't we just talking about this? Doing recon?"

Rebecca shook her head. "We've done recon on this site. It's free of security cameras and alarms. This isn't practice time any more. It's war. We fight or we die."

Camo man passed a balaclava to Taavi. "To be on the safe side," the man said. Taavi pulled the balaclava over his head, breathing deeply through his nose to calm himself.

"Those people back there weren't random members of the organization," Rebecca told him. "They're members of the cell you may be invited to join, a front-line direct-action cell. They were impressed by your answers. Now it's time to prove yourself to them."

Camo Man pulled out a box of matches for Taavi. Then he passed over a pop bottle filled with a liquid that gleamed yellow in the dim light. Gasoline.

"Be quick but careful," Rebecca said, checking her wristwatch. "Leave no fingerprints. Are you ready?" Taavi opened his mouth, but before he could think of something to say, Rebecca spoke sharply: "Okay, go!"

Taavi stood and jogged from the forest's edge toward the machine. Within moments he was staring up at it. The bottom of the cab was as high as his head, the cab door accessible by a ladder welded to the machine. Taavi put down the bottle and slipped the matchbox into his pocket. He climbed the ladder and tried the door—locked. He tried the hood of the engine compartment. It wouldn't budge.

The windshield was covered with a steel grille, but the side door had a smaller, unprotected window. Heart pounding in his chest, he dropped back to the ground, searching for a rock. He found a round stone the size of his fist. One-handed, he tossed it up at the door window. It bounced off the window without cracking it. Taavi looked for a larger rock and found a hunk of granite the size of his head.

Using both hands, he lobbed it at the window six feet above. It struck the door handle loudly and fell to the ground. Taavi glanced involuntarily at the place where the other two hid, beginning to sweat.

Taavi picked up the granite and cradled it under his arm like a football. He climbed the ladder one-handed, then balanced the heavy rock on his right hand, finally heaving the stone toward the window like a shotput.

The window collapsed inward, not with the satisfying thunk of the office windows at the tank farm but with a muted crunch. He retrieved the gasoline bottle. Uncapping it carefully to avoid spilling on himself, he reached into the cab and poured gasoline over the control panel, the seat upholstery, and a pile of greasy-looking rags. The fumes were enough to make him light-headed.

Tossing the bottle into the cab, he drew a single wooden match from his matchbox, struck it, and flicked it through the window.

The result was explosive. The cab filled with flame, a tongue of fire erupting from the shattered window toward his face. He ducked reflexively and stumbled backward off the ladder, landing hard. He grunted, found his feet, and backed away.

The cab's interior glowed infernally. Oily smoke poured from the broken window. The smell of gasoline was replaced with the stench of burning plastic. For a moment, the flames dwindled as they consumed the limited oxygen in the cab. Then there was the *clink, dink* of cracking glass, and another window shattered from the heat, admitting a gush of oxygen. The flames rose again, and Taavi watched in awe.

"Hey!" Rebecca called. "Get your ass back here!"

He ran back to her. She and the camo man had already gone a short distance up the trail. They began to run, and so did he, fleeing the flickering firelight and smoke.

They took a different branch of the trail, so faint that Taavi could barely make out a path. If he had been alone he would have been hopelessly lost. As they ran, a cramp grew in his abdomen. Before it became overwhelming, they reached a gravel road and stopped in a ditch at the edge. Taavi was gasping, but the other two seemed barely out of breath. He would have to start jogging.

Camo Man pointed a flashlight down the road and flicked it on and off three times. A pair of headlights replied, and moments later a minivan pulled up alongside them. The door slid open, the three of them piled in, and the van drove off into the night.

～

Summer came and went. The sun arced lower and lower in the sky. Leaves changed their colors and fell from the trees. The days shortened and the nights lengthened. Which was just fine for Helen; long nights made reconnaissance easier.

Helen checked the Halloween costume in her bathroom mirror. A witch. Not very creative, but the conical hat and wig covered the stubble on her head and obscured her face. She applied green lipstick. Took half a dozen pills with a swig of water.

She headed out her front door, looking up and down the street. She walked down the street to Elijah's house, which was thumping with party music. Elijah had invited her a dozen times to his Halloween party; she decided at the last minute to make an appearance. Elijah and his boyfriend were hosting, dressed as hurricanes with wide discs of cottony cloud around their heads. Topical, if not especially tasteful. Helen chatted briefly with people she knew—both Gwen and Apollo were away on a speaking tour—and then headed to the bathroom. There she removed her witch costume and replaced it with a rubber gorilla mask from her bag. The mask was realistic, though from the neck down she was simply dressed in dark wool clothing.

Helen left Elijah's house through the back door without saying good-bye. She walked through several alleys to a car she had parked on a side street the day before, an old field car that had been sitting behind Gwen's barn. Helen hadn't asked to borrow it, just picked it up one afternoon while checking on Gwen's animals.

She got into the car. To her relief, it started easily. She put it into gear, took a left at the first street, and drove out of town. Helen spent the rest of Halloween night in camouflage clothing at the edge of a pipeline construction site. She sprawled on a thick green mat on the frosty ground, a black toque pulled over her ears. She wore a lot of hats since her hair fell out.

Lymphoma—that's what the doctors said. Blood cancer. In retrospect, her symptoms seemed obvious: swollen lymph nodes she ignored, fatigue she attributed to overwork, creeping weight loss, low-level fever she attributed to a greenhouse summer. All those things were textbook warning signs.

The specialist had given her eight months to live. She didn't tell her friends that detail, didn't want to distract them from important organizing work. But she knew how much time she had left, and she planned to make the most of it.

The diagnosis was a shock, at first. Then it offered a strange sort of relief. She had felt so fatigued and depressed after the collapse of the tank-farm campaign that she was glad to have something to blame those feelings on. That feeling of relief diminished when she started chemotherapy.

Her friends were extremely supportive. Gwendolyn and Apollo had accompanied her to many treatments (though Gwen had since gone on a series of speaking tours, and Helen saw her much less). They kept her company before and after claustrophobia-inducing MRIs. No one pushed her to go to protests or blockades; her doctor even recommended she stay away from crowds and public events while she was immunosuppressed. The conspicuous surveillance of her apartment—which spiked after the bombing of the dilapidated petroleum depot—had dwindled and then disappeared after a few weeks.

There had been some court appearances for the SLAPP suit, but the judge allowed a lawyer could attend on her behalf, due to her illness. The lawsuit still loomed—a fifty-million-dollar monster that woke her in the middle of the night—but once she stopped appearing in court, she stopped appearing in the news articles as well.

Helen's original intent was not to fly under the radar. But once it was happening, she decided to take advantage of the opportunity. She had learned lessons from the tank-farm fight. The failure of the lobbying phase, followed by the middling success of the tank farm sit-in, followed by the decisive success of an underground strike—well, the implications were obvious to her.

"The aboveground campaign didn't *fail*," Gwen had insisted when Helen shared her interpretation. "It was *complemented* by underground action. Neither would have worked without the other."

This was how Gwen spoke in her videos, each of which got more than a hundred thousand views (at least half of them from people who despised Gwen). But Helen didn't fully accept Gwen's argument. Political problems could be solved by dialogue if both sides participated. But what if the side with more power insisted on cheating? On arbitrarily imprisoning people? On spying and following them? On using legal tricks to destroy their livelihoods? What options remained?

Philip Justinian insisted the only option was to embrace power. In the aftermath of what he described as "the tank farm debacle" he sent her dozens of lengthy text messages and voice mails, offering his father's help with their lawsuit—aid that was always *about* to appear but that never materialized—along with "career advice" and suggestions that she get a job at the PR firm where Philip was now a manager, thanks to his "social change expertise" and his family connections. The texts had been faux-friendly at first, though full of subtle digs against the other campaign organizers. After Justinian wrote a series of public op-eds in praise of the "realpolitik of the Industrial Revitalization Initiative," Helen stopped replying, and his messages veered into outright condescension.

Subsequent texts grew even longer, with Justinian sharing his personal theories on the climate emergency, public health, and political change. Philip Justinian believed climate apocalypse was inevitable, that anyone who claimed otherwise was posturing or delusional. He insisted the left had to "accept reality" and recognize that the earth no longer had room to support every human comfortably. He blamed global warming not on conservatives—since "capitalism will inevitably destroy the planet and can't be expected to change"—but on liberals. In his eyes, planetary doom was the fault of the privileged left who wanted the benefits of consumerism without accepting the cost. He blamed the left for being indecisive and self-involved, for ignoring the importance of political power and ecological limits in favor of cultural distractions like gender-reveal parties.

The thing was, in scattered moments she actually found herself agreeing. Not about gender-reveal parties—that was an antifeminist dog whistle—but about the timidity and self-delusion that held back organizations like her former employer, Friends of the Watershed.

All of which had led Helen to a pipeline excavation in the middle of the night.

Helen raised her night-vision scope. The construction site was still just a long, empty trench. The dirt walls were eroded, slumping after the recent passage of Hurricane Sigma. The excavation machines were stored overnight some ten kilometers away, in a fenced and locked pen. That pen was illuminated by floodlights, and a security guard watched the site all night from a trailer. Helen was happy the company needed expensive security measures, but it didn't stop them, and it made equipment sabotage difficult. Sabotage of the trench itself would be pointless. Any damage she could do overnight with a shovel was less than a hurricane and could be reversed by a high hoe in minutes.

The absence of security guards patrolling the trench was promising. Perhaps, with the help of a topographic map, she could pick out waterways and drainage routes. She could wait for a tropical storm and plug up key culverts, redirecting water into the trench and collapsing the sides through erosion. Or perhaps she could—

Helen heard a distant buzzing sound. A vehicle approaching? No, the sound was too high-pitched to be a car or truck. It was also high in *altitude*. She turned her scope down the length of the trench and saw it speeding through the air a hundred feet up, a tiny drone with spindly legs.

She pulled her mat overtop her body. The buzzing of the drone swelled and for a moment she thought it was hovering directly above her. Then the sound diminished, and the drone continued down the length of the trench and off into the distance. Soon the sound was gone.

So the trench *wasn't* unpatrolled, after all.

~

"Yes! Hit harder! Harder!"

Dee struck the punching bag with a quick jab and then a powerful right hook. It felt good. It felt exhausting.

"Okay, that's time," her Eskrima coach said, checking the clock. "Good work. Almost like you never had an accident. Hit the shower."

Dee headed to the sauna, sore all over from her workout. She rubbed the scar across her abdomen that turned an angry red when she exercised. It had taken Dee four months to recover from her accident. Her father never did.

Dee had shed her crutches, then her cane, and by fall she could walk as though nothing had happened. That made it easier to visit her father in the long-term-care facility where he had been moved once the hospital ran out of treatments. Dee's father was not aware of her visits; he never woke up.

The hospital had assigned a social worker to Dee, since she was a minor at the time of the accident. Rebecca, still posing as her cousin, fended off interventions in Dee's personal life.

But her father's attorney insisted on regular audits of her "donations," greatly reducing Dee's ability to launder money. She coped by making compromises to expand Kraken's clandestine revenues. She gave the fundraising circuit more latitude. It was finally making a profit, and then some.

She used some of her father's money to donate hundreds of thousands of dollars to perfectly legitimate, aboveground causes: the legal fund of the Newbrook Four, half a dozen Indigenous resistance struggles, a group of people occupying a farm in the middle of a quarry expansion and trying to found an ecological education center—she wrote a huge check to the "Thistleroot Institute for Resistance and Resilience."

She tried to cope with her disconsolate loneliness by spending more time with her network members—too much time, her paranoia told her—and by throwing herself into her work.

But she did not feel as capable as before. She got caught up in minor decisions. Which cell should this person be admitted to? What target needs reconnaissance? She still felt driven—autumn had brought the worst hurricane season in recorded history, a clear harbinger of climate catastrophe—but she was distracted, spread too thin.

She came to accept that she had a finite decision-making capacity, that through overuse she impaired her decisiveness, just as a muscle weakened with overexertion. And so she developed a rigid personal routine: Every Tuesday, get up, go for a run. Eggs for breakfast, chicken Caesar salad for lunch. Goat curry and rice for dinner. Wednesday morning, go for a swim and then eat granola. Lunch was cream of mushroom soup. For dinner, a military-surplus MRE. Thursday, oatmeal, martial arts (usually Eskrima), noodles, work at Greek church, Chinese takeout.

Dee tried to maintain hope that her father would awaken, an increasingly remote possibility.

Though now unable to launder her father's charitable donations, she refused to relinquish her role as financial hub for her circuits. Which was half the reason for her visit to the run-down YMCA across town where she studied Eskrima. She did not handle illegal product; that was a job for a separate division, carefully separated from political action cells by cutouts and firewalls. But at some point, she had to retrieve the cash. Which was a simple matter of good tradecraft, combined with a bit of money laundering courtesy of the café.

The close call with Corben and the Newbrook recruits had given Dee ample reason to exercise her paranoia. This trip to the YMCA was no exception. Earlier that day, she had driven her father's car to a nearby movie theater and parked it in their lot. She paid for parking and the movie ticket with her own debit card. She gave her movie ticket to a panhandler and walked to the nearest subway station. She paid with cash, never a transit card. She rode the subway to an aging shopping center ten minutes away. She zigzagged across the city in this fashion, switching coats, hats, and modes of transportation at crowded hubs.

It took her well over an hour to get to a gym less than ten kilometers from her house. While she exercised, she left her street clothes and empty backpack in a corner locker of the changing room; her combination lock bore a conspicuous scratch on one side.

After the sauna, she went back to the changing room and opened her locker. The empty backpack was gone. It had been swapped for an identical bag which was roughly half full. She peeked inside to see several large ziplock bags full of cash.

She dried her hair, changed back into her normal clothes, and went out onto the street to hail a cab.

⟝

"Large cappuccino to go," said the woman, "decaf."

"All right," said Taavi, ringing up the order. "And is that everything?"

"A cinnamon muffin and a copy of *Finnegan's Wake*."

Taavi's ears perked up. "We don't have any copies of *Finnegan's Wake* right now. How about *Gravity's Rainbow?*"

"Perfect," the woman said. Taavi rang her up. She handed him a bill and a handful of change. Amongst her coins was a microSD card, which he tucked into the cash drawer with the money.

"One moment," Taavi said. He made the cappuccino and put it in a cup for her. Then he ducked behind the counter and grabbed a paper bag. He threw in a metal canister and tossed the muffin on top, then put the paper bag on the counter with the cappuccino. He made a show of looking on the bookshelf behind the counter. "Actually, he said, "we don't have any *Pynchon* after all."

"Maybe next time," she said, and left.

Taavi's training for Kraken had been an ordeal. The days after the destruction of the excavator didn't include a welcome party. Rather, he was moved to the city and spent weeks alternating between tedious waits in hotel rooms and the performance of tasks assigned via texts on a disposable phone. One day he would be given a sealed briefcase to carry, using mass transit, from a post-office box to a dead drop in a train station across the city. The next day might bring an identical task, with instructions that he would being followed: shake his tail or fail the test. They never told him whether he succeeded or not.

Another day, he spent the morning in a window seat at a public library, writing down the license plate of every red car that went by. The day after, after receiving four documentaries on revolution, he had to record a fifteen-minute presentation on what he had learned about strategy and organization, which he left in a locker at a public pool. Sometimes the task was a surprise: on returning to his hotel after spending an afternoon in a Chinese café (having been told to "practice his powers of observation"), he was asked to write out the menu from memory. And so on.

He came to suspect that some tasks weren't what they seemed. Endless tasks of concentration were, perhaps, really tests of his perseverance in the face of stress and tedium. Perhaps the recall tests—like committing to memory the ever-growing list of every hurricane, typhoon, and tropical storm that year—were actually meant to reinforce the apocalyptic nature of their struggle.

They gave him a stack of assigned readings that took weeks to plow through—stories of historical movements, mostly underground networks: anti-Nazi resistance, Naxalite insurgency in India, secret intellectual networks in Soviet Russia, armed civil-rights movements like the Deacons for Defense. Samantha had probably read half of it *before* they went underground, just for fun. Taavi complained to Rebecca about the hundreds of pages he had been assigned. She told him it was the "short version," that the members of the movements he studied had been executed for sharing texts no longer than a pamphlet, and that Taavi should stop whining and be grateful for the opportunity to learn from their struggles.

After all those ordeals, they had assigned him to work in a coffee shop, of all things. "I'm not a fucking barista," he had told Rebecca. Him, a trained and experienced revolutionary! It wasn't even a proper café, it was a café-slash-*used-book-store*, which had to be just about the most humdrum post imaginable for someone who was truly ready to fuck shit up.

Taavi came to realize that the coffee shop was not so bad. It meant company. He moved into the apartment above the café, along with a cell of other radicals. The people in Taavi's new cell were sweet and kind. There were six of them, counting Taavi. Three were Kraken veterans, three new recruits.

The veterans had been in another cell called Cell Seventeen, which had sent explosive robotic crawlers into the tank farm's pipes and blown it apart. Cell Seventeen had split in two to accommodate fresh recruits. "Cellular mitosis," joked William, the oldest of the veterans at thirty-nine. William had an impeccable memory and a sharp eye for detail. He was also a perfectionist prone to bouts of insomnia.

Jennifer was laid-back. "I have to relax, I'm on vacation," she was fond of saying. She was a Texan who had worked at an investment bank until she was twenty-five. She went on vacation, read "every scrap of Edward Abbey I could find," and never made it back to her job.

Harrison was the quietest of the veterans. As a postdoctoral researcher he had studied a particular Amazonian salamander. On his third research trip, he found the salamander had been totally wiped out by a Canadian mining development, and he abandoned academia. Harrison mostly sat on the apartment's fire escape, reading chemistry textbooks and smoking tobacco from a pipe.

The other two new recruits were both women. Natasha was even younger than Taavi and volunteered little, though she sometimes told stories of living in Ukraine. And Shawna was a muscular kickboxer who had grown up in the Bronx before joining—and rapidly becoming disillusioned with—Greenpeace.

The camo man with the Scottish accent was not among them. And Rebecca, though she often visited to coordinate, was not part of their cell.

Taavi's new comrades were always asking him: "Tell me a story." It had to be a new story to satisfy them. He couldn't keep recycling stories, so he returned to his assigned readings with real intent. And from the stories told by his comrades, he learned about dozens of movements he'd never heard of: the Bolt Weevils, fighters for Timorian independence, the Nian rebels in China, the Diggers, the True Levellers, a half dozen different groups of maroons. He went to bed each night with his head spinning from the new knowledge and context.

Taavi liked his cellmates. He enjoyed their company, admired them, found them brave and brilliant and insightful. But he didn't feel close to them—not was as he had with Samantha. Perhaps it was because he had been instructed never to share his last name. Perhaps Corben's betrayal had made him hesitant to grow close.

Not that it mattered. After weeks of solitude, his only contact with his past life coming through Gwen's online videos, he craved company more than he ever had in his life. And he came to realize that his new workplace was far more than a coffee shop.

A regular visitor to the café would notice nothing unusual. It was a popular café; sometimes customers stayed a while, sometimes they bought a coffee and left. Sometimes groups played board games or booked a side room for a private party. Delivery people brought in packages or handcarts of supplies for the kitchen through the back entrance. Local bakers dropped off boxes of muffins and scones in the early morning. Sometimes people picked up sealed bags of coffee beans or particular books they had ordered in advance. Sometimes people sold books they didn't want anymore. On days with good weather there was even a rotating wire rack out front where people could buy a book and drop coins in a can without needing to come in. What was suspicious about any of that?

But Taavi had been steeped in the principles of underground resistance. He came to understand that the café was a perfect front, and that the city offered very different opportunities from small-town Newbrook. Hundreds of customers came in each day. Thousands walked past. The customers had diverse livelihoods and class backgrounds, so underground members with assorted cover stories could visit without arousing suspicion. And every time an object changed hands in the café—a book, a cup of coffee, a bag of roasted beans, a set of dice—was an opportunity for hidden communication.

No doubt he had seen, during his months at the café, members from every cell in the city. Yet they were indistinguishable from the tens of thousands of others who came in for coffee, browsed the rack in front of the store, or logged on to free Wi-Fi from a park bench across the street. The café was a perfect communications hub.

That business with code words and *Finnegan's Wake* was pretty rare—or so Taavi assumed. It was easier and safer to use dead drops. The canister had to be delivered in person for some reason. Taavi didn't question every detail. Sometimes he just got up, did his job, served coffee, trained, and went to bed. Patterns were important.

Rebecca had told him so when she gave him his clock a few weeks earlier. "You know what's going to keep you alive in this business?" she asked. "Routine—certain things you always do. Always wipe your prints. Always check for a tail. Use only a clean computer, use cash, follow crypto protocols. Pay your rent on time. Keep your car in good order and drive within ten percent of the speed limit." She had looked at him as he nodded assent.

"Do you know what's going to get you *killed* in this business?" She paused and stared at him again. "Same fucking thing. Patterns. Routines. Sloppy little habits you don't even think of. Do the basics right, and if everyone keeps their mouth shut, the only thing that can trip you up is pattern recognition. If we are predictable, if someone can anticipate where and when we communicate, we're done. Which is why we have this."

She held out a travel alarm clock. It looked cheap, a flimsy LCD display and a folding stand of black and gray plastic. "Humans follow patterns. Habits feel comfortable. This little gadget helps break routines that will get you caught." She fiddled with the clock and set it on the table in front of him.

"It's been modified with a pseudo–random number generator. The clock will go off at seemingly random intervals about two or three times a week." Obligingly, the clock beeped and flashed its screen brightly. The time was 11:04:23.

"It uses a complex algorithm, combining the current time and date with an internal store of pregenerated random numbers." Taavi looked at her confusedly. "You don't need to know how it works. Just know it produces a seemingly random series of dates and times that only repeats every twelve million years or so.

"We have a paired device. When your alarm goes off, you have a message from us. Every time. The message might just be 'everything is fine,' but it will be *something*. The message is hidden, and to retrieve it you go online."

She opened up her laptop. "Use a clean computer, like this one, with the Tor network. Or use a random computer—like one at an internet café—only once and never again for that purpose." She pointed to the seconds indicator, which had paused at *23*. "Here's a list of sixty information drops, in order. Memorize it. For now, find number 23—the Craigslist for Albuquerque, New Mexico. At that time, 11:04, we posted a message for you disguised as something else: a Missed Connection, a job offer, Aa garage sale. Within six hours, we delete the message whether you've read it or not, understand?" Taavi nodded. "Oh, and there's something else."

She pressed two buttons on the clock simultaneously, and the screen flickered. Instead of counting time *up*, the numbers counted *down*. It read eleven months, fourteen days, seventeen hours, eight minutes, twenty-three seconds. "What's that?" he asked.

"Our best estimate for the ecological point of no return," she explained. "It averages seven climate models and dozens of biotic indicators. We slow the megamachine, we win extra time. But if you hit zero, that's it. We pass too many tipping points, and the planet slides into irreversible climate holocaust. It's your personal doomsday clock."

Taavi checked the doomsday clock every morning when he got up and every night when he went to bed.

He lived a life of routine. He got so used to routine—working during the day, training in the evening—that he was surprised when he was given a mission outside the café.

"It's a simple dead drop," Rebecca told him in the café's small kitchen. "Just stick this to the bottom of the postal box at this address." She handed him a magnet (firmly taped to a memory card) and a slip of paper with an address. A street intersection.

"Why me?" he asked.

"This is already part of your job," she answered. "We can trust you. You're trained to move around without being followed. And," she added, "everyone else is already busy."

It took him an hour to zigzag across town. The destination was just an intersection in a residential neighborhood with one of those gray, utilitarian boxes that mail carriers used. Taavi knelt beside it and pretended to tie his shoe. He slipped the magnet under the bottom edge of the box, and it snapped onto the metal with an audible click.

He stood and began walking toward a bus stop a few streets over. It was a sunny fall day, one of the few that remained, and he enjoyed the feel of the sun on his face. He was relaxed to the point that he almost forgot his regular countersurveillance checks. He was nearly at the bus stop before he realized he was being followed.

⤚

Helen tried to keep a low profile during reconnaissance. But after her creepy drone encounter, she tried something new. Rather than staying low, she would get up high: she rented a plane.

Posing as a tourist, she hired a pilot and a small plane for an afternoon. Her flight path would take her over several potential targets.

"You missed the fall colors!" said the pilot through his headset as they flew. "They were better a week ago. Hurricane blew all the leaves away."

"That's okay," said Helen, snapping photos with an single-lens reflex camera and telephoto lens. "I'm doing an art project on fading beauty," she lied on a whim. "It's best if they're past their prime."

After twenty minutes flying roughly parallel to a pipeline, they reached a sprawling network of quarries. Helen couldn't believe its size. She had viewed aerial photos online, but they were years old and didn't include new security fences or equipment. She was awestruck by the size of the quarry network. Most things looked smaller from the air; the quarry system somehow looked *bigger*. She could only imagine how it would look if the separate excavations were consolidated into a single enormous quarry, as IRI demanded.

"How's that for 'faded beauty'?" The pilot's voice crackled through her headphones. Helen held down the shutter on her camera, taking a continuous stream of photos as they passed.

"It's a dramatic landscape," said Helen.

"I'll take you by again," he said. He made several passes over the site while Helen took hundreds of detailed photos. So far, the site didn't look promising as a target. Security was strong. It would be hard to get past the fences and topographic obstacles. And there was already an aboveground activist presence: several tree-sits were established in the area. In the middle of the quarry network was an old homestead that stalwart farmers refused to sell to the aggregate company. They hosted the main protest camp. Helen took several photographs of the farmstead with her telephoto lens. The farm had dozens of buildings. With a scaffold, someone was painting a mural on a large barn, a spiny plant with pink flowers twenty feet high.

On their fourth pass, the turbulence became too much for Helen. The chemotherapy had lowered her threshold for nausea. She had to stow her camera and retch into a paper bag.

"Sorry," said the pilot. "It gets bumpy so low."

After they landed, she went home to rest, shower, brush her teeth, and review the photographs. She was just getting started when Apollo knocked on her back door. She shut her computer.

"Good afternoon." He smiled and kissed her warmly on the lips. "I brought mangos and croissants," he said. "Mangos are not exactly local, but . . ." He shrugged.

"They look tasty," she said. Their romantic relationship had always been intermittent. They were both workaholics in their own ways, throwing themselves into projects and campaigns with a fervor that left little time for serious relationships. But their relationship had deepened. Apollo's time in prison and her cancer made each of them crave intimacy and intense lived experience. Sex wasn't the *only* aspect of it, but it was a big part.

Their relationship had its bumps. Helen's increased sense of her own mortality made her crave company, but chemo drugs didn't enhance libido. Apollo spent weeks at a time giving speaking tours on resistance and repression. But neither was looking to get married, and both enjoyed what they got out of it.

That afternoon, they sat on Helen's couch with the fruit and croissants. Helen sat sideways against the armrest, her legs comfortably over Apollo's lap. He gently caressed the stubble that grew on her head. Apollo had shaved his own head in solidarity a month earlier, revealing old tattoos.

"How's Gwendolyn?" she asked.

"Doing well!" he said. "We spoke together in Toronto last week."

"I thought you were in New York," she said.

"Was that last week?" Apollo said. "Cities are all smog, highways, McDonald's, Starbucks. Who can tell them apart?"

"I guess it doesn't matter," Helen said, "as long as Gwen's doing well. Any more death threats?"

Apollo shifted uncomfortably. "Best to ignore them," he said. "Giving those people more attention only encourages them."

"Who's sending them now? Neo-Nazis? Alt right? Literal fascists?"

"A mixed bag," he answered. "Best to pay it no mind." He grabbed a mango from the table.

"Have you heard anything about drones being used at IRI sites?" she asked casually.

"Oh yeah," he said through a mouthful of mango. "There was a talk about them at the last strategy consult. If you wanted to come . . ." She made a face. "Okay, okay! You know you're always welcome. But yeah, government announced a few months ago they were buying drones to patrol pipelines. Civil-liberties groups complained; government promised that they weren't armed, blah blah blah."

"Their batteries can't have much range," said Helen.

"The big ones run on gasoline," said Apollo. "They can fly for hours. They buzz the quarry with them nonstop. They're like fucking mosquito black helicopters."

"How are things at the quarry?" Helen asked.

"Not good," he answered. "The organizers there are serious. The camp at the old farm is awesome. There's a huge barn as a common space for meetings and activities, and a bunch of cabins for guests. But the infrastructure is ancient. The well doesn't work; groundwater is all fucked up by the quarry. They need a lot of money to make it liveable for winter. Otherwise . . ." He shrugged. "The cops are just waiting for eminent domain, or an injunction, or for people to stop paying attention. Then they can sweep in and arrest everyone at once. World won't even notice."

Taavi reached the bus stop. The person following him was still there, wearing a dark-blue hoodie with the hood up, a black cloth face mask. If Taavi got on the bus he could lure his tail onto the bus, too. Then he could jump off a moment before it departed. Or he could get off at a busy mall and lose his tail. Or he could—shit. They were coming closer, approaching to within striking distance. He turned toward them and raised his hands into a defensive stance.

"Taavi?" The woman's voice was muffled by her face mask. "I knew it was you." It took him a solid five seconds to recognize Samantha.

Ten minutes later, in a nearly empty doughnut shop down the street, they sat together. Samantha's shoulder-length hair had been cut short. Her skin was less pale, as though she were spending time outside. Her glasses were gone; instead, she wore dark eyeliner; the sort of thing which stood out on her face and which a passerby would remember, but which could be wiped away in a few seconds.

"You changed your hair," he said.

"Cover," she answered simply. "I didn't realize it was going to be you when I started following you."

"I thought I'd never see you again," said Taavi. "At least, not for a long time."

"I assumed they would put us in different cities," she said. "I did see Andy once. Well, sort of."

"What do you mean?"

"Andy was presenting as a woman. I think she goes by Annie now."

Taavi looked confused. "That disguise requires real commitment."

"I don't think it's a disguise," said Samantha. "I think she's transitioning. The business with Corben may have been the last straw for Annie, as far as masculinity was concerned."

"Huh!" said Taavi. "Well, good for her." There was a pause as they both gazed at one another. Out the window, in his peripheral vision, Taavi watched a police car drive past the doughnut shop, raising his heart rate. But the car didn't stop. Taavi returned his attention to Samantha. "Are you doing well?"

She gave him an odd look. "You know, technically, we shouldn't even be talking to each other. It was a breach of security for me to approach you."

Taavi frowned. "I thought maybe you were in a counterintelligence cell. Following people to—"

Samantha shook her head. "Taavi, something strange is going on with this network. Maybe something wrong."

Taavi drew back. "Everything's fine in my group. None of Corben's bullshit machismo. No guns. No stupid risks during midnight actions. If anything, it's a bit boring compared to—"

"Not what I mean," said Samantha. "Taavi, why do think we met today?"

Taavi considered. "Were you picking up the card at the dead drop?" he asked.

"After what happened with Corben," she said, "I swore never to fall into a trap again. After Rebecca rescued us, I asked myself, 'What do we really know about these people?'" Taavi watched her intently. "I went through the same training as you, I imagine. I was tested, evaluated, and assigned to a cell. I could tell that we were dealing with serious, well-organized people. That relaxed me, for a time.

"They put me in a logistics cell. In the beginning I was a courier. I moved messages. Supplies. Equipment. Occasionally people."

"People?" Taavi asked.

"Soon I was working our supply caches and safe houses. A few things became obvious: For one, the network was expanding rapidly. We set up new caches and dead drops constantly, not to replace old ones but because we needed space for new cells and operations. That's expensive—the safe houses weren't punk squats. People with serious resources bankroll us. I started to wonder—who has these kinds of resources?"

Taavi was afraid to speculate. Who would have enough resources to fund an entire network? A government? Not the United States, surely. China, perhaps?

"Half the time, I didn't know what we were moving," continued Samantha. "Locked equipment boxes, sealed containers." Taavi himself had carried a few of those. "Know what else was weird? We weren't the only people with a story about being rescued. A few people in my cell were under some kind of surveillance before they got recruited."

"I guess a bunch of us got lucky," said Taavi.

"Did we?" asked Samantha. "It's not like some group of anarchists has a list of all of the people under state surveillance, right? So, who would?" She let the question hang in the air for a long moment. "I started to get paranoid. I asked questions of experienced members, but they either didn't know or wouldn't tell me. I started reconstructing a model of the network so I could understand. On my off hours, I watched our own dead drops and caches for people from other branches of the network to show up. Then I followed them."

"Fuck, Samantha!" Taavi said. "That's a huge security breach."

"I know, I know—"

"Sam, there's a reason we aren't supposed to know everyone in the network! Compartmentalization is the *basis* of underground security. Knowing what you know is"—she hushed him as the woman at the counter looked over, and he lowered his voice—"dangerous. Imagine your wacky hypothesis is right: this network is a giant honeypot set up by the CIA or something. If they found out what you're doing they'd just fucking kill you."

"I know," she replied. "That's why I didn't tell anyone. I was a cell within a cell, quietly gathering information to support or disprove a dozen different hypotheses. I was satisfied to do my job, aware I was probably just paranoid, that there was probably nothing wrong." She paused. "Until three weeks ago. I was running a briefcase between two dead drops and decided to pick the lock."

Taavi smacked himself on the forehead. "Jesus, Samantha."

"I expected it would be full of files about targets, or recon equipment, or maybe just cash. But it was full of pills, Taavi. Drugs."

Taavi's eyes widened.

"I kept a few pills and delivered the package. Then I bought a test kit, like parents use to test teenagers' clothes for drug residue. Test was negative for the usual stuff—marijuana, ecstasy, PCP—so they must be high-end designer drugs. I think that's where the money comes from. We're trafficking drugs, Taavi."

Taavi was silent for a moment. "Don't your test results mean the pills aren't illegal? They could be nonprescription, like—"

Samantha gave an exasperated sigh. "No one goes to the trouble of smuggling aspirin or penicillin. That would be stupid. Designer drugs are the only thing that makes sense. But I didn't have anyone to talk to. Until *you* walked up to a dead drop I was watching. I couldn't believe my luck. I was so surprised I almost let you walk away."

Taavi was shaking his head. "Samantha, this doesn't make sense. The Revolutionary Council would never allow this sort of thing."

She reached out and seized him by the wrist. "That's another thing—the 'council.' Just who is on this committee?"

Taavi shrugged. "It's a secret, for their safety, but I know the outlines. Three women who used to be in the Weather Underground. A couple of hackers from Anonymous. Some Zapatistas, an exiled riot grrrl from the former Soviet bloc. A US special forces veteran who knows the system from inside out—what?"

Samantha was shaking her head. "I heard a similar fable. I think in our version the special forces guy was on a plane with captured members of the Movement for the Emancipation of the Niger Delta, and he faked a plane crash so they could escape, blah blah blah."

"I didn't hear that part," said Taavi.

"Because it's bullshit!" said Samantha. "Do you want the truth? I've talked to a bunch of people, and no one has met any of these 'council members.' I mapped out the different cells, the dead drops, the communications channels—"

Taavi rubbed his face. "Tell me you aren't writing this shit down!"

"—and you'd think that, for security, different parts of the network would be funded via different couriers. But they all connect through *one person.* I delivered a package to that person at a YMCA this afternoon and watched to confirm that she picked it up. That person is the fiscal and comms bottleneck to the committee, and she's getting deliveries of a *lot* of money."

"Who?" asked Taavi.

"A young woman, South Asian, looks like a teenager. I don't know who's really running this network. But *she's* the person in contact with them."

Taavi looked surprised. "There's a girl who Rebecca sees at our café sometimes. A courier, maybe Indian? But she's just a kid."

"Taavi," said Samantha, "pin her down. Find out what the hell is going on. But be discreet."

"She's not there every day," said Taavi. "But I'll try." Samantha nodded sharply. And then, as if she had checked off a mental agenda item and was ready to move forward, her expression softened slightly. She reached across the table and took Taavi's hand. His eyes widened. "Aren't you worried about breaking our cover?"

Samantha shrugged and stared into his eyes. "People will assume we're on a date," she suggested. "Lovers." She shifted her foot forward under the table and pressed it against his calf. Taavi swallowed.

"How long?" he said, "until you have to be back with your cell?"

She stood without breaking eye contact. "Wait sixty seconds," she whispered, "then follow me to the bathroom." She left.

Taavi checked his watch. He managed to wait seventeen seconds before he got up and walked to the back of the shop. By the time sixty seconds actually passed, she had already gotten most of his clothes off.

~

Helen enjoyed Apollo's surprise visit. But, as happened with growing frequency, she tired of company and sent him home.

Once he left, she pored over the aerial photographs she had taken, adding them to her project files, trying to assess the pros and cons of each target. The pipeline route she had reconnoitered the night before was unsuitable for clandestine action; there was not yet anything to damage. The sprawling industrial park being expanded to the south was too big for a solo operative. She lacked the resources and skills to build explosives, and though she could probably damage the concrete-forming equipment, there were round-the-clock guards. She would not get much done before being captured.

A dozen other small IRI sites were possible targets. A few had been shut down by community action. A new industrial waste dump to the west had been stopped dead when the nearest Indigenous community simply took over the facility and replaced anyone who was arrested with new volunteers. But most small sites attracted little popular resistance. This didn't surprise Helen; bigger, more obviously destructive IRI sites were bound to attract the most attention.

In any case, for Helen, the absence of an aboveground campaign was a deal breaker. She needed her clandestine act to be seen as representing the will of a community. Many communities *wouldn't* welcome underground action, which narrowed her scope of action greatly.

She kept circling back to the quarry campaign. The organizers had mobilized popular resistance. They had done well, so far, but were threatened by fatigue, the onset of winter, and the likelihood of arrests once their farm stronghold fell out of the public eye. They clearly needed *some* kind of help. And the quarry represented an immediate, tangible danger. Supporters would understand drastic action. Whole farms would simply be scooped off the face of the planet if the campaign failed.

Few other targets radiated that kind of palpable threat. For example, there was a refinery less than two hours away planning to *double* its capacity to process tar sands oil. But the upgrade was happening on land the refinery already owned, and ultimately the biggest threat there was worsening global warming. Climate change was amorphous; it didn't provoke the intense popular sentiment of the quarry or tank-farm campaigns.

Helen flipped through her aerial photographs of the quarry. Heavy equipment was the obvious target. She had read that IRI had supply chain problems due to rapid expansion. They had been barely able to keep up with the demand for large bulldozers, dump trucks, and excavators. At the quarry this equipment was already in place, parked above the pit in a well-fenced area accessible by a single gravel road.

Access was the major obstacle to an action at the quarry, as far as Helen was concerned. It was terribly hard to get into, and that inaccessibility was probably the reason they were using drones instead of a human security guard. There were only two passable roads into the area: one that came from the north and ended at the farm, and one from the south that ended at the quarry's equipment yard. There was more than a kilometer of pits and cliffs between the two, and the equipment yard itself was surrounded by an array of deep excavations kilometers across. If she were spotted by drones, she couldn't escape across the rugged terrain. And planning escape was the first task of any clandestine action.

Or was it? She rotated the map of the quarry in front of her and pondered. She could turn the inaccessibility of the site to her advantage. If she could block off the main road—even for a short time—it would be impossible for security or police to get into the site. She could do whatever damage she wanted to the equipment.

But only if she didn't *need* to escape.

When Taavi got home from his unexpected visit with Samantha he didn't know to feel. Should he be suspicious? Frightened? He was elated, glowing.

He had an hour until dinner. Everyone in the cell participated in training after dinner. There was always a physical component—usually some stretching, strength training, and self-defense—and a mental component. Sometimes they would play strategy games, which Harrison usually won; sometimes they would watch a political film and then discuss it.

Samantha had warned Taavi to be discreet, so Taavi decided to use his hour to gather information. He did a quick check to see who was home. Rebecca, who visited often but lived elsewhere, was not present. Neither was the mysterious courier. Jennifer and William were downstairs, running the café. Natasha and Shawna were in Shawna's room with the door closed. And Harrison was in the apartment's kitchen, preparing dinner. Taavi went to Harrison and offered to help.

"Chop carrots," Harrison said, handing him a knife. Harrison was like that: concise.

"Sure," agreed Taavi. "So, is Rebecca going to be around for film analysis tonight?"

"Nope," said Harrison. "William's running discussion."

"How about that courier?" said Taavi. "She hangs around a lot; she should come join us some time."

"I doubt she would," replied Harrison. "Not her style."

"She's pretty young for a courier," Taavi said as he chopped.

"Probably why no one suspects her," said Harrison.

"She seems pretty slick," said Taavi. "Capable. Must have a lot of experience."

Harrison shrugged. "I heard her dad was a Tamil Tiger. She was the one who brought me my message from the Revolutionary Council," he said, "inviting me to form my first cell."

"Huh, so she's been around since the beginning," said Taavi. The wind began to pick up outside, rattling the window panes. The remnants of another hurricane were approaching.

"*My* beginning, at least," said Harrison. "But I wouldn't ask too many questions about people outside our cell. People might take it wrong."

"Sorry, man, I didn't mean to—"

"It's fine," said Harrison. "But be careful spreading personal information and rumors. Not everyone we encounter in this business has our best interests at heart."

That, thought Taavi, *is exactly what I'm worried about.*

～

Dee spent most afternoons working, in accordance with her routine. After a few hours at home, she grew lonely in her father's absence. Watching the news alone was little consolation, in part because it had grown so repetitive: yet another tense naval encounter with the Chinese fleet in the western Pacific, yet more hopeful reporting about the growth of the economy and the latest must-have gadgets, yet more drone footage of wildfires. Yet another breathless storm watch, more footage of ruined islands in the Caribbean or East Asia, more video of homeless people desperate for water. Yet again they had run out of names for tropical storms, and the latest storm on the way up from the Gulf of Mexico was "Hurricane Tau." Dee found it all pretty depressing.

So, after dinner, she put on her shoes and walked to the café, as she did with increasing frequency. Rebecca was glad to see her, and they visited in the store room.

"How've you been, little sister?" asked Rebecca.

"Mostly okay," said Dee. This wasn't a prearranged code; they had dispensed with those. Dee was answering honestly.

"Being a solo courier seems lonely," said Rebecca. "Always connecting people but never connecting *with* them. Maybe you should ask to be assigned to a regular cell, have some friends and comrades you can talk to."

Dee sighed. "I don't think the council would be willing to assign me to that role. I'm needed to move about."

They chatted until they were interrupted by a knock at the storeroom door a few minutes later. It was the young blond man, Taavi, who had been added to this cell a few months earlier. She had reviewed video of his midnight "interrogation" in the forest, pronouncing him trustworthy before deleting the encrypted files. Dee had never spoken to him—she never spoke to anyone outside of her primary contact in a given circuit—but the sight of him made her scars itch.

"Sorry to interrupt," he said. "Rebecca, there's a message for you on the drop. Also, I need coffee filters."

Rebecca apologized to Dee for leaving abruptly, offered a welcome hug, and left the room, shutting the door behind her. The young man staying, fiddling with the shelves, pulling boxes on and off, adjusting things that didn't need adjusting.

Dee, despite her habit of silence in front of cell members, became impatient. "Coffee filters are there," she said, pointing to a clearly marked box in the middle of the shelf.

He ignored them, put down the box he was holding, and slowly turned to her.

"I don't know who you really are," he said, "but you're going to give me some answers."

19

2051

Layth and Gwendolyn travelled for six days, mostly bicycling over unmaintained gravel roads. As they approached the Thistle they were intercepted by a three-person militia patrol. After persuading the patrol they were friendly they received directions to the Thistle—and instructions to follow them exactly. Gwendolyn was exhausted by the end; they had to walk their bicycles the last kilometer, continuing an intermittent conversation they'd been having for days.

"What went wrong back then?" asked Layth.

"With me?" asked Gwendolyn.

"With resistance in general. After K-Day there was real potential for change for the better. But things got worse."

"Why Kraken Day?" said Gwendolyn. "That was before you were born."

"That's the last time revolution seemed likely. And before that, the seventies, maybe."

Gwendolyn shook her head. "K-Day didn't have the revolutionary potential you imagine. There weren't actually many people involved. And it wasn't just one day."

"Right—days of action!" said Layth. "Across the continent! I wish we could coordinate even in one city. We can barely hold our safe houses and escape lines together."

"Kraken wasn't so big," she said. "They worked very hard and burned themselves out. Got isolated. Actually, that was the problem: not enough aboveground movement building to sustain a serious underground. A resistance movement is like an iceberg upside down. Ninety percent has to be above the surface."

"So why didn't outreach happen when it was easy? We can't even have a ten-person book club without the risk they'll all get triaged. News is controlled. We can't cross town without hitting six checkpoints."

"People were afraid, I guess," said Gwendolyn. "There was surveillance then, too. People were more afraid of getting in trouble or going to jail than they were of global warming or soil erosion or creeping fascism."

"They were complacent," concluded Layth. "Self-interested. Short-sighted."

Gwendolyn looked uncomfortable. "Not everyone. Certainly some."

"If they knew what would happen, how bad things would get, would they have done something?"

"People have great powers of self-delusion," said Gwendolyn. "But it's not fair to say they did *nothing*. People protested and recycled and wrote letters to their congressman. It just . . . wasn't enough."

"It was the wrong *kind* of action," said Layth. "They had options we don't have. You can jaywalk now and end up in a triage camp. Walk out your front door, and a drone is already watching you from above. People should have fought before things got desperate."

"I guess it's human nature," sighed Gwendolyn, "that most people don't fight until they have to. Until they're already desperate."

"If I were alive thirty years ago, I'd have torn the surveillance state apart with my bare hands," said Layth, anger on his face. "And the coal plants, and all the rest. Brick by brick. Like the Germans did to the Berlin Wall and Stasi headquarters."

"You forget, they lived under authoritarian rule for decades before that."

"I don't forget." Layth sighed. "I just wish humans would fucking learn something from history. I wish—I wish they had left us a different world to live in."

They had reached the farmstead; Layth was surprised to find it nearly silent. Had people already evacuated and moved to a safer location? Were they in hiding nearby? Had they relocated to Newbrook? Surely this farm, surrounded on three sides by steep cliffs and deep gorges, was a suitably defensible location? He looked around. A large shed nearby had an open garage door facing the driveway; inside, a woman sat on a stool in front of a large table covered with rifles. She watched him intently, a rifle in one hand, a bore brush in the other. She had a pistol and a knife strapped to her belt. Layth stepped off his bicycle and lowered it to the ground, keeping both of his hands open and visible.

"I'm Layth," he said loudly, "representing the armed urban wing of the Cluster of Revolutionary Action Cells. My comrade, Gwendolyn, has important intelligence about the Authority."

The woman lowered the rifle and brush and approached him, offering her hand. "I'm Lieutenant Dumont, community militia. Patrol told us you were coming. Is your comrade sick?" Gwendolyn was pale, leaning on her bicycle as through she could barely stand.

"It's not contagious," said Layth, "it's a chronic illness. She needs rest."

"Rest in the library," said Lieutenant Dumont, "until the housing coordinator returns to give you proper quarters. Park your bikes here." Layth wheeled them in and glanced at the rifles Dumont was cleaning. They must have been in storage—most were coated in heavy oil. The rifles looked old; a few had hammer-and-sickle symbols and Cyrillic letters stamped into the barrels.

"I expected more people," said Layth, lending Gwen his arm.

"Many are patrolling," replied Dumont as she guided them to the farmhouse. "And we had trouble with a collaborator named Farnham; we sent a militia contingent to secure that farm. Most people are prepping for a fight: burying supply caches, digging foxholes, gathering arms and making them ready." She nodded over her shoulder at the table of rifles. "We had two people go missing on a radio transmitter run, so a group went to search."

"What about Charlotte, Sara, and Evelyn?" asked Layth.

"I don't know all the newcomers by name," said Lieutenant Dumont, ushering them into the main farmhouse. "But Charlotte went down the valley for target practice. Should be back by nightfall."

The library was spacious, with couches and reading chairs. Gwen lay down on a couch and closed her eyes.

"There's food in the kitchen," said Lieutenant Dumont. "I should return to my post and finish cleaning rifles while the light is good."

Layth thanked her, and she left. He turned to Gwen. "Are you hungry?" he asked. She didn't answer—she had already fallen asleep. He, too, was more tired than hungry. They'd traded antibiotics for food on the trip.

Layth slumped into a reading chair and closed his eyes. He wanted to sleep. He wanted to be *able* to sleep. But his work was not done. So, he stood, despite the aches and stiffness in his protesting legs, and walked the perimeter of the library.

Displayed on one wall were maps at various scales. Another wall held painted portraits depicting people he didn't recognize. His eye was drawn to a colorful painting of a lively woman with bright-green eyes who seemed somehow familiar. He read the plaque: "Helen Kasym (1995–2028). Community organizer. Friend. Warrior. Martyr." He inspected the other plaques, realizing that everyone depicted had been dead for decades.

Beside the smaller portraits was a single enormous painting that depicted a flaming pile of heavy equipment—bulldozers and dump trucks and the like—visibly crushed together. An impressionistic rendering of a woman's face was subtly visible in the eddies of rising smoke.

The regular shelves contained how-to books, novels, old magazines, reference texts. There was a whole section on "peak oil." He thumbed through a thick tome full of graphs and charts. He found the whole idea somehow quaint; most of the people he knew hadn't thought about peak oil in years. All they worried about was being post-pandemic, post-hurricane, post-blackout, or post-curfew.

He flipped through the political zines. There was a whole box about the area's history of activism, going back fifty years. He picked one at random. He had trouble concentrating on the text—his tired eyes slide across it—but he did find a tiny, black-and-white photo of Gwendolyn at a protest, corroded fuel tanks looming in the background. He recognized her only because of the caption. Time and illness had obviously taken their toll.

He sat in a comfortable chair and flipped through the zine. He must have fallen asleep; the next thing he perceived was someone shaking him gently. He opened his eyes and smiled.

"Charlotte!" he said. He stood and they hugged, a close embrace that lasted thirty seconds. Finally, he leaned back and gripped her by the shoulders. "I'm sorry about John."

She pressed her lips together tightly and nodded. "I'm sorry about Noah."

Layth closed his deep eyes for a long moment. Then he reopened them and took in the sight of her. "You look good!" he said. "Well fed."

"You look like a goddamned skeleton," she replied. "Have you eaten since you got here?" He shook his head, and she dragged him down to the kitchen as he tucked the half-read zine into his pocket.

Minutes later, he was devouring a bowl of fried potatoes and beans. "This is amazing," he said, shovelling food into his mouth. "I didn't think I was hungry, but . . ."

"It's pretty good here," said Charlotte looking around the warm kitchen as people began trickling in for dinner. "Warm. Cozy. Plenty of food. It feels safe here." She lowered her voice. "Intellectually, I know it's not. They lost two people just this week. But it *feels* safe."

"They lost people already?" said Layth, swallowing his mouthful. "I thought the fighting hadn't started yet."

"Folks went to use an old radio tower one night," said Charlotte. "Didn't come back. Our militia found the tower, and their truck had been blasted. Drone, probably. Authority patrol showed up, and our team had to run."

"Shit," said Layth.

"Yeah. And get this: the woman who got blasted? She's who X said would help us."

"Wait," said Layth, putting down his spoon. "*She's* the woman who—"

"Yeah," said Charlotte.

"Fuck," said Layth. "They couldn't even bring the bodies back for burial?"

"They didn't actually *see* the bodies," said Charlotte. "But let's be honest: a drone strike, in the middle of a winter night, and nobody sees them for a week? It's not looking good."

"Hmmm," agreed Layth, and he kept eating. "Still," he added, nodding at his bowl, "we should enjoy what we've got. How are Evelyn and Sara settling in?" he asked. Charlotte gave him a quizzical look. "Sara. Evelyn. Their little boy, Sid. They got smuggled out of the city by our network."

Charlotte's face turned grim. "You're the first from our network since I got here. I was supposed to welcome two women and a child, but another message downgraded that to just the one woman. Same message that said headquarters was relocating; stand by for instructions. Haven't heard a thing since."

Layth put his hand to his forehead, struggling to remember a conversation X had been having on the phone the night of the assassination. The rescue attempt had failed, he realized. Or had been aborted. Thanks to the evacuation of headquarters, Sara and Sid were never pulled out.

"As for the last woman—Evelyn, you said?—she just didn't show up. Smugglers came through Newbrook a while ago; she wasn't with them."

Layth stood up abruptly. He walked to a larder on the side of the kitchen, swung open the glass door, and began grabbing biscuits and hard sausage and dried fruit from the shelves.

"What the hell are you doing?" Charlotte asked.

"I'm going to find Evelyn," he replied.

—⟳—

Each day, Evelyn tested her ankle with more weight. It was painful, but she had no choice; she had eaten her provisions, including the canned albacore and the nearby edible plants she recognized. The swelling was down by fifty percent, she guessed. She would have liked to let it heal fully, but she was losing weight. Her daily caloric deficit had become a greater threat than her inflamed ankle.

At first, the thought of leaving the cabin's relative safety had frightened her. She could get lost in the dark and freeze to death. She could break her leg or run into wolves. Wait, had wolves gone extinct? She couldn't remember.

But it became clear the smugglers were not returning for her—and equally clear that if she stayed in the cabin, alone, she would starve or freeze long before her ankle healed.

Evelyn could walk, albeit slowly, with a walking stick and frequent breaks. There wasn't much wilderness near the city. If she walked straight until she found a watercourse, and then followed it downhill until it joined a river, she probably wouldn't have to walk more than ten kilometers before she came across a village or a road or a farm or something. She surely wouldn't have to travel more than a day or two.

She found an old pair of hiking boots in a back closet. They had been sitting there for decades, too worn out for people of the time. But they were fine by modern standards, with good soles. The laces had been nibbled by mice, but she didn't plan to lace them all the way up. Her ankle couldn't stand the pressure.

So, at sunrise on the tenth day she rose, rolled her sleeping bag up in her reflective cloak, packed a few stubby candles and a canteen in a small bag. She put on the big hiking boots and stepped outside.

It was an overcast winter morning; she couldn't *quite* make out the sun. But she could tell which quadrant of the sky it was in, more or less. So, she started walking away from it, headed west. Or north. Or northwest. She wasn't sure, but she would find a creek, and then she would follow it.

And then, soon, she would find people.

Layth planned his bicycle-based search. Evelyn was poorly dressed and inexperienced with camping. If she had been caught in the open during the coldest nights of the past week, she would simply be dead. Also, several advancing YEA fronts were moving through the countryside, seizing territory. If she had fallen behind their lines she'd have been biometrically scanned, recognized as a wanted assassin, and sent on an express train back to the city for a neurologically invasive interrogation.

Those macabre realizations narrowed the search tremendously. If Layth was to find her alive she must be in a village or building of some kind away from the front. Charlotte told him the smuggler's route *she* had come on, which left a small wedge of territory to check.

He visited three villages to no avail. But he realized the smugglers would need to travel fast, off road, hidden from drone surveillance. That meant forested areas with mostly continuous strips running northwest toward the Thistle and Newbrook. That reduced the search area even further; most of the forest had been stripped for charcoal production.

He moved southeast along the expected route, looking for hunters' cabins, logging camps, any remote structures that might make good shelter. Twice he had to change routes or hide to avoid YEA activity and low-altitude drones. He checked four places before he found a hunters' cabin that had recently been occupied. Someone had swept the dust off the kitchen counters, and there were footprints in and around the building. It had to be her. But which way would she go?

He wasn't a tracker or a hunter or a forest guerrilla. He was an *urban* guerrilla. He couldn't trace where Evelyn had gone by looking at bits of broken twigs or overturned pebbles. But he could try to *think* like she would. If she had become separated from the smugglers she would have few provisions, no way to hunt, few recognizable plants to gather in midwinter. She would seek a place with food, warmth, and people. If she was smart—and he knew she was, despite her difficulty recognizing what truly went on in the triage camps—she would continue along the same direction the smugglers had been headed, west, or northwest. If she were injured or weak from hunger she would follow the path of least resistance, keeping to forest cover—which meant she would soon be blocked by the wide, icy river he had passed on the way.

A river that would soon fall behind Authority lines.

He turned his bicycle toward that river and began to pedal.

—◆—

Adelaide and Carlos hid as best they could. The countryside west of the city was swarming with YEA patrols, triage squads, and airborne drones. After fleeing the drone strike on the transmitter, they had hunkered down in a cedar thicket an hour's jog from the abandoned airstrip. There was no snow on the frozen ground, so they left no foot-prints to be followed by the Authority patrol that would inevitably follow the drone strike that had destroyed their transmission tower, their radio equipment, and their sole means of transportation.

Travel with so many drones in the air was prohibitively dangerous, so they built a tiny hut out of branches and cedar boughs beside a fallen tree. Carlos found a supply of oyster mushrooms on a stump a short distance away and some cattail roots in a pond. Addy recognized a stand of white oak up the hill and filled her hat with acorns. Then she found a maple tree and bored a tiny hole just above the ground with the point of her knife. She propped her water bottle there to collect sweet-smelling sap. Their shelter wasn't luxurious or warm, but there was enough food to keep them alive while they waited out the patrols.

After two days, they went north, and after twelve hours of walking came to a friendly town. The local community militia had a working car and enough battery charge to drive them home.

Their return to the Thistle—alive and in good health—immediately triggered a party, though what they wanted most was to sleep in their own beds as soon as possible. Carlos barely made it past lunch before he fell asleep on a couch in the common hall. Addy herself sat on a couch and sipped her drink.

"Sounds rough out there," a woman said to Addy. Addy turned to see a green-eyed, white-haired woman she didn't recognize sitting on a chair a short distance away.

"A lot of patrols," agreed Addy. Her physical fatigue had been transmuted into general sleepiness by half a glass of warm mead. She wasn't interested in chatting with a stranger. She had bigger problems on her mind. She was mentally reviewing her conversation with Simón, word by word, and wondering if they had correctly transcribed the string of digits Simón had send moments before the drone strike.

"You know, I never got a chance to thank you for what you did," the green-eyed woman said. Addy gave her an inquisitive look. "We never met in person," said the woman. "You'd have seen my photograph, but I look pretty different. I wouldn't have recognized you either. Charlotte told me who you were."

"Did she," said Addy, nonplussed.

"You saved my life, you know," said the woman. "Well, you and Rebecca."

Addy's eyes widened. She gave the room a reflexive visual sweep for eavesdroppers, a habit she hadn't used for years. She sat in a chair beside the woman. "I didn't catch your name," Addy said.

"I guess I go by Gwendolyn," the woman said. "And for a spell before that, Gladys, and earlier, Gwen . . . And before that, well . . ."

"I remember," said Addy. She remembered everything. She remembered the day when Rebecca decided to help Gwendolyn. That terrible day. A dreadful week, a horrible month.

"I guess nothing turned out the way we expected, did it?" said Gwendolyn. "I didn't expect to live another couple of decades. I wouldn't have, without you."

Addy nodded. "I hate to break it to you, but none of us has a long life expectancy right now."

Gwendolyn shrugged. "Individuals die. That's nature. I got more time than I expected, and I'm not scared of dying. Well, less scared than most, anyway. Communities, on the other hand, are meant to live on. So, if I can die in a way that helps my community, the community of life, so be it."

"I used to think that, too." Addy smiled. "I guess I never thought I'd get this *old*. I imagined I'd sacrifice myself for the cause."

"Many people sacrificed themselves," said Gwendolyn. "It's good that you didn't. We need you now."

"I don't have much to offer," said Addy. "I'm not even a good shot."

"Bullcrap," said Gwendolyn. "You're a resistance mastermind. An organizational genius, that's what I was told."

"That was a long time ago," said Addy. "We saw how that turned out. And the odds are not in our favor this time."

"They rarely are, but we fight anyway," said Gwendolyn. Then she brightened. "Besides, you don't know what I know. Show me a map, and I'll show you all the gaps I've found in the Authority's armor."

And with Gwendolyn leaning on Addy's arm, they slowly left the party.

—⁄

Evelyn walked along a stream. As the day wore on she expected the morning fog to dissipate. Instead, it seemed to worsen. The smell of wood smoke was in the air, so she must be nearing a village or town.

She followed the creek along the bottom of a ravine, then heard sounds of people and tools from above. She grinned. Soon she would be warm and her belly would be full.

She picked her way carefully up the slope, ankle protesting as she climbed. She grasped every handhold and branch she could to help her ascend. Finally, she reached the lip of the ravine, but once she could see over she dropped to her stomach.

The woods ended at the edge of the ravine. Beyond was an open field of mud and stumps. A few hundred meters away she could see work crews piling chunks of wood into mounds. Other teams were covering the mounds with dirt. Some mounds, already covered, were smoldering, filling the clear-cut with smog. On the workers' clothing she saw red tags gleaming in the light.

She slowly slid back down into the ravine. She would have to find another way.

—✦

Layth abandoned his bicycle not far from the Authority front. It pained him to leave it when he was so desperate for mobility, but he thought he had seen a drone following him. He needed to get off the roads and into the cover of brush, even though his feet were already blistered and walking made it worse. He traversed a deep ravine where the trees had been spared because the ground was too steep to cut them easily. And then, a few hours later, he found Evelyn. She was limping along in a daze, barely conscious of her surroundings. He called her name and she looked up in disbelief.

"What are you doing out here?" she asked.

"I came to find you," he said, his voice faltering. "But there—there's something I have to tell you."

—✦

Evelyn wanted to cry when he told her. To weep. But she couldn't. She was too tired, too cold. The tears were frozen inside of her. He tried to apologize, to take responsibility for the fact that her family had ended up in a triage camp instead of a sanctuary. But she didn't want to hear it. She only wanted to push forward.

The forest was damp and cool as Evelyn limped along with Layth at her side. Soon the forest would be dark, and moisture on the dead leaves would congeal into ice and hoarfrost. For now, damp kept the leaves underfoot from crunching loudly.

They stayed off the roads and smugglers' trails, moving as swiftly as they could to avoid the advancing Authority front. Layth speculated darkly about why the hired smugglers had failed to return for Evelyn in her cabin. Had they simply abandoned her and taken her fare? Had they been captured themselves and faced triage and interrogation? Or perhaps, as Layth put it, they were simply "racist, nationalist shit-heads" who would leave someone for dead because they didn't like where their grandparents were from. In any case, the smugglers had vanished.

So, Evelyn and Layth travelled like wraiths along misty hedgerows, using ravines and deep cedar cover where they could find it. Where they could not, Layth consulted a topographic map he had borrowed from the Thistle and plotted the shortest route to the next patch of cover.

Evelyn did not know if Layth was taciturn by nature. Perhaps, in happier times, he was cheerful and loquacious. But he had rarely spoken on this trip, his jaw perpetually clenching and unclenching, his brow furrowed over deep eye sockets. The tension that lined his sallow face made him look years older than he was, and his cheeks had been scratched by hawthorn branches. Evelyn knew, from a recent glance in the surface of an ice-free pond, that she looked worse. Her reddened nose ran perpetually in the cold, damp air.

She thought constantly of Sara and Sid, trying to recall her best memories with them: Planting seeds in the balcony garden with Sid. Meeting Sara when Sara was making her rounds during a blackout, ensuring everyone was warm enough. Walking with them on the grounds of the apartment block on a sunny day in spring. But her mind kept drifting back to their imprisonment in the triage camp, to compulsory labor, and to the horrors they would face if the camp warden ever figured out they were associated with a wanted terrorist.

She was locked in her own imagination when Layth, beside her, stopped suddenly and grasped her arm. She looked up to see they were in a section of forest with an open understory and tall, closely spaced birch and aspen. To her right the ground sloped downward, and she could hear running water some distance away. She heard a snap in the distance, then another. Her eyes widened. "Are we being—"

Layth cut her off with a sharp shake of his head. He pointed at a large yew bush about twenty feet away. They walked swiftly and silently to it, slid their small packs underneath, and rolled beneath its lower branches. Layth spread his camouflage cloak over both their bodies. Then he put his finger to his lips in a shushing gesture and silently drew a pistol from the folds of his coats and sweaters.

They did not wait long to learn the source of the sounds. It was not deer or porcupine, but two Armor Security officers, armed with rifles. They walked side by side, seemingly unconcerned.

Sixty seconds later, the soldiers were a stone's throw away, walking and chatting as if they were taking a Sunday stroll in the park. Then they stopped walking, went silent, and each put a hand to their left ear. Layth moved with glacial slowness to raise his pistol and draw a bead on them. Suddenly one of them barked out: "We're almost to the bridge. Confirm when convoy is ready." They marched on at double pace. In seconds, they were out of sight, but their noisy footfalls persisted a few moments before fading away.

Layth rolled toward Evelyn and pulled out his map. "There's a bridge not far from here," he whispered. "I'll check it out." He handed the map to her. "If I don't come back within two hours, follow this to 4500 Quarry Road." He slid out from the bush, leaving her the cloak, and padded silently in the direction of the running water.

She pulled the cloak over herself, leaving a tiny gap near the ground to breathe through. As she suppressed the urge to shiver, she heard the soft rumble of diesel engines in the distance.

—⟋

Layth followed a game trail downhill toward the river. The sound of rushing water grew. It concealed his footfalls but would also hide the steps of any sentries on patrol.

Minutes later, he was at the water's edge. The water level was low; stony banks sat high and exposed. Fallen trees offered some cover. Layth dropped to the ground and belly-crawled alongside a larger trunk. When he reached a crook, he peered through it downriver. An old iron bridge, brown with rust, squatted over the crossing on weathered concrete abutments.

He drew out binoculars and focused on the bridge. Several soldiers stood there, looking back toward the side of the river Layth had come from. A soldier gestured, and a transport truck began to inch across the bridge. It travelled at a walking pace; perhaps the soldiers were concerned about the strength of the bridge, or with saving fuel? It held a shipping container with peeling markings. Layth could not guess its contents. Behind it came several army trucks and a school bus. Troop transports, perhaps?

A moment later, Layth saw the reason the convoy moved at walking speed. A foot column of soldiers, and then civilians, appeared on the bridge. Layth steadied his binoculars against a thick branch. The civilians held their arms together stiffly in front of themselves, as though their hands were bound. Soon they were over the bridge and out of sight.

Next, a clattering sound, like hundreds of blacksmith's hammers pounding in series. A tank appeared and began to cross. Layth wished for a rocket launcher. He prayed the extreme load would crumple the bridge and send the tank into the river. No such luck.

Layth swore softly under his breath.

—✒

Adelaide led Gwendolyn to the library as the party continued in the common hall. Gwendolyn spent a long time staring at the portraits, the painting of the crushed and burning equipment. "Our memorial wall," Addy explained. "Our farm wouldn't exist without—" and then her voice softened. "You knew her, of course."

"Very well," said Gwendolyn. She lay on the couch, and Addy

found a chair. "We've been at this a long time, you and I," said Gwendolyn, her eyes closed.

"You longer than me," said Addy.

"We've lost a lot of people." Gwen sighed. Addy was silent, so Gwendolyn continued. "We'll lose more before this is over."

"This time, I'm afraid we'll lose all of them," said Addy.

Gwendolyn coughed several times, and Addy got her a glass of water. "You should read Authority correspondence, like I have," said Gwendolyn. "*They* talk the same way. Desperate. Beleaguered inside and out."

"It doesn't feel that way," said Addy.

"That's the isolation, Dee," said Gwendolyn, "the absence of news that isn't censored or synthesized for propaganda purposes by a damned supercomputer. I'm sure people in North Korea thought their government was invincible before it fell."

"Last time a government fell here," said Addy, "it wasn't exactly an improvement."

Gwendolyn opened her eyes and locked them onto Addy's face. "Don't feel guilty for your part in that. It would have come down eventually, no matter what. You did a lot of good."

"The Authority has undone that good—stripping forests for charcoal, selling people into slavery."

"Near the city, that's true. But you didn't invent colonialism. This is just their last gasp. Away from here—up north, in the oceans, in Latin America, in the Pacific, humans *and* other living creatures are faring better than they would have been."

"How can you know for sure?"

"I can't," said Gwendolyn. "No one can. But you acted, Dee. You did your best when others were afraid to do anything. You didn't make things worse, I'm certain of that."

"And if the Authority falls?" said Addy. "What then? A few town councils in the countryside don't make a democratic society. Maybe China will expand their protectorate. Maybe whatever foreign powers sponsor urban resistance will march in and set up a puppet state. Maybe Authority generals will nuke the whole territory to keep someone else from getting it, just like that rogue general with the tar sands."

"How do you know you won't slip and break your neck walking to the chicken coop tomorrow? Why eat breakfast if the sun will go nova and burn the earth to ash someday? There are no guarantees. We keep fighting, trying to make things better at whatever scale we can, for as long as we can. Otherwise, what's the point of being alive?"

Addy was silent for a long while. Unsatisfied.

"Maybe this will make you feel better," said Gwendolyn. "I know from the inside the Authority is weaker than it looks. Fractured. Brittle."

Addy pointed at a map of the region, showing the concentric red lines of growing YEA borders. "Their front has expanded every month of the last twelve."

"Exactly! They're overstretched! Desperate for new resources and land and workers," said Gwendolyn. "Every empire has a primary mechanism for expansion. The Romans conquered and looted to pay their troops. The industrial powers used technology and colonialism to get oil. The Authority triages to steal people's property, sell their scrapped infrastructure, force them into servitude."

Gwendolyn sat up, sipped her water, and continued. "Eventually any empire reaches its limits, but they're stuck in their pattern; they keep doing the *same thing more*. Rome ran out of loot and conquests, pissed off the Gauls, couldn't pay their army, and got sacked. When oil started getting expensive for the industrial states, they got into a bunch of foreign wars, destroyed their soil and groundwater trying to get the dregs, and squandered the little petroleum they had left. The Authority is going to do the same thing with triage. They've triaged almost everyone they can. The triage camps are burgeoning; they've stolen all the resources they can and burned the forests for charcoal, and their outer patrols would raid a homestead for a half a sack of moldy potatoes. Don't you see they're on the edge?"

"Maybe they'll just kill everyone in the Red Zone and force mind-control implants on anyone who causes trouble," replied Addy.

"Well, kid," said Gwendolyn, "that's why we've got to get our butts in gear."

—⚓

The arrival of Layth and Evelyn to the Thistle was joyous, but only briefly. Charlotte embraced Layth warmly, but her smile evaporated as soon as Layth relayed the proximity of YEA troops. Evelyn's relief at her arrival was soured by the fact that Sara and Sid were still captured. She had spent so long imagining the reunion that their absence was almost a physical agony. While both Layth and Evelyn were glad to rest and eat and be warm, their feeling of safety was tenuous at best.

They had only hours to recuperate before Charlotte insisted on meeting at the big kitchen table to talk action. Charlotte, Carlos, Lieutenant Dumont, Adelaide, Layth, and Evelyn clustered around that table late in the evening. Gwendolyn, looking increasingly frail, lay on a couch slightly to the side.

"We need a plan of action, and soon," Charlotte said. "Villages to the southeast have been emptied out, triaged."

Lieutenant Dumont nodded. "We've lost contact with several friendly towns this week. The Authority is preparing a full-scale assault."

"We should hunker down and avoid a fight," said Carlos. "What choice do we have? Send the most vulnerable further away, as far as Dakota territory if we need to. We're in a defensible location. We need to stall and get Newbrook's town council to negotiate with these people."

"Negotiate?" asked Layth with surprise. "These people won't *negotiate*. They want your land and your labor, and they'll try to crush anyone who gets in the way."

"See, labor," said Carlos, "that's what I'm talking about. Send an envoy, convince them that farmers are useful. They need us. If they relocate everyone, who will run the farms?"

"They'll run farms with triaged prisoners," said Gwendolyn. "Indentured servants, basically."

"They can't do that *everywhere*," said Carlos. "It makes no sense. That would happen in colonial Africa, or Nazi Germany. Not here."

"I grew up on a reserve," said Lieutenant Dumont. "Do I need to spell this out for you?"

"The rich have been looting the planet for centuries," said Charlotte, "as far as they could reach. The Authority is doing the same thing as always. They just can't reach very far."

"Can we stop arguing," said Layth, "about whether what's *clearly happening* is actually happening and focus on the battle plan?"

"That's another thing," said Carlos. "Battle plan? What battle plan? We can't fight a war against these people and win. Think about it; half of the people at this table spent the last week lost in the woods. We can't even keep a *dozen* people provisioned in the field, let alone an army."

"You don't get to decide whether or not there's a war," said Layth, his voice rising. "They've declared war. You just have to decide whether to fight or die."

"I can tell you're getting upset," said Carlos. "But it's not up to us to decide anything by ourselves. The town council should make any big decision. We can't go off half-cocked. It would be undemocratic and make things worse!"

Several people snorted in distain. "That would take too long," said Lieutenant Dumont, "Newbrook won't do anything decisive anyway."

"Maybe," Carlos began, "but—"

Addy cut him off. "Carlos, I love you, and what you think matters to me," she said. "But you need to be quiet and listen to these people." Carlos raised his open palms resignedly, then crossed his arms and stared down at the table.

There was a brief silence before Charlotte spoke. "When I arrived here, I was skeptical whether anyone here would fight back. Whether we would get along. Now I feel more at home than I have in years. I think people here can learn to fight. I think they have true revolutionary potential." Carlos frowned slightly but wisely said nothing. Charlotte continued: "But they need time to prepare. To train."

"Not everyone needs time," said Lieutenant Dumont. "I've trained my whole life. I'll do whatever it takes to defend our land and our community," she said and turned her head slightly toward Carlos. "And I won't back down. No matter what."

Gwendolyn coughed slightly. It might have been involuntary, but the others took it as throat-clearing and turned to listen. So, she spoke. "I know it looks bad," she said. "But the Authority is not invulnerable. I spent years reading their private correspondence. They're terrified of how brittle their rule is. At first, they funded themselves by cannibalizing infrastructure; chopping up buildings, stripping out copper and aluminum and scrap metal to sell overseas. But that's nearly gone. They're cannibalizing the living space of their own workers. There's never enough food in the cities, even though they've conquered enormous tracts of prime farmland. Even charcoal is running out because they've cut so many trees.

"They squabble internally. Half of the troops haven't been paid in months. Their private security contractors have turf wars other over ruins and sacrifice zones. They're on the brink, and if you can push them hard enough the whole system might topple once and for all."

"But won't that make it harder for people on the bottom?" asked Evelyn suddenly, surprising herself. "Won't they crack down harder on people in the triage camps?"

There was a moment of silence before Dumont cut in. "Why exactly is this person sitting here?" she asked. "Didn't she work for Triage Administration? Why are we discussing our battle plan with someone who worked for the enemy until two weeks ago?"

Evelyn flushed. "I was *transferred* to do paperwork for Triage Administration. I came to understand what they do is wrong. My own family is in a triage camp right now."

"Will they testify at your war crimes trial?" asked Lieutenant Dumont.

"Jesus, LT," said Addy under her breath.

"Camps aside, don't you know what they do to people in the basement of that building?" said Dumont. "To their brains?"

"That's just a rumor," said Charlotte.

"Look, I trust Evelyn," said Layth firmly. "She and her partner fed information to the resistance that saved lives. When the time came, she shot the director of Triage Administration herself. She's here as a member of my organization, okay?"

Lieutenant Dumont said nothing to agree but did not challenge them further.

"Getting the conversation back on track," said Charlotte, "yes, they probably will crack down on people in the triage camps. But we're out of time. And toppling the Authority—destroying the triage system— is the only way to help those people in the long term." She turned toward Gwendolyn. "What specific weaknesses we can exploit *now*, to buy time?"

Gwendolyn pulled herself up to sitting, wincing in obvious pain. "Most troops have been moved out of cities to the borders, to loot smaller towns and secure farmland and living space. Others have moved from urban triage camps to smaller industrial towns. There are few organized troops in the city. Most that remain are paramilitaries and triage squads. They're poorly paid, poorly equipped, poorly disciplined. They bicker with each other. They'd run or crumble in the face of a decent uprising."

Layth leaned forward, a look of obvious skepticism on his face. "We've discussed this in the underground dozens of times. The mass of people in the city will not rise up. They haven't developed the necessary political consciousness. They don't see themselves as a group of workers or a people oppressed by their rulers; they're just competing for scraps."

"You dismiss them too easily," said Charlotte. "You in the armed wing think that because they won't pick up guns they don't have political consciousness. Plenty of people in the triage camps understand what's going on. But they won't risk their lives and families in an uprising unless they know it can succeed."

"It'll never succeed unless people take risks!" said Layth. "Someone has to start! We've tried small uprisings before, but the people didn't follow, because they weren't ready. How many times do they have to disappoint us before you understand—"

"Maybe instead of leading and expecting them to follow," interrupted Charlotte, "you take the lead from the people and support them when a revolutionary moment emerges."

"That's a semantic difference," replied Layth. "Revolutions don't just *happen*. They need to be organized, they need—"

"What do you think I've been doing my whole life?" demanded Charlotte. And the two of them began to speak over one another, until Addy cut in.

"Enough!" she said sharply. "We're not going to solve every political difference tonight. We need to know, what can we realistically achieve?"

"I'll be honest," said Layth. "Our resistance network is in shambles. We've lost key safe houses. Our cells are in disarray. The Samizdata system we use to communicate is overwhelmed by spam. A little girl in an abandoned building showed me a fix, but reaching my organization is difficult."

"Can you access the YEA network?" asked Gwendolyn.

"The farm has a landline to Newbrook," said Adelaide. "Radio is dangerous."

"Actually," said Lieutenant Dumont, "we have comm equipment taken from Woodborough—our Authority prisoner," she added to Gwen. "But we don't know his passwords."

"If you've got gear, I've got logins," said Gwendolyn. "Thousands of passwords I've collected over the years."

"Huh," said Charlotte in surprise. "So, we could get a message to our people. Saying what?"

"We've been offered support via the water route," said Addy. "From an old friend, Simón."

"Can he send arms?" asked Layth. "Military support?"

"We don't need guns," said Charlotte. "We need to make Samizdata work again. To connect people at the grassroots so they realize they aren't alone."

"Our conversation was cut off," said Addy. "I can contact them via the water route."

"If Gwendolyn gets us on the YEA network," said Layth, "I can get you on that submarine in person."

"They said I could use something called a Samizdata override?"

Layth swore loudly, and Charlotte looked excited. "Why didn't you say you had an override token?" Layth asked. Addy looked confused. "It's a one-time-use root password. We can use it to send a message to the whole Samizdata network at once."

"Send instructions," added Charlotte, "from that little girl on how to clear the spam, make the network useful again. Remind people they aren't alone!"

"That's great," said Layth. "But how does that stop us from being overrun by YEA troops next week? You ask people to ride their bikes to the countryside and join the barricades?"

"No," said Gwendolyn hoarsely. "You go there."

Adelaide nodded. "Like the Weather Underground—you bring the war home," she said. Everyone looked at her. "Layth and Charlotte's network may be in shambles. But there are hundreds of people in our community militia. LT can raise a squad of volunteers and sneak into the city, attack YEA targets there. Destroy wireless jammers. Take over propaganda transmitters and send our own messages. Burn checkpoints. Liberate medical stockpiles. Help the resistance in the city, and simultaneously force the Authority to withdraw their troops from the countryside. Show people in the city that the fight isn't over, and give us on the frontier some breathing space." Addy could tell she was getting through to people; Layth and Charlotte were grinning, Lieutenant Dumont looked thoughtful, even Evelyn was engaged now.

"We'd need a cover story," said Lieutenant Dumont. "Disguises. I can get volunteers, especially with the right targets."

"There's only one target for me," said Charlotte. "Triage Administration."

"I'll guide you," said Evelyn. "I know the building plan. But my family needs to be rescued."

"We have sympathizers in the triage camps," said Layth. "Including a priest. If we can rescue him, it will help us win friends abroad."

"A few attacks are no good if the people don't know about them," said Charlotte.

"We can send transmissions from the Electronic Countermeasures building next to Triage Administration," said Layth.

"That's too late," Charlotte said. "People need time to reorient *before* things start blowing up."

"There's an Authority wireless station on the roof of my old building," said Evelyn. "We could go there first."

"The apartment block is empty," said Layth. "We could get in. But there's something we haven't discussed. If our goal is to stir up the hornet's nest, if we're going to sneak people in and rescue prisoners, troops from outside the city will flood back in. They'll shut every checkpoint in the city, and we'll be stuck right in the middle of it."

"The water route," said Evelyn. "That submarine is the size of a bus.

And there's a huge amount of room on the container ship. We could sneak hundreds out through the water route."

"Most imprisoned organizers in the triage camps won't want to leave the city," said Charlotte. "They'll want to get back to their families, their communities. To reignite the resistance the Authority has smothered."

They spoke late into the night, brainstorming, arguing, hammering out details. They summoned Sridharan, who had helped install pre-Authority computer networks, to walk them through technical problems. Carlos left to go to bed in the small hours, and Gwendolyn fell asleep on the couch. By dawn, when everyone else began to lose steam, they had the skeleton of a plan, had put things in motion.

As the sun rose Addy crawled into bed beside Carlos, who was just waking up for his morning chores.

"Did you figure it out?" he asked.

Addy nodded. "Rendezvous in disguise at an Authority train station in three days. Sneak into the city on their own rail cars."

Carlos sighed. "I wish they wouldn't do this. We can't afford to lose LT. And Charlotte has a small child to take care of."

Addy bit her lip. "Charlotte's not going. She wants to stay here, help train people, make connections. Gwendolyn's staying too; she's too sick to travel."

"That's wise," said Carlos, sounding relieved.

Addy swallowed. "I'm going." Carlos's eyes widened. "I need to go. To finish things I started a long time ago."

"It's suicide," Carlos said.

"Maybe," replied Addy. "But it's the only option we have left. And I don't want to have an argument about this."

Carlos didn't argue with her. He held her, and wept, long after the sun had risen.

Three days later, a train pulled out of a rural station northwest of the city. Layth was glad—if incredulous—that Felicity had managed to arrange a private car for the two dozen disguised community militia members. Even better, she had sent boxes of uniforms from a small-time YEA contractor named Chonthus Supplemental Security. Most of the uniforms barely fit—Evelyn and Adelaide looked particularly uncomfortable—but they would have to do. Lieutenant Dumont had found one that fit and looked suitably commanding.

While Layth was changing into his uniform, he found a folded zine in his old clothes—the yellowed zine he had tucked into his pocket at the Thistle's library a week earlier, just before he had rushed off to find Evelyn limping through the wilderness. Normally he would hide or destroy a piece of incriminating evidence like a political zine, which could ruin his cover. But there was a little time before they reached the first checkpoint on the edge of the city and transferred to a municipal subway train, so he put his feet up and leafed through it, reading about a thirty-year-old struggle to stop a petroleum depot.

He flipped past the page with the tiny group photo of Gwendolyn and the others in front of rusted tanks. And then he found a page with a full, crisp headshot of a woman in her forties shouting into a megaphone. "Gwendolyn Gibson addressing a rally," read the caption.

Layth's whole body stiffened. He looked at the photo again, then down at the caption to double-check, and then back up to the photograph. The photo was large and clear. The woman in it looked nothing like the woman he had pulled from the old folks' home and brought to the Thistle. Even with decades of aging, it was obviously not Gwendolyn Gibson he had spent the last week with.

Layth began to sweat slightly in the cool train car. *Who exactly gave us the intelligence to plan this raid into the city?* he thought to himself. *Who the fuck is the woman I left behind with Charlotte at the Thistle?*

20

2028

"I am Helen Kasym," she said, speaking into her video camera. "You're watching this because I'm dead."

She took a breath. "I died fighting the enemy that's destroying our planet. Call it capitalism, imperialism, colonialism—it's a monster by any name. This quarry is only a small part of that, but it's the part I can reach.

"I've been a community organizer since my teens. I realize now that if we ever start to win, those in power surveil us, frame people, put them in prison. Community organizing tools aren't enough.

"This isn't a suicide note. I'm already dead. I have lymphoma, a cancer caused by industrial pollutants. I want my death to *mean* something.

"Colleagues and friends, don't mourn my death. One death is a small thing if it can make a difference. People die in struggle: Civil rights workers in the South. Monks immolating themselves in Vietnam. The Disappeared in Argentina.

"I'm only giving up a few months of extra life. I've spent much more of my life on campaigns that failed. And I'd rather be decisive than . . . than to spend that time chained to a hospital bed in prison.

"So be brave, friends, be brave. And step up. I chose to turn quarry equipment into wreckage. You'll fight back in your own way. But you *must* fight if we are to win. Love and solidarity. Good luck, and good-bye."

She stopped recording and scheduled the video to post automatically at three in the morning. Within a day, she expected, a million people would see it.

She checked the radar weather. A massive torus of precipitation, the remnants of Hurricane Tau, was rolling north toward them. Right on schedule.

Helen slid away from her desk, shouldered a pack full of equipment, and walked to her back door. She left two personal letters—one to Apollo and one to Gwen. Helen paused in her doorway and heard the rumble of thunder in the distance. Then she turned off the lights and closed the door behind her.

⚞

The young blond man, Taavi, was obviously angry. Dee tried to deflect his anger with body language. She smiled, interlaced her fingers, and took on the small and unassuming posture she used to make people like Taavi ignore her.

"Where's the Revolutionary Council?" demanded Taavi. "I need to talk to them."

"You can't," said Dee, smiling apologetically. "Compartmentalization. Unfortunate, but necessary."

"Bullshit," said Taavi. "I can't talk to them because they don't exist."

Dee widened her eyes, an infinitesimal moment of surprise. She tried to hide it, but Taavi saw through her pretense.

"Taavi, they're at a hidden location—" began Dee, but Taavi cut her off.

"More bullshit," said Taavi angrily. "I think every cell in this network heard a different story about who's in charge. I know underground movements need secrets. I get that big networks need coordination. What I want to know—if you expect me to stay beyond the next thirty seconds—is who the fuck am I working for?"

Dee nodded thoughtfully. Then she stood from her seat, strode toward him and—though she was a foot shorter—looked him in the eye with great authority.

"You're working for me," she said.

⚞

It began to rain just as Helen pulled up the quarry's access road in her rental car. The winding gravel road was dark, surrounded by dense brush. Drops of cold autumn rain spattered her windshield.

She drove halfway up the entry road, stopping where it began to climb uphill. The timing of the weather was perfect, as she had anticipated. Surveillance drones would be grounded by the storm. But she had to ensure that any ground access would be delayed. At the bottom of the hill she made a five-point turn to park the car perpendicular to the narrow road's direction of travel. No police cars or security vehicles would be able to sneak around her.

Helen needed to be certain of this. She guessed it would take two uninterrupted hours to do her work. She had considered elaborate solutions: scattering caltrops across the roadway to puncture tires, driving sharpened rebar stakes into the gravel surface. But such approaches were technical and time-consuming. She needed simple solutions.

She popped the trunk, got out of the car, and pulled on a waterproof coat to shield herself from the pelting rain. From the car's trunk she removed a large, waterproof, yellow-and-black sign. It read, *Car contains motion-activated bomb. DO NOT APPROACH.* She affixed it to the side of the car. The sign was false, of course. But that didn't matter. By the time any responding security officers called in an out-of-town bomb squad to inspect the vehicle, her job would be finished.

Her second solution was cruder. She pulled several bags full of garbage from the trunk and stuffed them into a culvert just uphill of the car. At the rate rain was falling—there was already a steady stream passing through the culvert—the road would be flooding within twenty minutes, and washed out within an hour.

Helen closed the trunk and proceeded by foot up the final hill toward the quarry, carrying only her backpack. She was dressed warmly but had lost much of her body fat during the course of lymphoma treatment. She felt a chill seeping through her, even though she was still dry under layers of Gore-Tex and wool.

The quarry gate was a ten-foot-tall chain-link panel topped with barbed wire and illuminated by floodlights. Helen knew there were security cameras pointed at the gate, so before reaching it, she turned through the woods toward a dark section of fence. She drew bolt-cutters from her backpack and cut herself a vertical opening in the chain link.

She was through in less than a minute. She gave the portable buildings on the site—also illuminated by floodlights—a wide berth and headed for the newly delivered heavy equipment, which was parked in neat rows. In her backpack she carried a toolkit and lock-picking set she could use to break into the equipment. She had spent weeks practicing and become quite good at picking locks.

She approached her main target: an enormous yellow bulldozer two stories high. It was the largest piece of equipment in the lot. It was so large that a minivan could fit into its enormous scooping blade. A ladder was welded into the frame so she could climb up to the cab a story above. She climbed.

Crouching in the rain at the door, she reached into her backpack for her tools. The metal beneath her feet was slippery, so she grasped the door handle to stabilize herself.

The door latch clicked. She stared for a moment and pulled the door all the way open. She entered and sat on the dry chair. The cab smelled like the inside of a new car. The keys were in the ignition. She turned them, and the engine rumbled on.

Helen laughed.

Taavi stared at Dee, wide-eyed and wondering at the strangeness of the situation, at the young woman's sudden shift from mild-mannered courier to confident revolutionary. Then he laughed out loud.

"What?" he said. "You're joking."

She maintained steady eye contact, waiting for his grin to fade before she answered. "I'm dead serious."

Taavi worked his jaw, trying to think of something intelligent to say. "You're telling me I've been working for a teenaged girl?"

"You've been working for the future of this planet," she snapped back. "I'm just passing on orders."

"Sounds like you've been drafting orders," Taavi said. "Playing at courier. Bringing messages from the 'central committee' or whatever crap you've come up with. We've been going along assuming there were grown-ups somewhere in the chain of command. What exactly are your revolutionary qualifications?"

"I've never joined a cell formed by an agent provocateur, if that's what you're asking," said Dee.

Taavi jerked back as though stung. "Where do you get off telling me—"

"I saved your ass," she said. "Me, and Rebecca, and a few others who took real risks. Without me, you'd be in jail or dead. So don't lecture me. I don't have time for ageist crap. I stepped up and did what needed doing."

Taavi shook his head and sat down, placing his hands over his face for a moment before looking back up. "I don't get it. Were you, like, raised by Naxalites or something?"

Dee remained standing. "My family is Bangladeshi, not Indian. And no, I didn't grow up in the jungle with a bunch of guerrillas. You don't need to be a guerrilla to start a movement. Some people think you need AK-47s and combat fatigues. They're wrong."

"How did you do this? *Why* would you do this? When I was your age, I skipped class every day and got stoned."

Dee thought a moment, glancing toward the ceiling, releasing him from the continuous stare she had fixed him with since he confronted her. "Do you know the old folk tale about stone soup?" Taavi shook his head no. "A traveller comes to a village. He's hungry. People in the village are hungry, too. They have a little, but won't share.

"The traveller fills his pot with water from the well. He throws in a rock he brought with him—a stone. He knocks on a door in the village square. A woman answers, and the traveller says, 'I'm making stone soup, and you're welcome to have some, but it's a little bland, and it would be nice to give it more flavor.' The woman gives him an onion. He chops it up, puts it in the soup.

"The onion is boiling away in this pot in the town square, and a villager walks by and says, 'Oh, that smells good.' The traveller explains, 'It's stone soup! You're welcome to eat, but it could use something to give it a little color.' So the villager goes home and brings back some carrots, and together they chop them up and put them in the soup.

"Another villager walks by and she smells the delicious soup, sees how nice and orange it looks. The traveller tells her he's making stone soup, and it's very nice but could use something to thicken it. So that villager gets some potatoes and puts them in the soup."

Taavi raised his hands plaintively. "Why are you telling me this?"

Dee plowed on. "More villagers saw something happening in the square and came to look. The traveller convinced each of them that *they* should bring something to add. Soon there was an enormous pot of thick, delicious soup. All of the villagers ate together and shared with each other for the first time in a long while."

Dee paused to let Taavi consider this. Taavi just shook his head and said, "If you think telling me a children's story will convince me you're mature enough to—"

"It's simple. I did it because no one else was doing it. I'm not saying I have all the skills needed for revolution. I know I *don't*. That's *my* strength, what I understand that radicals often don't. You need other people and other skills. I brought them in, I brought them together. I started with nothing. I made stone soup into something real. I broke through the insularity that kept militants from cooperating. Sure, people got different versions of the details. But they're all getting the movement they yearn for."

Taavi had one more rhetorical barb to deploy. "Maybe so. My question is, how many of them know their movement is trafficking drugs? And how long would they stay if they found out?"

∾——

Helen's plan, like most good plans, was simple. She used the tools she had at her disposal—in this case, a hundred-ton bulldozer and a two-hundred-foot quarry cliff.

Helen shifted the bulldozer joltingly into gear; its metal tracks began to clank raucously. She switched on the headlights. She needed them; the hurricane's rain had become truly torrential. She zeroed in on the nearest piece of large machinery, a wheeled front-end loader used to lift huge buckets of gravel into trucks. She rammed the loader. The bulldozer shuddered for a moment from the impact and then began to creep forward again.

The wheeled loader slid loudly across wet gravel, its locked wheels gouging shallow trenches in the ground. Helen pushed implacably forward with the bulldozer until the loader suddenly shifted, its near end rotating up and away from her. And then it disappeared, falling downward. She hit the brakes. A few seconds later she heard a distant, echoing crash as the loader struck bottom. She grinned, shifted the bulldozer into reverse, and peered through the black sheets of rain to find her next target.

✦

Dee frowned at Taavi. He would, of course, bring up the drugs. There was no point in denying; she had hidden certain things from new recruits, but she couldn't lie outright about a fact he obviously knew. She made a mental note to talk to Rebecca about problems with compartmentalization.

"Nothing dangerous. Designer drugs," she responded. "We have excellent chemists. It was our best fundraising option. We can't rob banks. No money in it, and we aren't armed. But synthetic recreational drugs, sold to rich kids, make us a *lot* of money."

"So, we're profiting off addiction?"

Dee shook her head. "This is not heroin. It's not crack. They're party drugs for the kids of the elite. Don't pretend to be a puritan about this."

"I need to know this organization is ethical."

Dee shook her head again and spoke softly. "You already know more than you should. You've broken the network's compartmentalization. Your personal sense of moral comfort is not more important than the safety and security of the entire network. Your behavior is reckless and selfish. Tomorrow you'll have to face the consequences of—"

She was interrupted by a knock on the door as Natasha stuck her head through the crack. "Hey, guys, you've got to come see what's on TV!"

✦

Most of the machines were much smaller than the bulldozer; Helen shoved them over the edge with ease. There were a couple of regular pickup trucks parked near the portable buildings. They were so light, by comparison, that it felt like nothing at all to push them over the edge.

The empty prefab buildings were too brittle to move, so Helen simply smashed them with the dozer blade. She smeared them out across the gravel expanse and crushed the debris under her treads. There had been security cameras on the buildings. Anyone looking at the monitor would see her bearing down, see the cameras go dark. Were there even people on the other end of those cameras?

It didn't matter. She was almost finished. She thought she would feel more strongly at the end. That she would feel afraid. Or sad. She had felt both of those things with great intensity for months. Perhaps, now, her mental circuits for those feelings were burned out. She had felt a thrill of excitement when the first pieces of machinery were destroyed. But by the end she felt only cold, and tired, and ready for things to be over.

Only one piece of equipment remained, an enormous dump truck large enough to carry a small herd of cattle. She approached it carefully, lining up the blade of her bulldozer with the front grille of the truck as though she were locking horns with it. She made contact with the blade of the bulldozer and pushed.

Nothing happened.

The ground had become saturated by rainfall, the gravel churned into slippery mud by her repeated passes with the dozer. Her tracks turned, but the cyclopean dump truck did not move. Perhaps she could get it to slide with enough momentum. She backed up forty feet and then drove at full speed toward the truck. The sudden impact caused her knees to slam painfully into the control panel. Metal crunched loudly, the blade of the dozer biting deeply into the dump truck's radiator. But it worked. The truck began to slide slowly toward the abyss.

She kept the engine revving at full speed and closed her eyes, bowing her head slightly. There was a subtle tremor as the truck reached the edge. The cab of the dozer began to rotate, and she waited for the sense of free fall.

But the feeling did not come. The bulldozer tracks turned, but she felt no motion. Helen opened her eyes. The truck was snagged on the cliff edge, its undercarriage resting precariously on the lip, its back wheels hanging over the precipice. She shifted into reverse, trying to dislodge herself, but the blade of the dozer was caught in the mangled metal of the truck's grille, and the rotation of the truck on the cliff edge had lifted the front of the dozer slightly. She had no traction.

As she stared wide-eyed out the window she saw a minor avalanche. The cliff edge shed several tons of gravel and mud. The weight of the truck shifted, and slowly, it pulled Helen and the bulldozer toward the void.

～

The big TV above the counter—the one they used to display menus and daily specials—was playing CNN. At first, Taavi just watched the images: a satellite photo of a small cluster of islands in a deep blue sea, American fighter jets in flight. A naval officer, looking out to sea through binoculars. The news ticker read THREE HUNDRED DEAD ON GULF COAST IN AFTERMATH OF HURRICANE TAU. SITUATION ESCALATES AFTER CHINESE 'SCIENCE' TEAM LANDS ON DISPUTED ISLANDS.

The view cut to a news reporter on the deck of an aircraft carrier. The sky behind was a clear, bright blue. "I'm here on the deck of the USS Gerald R. Ford, less than a hundred kilometers from the disputed Senkaku Islands between China and Japan," she said. Taavi could see several other ships behind the reporter. "The mood is tense. China, Japan, and the United States have all scrambled fighter jets."

The image switched to a side-by-side shot of the reporter and a news anchor. "Jane, is China still insisting this is purely an issue of scientific research?" the anchor asked.

The field reporter nodded. "They're saying they've landed on the island to study the natural ecology. But given the enormous undersea oil and gas reserves in this area, each country claiming sovereignty over the islands has a lot to—" She was interrupted by the rising wail of a siren, loud even over the TV. She ducked as if startled, and the camera panned abruptly to the right.

One of the ships behind her erupted with smoke, and then that smoke became a column of flame as a missile emerged from the ship's deck and ascended rapidly into the sky.

The siren and rocket noise were cut off, and the news anchor spoke. "One of the American ships has launched a missile . . . we're not sure if that's a surface-to-air missile or what the target is." He continued to babble; the camera panned up and followed the missile as it disappeared into the heavens.

The bulldozer's tracks churned frenetically as the dozer slid toward the edge of the cliff. In the headlights, beyond the body of the dump truck, Helen saw only cold rain and darkness.

She was seized, finally, by feelings of alarm and a sudden, overpowering urge toward self-preservation. She opened the door and flung herself out of the cab and down eight feet to the ground. She rolled out of the impact and ran thirty feet, as fast as she could, away from the cliff edge. Then Helen stopped, and turned. What was she doing? Where was her resolve? Was she giving up so easily?

She took a tentative step back toward the bulldozer. Then another. And then, as she stared, the dozer slipped almost silently over the edge of the cliff. A long second passed, then another. The crash came, barely audible over the sound of the downpour around her. She walked slowly to the edge and looked down. One of the dozer's headlights, still lit, faintly illuminated the great heap of wreckage she had wrought. She felt a moment of pride.

Helen leaned forward slightly, into the wind, measuring her desire to finish what she had started. Preparing to hurl herself onto that mound of metal. To become its figurehead.

The wind pushed against her as she leaned out ten degrees, and then fifteen. She yelled wordlessly into the gale.

She closed her eyes. And stepped backward. Away from the edge.

In that moment, she realized she was not ready to die.

She did not know what to do. She had not planned for survival. She had planned only to avoid capture. Despite the fact that she had ruined a dozen security cameras, no police and no security had arrived.

Helen began walking back to the rent in the fence, toward the long driveway, toward the rental car. She would see Gwendolyn. Gwendolyn would know what to do.

~~~

Dee and Taavi spent a few more minutes watching the news with the others in the bookstore-café. Then Dee grabbed Taavi by the elbow and pulled him over to a quiet corner.

"Do you see what's happening on that screen?" she asked. "The same thing that always happens, but worse. Global elite are fighting each other over the dregs of this planet's resources. A little war is good for business. The people who will suffer are the same as always: The working class and poor people sent to be maimed and killed in war. The Indigenous and traditional people whose land and water will become a battlefield. The people made homeless by wars over fossil fuels and by the climate catastrophe those fuels will cause. Are you listening?" Taavi nodded.

Dee continued. "This is what we predicted. Resource wars. Between nuclear powers. We can stop it. We can do what the Weather Underground did and bring the war home. But not if we're too busy fighting one another. We can sit here and squabble, because that's our privilege, but it's people without privilege who will suffer if we don't act.

"Things are changing fast," she said. "We'll escalate. Our time frames will accelerate. This is the moment we've trained for. We don't have time for internal conflict. We need to focus. To work harder than ever before. All I need to know is: Are you in? Or out?"

Taavi set his jaw.

"I'm in."

Before Dee could say any more, her burner phone rang. She excused herself from Taavi and went into the back room to answer. "Hello?"

A synthesized voice came on when she picked up. "I'm sorry to call you directly but it's an emergency," the robotic voice told her.

"Who is this?"

"Your friend from the Lucky Lion," it answered after a brief pause. *Simón,* she realized. "I just learned through police botnet that some are very angry about escape of three people from Newbrook earlier this year. About end of tank farm."

"Obviously," she answered.

A pause, then: "They plan retribution. Egging on right-wing militia, giving money, promising immunity."

"To do what?"

"The veterinarian," said the voice. "Get to her."

Helen pulled up to Gwendolyn's farm, still driving the rental car, well after midnight. To her surprise the lights in the house were still on, as were several in the barn. She pulled up to the house, got out, walked to the porch. The rain had diminished—it was falling in a mist, now—but Helen felt chilled to the bone. She couldn't wait to lie on Gwen's couch, drink hot chocolate, and tell Gwen everything.

"Gwendolyn?" she called out cautiously. She didn't want a shotgun-toting Gwen to be spooked by the sight of a strange car. "It's me! Helen." There was no answer. She opened the front door, calling several times for Gwendolyn. No response. She must have gone out to the barn to check on the animals.

Helen walked across muddy ground to the barn and entered through a side door. But in the barn's main corridor she saw something shocking. A horse was sprawled in a stall opening. It was clearly dead, wedged awkwardly against the stall door. Its mane was caked with gore, a bloody wound in its head.

Helen continued walking with trepidation through the barn. The corridor seemed to recede into the distance before her. Two goats stared at her silently from the far corner of the next stall. An enormous sow peered out from beneath a blanket of straw.

"Gwen?" Helen called, her voice quiet and catching in her throat. "Gwendolyn?"

And in the last stall Helen found her, lying face up on the straw bedding, a halo of clotted blood encircling her ruined head.

21

2051

The subways had been taken for military use years earlier. The tracks allowed troops and supplies to move quickly across the city, avoiding the "epidemic risk" posed by mixing with crowds. When economic and energy crises sent the sprawling suburbs into disarray, the subway become the new backbone of the city.

Electrically powered by nuclear reactors, the subway system ensured the urban elite could move around quickly and comfortably in new first-class subway cars. They could pass swiftly underneath the burgeoning ghettos and work camps and walled-off quarantine zones above, never pausing at a checkpoint or risking exposure to disease. When the occasional uprising flared, troops could bypass hastily erected street barricades and avoid debris hurled from rooftops, emerging from the underworld to suppress unrest.

Addy hadn't ridden a subway for over a decade. During her time on the run, she avoided major cities and especially subways, which bristled with surveillance cameras hooked into facial recognition systems. The subway was vastly different from what she remembered. YEA guards replaced commuters. The fold-away seats used to accommodate wheelchairs were occupied by storage boxes and ammo crates. Each station was full of troops, sitting on backpacks and lawn chairs while waiting for their trains.

Some cars had been converted into private luxury coaches for the Authority's higher-ups. Others had their walls cut away, turning them into improvised flatbeds for freight that could be rapidly loaded and unloaded.

Addy shifted uncomfortably in her YEA uniform, adjusting her armbands. The uniform fit her poorly—it was for a much taller person—which made her feel even more out of place.

She did her best to blend in. The train car held two dozen resistance fighters, posing as Chonthus Supplemental Security officers. Chonthus was a small-time franchise that had gone bankrupt before X arranged the theft of surplus uniforms.

Addy stood next to Evelyn and Layth. Both were dressed as soldiers, their faces partly obscured by gear: goggles, green-and-black scarves, helmets and medical masks. It was necessary that they be fully disguised, since they could be recognized. But they would not be travelling with Adelaide. They would peel off from the main contingent and proceed to a high point for observation before sneaking into the triage camp where Sara and Sid were held.

Layth had looked uneasy during their trip. Addy assumed he was nervous about the mission. But as they neared the first of their stops, he leaned close: "How well do you know Gwendolyn?"

Addy drew on old memories. "She's been with the network for decades. Not exactly a raw recruit."

"But do you trust her?" Layth asked. "With our lives?" Addy gave a vague gesture toward the others, as if to say: *We're here, aren't we?* Layth persisted: "Can you vouch for her, personally, from back then?"

Addy snorted. "I didn't know her *personally.* Compartmentalization is—"

"—rule number one, I know, but are you sure she is who she—"

"You just spent a week with her. You tell me, do *you* trust her?" Addy asked. Layth worked his jaw back and forth, saying nothing. Addy sighed. "It's a simple risk matrix. Either she's trustworthy or not. Either we attack or not. If we don't attack, we lose the Thistle, whether she's trustworthy or not. If she's playing us, we lose either way. Our only option is to *act* as though she's trustworthy and attack, because that's the only outcome on the risk matrix that leads to victory."

"Even if it means we're on our way to a trap," said Layth.

"Even if," said Addy.

Over the next few stops, resistance members disembarked in threes and fours. They would walk to their rendezvous in groups too small to draw attention. As she disembarked, Addy turned to Layth. She opened her mouth as if to speak, but after a pause she closed it again and gave Layth a firm nod. The doors shut, and the train slid away.

—✔

Once Addy disembarked, only three resistance members remained: Layth, Evelyn, and Sridharan, who would serve as radio engineer and accompany them to Evelyn's old apartment block. Layth turned to Evelyn, who was sitting silently at the side of the train, staring out the window at subterranean walls as the train got back up to speed. "Are you okay?" he asked.

She shook her head slowly.

"Are you nervous?" he asked.

She shrugged.

"We shouldn't have any trouble with checkpoints in our uniforms," Layth said. Evelyn said nothing.

—✔

When Addy arrived at the rendezvous point, a boat was already waiting, bobbing gently by a ruined concrete pier in the shadow of an abandoned warehouse. The boat was a battered old canoe, its mottled gray paint matching the color of the water.

Resistance members assembled in the warehouse, standing or crouching on a cracked cement floor littered with splinters from wooden pallets. It reminded Addy of a poultry abattoir she had hidden out in years earlier, where the floor had been scattered with the feathers of chickens long-perished.

Lieutenant Dumont had arrived first and had the situation in hand, as usual. "The boat is here, and he's ready to go," said Lieutenant Dumont, "but there's only one guy."

"There were supposed to be two," said Addy. "Where's the other guy?"

"Late, apparently," said Lieutenant Dumont. "Old guy in the canoe says there are extra checkpoints today. Other guy might be delayed."

Addy checked her watch. Her stomach twisted uncomfortably. "I'd better go. We can't waste time."

"What help do you think they'll give us?"

Addy shrugged. "Maybe I'll come back with proper ordnance. Some explosives?"

"How about a cruise-missile strike on YEA headquarters and a platoon of Ecuadoran paratroopers?"

Addy smiled. "Sure. Why not?" She walked to the dock, toward the canoe. In the distance she saw the container ship, slowly rusting in the harbor.

—⚡

Evelyn's apartment had been so effectively stripped that she barely recognized it. Even the front door was gone. She knew her unit only from a set of holes in the drywall where Sid had once thrown a set of darts. Their personal possessions were gone. Evelyn knew items of value had been taken by soldiers, the rest left for salvage teams or thrown out the window to be burned as part of the neighborhood's sterilization. The enormous burn pile below, that's where their threadbare bedding would have gone. Their books, too—all ash.

Electrical fixtures, switches, and outlets were gone. Drywall was torn open in a hundred places to pull wiring. The stainless-steel sink was pulled from the kitchen counter, the doors from the cabinets. The old building's copper pipes had been removed carefully. Evelyn imagined all of it was already on a boat, heading to be sold overseas.

The glass patio doors of the balcony had been removed along with other windows. Perhaps they had been added to a brand-new greenhouse in some company town. The balcony's steel balustrade was gone, too; there was nothing to keep a person from walking straight through the apartment and over the edge.

The structure of the building was still there, and the brick façade. Evelyn knew those would be dismantled as soon as the Renewal Administration could allocate cranes and heavy machinery to break down the whole building from top to bottom. The city would devour itself.

Evelyn turned to Layth and Sridharan, who waited in the hallway. "Let's go," she said. They went to the stairwell that led to the roof.

—⚡

The view from the top of the apartment building was remarkable, Layth observed. The day was overcast, but the cloud ceiling was high, and he could see a great swath of the city below. To the far north lay the sprawl of the old suburbs, with many neighborhoods stripped for salvage and repurposed for urban pasture and garden allotments; to the east, industrial park after industrial park, most of them silent. Here was a warehouse missing its roof, there the stub of an old brick smokestack partially dismantled.

To the west were the skyscrapers of downtown, faintly wreathed in their usual halo of smoke. To the south, the docks and piers of the waterfront. Past the port he could see the harbor islands, and beyond them the scabrous hulk of the cargo ship.

"Is it safe to use my radio?" Layth asked Sridharan.

"Plenty of public safety traffic in the city," Sridharan answered without looking up from a tablet. "You'll blend in. But keep it short."

Layth raised his radio. "Chonthus one-four-three, radio check."

A moment's pause, then his radio crackled with Dumont's voice. "Read you five by five," she said.

"I'll get started," said Sridharan, popping open an access panel below the antennae.

"We'll keep watch," Layth replied. That would be his job alone. Evelyn sat on a folding chair left behind by YEA snipers who formerly occupied the roof. She stared vacantly toward the main triage camps. She'd barely slept in days.

Layth pointed his binoculars toward the cargo ship. He caught a glimpse of the canoe as it disappeared into a tear in the hull. He checked his watch and then turned to Sridharan.

"How's it going?" Layth asked.

"Fine," said the engineer, glancing at a tablet he had plugged in to the nest of wires connecting the antennae. "Good signal, open bandwidth on the correct channels. I can transmit a message to all Samizdata coins within ten kilometers. I just need—huh." He stared at his tablet. "That's weird."

"What?" asked Layth, his pulse quickening.

"They just changed jamming frequencies. Right now."

"Something you did?" asked Layth.

"No," said Sridharan. "The jamming system, all the cyberwarfare stuff is at the government complex near Triage Administration. It's weird they changed in the middle of the day, instead of at midnight as usual. Don't worry, I can still send the Samizdata broadcast, assuming Addy gave us the right code."

"Do it quick," said Layth, tensely. He knelt near the edge of the rooftop and panned across the city with his binoculars. At first, he saw nothing unusual. Then he checked the waterfront. A convoy of heavy green security trucks was driving up onto a government dock, towing long, canvas-wrapped machines.

The edge in his voice had drawn Evelyn out of her reverie. "What are those?" she asked.

Layth squinted at them. "I think those are howitzers. We need to warn them." He lifted his radio, but when he tried to use it got only the characteristic chirping and buzzing of a jammed frequency. "Fuck!"

—⚞

The canoe pulled up to the improvised dock in the dim ruins of the cargo ship; Addy paddled at the bow, having taken the place of the missing man.

As they coasted to a stop, Addy checked her watch for the seventh time in as many minutes. Archie noticed and spoke softly. "There's no rushing things. The submarine travels slow near the harbor so they don't attract attention. When they do get here, they'll only send a message at exactly the appointed time. That's hours from now. Why don't you go have a smoke or something?" Addy just fidgeted and tapped her foot anxiously on the aluminum of the canoe. "If it makes you feel better," Archie said, "we can get the Gertrude now."

Addy nearly leapt from her seat. "Let's go!"

The older man sighed, pulling himself onto the dock. Once they tied up and disembarked, the man produced a flashlight and started walking down one of the corridors. Addy followed him closely, racking her brain for military communications jargon. "So, Gertrude is a radio?"

"Radio doesn't go far underwater. The Gertrude transmits ultra-sound. We only use it at short distances. Talk too loud, *they'll* overhear."

They made their way to the cargo stack, ducking through jagged openings and climbing up makeshift ladders. They passed through a dozen dark containers that held only scattered bits of filthy cardboard and fragments of shipping pallet. Addy was hopelessly disoriented. "I'm surprised you keep it so far away," Addy said.

"If there were a raid, they'd never find it," Archie promised. "If those goons ever figure out what goes on here, they'll get lost searching the stack and either give up or sink the damned thing out of frustration!" He chuckled. Addy, feeling lost and slightly claustrophobic, didn't respond. They continued to wind through containers in a lopsided, upward spiral. Soon, Addy thought she could hear a distant whistling sound. Perhaps the growing wind of a coming storm. They must be at the top level.

"We're almost there," Archie told her. "We just have to—" he stopped abruptly as a rumbling sound reverberated through the container stack.

In the dark, Addy's eyes went wide. "Is the ship shifting?"

The older man listened for a moment. "We're firmly on a sandbar," he muttered. "There's no way—" He was interrupted again by a roar of tearing metal that echoed through the stack. Somewhere in the noise Addy recognized the sound of an explosion.

"We're under attack!" she said with certainty.

"That doesn't make any sense," Archie muttered, confused. Another explosion, this one so loud that Addy's ears rang and dust was stirred from the floor of the container.

"We've got to *move*," she yelled over the ringing in her ears, "Now!" He hustled for the next doorway, running with speed and suddenness that surprised her. There was another explosion, and then another. The floor of the container seemed to shift beneath her. Her legs felt numb with panic; her hands shook violently.

As he entered the next container a few meters ahead of her there was another explosion, this one so close that she nearly fell over from the concussion. The air was filled with dust and smoke; she could see spears of daylight from fresh holes in the container ceiling. The old man collapsed. She called, "Are you okay?" But there was no reply. She could not even hear her own voice, only a high-pitched buzzing.

She reached out to touch the man where he lay in front of her. Her hands on his torso felt wet and sticky. Archie turned to her, his face a dim blur in the gloom. He shone the flashlight on his own face, which was ashen gray. He shouted something; she read his lips: *Get the case!* He pressed the flashlight into her hand, and she glimpsed the red that coated her palms and his shirt, the fragments of metal dust and shrapnel across his body.

She took the flashlight and ran forward. She travelled the last three containers in an eyeblink. She tried to plan; when she got the device, would she be strong enough to drag him back? If he went unconscious, could she find her way back down to the canoe? She doubted it.

She ducked through a three-foot-high opening to reach the final container in the tunnel and shone the flashlight into that dead end.

The container was empty.

There was another dull explosion, and then two more in quick succession; she felt them but heard only buzzing. The container shifted beneath her feet, and she stumbled to hands and knees. She raised herself into a crouch and looked ahead once more with the flashlight, but there was nothing there.

It must be the wrong container. She turned to go, panicked and confused. But once she turned, she saw something: a shadow in the upper corner of the container, just above the entryway. And there it was: a hard-sided orange plastic container the size of a suitcase, strapped to the ceiling with bungee cord. She retrieved it and ducked through the single door into the previous container. She broke into a run, only two containers away from the old man.

She found herself, a moment later, facing daylight and cloudy skies. In front of her was a wide expanse of shipping-container tops. The containers that should have been on her level—including the one holding Archie—were all gone. They had been blown clear off the ship.

—✺

"My god," said Evelyn. "The ship!"

Layth put down the useless radio and raised his binoculars. Artillery had zeroed in on the vessel. Their barrage was knocking it to pieces. Many containers on the shoreward side had been crushed by the explosions, cratered or crumpled into scrap. Whole rows had been blasted from the top by a string of direct hits.

"We need to do something," said Evelyn. "Send a team to attack the artillery!"

Layth wanted to explain that, for a beleaguered insurgency, any successful operation was planned days in advance. That by the time he even got in contact with any combat team, the ship would be rubble. That everyone on board was doomed. But he just closed his eyes and said, "There's nothing we can do."

—⚡

Addy ran forward on rubbery knees. She needed to find a container she could enter, an access point to the interior of the stack, a safe way to descend. But it was clear she would not. The remaining containers on her level were ruined, everted flowers of jagged steel.

She slowed to a jog, still holding the heavy plastic case, barely able to think through the panic. Another artillery shell burst on some distant part of the ship. She felt tiny pricks on her skin as shrapnel cut into her.

The sharp pain cleared her head. She had two choices: She could stay on the exposed surface of the container stack, and in the next ten seconds a high-explosive artillery shell would hit close enough to kill her. Or she could jump. She turned toward the nearest edge, ran directly toward the incoming shells.

If she had slowed or stopped she might have looked down. Might have considered the horrifying distance from the top of the stack to the waves below. But she didn't slow. She didn't even jump when she reached the edge. She just kept running, legs pumping as she plunged into emptiness.

—⚡

Within minutes the cargo ship was obscured by dust and ash. Through the binoculars Layth could see eddies twist off the column of smoke as a circling drone inspected the wreckage, stirring up wisps with its rotors. Then he lowered his binoculars decisively.

"We're going," he said. "Now."

"Cauterization," Evelyn said, gesturing distantly. "They're trying to burn out the infection."

At first, Layth thought that she meant the ship. But as he followed Evelyn's gesture he saw several more columns of smoke rising above the city's usual haze. They seemed to emanate from quarantine zones.

Evelyn stared at the distant fires and shook herself. "Okay," she said, "we'll have to hurry."

Layth nodded. "We need to get to the warehouse rendezvous before the subway is shut down."

Evelyn gave him a confused look. "That's going backward. We need to liberate the triage camp."

Layth shook his head. "I'm sorry, Evelyn. That's not going to happen right now. We needed the submarine and the container ship to get people out. There's no way we can smuggle dozens of people out of the city undiscovered. The plan is scuttled. The Authority must have known."

Sridharan cleared his throat. Both Evelyn and Layth ignored him.

"Not good enough," said Evelyn. "We made a plan. That's why we're here."

"That plan won't work," said Layth. "We have to get back to the others. Regroup and reconsider our options." Sirens and alarms began to sound, their echoes growing and overlapping across the city.

"Hey, listen," began Sridharan.

"We can't retreat," said Evelyn. "You said it yourself. They're in confusion. Disarray. This is the perfect time to attack."

"They're on *alert*," answered Layth. "We can't do anything rash, can't draw attention to ourselves."

"Fine," said Evelyn. "I'll go to the triage camp myself. With my credentials I should be able to at least get my family and a few others out."

"That's ridiculous," said Layth. "You can barely walk, let alone stage a prison break."

"If I'd known my family was trapped there," Evelyn said, an accusatory edge entering her voice, "I never would've left the city."

"You two, we really need to move," said Sridharan.

"That's what we're discussing!" said Evelyn.

"Are you ready to send the Samizdata transmission?" asked Layth.

"That's the thing," said Sridharan, his voice tight. "I sent it two minutes ago."

Layth glanced up involuntarily, his eyes flicking across the sky in search of a meandering sniffer drone or an electronic countermeasures missile zeroed in on the antennae. Layth turned to face the tech directly. "Get your tools; we go now. *All* of us. Evelyn—" He turned back toward her, only to see her disappear through the door to the stairwell.

—⚊

The whole route between Evelyn's old apartment and the landfill triage camp had been zoned red: passage to authorized emergency personnel only. Limping along, Evelyn felt as though she had wandered backstage during a play. The façade of security theater was gone. Gone was the pretense of control and authority, the carefully staged checkpoints, the long and deliberately tedious queues. What Evelyn saw was barely repressed panic, the buzzing of wasps in a hive torn open.

Triage officers, soldiers, and riot police ran back and forth. Pickup trucks filled with them squealed down the street. Officers checked maps and yelled orders. And all of them ignored her. In the Yellow Zone, in her civilian clothes, she would be stared at, videoed, followed, frisked, interrogated. But here, in her ill-fitting uniform, one boot unlaced to accommodate her still-swollen ankle, they didn't even glance at her. She felt like a ghost haunting her old neighborhood.

Most soldiers and cops were going in the opposite direction. They were headed to the edges of their zone of control, to the Yellow Zone, toward unrest. Evelyn headed deeper into their territory. Into the hive.

Her mind was blurred with fatigue. Her constant fear for her family became background noise, a continuous psychological buzzing that drowned out her personal feelings from moment to moment. She tried to concentrate, to devise a plan. An emergency prisoner transfer, perhaps. Something off the books. With the confusion around her, it seemed plausible.

As she considered, a Homeland Patrol cruiser passed her going in the same direction. Then it stopped. She kept walking, trying to ignore it. "Hey!" a man called from the passenger side window. "Hey, get in!" She pretended not to hear as she passed the car. But the car crawled forward, keeping pace with her, as the security contractor in the front seat continued to call to her. "Hey, limpy! Are you deaf? We'll give you a ride."

She shook her head. "I can walk."

The car stopped, and the man got out and opened the back door for her. "Come on," he said. "We're going your way." She looked into the car. It had a transparent divider between the backseat and the front, like an old police car. "What's the problem?" the man asked.

Evelyn tried to smile normally. "Nothing," she said, knowing her own hesitation was cause for suspicion, that the more she delayed the stranger she seemed. Why wouldn't she take a ride from a fellow public safety officer, after all? She smiled again, vaguely, and got into the backseat.

The man closed the door behind her and climbed back into the front, and the car began to move.

—�li

Addy came to awareness in a dark place with still air. Her right shoulder and hand throbbed painfully. Her spine felt as though pins had been thrust into the gaps between each vertebra. Her lungs felt heavy, swollen, and wet. She coughed several times, loudly and involuntarily, each paroxysm worsening the pain in her spine.

She came up slightly on her left elbow—her good arm—and looked around. A confined and dimly lit space, long and narrow, lined with pipes and cables. Near her, a few bunks, unoccupied. Stowed beneath her bunk was a bundle of wet cloth—her phony uniform. Farther away, figures were huddled in hushed conversation. The whole place was perhaps the size of a city bus. The submarine, she realized.

"Hello!" she called, her voice hoarse. "Salud!"

One of the figures walked over and sat on the bunk opposite her. "You must try to rest and be quiet," he said in lightly accented English. His voice was oddly muted; she wondered if she had water trapped in her ears. "It's dangerous to make loud noises close to the city. There could be underwater microphones. You have been hurt, but you are safe now. Sleep, if you can."

"Where are we going?" she asked. "Señor . . ."

He held a finger to his lips as though she were speaking too loudly. "I am Juan. We go south," he said. "Away from the city. You'll get medical attention and be debriefed. Then you can go down to Latin America, if you wish. It's much nicer." He smiled, kindly. The man's clothing was clearly based on a uniform, but it was dark and conspicuously devoid of insignia, flags, or rank markers.

"I'll meet with Simón?" she asked.

"It is better to speak once we are safely away," Juan said and made as though to stand.

"Wait!" she said, too loudly, and he settled back down. "We can't leave. My allies in the city need help."

He shook his head, slowly and sadly. "We can't go back. Too dangerous. We were ordered to aid and retrieve you. We have done this. The escalation of hostilities makes it too dangerous to, how do you say, linger."

Addy sighed. She hadn't anticipated that she, *personally*, would be the object of Simón's assistance. "Other personnel need to be retrieved. High-ranking resistance members, political prisoners," she improvised. "If they remain, they will surely be killed."

Juan raised his eyebrows. "They are ready for pickup?"

"We'll have to send a team ashore," she said, "to meet them."

He looked sad. "I'm sorry, but we can't risk an invaluable military asset," he said, gesturing to the submarine around them, "for an unplanned rendezvous with foreign nationals. Our orders are to avoid—"

"They aren't foreign nationals," she interrupted. "There are international prisoners. A man—a priest—came to the city on this boat. He's in terrible danger." Addy was thankful that Charlotte and Layth had been forthcoming about the situation in the city.

"We lost contact with him. You know him to be alive?"

"Yes," she lied. "He is injured and in need of care."

The submariner nodded. "I will discuss it with the others. But understand we have limited room; we can only bring a few people aboard."

"How many?" she asked.

He looked thoughtful. "Six, at most."

"There's plenty of space!" Addy insisted. "You could fit fifty people."

"It's not a question of space. It's a question of oxygen. With a crew of ten we can stay submerged for a few days before the scrubbers are overwhelmed. But with sixty people"—he made a quick mental calculation—"our air would be unbreathable within an hour."

"So how far could you take us in that time?" she asked.

"Submerged we travel at eight knots, so perhaps fifteen kilometers. Still well within the city limits."

But maybe, Addy thought to herself, far enough.

—⁄

In the security cruiser's dashboard Evelyn saw a camera which pointed straight back. She avoided looking at it, gazing instead out the window at the streams of security contractors they passed.

"Chonthus, eh?" said the officer in the passenger seat. "Didn't know you were still in business. Where are you headed, girl?"

"Landfill reclamation camp," she said.

"Ooh," said the driver. "You're tough enough to handle the politicals, eh? Maybe you aren't as fresh as you look." Evelyn said nothing.

The radio crackled. "All Homeland units, be advised of riot underway at checkpoint in Yellow Fourteen. All temporary checkpoints, cease operations and regroup at hardened locations."

"Jesus Christ," said the driver. "They're pissed off in the Yellow Zone today. Armor probably screwed it up again."

"Fucking residents," said the other man. "Crybabies can't handle it if they don't get their chocolate rations." Evelyn knew that no one in the Yellow Zone got chocolate rations. The man in the passenger seat turned back to Evelyn. "Hey, girl! Give those politicals some extra whacks for me. Stirring up shit everywhere . . ."

Evelyn frowned. "I'm not a 'girl.'"

The man in the passenger seat looked confused for a moment, stared at her, and then flicked his eyes up and down her body before realizing what she meant. "Woohoo, Steve, we've got ourselves a feminist!" They both laughed.

The radio crackled again. "All units, repeat, all units. Do not enter the Yellow Zone in groups smaller than twenty. Smaller groups, relocate to the border and await reinforcements."

"Shiiiiit," said the driver.

The passenger was reading something on his handheld device and started laughing. "Check out this bulletin: immediate power-down in the Yellow Zone."

"That's just going to piss them off," said the driver.

"Nah," said the passenger. "No food, water, or heat? They'll chill out once the sun goes down, just like always," he replied. "But we'll get to crack some heads tonight, that's for damned sure."

"Make sure to leave a few heads intact," said the driver, "so the Authority has something to *clamp down on*." They chuckled like this was an old joke.

The cruiser almost sped past the main gate of the reclamation triage camp before the front passenger prompted the driver, who screeched to a halt just past the gate. Evelyn tried the handle of her door. It was locked.

The passenger laughed. "Now, now," he said. "You do know those things don't open from the inside?" He got out and opened the door for her with theatrical gallantry.

"Thanks," she said, without looking at him, and limped into the guardhouse at the camp gate.

Two Armor guards waited inside. They were well equipped, with newish-looking helmets and heads-up displays in their goggles. They sat in swivel chairs, looking bored.

"I need to get through," she said, gesturing to the door on the opposite side of the gatehouse, which led to the camp itself.

"We're on lockdown," said one of the guards, "because of the riots."

"You may be on lockdown," she said, with more authority than she felt, "but some of us still have jobs to do."

He rolled his eyes and then stood to walk toward the locked door. Suddenly he stopped. His digital goggles flickered, and the slack-jawed look left his face. He made sudden eye contact with Evelyn.

She barely had time to flinch before they tackled her.

—✒

When Layth reached the dockside rendezvous point, he felt exhausted. He had been up since well before dawn, and marching across half the city in poorly fitting uniform boots had only drained him further. As he entered the warehouse—alongside Sridharan, who could barely keep his eyes open—Layth expected to find the rest of the resisters in a state of emotional chaos, paralyzed by the loss of their plan and their friend, Addy.

This was not at all what he saw. His comrades had, in fact, set up some kind of improvised operations center, using rusted old spools as tables and chairs. About a dozen fighters had formed into a circle— the remainder no doubt active as sentries—where Dumont was conducting a strategy session on a pocket notepad.

"Glad you're okay," said Lieutenant Dumont. "When we lost contact, we assumed the worst."

"I wasn't sure you'd still be here," said Layth. "Do you know why the ship was attacked? And the jamming frequencies changed?"

Dumont shook her head. "I was hoping you knew. One of the canoe paddlers didn't show up today. Maybe he was captured and interrogated."

Layth nodded. "Maybe," he said. Or maybe they had been betrayed by the stranger who called herself Gwendolyn Gibson.

Dumont continued. "Your timing is good. We were about to have a vote. Did the transmission succeed?" Sridharan nodded. "Wait," asked Dumont, "where is Park?"

Layth frowned. "Evelyn went to find her family."

"Alone?" asked Lieutenant Dumont with surprise. "You let her go? If she gets captured and talks—"

Layth grunted in exasperation. "I couldn't stop her. What's the vote?"

"We've been brainstorming options," said Lieutenant Dumont.

"With the borders locked down, and without access to the cargo ship and submarine, we have no escape options. We have to decide whether to try to retreat, or go ahead with the attack without an exit route."

To attack without an exit plan went against every grain of Layth's training. But he was tired of retreating. And the thickening smoke in the air made it clear that few people in the city had escape options anymore.

"If we do attack, what then?" Layth asked.

"A two-pronged effort," said Lieutenant Dumont. "One attack to draw out the defenders of the administrative district into the quarantine zone. There we can snipe at them, use booby traps, distract their troops. With the other prong, attack the administrative district and destroy the jamming apparatus."

Layth's heart sank. It was a ridiculous plan. A dozen rural hunters and farmers—though they might know every creek and edible plant at home—could not possibly wage an urban guerrilla conflict on terrain completely unfamiliar to them. They would be surrounded and obliterated in minutes. And the other dozen—better suited to consensus discussion and milking goats—could not wage a head-on assault against a facility guarded by hundreds of well-armed security professionals who wouldn't hesitate to fire.

There was a sharp, short whistle. Everyone in the circle turned toward it, firearms in hand. A few moments later, one of their sentries appeared, leading a blindfolded woman whom Layth recognized immediately. He smiled.

"Felicity."

Evelyn's cell was brightly illuminated and walled with white tile. It reminded her of a 1950s hospital room. There was medical equipment mounted on one wall—an oxygen nozzle, or something, and a few empty brackets. On the ceiling, two security cameras were mounted at opposite corners, covered in protective housings.

Unlike in a hospital room, however, there was no bed and no white sheets. There was no toilet or bedpan. There was a concrete floor which sloped almost imperceptibly to a single drain in the corner. And in the middle of the floor was a steel eyebolt, to which Evelyn, via her handcuffs, was shackled.

They had taken her phony uniform, her helmet and boots, and everything else down to and including her underwear. They had given her a hospital gown that was too large and that gave no protection from the cold, abrasive concrete floor beneath her bare legs.

The room had no means of telling time, no windows. The gray steel door had one slot in it—presumably for food—and one small peephole through which the guards could look but that was useless to her. She could hear footfalls outside the door occasionally, and sometimes brief shouting or screams. But nothing in words she could understand.

She had no idea how much time she spent staring at the blindingly bright lights in the ceiling before she heard a key in the lock of her door. Reflexively, she tried to come to her feet. But the chain that held her wrists was too short and allowed her only to kneel.

The door swung open. Through it she saw a short section of hallway and other cell doors. A blue-gloved guard appeared in the doorway, wearing a disposable medical mask and tinted goggles. She couldn't see his eyes. He dragged in an aluminum chair and placed it near the door, just out of her reach. Then he stepped back out to the hall.

And in walked Director Justinian.

22

2028

When Helen found Gwen's body, time stopped. Helen slumped against a corner of the barn and stared for . . . minutes? Hours? She knew not how long.

Until a man with a shotgun appeared in the doorway of the barn. "There's a woman in here!" he called over his shoulder in a thick Scottish brogue. Then he walked toward her. They must have come back, she thought. The assassins, the murderers. In slow motion, she struggled to stand, reaching for the pitchfork beside Gwen's body.

"Are you hurt?" the man with the shotgun asked. He stared at her, then followed her gaze to the back stall. "Jesus!" he said, covering his mouth.

Two women entered the barn. One was armed with a rifle, checking each stall. The other was unarmed, with long black hair. Her eyes were locked on Helen.

"There's a woman in the stall, dead," said the shotgun man. "The veterinarian."

"Check out back," said the woman with long hair. She turned to Helen, speaking in rapid, soft tones. "My name is Rebecca. I'm here to help. We got warning that vigilantes were on their way. Are they still here?"

Helen shook her head slowly. "I don't . . . think so."

"Are you hurt, Helen?"

Helen blinked slowly. "How do you know who I am?"

Rebecca reached out, grasped Helen by the hand. "I'm a friend. Tell me what happened. We don't have much time." Rebecca turned to the woman with the rifle. "Find her a blanket; she's freezing."

"We should leave," the other woman said. "We're too late. And she's too dazed to tell us anything."

"She's had a traumatic event. Give her a moment." Rebecca turned back to Helen. "Can you tell me what happened tonight?"

And, haltingly, Helen began to tell her.

———

In the café's back room, CNN audible through the closed door, Dee opened her computer and checked her timelines. She had wanted another six months. Not everything was ready. Things would have to be rushed, K-Day moved forward. Cells would be strained to the breaking point. Some, she knew, would be lost. People might be injured, captured, overwhelmed by the pressure. It was terrible. But innumerably more people had it worse in slums and sweatshops and reservations. Which was why they fought.

Dee's visits to Rebecca and the action cell kept her sane. But she was too exposed with them. If a member of the cell were captured it could lead back to her. She would move to a safe house, run the operation from there with handpicked colleagues. Many of the people she had in mind were scattered, too far to be brought back in time. She would recruit locally to assemble a 'mission control' group for K-Day. The new logistics organizer Samantha was frighteningly intelligent and capable. Dee put her name at the top of a mental list.

Dee's phone buzzed. An encrypted text message appeared from Rebecca. "Tip correct. Too late for GG, she didn't make it." Dee swore aloud. "HK present. Sit v. complicated. Invite?" Dee swore several more times, loudly. The war had barely started, and a member of the organization was already dead, killed by goons in a proxy assassination.

Dee texted Rebecca back. "Your call."

———

Taavi lay in his bed, silent. Below, the TV blared as his comrades watched the news late into the night. He felt anxious and lonely. If he went to a comrade and asked for solace—a hug, a backrub, a cup of cocoa—they would offer it. But he thought only of Sam. Yearned to be with her. He wondered what would happen if he went back to that same mailbox where she had watched him. That same coffee shop. Did she live in that neighborhood?

In the distance, he heard sirens over the rain and wind. His heart thumped, as it did every time he heard sirens. He thought suddenly of Grandma Eevi, back in Finland, sleeping in her boots each night, waiting for the tsar's men to burst through her door. Taavi breathed deeply to calm himself as the sirens faded.

He knew it was impossible, with the acceleration of Kraken's plans, to see Samantha soon. He might not see her for a long time. So, he stared at the dark ceiling, and pictured her face.

⁓

Once Helen had recounted her story to Rebecca, where they sat on the couch in Gwen's living room, Rebecca was silent for several long moments. Then Rebecca asked, "So you've already published your confession?" Helen stared into the middle distance, thinking of how Gwen's body looked in the stall. Rebecca reached out and held Helen by the shoulders. Helen jumped. "I know you're tired and in pain. I need you to concentrate a few more minutes, then you can rest."

Helen checked her watch: 3:20 a.m. "I sent my confession. It's out of our hands."

"Helen, you need to make a choice," said Rebecca. "I can take you to safety. You can work with an organization that specializes in doing the kinds of things you did tonight. But if you come, your old life will be gone.

"Or we can leave without you. But from what you've told me about your cancer you'd probably spend the rest of your life in prison."

"I'd rather die," replied Helen.

"Come with me," said Rebecca. "For the time you have left we can protect you. You can work with us. I have a plan to deprive those murderers of their victory, keep them from using this tragedy to intimidate people."

The man with the shotgun cut in. "Rebecca, we don't have time for this. We've been here thirty minutes."

Rebecca raised a hand without looking away from Helen. "Can you decide?" she asked.

"Yes," replied Helen. "I decide yes. I'll come."

"Have you ever had any cavities?" asked Rebecca. "Any fillings?"

Helen felt befuddled. "Uh, no," she said, "not that I can remember."

"Okay," said Rebecca. "Give me your wallet and go wait in the car."

Helen handed Rebecca her wallet. As she walked out the door, she could hear Rebecca giving the man instructions. "The straw needs to be saturated with diesel. We leave in three minutes."

Helen got into the backseat of Rebecca's car. She shut the door, leaned her head against the window, and closed her eyes, feeling dizzy. A moment later, Rebecca opened the back door and sat next to Helen.

"Don't fall asleep," she said.

"I'm so tired," Helen said, slurring out the words.

"Stay awake," said Rebecca. She smelled of smoke. "Sleep is how the brain keeps memories. If you sleep now the trauma memories will be stronger. You need to stay awake, short-circuit the trauma mechanism."

"How do you know?" asked Helen.

Rebecca reached out and gently took Helen's hand. Helen leaned toward her, and Rebecca put an arm around Helen. "I know," Rebecca said.

Two minutes later, they pulled out of the driveway. Behind them, the barn was already consumed in flame.

✦

Dee called a meeting above the bookstore-café the morning after Hurricane Tau rolled through, the morning after missiles were fired near the Senkaku islands. Everyone had stayed up watching TV until high winds knocked out the power in early morning. The café was shut down, like much of the city, during the blackouts that followed.

Dee asked Taavi not to share her secret with the cell. She had no idea what he would do. But she couldn't expel him. She needed everyone.

Rebecca arrived at nine o'clock and rousted the crew. "Everyone up! Meeting in five." She had dark bags under her eyes.

Dee raised her eyebrows inquisitively: *How did it go?*

Rebecca frowned and shook her head once, tersely—*Not good—*

unwilling to say more with the others in earshot. A few minutes later, Dee and Rebecca were sitting with Taavi, William, Natasha, Shawna, Harrison, and Jennifer arrayed around them, drinking coffee and tea made on a gas stove. They looked sleepy and grim, save William, who fidgeted restlessly and appeared not to have slept at all.

"Am I the only one," asked Harrison, "in an apocalyptic mood this morning?" There were nods of agreement.

Dee spoke. "You all know me as a courier," she said. "Things have changed. I'm here now as a direct representative of the Revolutionary Council. They've sent me to explain why we are escalating sooner than we might have liked." She looked at Taavi. He didn't make eye contact.

"Isn't it obvious?" asked Shawna. "Worst hurricane season of all time. Global warming no one can ignore."

"A war starting over oil," said Natasha, "again. I'm just not clear whose side we're on."

"We're the side of the oppressed," said Rebecca. "I don't support the Chinese government. Fuck, they're more capitalist than the capitalists now. But the American military is the aggressor, and we can intervene here."

"It's more Euro-American colonialism in Asia," said Dee. "Going back to Vietnam, and the occupation of the Philippines after the Spanish-American War, and the Opium Wars before that. But we have the chance to nip this war in the bud."

"It makes no sense for the United States to do this now," said Natasha.

"They're desperate," replied Dee. "Losing the grip they've had on the Pacific Rim since World War Two. And they're threatened here by economic trouble and protest movements."

"Right," said Jennifer, "but they can't actually win a war with China. It's stupid to start one."

"Absolutely," agreed Rebecca. "But from an imperialist perspective it's perfect. War is great for the economy and bad for dissent. Most of you are too young to remember this, but after September Eleventh, social movements were terrified of seeming unpatriotic, so they got quiet. This war will accomplish the same."

"That's what war always does," added Harrison. "Feds used the same excuse to crack down on Wobblies and union organizers in World War One. Even the suffragists put themselves on pause."

"Exactly," said Rebecca. "Most people will cheer on the war, support the troops, all that. Liberals will silence themselves. The serious resisters will be quietly suppressed, COINTELPRO-style. Radical movements will be snuffed out for another five years, or ten years, or a generation."

"Our planet can't afford to wait ten years," Dee said. "Meanwhile, both the United States and China understand that the global resource pie is shrinking. There's only going to be room for one superpower in the world. They both want that spot, even if it means a devastating war."

"So we move up the timetable for K-Day—stop them now," said Rebecca, "before war is inevitable."

"To bring the war home," said Dee, "before it becomes a world war."

There was a long silence as members of the cell considered this. Some nodded in thoughtful agreement. William, twitching slightly, asked: "Shouldn't we meet directly with the Revolutionary Council about this?"

Taavi began to speak, and Dee held her breath. "It won't be possible to meet them," Taavi said. "Their identities are . . . too secret." He looked directly at Dee. "Probably we'll never meet them. Compartmentalization." Dee looked at Taavi, nodding slowly.

Harrison spoke up. "What does this mean for us?" he asked.

Rebecca spoke. "It means the end of cautious, piecemeal sabotage. The intelligence circuit has a list of targets across our region, ranked by priority: power grid infrastructure, transformers, natural gas lines, fiscal telecommunications. Action cells will attack them in a synchronized fashion, simultaneously."

"That will affect civilians, too," pointed out Shawna.

"So does war," said Rebecca. "So do gigantic greenhouse hurricanes."

"We'll focus on military infrastructure and climate criminals," Dee said, plowing forward. "Each cell will attack targets in quick succession—sometimes two actions in the same day—until the war is stopped or the cell can't go on."

"If anyone is caught, say nothing," reminded Rebecca, "not even your name or address. The rest of the cell will relocate to emergency redoubts for new missions."

"Even if some are captured," said Dee, "enough of the network should stay intact to finish the job."

Jennifer spoke: "We've always been told to be cautious—to plan escape first. But now you're telling us . . ." She trailed off.

"Be careful," said Rebecca, "but be bold. Quick and audacious attacks won't be perfect, but you're experienced revolutionaries now. Lightning attacks will happen faster than the police or military can respond. Meanwhile, the economy will be in disarray, hopefully stopping the war."

"And making a clear connection for the public," said Harrison, "among war, climate catastrophe, and the normal functioning of capitalism."

"And opening breathing room for our allies," said Dee, "whether those are people living in Asia on the Pacific Rim, peace activists here, or Indigenous organizers fighting against encroachment on their land."

Dee went quiet for a moment, thinking of what else to say. Several of the cell members began to murmur to one another. Dee looked at Rebecca and shrugged.

Rebecca rubbed the bags under her eyes and spoke slowly: "I want you to all turn to your comrades and reaffirm your commitment to our goals and to them. And if there's something you need to say to someone in your life—your family, a friend, a lover—go write them a letter."

After the meeting, Taavi went downstairs to the still-closed café to write a letter to his mother. Before he had finished, Rebecca came down and gave him an address and a unit number. "Urgent pickup from logistics," she said.

"What?" he asked. "I'm not a courier."

"They requested you," she said. "Their people are busy."

"*They requested me?*" he asked. "How did they—"

"Get going," she said, "it sounds urgent."

He grabbed a backpack and left, taking an indirect path for countersurveillance. When he got to the address, he found it was a motel, and that the number was for a room. He went up to the door and paused before he knocked. It was odd that he had been assigned this mission. Perhaps Dee, perturbed that he had discovered her secret, had sent him here so some armed goon with a Scottish accent could—

The door swung open to reveal Samantha in a bathrobe. She smiled. So did he. And then she pulled him into the room and closed the door.

Afterward, lying naked in the bed, Taavi turned to her. "This is dangerous, you know. Meeting again. Breaking the rules."

She stared up at the ceiling and then asked, "What would you do if you only had a few days to live?

He frowned. "Do you know something I don't?"

She faced him and grinned mischievously. "I know a lot of things you don't."

"I'm serious," he said.

She nodded soberly, ran a hand across his bare abdomen. "So am I."

He thought for a moment. "I would do something that matters in the big struggle. Something no one would forget. I would eat an enormous meal with all my friends; we'd feast and dance through the night. Then I would swim naked in a river at sunrise."

"You know it's fucking cold out there, right?" she asked.

"And," he said, "I would tell my mom, the people I care about, that I love them." She nodded, silently, and ran her fingers through his hair. "What about you?" he asked.

"Oh, I have quite a few decades left, thanks."

He mock-punched her in the arm. "No fair!" he said.

She pursed her lips. "I would go see a movie."

"Which one?" he asked.

"It doesn't matter. I've been too busy to see a movie for six months. I would smoke some pot and go to the theater. Maybe a comedy. I would eat a lot of popcorn. With real butter, of course," she added.

"Of course!" he replied.

"And then," she said, her eyes turning flinty, "I would track down Corben and shoot him in the head."

Taavi's eyes widened. "That's pretty dark," he said.

"Turn on the news," she answered, again staring at the ceiling. "We live in a dark world." She paused, as though considering something. "There's a cell in the intelligence circuit," she began, "whose job is to mass-produce action plans. They have binders full—well, encrypted disks full. They review every infrastructure target and draw up plans to shut it down with everything from protest to sabotage. They've been doing it for years, cribbing suggestions from official vulnerability reports."

"How do you know this?" Taavi asked.

"There are literally thousands of these plans," she said, "ranked by impact, sorted by the tactics required to shut them down, listing coordinated actions to cause the most disruption. Some are underground tactics, some aboveground mobilizations, some are both. I got drafted to check plans, to make sure they're up-to-date. I'm pretty sure the leadership—mostly Dee, from what you've said—wants to run through as many actions as they can in the next week."

"Hmm," Taavi said in response. Then he rose up on his elbows and stroked her cheek gently. "I love you," he said.

"I know," she replied. Then she added: "I love you, too."

⚡

Dee's suburban safe house was not far from a commuter rail station. Dee had considered using one of the rural safe houses, but they were visited infrequently. She didn't want to draw neighbors' attention with a sudden burst of traffic. Nor did she want to get stuck downtown in a traffic disruption or a blackout—both of which she might *cause* in the coming days. So, the suburban safe house—with its back entrance through a park and proximity to mass transit that would help guests avoid being tailed—was a suitable choice for K-Day mission control. And since no one lived there, unlike most other safe houses, there was room to convene her team.

They had leased the house a year earlier; the logistics circuit wanted its basement as a chemistry lab. That lab had been scaled up and relocated, leaving the house available for Dee. Few people knew the location; even Rebecca did not.

When Dee arrived, entering through the back door, the house was empty. There were crates of nonperishable food and snacks in the kitchen. Dee went into the unfinished basement. The windows were covered. There was no evidence of the chemistry lab; the place had been stripped clean. She went upstairs to the den. There were blackout blinds on the windows, a ridiculously large high-definition television, chairs and couches that looked comfortable. The room would do. Soon the others would arrive with flip-chart paper and markers and their own encrypted laptops. She would have them make coffee and drag a table into the room with the TV.

Meanwhile, she connected her computer to the enormous television and displayed a map from the intelligence circuit, A multilayered composite of the major industrial and military infrastructure in North America.

She checked her travel clock. The doomsday counter ticked downward. Their preliminary actions would begin in mere hours.

Dee realized, suddenly, that she was supposed to visit her father that morning but had forgotten entirely. She cursed aloud. She wanted to call his doctor to check in but had left her personal phone at home so she couldn't be tracked with it. It was too risky to use her burner phone. He wouldn't be aware of her absence. It would have to wait.

As the sun set, Taavi and his cellmate Natasha stood in the cover of trees on a low ridge, looking over an industrial park bathed in pink light. They were dressed in dark camouflage. They were hunters, went their cover story. Taavi thought they looked scrawny for hunters, but hopefully they wouldn't see anyone who cared. The cover story was important, though, because it explained the shotguns they carried.

The cell will split into three, Rebecca had explained at the rushed briefing that morning. *Two groups will pose as hunters. Natasha with*

Taavi, Shawna with Harrison. They'll approach from the west and the north at sunset.

Taavi checked his watch. "It's time," he said. They loaded their shotguns and walked along the ridge, Taavi checking his handheld GPS.

The industrial park hosts several manufacturers. Our target is the AMMOCOR factory. They make bullets for police and the military. They got rich during the Iraq War and Afghanistan. Now that things are heating up in the Pacific, the factory runs triple shifts to stockpile munitions. And the whole industrial park is expanding under IRI.

Forest gave way to low grasses. In the dimming light, Taavi could see the looming angular frameworks of steel towers and electrical lines. The light of the setting sun glinted off shining bolts and glass insulators. He paused to watch for warning signs—police cars, security trucks, the flash of binoculars in the distance.

"Tank *farms*," said Natasha. "Industrial *parks*. Bullshit. The whole world is upside down."

There is one access road and two power lines feeding the site. The armed teams will move to the vulnerable points on those power lines. At exactly 6:03, they'll act simultaneously.

Taavi clicked off the safety on his shotgun and raised it to draw a bead on the nearest glass insulator, while Natasha kept watch. He had been given little firearms training—"not in our tactical repertoire," Rebecca had explained months earlier—but he had used shotguns twice before and was assured they were easy to aim because of the wide spray of pellets they fired. He exhaled slowly as he aimed, listened to the soft sounds of wind rustling fall leaves. A distant gunshot echoed across the hills as the other team fired. He pulled the trigger.

The kickback felt like someone had punched him in the shoulder. The noise was worse; his ears rang, drowning out the rustling leaves. "Fuck!" he said. "I forgot my earplugs."

"You hit the insulator," Natasha replied, offering a pair of earplugs and shifting from foot to foot anxiously. "Let's get this done."

"Keep watch," said Taavi. He stuffed in the earplugs and racked a new shell into the chamber. With gloved hands, Natasha picked up the empty cartridge that was ejected, tucking it into a bag. Taavi pointed at the next insulator and fired.

While the armed pairs are at work, the third pair—Jennifer and William—will drive up the main access road to the parking lot. They'll turn around, and as they leave they'll scatter caltrops across the road. Any utilities trucks or police who respond will have their tires punctured as they arrive.

Taavi fired four more shots, hitting three more insulators. With each hit, an electrical line sagged lower. "Just one more," his companion encouraged. Taavi sweated profusely. He fired again, hitting his fifth insulator. With a bright blue flash, the power line struck the steel of the tower. "Awesome!" exclaimed Natasha. "It's shorted out."

Taavi looked toward the industrial park in the twilight. He had a moment's glimpse of floodlights and lit windows, then the whole thing went dark. "Great," he said. "Let's get the fuck out of here."

꜊

When Helen awoke, the sun's light shone pink through curtains in a strange room. She had a millisecond of comfort in a soft warm bed before she remembered what had happened. The flood of imagery was debilitating. She had a sudden and powerful urge to vomit. She stumbled into the hallway to find a bathroom, failed, and dry-heaved into a wastepaper basket.

She wiped her mouth with the sleeve of the soft pajama shirt she wore, a shirt she did not recognize. Rebecca and the other two had brought her to this cabin after Gwen had been murdered. They kept her up until after dawn, speaking in calm voices, giving her food and hot chocolate, until she fell asleep sitting up. Helen remembered something about disrupting traumatic-memory formation. They had succeeded, at least, in disrupting her memories—she had no idea where she was, how much time had passed.

She looked out the nearest window at the sky. For a moment, she thought it was sunrise; the horizon was bright with the sun just beneath it. But the colors were bloody red, and there was no frost on the forest floor. Sunset, she decided.

She went downstairs. The cabin was quiet, though she could hear someone trying to start an engine not far away. A generator, perhaps?

Helen filled a glass of water from the tap and drank it. She felt eerily calm. She thought of another cabin she had visited as a child, years ago. A violent fall storm had whipped up the lake into a froth. Her parents had tucked her in to the sound of howling wind and breaking branches. When she had risen in the morning, before anyone else, she looked out the windows to see a cold snap had set in. The lake had frozen. White-tops had turned to dark ice, like glass.

Helen filled a kettle and put it on the propane stove. The cabin was warm, but her fingers were numb and clumsy; it took a few tries to get the stove lit. She turned to the counter. There was a box of individually sealed hot beverage packets: tea bags, coffee, and—she hoped—more hot chocolate. She flipped through them with clumsy fingers. It was poorly organized, jumbled together. She kept pulling out foil packets she thought would be hot chocolate, but each turned out to be a different kind of freeze-dried instant coffee. At first it was mildly irritating. But as it happened again and again, she grew incensed.

She lifted the box and hurled it across the room. "Fuck!" she yelled. Little packets scattered everywhere: onto the couch, behind bookshelves, across the floor, and under a cabinet holding the television.

The television. Rebecca had told her to avoid TV, to avoid the radio, to avoid newspapers. That she had to rest and heal, and that the news would upset her.

Helen crossed the room and turned on the TV. She tried a few channels before she found the news. Once she found it, she jerked back from the TV, because she was looking at her own gaunt face.

". . . left a detailed suicide video," a voiceover was saying, "explaining her reasons for destroying quarry equipment."

They played snippets of the video she had sent out. "I want my death to *mean* something . . . Don't mourn my death. One death is a small thing if it can make a difference."

There was a brief drone shot of the quarry, showing heaps of ruined trucks and bulldozers piled on one another, then a cut to a police officer. "We believe that the suspect, Helen Kasym, destroyed the machinery before proceeding to the farm and killing herself. It's not clear whether she set the barn on fire on purpose or if that was an accident."

Then a reporter in a newsroom: "Now, this may be slightly confusing, but the farm where Helen Kasym's body was found is the *same* farm where Gwendolyn Gibson lives—or where she *lived*, rather, before she went on the run a few days ago because of death threats." Helen furrowed her brow in confusion.

"Let me get this straight," said the news anchor. "Gwen Gibson, who appeared on this program a number of times, received death threats and went into hiding."

"That's right," said the reporter.

"After she left, Helen Kasym pushed equipment into a quarry, went to Gibson's farm, and killed herself?"

"That's the narrative the police are working with," said the reporter. "Her rental car and personal effects were found at the scene. Due to the intensity of the blaze, we may never have a cause of death for Kasym."

"Both women have been high-profile activists, and two press conferences were held today by their colleagues in Newbrook." The first press conference showed Leon, Philip Justinian, and the police chief decrying Helen's actions. Leon apologized to the quarry company on behalf of Friends of the Watershed, and Justinian—who was wearing a suit—explained that the Industrial Revitalization Initiative included funding for wind turbines, making the late Helen Kasym's actions especially counterproductive.

Then the image cut to a second press conference at which she recognized Apollo, Teresa, and Elijah. Apollo was openly weeping. She reached out, abruptly, and turned the television off.

Behind her, the kettle began to whimper, and then to scream.

~

CNN had played all day at the mission-control safe house, with coverage increasingly dominated by Kraken.

"So far, it's been a complete success," recounted Samantha. "Eight direct actions so far. Five military contractors had to stop operations, and three oil companies. No injuries among civilians or among our people."

"Cell Fourteen had a run-in with police," added Security. To protect identities, those at mission control were addressed by their roles rather than their names. "A traffic stop near a fracking targets. But no arrests."

"Good," said Dee, a takeout box of fried rice cooling on the table in front of her. "What's the public response, Media?"

Media looked up from her laptop, tugging absentmindedly at her long, curly hair. "Social media response is mixed—no surprise. Some are calling it terrorism. Some are blaming Chinese people for sabotage."

"We'll need to respond," said Dee. "Make a note for the next communiqué: 'We're in solidarity with Asian peoples, but our ethnicity is diverse,' or something like that." Media tapped at her keyboard.

"What about other social movements?"

There was a pause at the table. Media began: "They're not exactly stepping up to the plate . . ."

Intel jumped in. "They haven't all been critical."

Dee asked, "They're holding their tongues?"

Intel shook his head. "Not necessarily. The organizations who respond negatively are better established, more conservative. They have the money for full-time staff and PR people. The grassroots groups, the radicals, aren't issuing press releases yet."

"Okay," said Dee, "but they'll be on social media."

"Some are posting in support," said Media. "Cautiously. They know they're being watched. With the political climate . . ."

"Fine," said Dee, surprised at the disappointment she felt that there had not yet been a groundswell of activist support. "What are the next targets on the docket?" She turned to the whiteboard where targets, locations, and cells were listed and color coded. She pointed her finger to one near the top. "Coal plant. Running on coal from mountaintop removal. Perfect. Let's shut that down."

～

"We have the go-ahead for our next action," Rebecca told Taavi and the other members of his cell. "You've got twelve hours to study the plans and prepare." She placed a map on the coffee table of their apartment above the café. "Coal-fired power plant. Details here."

Taavi picked up a sheet of paper: an intelligence report on the plant, evaluating each major component and options for disabling it—not just bombs and wire cutters but aboveground protests as well.

"Who makes these?" Taavi asked, waving the sheet.

"Intel circuit," said Rebecca. "Now, there are two premission tasks to carry out—"

"It has typos in it," said Taavi.

Rebecca paused, looking up at Taavi. Then she shrugged. "It was a rush job. We don't have a copy editor. Okay, this mission has six roles. One person goes to the dead drop at seven a.m. tomorrow, picks up the vehicle. The explosives and timers are already assembled in the van. Two people will go tonight for a final recon. Where's William?"

There was an awkward series of glances around the table. "William is ill today," said Natasha.

"With what? Flu? Food poisoning?" asked Rebecca.

"Severe nerves," replied Taavi. "Anxiety. He . . . took some tranquilizers this morning and he's been sleeping all day."

Rebecca swore under her breath. "That gives us only five people." She checked her watch and looked resigned. "Okay, I'll join you. Everyone, memorize these plans and be ready to review them at breakfast tomorrow."

～

"Shouldn't we talk to the council about this?" Security asked, scratching the fresh stubble on his face. "Approving or denying plans?" Samantha gave Dee an inquisitive look.

"The Revolutionary Council has preapproved all these actions," replied Dee, her face calm and blank. "It's our job to carry them out as we see fit."

"Okay," said Intel, "but we don't *have* to do them all right now."

Dee looked puzzled. "We don't *have* to do anything. We *chose* to be part of this organization, which exists to carry out direct actions."

"Of course," said Security. "I'm just saying, K-Day is going well—

no arrests, all actions reasonably successful. It's almost miraculous how well things are going. Maybe we shouldn't push it."

"What," said Dee, "you want to quit while we're ahead?"

"I'm just wondering," said Security, "if this is a good time to pause and learn from our experiences. A lot of these recruits are very fresh."

Security glanced at Recruitment, who nodded in agreement and added: "If we want to *maintain* the same rate of success . . ."

Dee, stared at them evenly. Security changed tack. "Look, I've been an activist a long time. Probably twenty years longer than you. I'm not trying to be competitive—I respect your commitment to the movement and your connections—I'm just offering my perspective. I would be proud to have been part of *any one* of these actions in my career." He gazed at her, not as a challenge, but to gauge her level of agreement. "And I'd much rather be proud *outside* of prison than *inside*. You could say I'm satisfied with my current cellmates."

There were a few chuckles, but people looked serious, and several nodded, including Intel. Intel added, "Maybe now isn't the best time to escalate further. Our people are tired. We've taken the best and easiest targets. The risk rises dramatically from here."

Logistics spoke up. "We're low on vital supplies. Caltrops, for example. They're hard to transport and take forever to make."

"We can get by without caltrops," said Dee.

"Explosives, too," persisted Logistics. "We need time to solder electronics, check timers, assemble detonators. If we escalate we might not keep up."

Dee held up her travel clock so they could all see it. The doomsday clock was ticking down from six months. Dee spoke with as much authority as she could muster. "We'll improvise. Resisters always improvise. We can't back down. We escalate until we win. That's our job. If you don't want that job any more, fine; you can resign. But the council wants this, and if you don't, someone else will step up to take your place at mission control." Security looked away. Several others at the table looked down, awkwardly.

Samantha surprised herself by speaking up. "I think this is exactly the time to escalate," she said. The rest of the table looked at her. "When have we ever had an organization like this? When will we have one again if we quit now? Remember why we're here. Remember how many lives will be lost if war in the Pacific goes ahead. Consider how many will die if we don't stop climate catastrophe. You talk as if we have a *choice* of when to act. The choice isn't *when*, it's *whether*. We act now—or never."

There was another pause. "It would be good," said Intel, "to bring this problem to the Revolutionary Council and get their opinion."

Dee suppressed the urge to roll her eyes. "I'll do that tonight," she promised.

The scale of the coal plant was outrageous to Taavi. He had closely—albeit briefly—studied its maps and plans, but its size had not been fully clear. The coal stockpile, which looked large in the aerial photographs, was in person a mindboggling expanse of solid greenhouse gases. The smokestacks, foreshortened stubs on Google Earth, towered impressively in the red light of the setting sun; the electrical substation, a small fenced enclosure on the map, had the same footprint as his high school. Each of the cylindrical transformers—their true targets—was as large as his mother's minivan.

Beside him, lying prone on the crest of a low hill a few hundred meters from the plant, Rebecca lowered her binoculars and checked the time on the travel alarm clock she always carried. "Five minutes to sunset," she said, a cigarette smoldering between her lips. "Almost time to go. Ready?"

Taavi laughed. His stomach churned with anxiety. "Operationally or emotionally?"

She gave him a look that was both sympathetic and diagnostic. "Either. Both."

He shrugged. "Yes and no. I'll go ahead with things, but I'm hoping for a long break after this."

She smiled faintly. "I can't promise that," she said. "But I can tell you, once we're done here, I'm going to have a truly spectacular nap." She checked her clock again and threw her cigarette into the wet, yellow grass. "Thirty seconds. Back to the van."

Their vehicle, which Taavi had picked up at a dead drop that morning, was a nondescript white utility van. Rebecca was the driver, and Taavi sat beside her. In the back were four other members of the cell—Harrison, Jennifer, Shawna, and Natasha—crowded among four very powerful explosive devices. Each device was bolted to a two-wheeled delivery dolly and cargo-strapped to the walls of the van. There were no markings except a single yellow sticker on each, which read, *Handle gently and with extreme care.* Taavi knew without being told—from the sturdy look of the transformers and the implied energy needed to destroy them—that an accident with the bombs would vaporize the van and everyone in it.

Rebecca started the van and drove the short distance to the gravel road that entered the transformer station. This road avoided the gate-house and security guards at the plant's main entry.

They pulled up to the gate of the tall barbed-wire fence that surrounded the substation. Taavi glanced around. His heart thumped steadily in his chest. Still no sign of trouble. In the back of the van he heard an abortive gagging sound, as though someone was about to vomit. "Sorry," came Jennifer's voice. "I get carsick." Taavi knew exactly how she felt.

Rebecca put the van into park, leaving the engine running, and they both got out. They wanted to delay bringing anyone out of the back of the van, to put off as long as possible unusual behavior—like a contractor's cargo van with too many people in it. So, it was Taavi who produced bolt cutters from inside his jacket and Rebecca who stood casually between him and the main plant, obscuring the view as he cut through the chain that held the gate closed.

Rebecca got back in the van and drove into the fenced lot as Taavi pushed the gate open. His fingers trembled slightly against the cool metal. He shivered in the fading light of the late fall evening. The sun was totally beneath the horizon; they had only fifteen minutes of twilight left.

The van came to a stop in the center of the substation, and everyone burst into action. Each of the four people in the back was responsible for placing a single device. It was Taavi's job to keep watch for trouble and Rebecca's job to keep time. He stood by the gate and panned his head continuously back and forth, checking his own watch compulsively. Within thirty seconds, his cellmates had unlatched the first device and carefully slid it out of the van so that the wheels touched the ground. Taavi panned left again. The horizon was clear; there were no vehicle lights on in the distant parking lot of the plant.

"Pssst!" Rebecca beckoned Taavi over to where Natasha was struggling to roll the heavy device over loose, wet gravel. "You help. I'll keep watch."

Taavi and Natasha dragged the device over to the first transformer. "Don't drop it," Taavi said. Natasha chuckled nervously. "I wasn't kidding," said Taavi. They parked it against the bottom of the transformer. Taavi involuntarily winced as Natasha reached out and flicked the switch that would arm the device. But there was no explosion. A single red LED illuminated. That was all.

Taavi checked his watch. Two and a half minutes had passed since they parked the van. Only one device was armed, and another just being rolled up to its transformer, because it was taking two people to move the bombs over gravel. The action plan called for them to depart after only three minutes. "Next one, quick," Taavi said to Natasha.

Taavi and Natasha were unloading the fourth device when Rebecca cried out raggedly. "Cops! Quick! Everyone in the van!" The pair placing the third device ran toward the van. Taavi looked and could see two police cars, lights flashing, driving directly toward them up the gravel road. "Fuck!" he said. He pulled on the fourth device, which was halfway out of the van and resting on the rear bumper. "It's stuck!"

The van's engine started and roared. Rebecca looked back from the driver's seat. "It's stuck on that cargo strap!" she said. A strap was hooked onto the bomb's handle, keeping it attached to the van. Shawna vaulted into the back of the van and unhooked it. Taavi pulled as hard as he could, and the bomb rolled out onto the ground with a loud crack. Everyone looked at it in horror, but it did not explode. "Get in, now!" roared Rebecca.

Everyone else was already in the back. Taavi flicked the switch to arm the final bomb and leapt into the van, which was already beginning to accelerate forward. Many hands grasped his arms and shirt and pulled him in. Rebecca swerved through the gate, and the back door slammed shut.

"Taavi!" commanded Rebecca, "we need a distraction to escape. Get the detonator!"

Taavi reached for the remote detonator in the box between the front seats. Shawna spoke up: "We're supposed to be five hundred meters away!" Taavi found the remote detonator and pulled it out of the box. Lifting it up, he could see through the windshield that the police had stopped a short distance up the driveway from them, blocking their path, standing behind open car doors with guns drawn.

"We won't get far without a diversion," said Rebecca. "Everybody lie down!" She gunned the engine and accelerated toward the police. "Taavi, are you ready?"

He flipped on the power switch beside the detonator's antenna. A green LED glowed. There was only one button, a button with a safety cover he slid to the side. "Ready," he said.

Before Rebecca could answer, the windshield began to fracture. A dozen spiderweb holes appeared in quick succession. Taavi felt sharp bites in his neck and chest. The van swerved off the road and tilted to one side.

Taavi pressed the button.

23

2051

Justinian looked pale, dapper, and very much alive as he stood in the stark light of Evelyn's cell. In his right hand he held a cane of polished ebony, which he leaned on only slightly. His left arm was in a sling— not a temporary sling of white cloth but one stitched from dark linen. It looked tailored. Permanent.

He noticed her staring at it. "Recognize your handiwork?" he asked. "Nearly complete paralysis of the limb, I'm afraid. They tell me your"—he winced in recollection—"little firecracker severed my brachial plexus. Oh, and my subclavian artery. Which . . . well, you remember all the blood." He reached out with his cane, placed its point against her chest just below her left collar bone. "You aimed *high*. You should have aimed here." He slid his cane down to point at her heart; she looked away with a sneer on her face. "You closet liberals, you bleeding hearts, never could get the job done. You lack killer instinct. At the vital moment, you pull your punches. You compromise when you should be decisive."

A guard placed a chair for Justinian, who sat without taking his eyes off Evelyn. "I hope you've been treated well. I mean that." He smiled at her, as during their previous encounters, but something in his eyes was subtly different. Perhaps, she thought, he was faking the smile as he stared across the cell. But something made her wonder if the smile *before* had been phony—if she were only now seeing the real one.

"That's the difference between you and I," he said. "To grievously wound me, to leave me bleeding to death . . ." He shook his head slowly. "I wouldn't do that to my worst enemy."

"Bullshit," she spat, while shackled to the floor. "I saw photos of people you tortured to death."

He raised his right hand in a calming gesture; his left fingers twitched ineffectually. "*I* didn't hurt those criminals. Public safety officers, the rightful enforcers of law and order, used proportional force to apprehend them. If criminals were injured, that only reflects the violence of the criminals."

He gazed at her unsmiling, unblinking. Then he issued an abrupt laugh, like a bark. "Is *that* what you think will happen to you? Torture?" He laughed again, a slow grin spreading across his face. "Evelyn, Evelyn, Evelyn! Clear such thoughts from your mind. We don't torture people. You aren't in the custody of some teenaged constable who doesn't know the strength of his baton arm! You're in good hands." She glanced involuntarily at the twisted fingers of his left hand. He saw, and his grin widened.

"We aren't *monsters,* Evelyn. Is that honestly what you think of us? That you're in a medieval dungeon? That we're the Gestapo?" he shook his head. "That's the barbaric past we've swept away. That's the savagery *your* people represent. Don't worry. We won't pull out your fingernails, won't put you in a glass box and erase your emotions with X-rays. We won't stick your head in a cage of rats in Room 101."

She stared back in horrified confusion.

"We don't use terror, Evelyn," he said. "We're civilized. What should frighten you is this: we will win. And that empty, stupid look, *that's* why. The Authority has a *tradition* of power and discipline. You don't even know your own history! Zamyatin? Orwell? I allude to them; you understand *nothing*. You haven't even read them! I've read them. I've read *Animal Farm.* I understand it better than Orwell."

He leaned back in his chair and sighed.

"How long did it take, Evelyn?" he asked. She said nothing. "I liked you. I truly did. I thought we could become . . . close." She looked away in disgust. "Tell me: how long did it take your organization to place an assassin in my inner circle?"

—⟍

Adelaide walked ashore in a wet suit after sunset, Juan at her side. The submariners refused to surface within view of the city. So, they parked underwater near the mouth of a creek—what had been a creek, before the city had entombed it in concrete and culverts—leaving Addy and Juan to swim to the surface.

In the cold, open air, Addy could smell the stink of the creek water. Her skin itched from it; she tried to convince herself the feeling was psychosomatic.

They hid their flippers and wet suits beneath an empty barrel on the gravel shore and changed into dry, dark coveralls, warm coats, and rubber boots. Changing clothes was painful and slow for Addy; every joint in her right arm was inflamed, despite the painkillers Juan had given her.

Once she had changed, Juan looked impatient and anxious. He was a submariner, not a commando. At least he was used to sneaking around. Any attempt at a stand-up fight would surely get them killed.

They put on reflective antidrone cloaks on over their clothing; Juan lifted a dark-blue equipment bag.

"Which way?" Juan asked. He spoke at normal volume; Addy heard it as a whisper. She wondered if her ears would ever recover from the damage of the artillery bursts—if she would live long enough for it to matter.

Addy shone a red flashlight on the tiny, laminated map of the city that Layth had given her. She could see her own breath in the ochre glow. Layth had explained that wastewater from the triage camp at the old landfill was pumped into this creek through an enormous culvert. It should be easy enough to find.

"Follow me," whispered Addy, walking along the creek bed. She switched off her flashlight so it wouldn't draw attention. It was overcast above. No moonlight, but the faint reflection of city glow from the cloud layer helped them find their footing. She prayed, silently, that she could locate the access to the camp quickly and safely. And she reflected morosely on her life—that well into middle age she was still leading people along dangerous paths while displaying greater confidence than she felt.

The camp's drainage culvert was easy to locate; it was a concrete tunnel five feet in diameter. It emanated strong odors that Addy didn't smell so much as *taste* at the back of her mouth. Sniffing the air of the culvert was like chewing a copper penny. She grimaced but moved forward.

"Why is it dry?" asked Juan, ducking into the culvert behind her. It was true, Addy saw. The culvert was strangely dry at the bottom, exposing an encrusted rainbow of flaking residues. She had been told the culvert was continuously in use, draining the water from the pit of the landfill mine.

She did not have an answer until they reached the end of the culvert and looked through a steel grate into the camp itself. The whole camp was dark, save a battery-powered floodlight near a guard station. "No power," she said. "Pumps aren't running to drain the pit. It must be filling, slowly."

"Perfecto," said Juan. "In the dark it will be easier to move around the camp, to find our people and bring them back down the culvert." It was dim but not silent. Somewhere nearby—an adjacent camp—there was loud, rhythmic shouting. Chanting by hundreds, if not thousands, of people. Addy could not make out any words, but she could tell from the tone that they were angry. Determined. She felt her skin prickle. Goosebumps. A buried but once familiar feeling of excitement stirred in her, like fiddleheads pushing through leaf litter in spring.

Juan pushed at the steel bars over the culvert opening. The bars moved slightly; the barrier was locked. From his bag he produced a cylindrical object the size of a water bottle, with a set of shiny nozzles at one end. "Shield your eyes," he said, and she looked away.

There were indigo flashes and a sizzle like frying bacon. When Addy looked back, the hasp of the lock was sheared in two, the cut edges a cherry red that faded to dull black. She pushed the gate open. Its rusted hinges squeaked noisily, but there was no reaction from the distant guardhouse. They crossed the shallow, muddy tailings pond that fed the culvert.

From the edge of the pit, Addy scanned the outlines of darkened structures on the opposite side. There was a hundred-year-old brick structure, once a school, where triaged workers sorted junk for precious lithium and rare metals. The workers, apparently, were less valuable. Most were housed in nearby tents and shacks of scavenged materials.

Addy and Juan walked carefully around the edge of the pit, step-ping quietly, wary of accidentally kicking some century-old tin can. They soon arrived at the small shantytown near the school building. Addy heard whispered conversation in one shack, and she stopped to listen.

". . . believe what the Samizdata coin says?" a deep voice was saying. "We all like the idea of an uprising. But we saw what happened in Detroit. If we—"

"This is different," interrupted a woman's voice. "The Authority is weak. Outnumbered. Some security contractors haven't been paid in weeks. Central Triage is bursting at the seams. We should—"

Someone shushed the other two abruptly. "Listen! Outside."

A plastic door flap was pulled open, revealing a dim flashlight bulb and a dozen faces that stared at Addy.

Addy smiled and stared into the darkened shack. "My name is Adita," she said, "and I'm here to rescue you."

—⤙

"I'm so glad to see you," Layth said, hugging Felicity tightly.

She squeezed him back. "Until we got your message," she said, "we thought you might be dead."

"We appreciate the train ride," he said, releasing her, "and the uni-forms."

Something strange flicked over her features for an instant, then her expression returned to normal. "Glad to be of service," she said. "But everything has changed."

He nodded, looking through a glassless window toward the con-tainer ship. Once the sun had set, they could see only occasional sparks from the smoldering fires aboard. "We planned to exfiltrate political prisoners via the water route. But now—"

"We're on our own," she completed his thought.

"As usual," he replied.

"Well, I have good news and bad news," she said. "X has done some-thing rash. She thinks this is our last chance to turn things around; she's burning through every asset we have."

Layth nodded. "You'd better tell everyone," he said, gesturing to the circle of militants.

She looked surprised. "There are dozens of people here," she said. "It's a security risk just showing our *faces* to so many people. Any of them could identify us if captured. Security culture—"

He raised a hand to interrupt. "Compartmentalization is important," he said. "But the only thing we can do now is to act swiftly, as a group, before the authority finds and kills us."

Felicity looked reluctant but agreed, and Layth called the others together. They crouched in the dim light of a few red flashlights.

"The city is on the verge of complete upheaval," Felicity began. "There have been riots over food shortages. An Authority stockpile in the Yellow Zone was liberated—the news says officers were charged by a mob—and several civilians were killed. Yesterday, the families of the dead defied the prohibition on mass assemblies and held a public funeral march. The YEA cracked down, kettled the procession, and triaged the marchers."

There was a murmur in the circle. "We hadn't heard," said Layth.

Felicity nodded. "You've arrived at an auspicious time. This morning, in a coordinated action, people in five neighborhoods refused to submit to checkpoint searches—civil disobedience. The first four hundred were arrested. After that, the Authority simply shut down the checkpoints. Crowds began to form at the closed checkpoints—crowds of more than ten people."

"Another breach of the law," surmised Lieutenant Dumont.

"Exactly," said Felicity. "The guards retreated to their gatehouses and sniper nests. By noon, groups of citizens were brazenly jumping fences, running across the quarantine lanes, and moving between zones. YEA troops opened fire, used incendiaries to attack buildings in the Red Zone."

"We saw from the rooftop," said Layth, "while they attacked the cargo ship."

Felicity nodded. "They think unrest is being coordinated by a foreign power. Your mass transmission to the Samizdata system reinforced their paranoia." Layth frowned. "After guards opened fire on civilians, people in the Yellow Zone escalated. They used Samizdata to report on atrocities. To coordinate. They began to destroy Authority property in the Yellow and Red Zones. Temporary checkpoints, abandoned by retreating guards, were smashed. Prisoner transport buses, left empty in the street, were burned."

There were excited mutters from the circle of militants.

Felicity continued. "The YEA response was to shut off all utilities outside of the Green Zone. Most of people in the city are now without water, electricity, heat."

"Those were never reliable in the Yellow Zone," said Layth.

"No," said Felicity, "but now even the sewage systems have been shut off and are starting to back up. It's untenable. A few days of this and people will either surrender or be in full-scale revolt. X— our network coordinator—believes this is a moment of revolutionary potential." She faced Layth directly. "It's what we've been waiting for. The mass of people are angry. They have little to lose. And they vastly outnumber their wardens."

"Security contractors have them outgunned," Lieutenant Dumont said.

"Which is why X ordered something drastic," said Felicity. "A false-flag operation. Your uniforms were not our only fakes. Months ago, we began manufacturing, assembling, and stealing uniforms from Armor Security." There were a couple of knowing *oohs* from the circle, but most people looked blank. "It's the second-biggest security contractor in the city," explained Felicity. "Their competitor Homeland Patrol is number one. As we speak, five cells of resistance fighters in Armor uniforms and stolen Armor vehicles are staging hit-and-run attacks on Homeland facilities." There were a few gasps.

"Can that work?" asked Lieutenant Dumont. "Surely they coordinate through the Authority."

"The companies are mutually suspicious," said Felicity. "They've had fistfights between patrols where the two companies tried to set up checkpoints at the same intersection. There's no trust. Homeland will believe that Armor is using public unrest as cover for a coup. Armor will believe the same once Homeland counterattacks. Eventually, they might figure it out. But we have a few hours—even days—during which they'll be confused."

"And a lot of them will die," said Lieutenant Dumont, "on both sides."

"So we're using divide and conquer against the rulers for once," said Layth.

"Exactly," said Felicity.

"That can't be the whole plan," Layth said. "Most people in the Green Zone still support the Authority. They've got resources, tools—"

"The plan is to drive a wedge not just between security contractors but between different ideological factions in the Green Zone," said Felicity. "Most people are still ignorant of how bad conditions in the triage camps truly are. By releasing information about those atrocities, using the YEA's own broadcast system, we can turn elites against each other. Agitprop packages have been prepared for broadcast. We just need to plug them in."

"That's a terrible gamble," replied Layth. "Most people in the Green Zone don't care."

"Perhaps," agreed Felicity. "But if we take over the Electronic Countermeasures center, shut down the jammers, and regain contact with the outside world, we may be able to unite larger forces against the Authority."

"Most YEA troops are outside the city," pointed out Lieutenant Dumont. "But they're probably recalling whole companies already. A few dozen guerrillas can't do much against ten thousand armed goons."

"Absolutely, once troops return," agreed Felicity. "But tonight, the guards are afraid of both rioters and other guards, while we can move quickly and freely. You'll have both Layth and myself to show you the territory. But if we're going to act, we have to go now."

There was a brief pause and some muttered discussion before Lieutenant Dumont pointed out the window. "Look, power is back in the Yellow Zone!" The bottoms of low clouds glowed with pulsing orange light.

Layth realized at once what was happening and grimaced deeply.

"No," he said. "The Yellow Zone is on fire."

In the basement cell Evelyn pursed her lips, waiting in silence. Justinian repeated his question. "How long did they train you?" he asked. "How many months did it take them to move you through the bureaucracy to a place where you could literally shoot me in the back?"

She said nothing. He shifted his chair closer. The scrape of its metal feet on abrasive cement reverberated through the cell. "Did you think that would change things?" he asked, gazing down at her. "Not everyone in the Authority is as thoughtful as I am. If you got rid of me, there could be some really nasty people in charge." Evelyn was silent.

He sighed and looked away. "It doesn't matter. This isn't an interrogation. We know everything. We know about the smuggler's cove in the wreck of that container ship. We've known for years, but it's better to keep an *eye* on these things. If we had cracked down, the smugglers would have gone deeper underground. But now there is no underground, and that ship is obliterated.

"Your last-ditch attempts at public unrest will fail. Your foreign sponsors are doomed. We know about the submarine in the harbor; a torpedo drone is the way. I'm not a military man, but I'm told there's a fifty-fifty chance your friends will drown, versus being killed by the explosion of the torpedo itself." He shrugged one-sidedly.

"But who cares about them? It's time to talk about *your* future. Such as it is."

—✓

It took Addy only moments to learn three important things. First, Sara and Sid were alive and well in the very shack she had stumbled across, and were ecstatic to know that Evelyn was fine and waiting to meet them in the city. Second, the people in that shack had already been planning their *own* prison break but were stymied by their lack of an escape route that was passable for their children. Most people in that part of the camp, it turned out, were family of resisters who had been disappeared into the triage system. Nearly a quarter of those in the camp were children.

And third, Addy learned the priest was quite dead, and had been for at least a week.

Juan glowered at her when he found out. "You lied to me," he accused in a hushed voice. "You said you were certain."

"Old information," she dissembled apologetically.

But, literally surrounded by children who were in imminent danger of being killed, Juan agreed to help smuggle out as many as they could on the submarine. Addy discovered that, to her dismay, this would be simpler than expected. Most of the people in this camp had been removed without explanation in the preceding days, leaving fewer than a hundred prisoners. Everyone in the infirmary had been taken.

"If we prioritize putting children on the submarine," suggested Sara, "adults who won't fit can try to escape on foot." And so, with exceptional speed and quietness, the prisoners snuck single file through the dry culvert and down to the stream. As they walked, the sound of chanting from the other camp faded away.

When they reached the end of the culvert, Juan held up a hand and stopped them. "Wait here," he said, and cocked his head. He seemed to be listening, but Addy couldn't hear anything. He pulled out his binoculars and panned across the harbor. Then he began cursing wildly under his breath in Spanish. He dropped the binoculars and pulled out a tiny device that looked like a walkie-talkie with a blunt, flattened antenna. He began to frantically press buttons on it.

Addy picked up the binoculars; through them she could see everything as bright as day—there were light-enhancing optics packed inside. In that augmented view, the helicopter over the harbor stood out like a comet. She focused the binoculars and realized it wasn't a normal helicopter—it was too small; there was no crew compartment. Underneath the rotors and between the skids hung two cylindrical objects she couldn't quite make out. Bombs, perhaps, judging by how panicked Juan was.

Or torpedoes.

"Are you warning them?" she asked Juan.

"Calling backup," he answered. *Another submarine?* she wondered.

The helicopter moved back and forth across the harbor in a systematic pattern. It would slide fifty meters one way, and then jump forward, and then slide over again. Addy was trying to anticipate its next move when, without warning, one of the torpedoes fell. "It dropped one!" said Addy. Then the other was released. Juan fell to his knees. A few seconds later a deep rumbling sound reverberated below their feet. The surface of the water leapt and frothed. Juan stared out over the water.

"I was too late," he choked out, tears in his eyes. Then he raised the device in his hand and switched it off. He looked up. "This beacon is very powerful. They will have triangulated our position. We must run. Now."

—≁

"Your future," Justinian mused, staring at Evelyn, "is tied to the future of this city. Both of you will be healed, in time. Cured."

"You are a cancer," spat Evelyn. "The people of this city will destroy you."

"We have experience dealing with that attitude."

"I remember Detroit."

"Detroit? Detroit! Hah!" He stood and began pacing, his walking stick clacking against the floor. "You don't understand," he said, "the simple power of the medical approach. You are an infection. Your ideology is an epidemic. We contain it. Quarantine it. Cauterize necrotic tissues.

"Do you know what we learned from movements of the past? You thrive on *martyrs*." He spat the last word, a spray of saliva bursting from his sneering lips like gun smoke from a pistol's muzzle. "We imprison a leader, we kill them? That only encourages distorted thinking! People love the underdog. Some of our contractors have been slow to learn this. Hanging people in front of courthouses! Killing the family of an insurgent and throwing the bodies into a river. *Ridiculous*. A public-health nightmare.

"You put a corpse rotting with dysentery in a public square, and *it will spread disease*. Simple epidemiology!" He tugged at his sling, agitated. His voice rose. "The same with infectious ideology. You *triage* people. You *quarantine* those you suspect. And if someone is infected, you remove them. If villages are infected, you sterilize them. You do what must be done!"

His voice fell to a whisper, and he leaned in close to her face. "You do not give the rabble someone to *fawn* over. You do not make martyrs out of rebels. You do not give them a coffin to march or an underdog to celebrate. You do not censor a radical newspaper. That propaganda is only *pus* oozing from a wound in the body public. You do not poke at a suppurating wound."

"To save the body, you cauterize the wound! You excise the tumor!" Then Justinian's voice fell to a whisper. "This medical approach avoids the cruelty of the past. Do you know how many people were in prison on this continent before the fall? More than two million, wasting away in nonproductivity, unable to work. Actually *costing* society money! If you include the people on parole, in the court system, you can add millions more. That bankrupted the state as much as anything else. And it was pointless. Cruel. We don't punish social disharmony.

"There are only two options. Option one" —he gestured with his right hand—"restitution. A citizen's misbehavior has a cost to society. We require them to pay society for the costs they incur through the triage camps and labor crews. Option two"—the fingers of his immobilized left hand twitched—"treatment. Sometimes people continue to misbehave. That's no longer an economic problem. It's a medical problem—a problem we can cure."

He looked down at his arm in its sling. "Nerves are delicate, fragile things. The nerve clamping doesn't damage them. It's not a lobotomy. It suppresses parts of the nervous system that cause problems in our patients, neural circuits that make them upset. It makes them productive members of society—better workers, if the task isn't too demanding. They aren't cyborgs, like the rumors say. Nerve clamping is more—"

A guard entered the room, looking apologetic, and whispered something in Justinian's ear. The director nodded. Then he stood and lifted his cane. "I'll check on you afterward. Hopefully you'll recognize me. Memory loss is common after the procedure." He shrugged his right shoulder. "But if you suffer some . . . disorientation, we can have a fresh start then, can't we?" He smiled again as he stepped out of the room. Evelyn knew, in that moment, that the smile was genuine.

—⚡

A sentry on top of the warehouse confirmed to Layth and Lieutenant Dumont that several blocks in the Yellow Zone were engulfed in flame. The circle of militants finished their discussion quickly.

"The YEA won't send firefighting crews with the district on lockdown," said Felicity. "It happened at a camp three years ago. Guards made fire trucks wait outside the gate until everything burned down."

"Won't the residents fight it?" asked Lieutenant Dumont.

"They'll try," said Layth. "But with water shut down, the fire hydrants in the zone won't work."

"It's been so dry this year," said Felicity, "there's no snow to slow the fire. It could spread through the whole zone by tomorrow—with everyone trapped inside."

"Okay, people," called Lieutenant Dumont. "Get your shit; we move out now!"

Their nocturnal march to the administrative district was far different from their infiltration into the city at dawn of that same day. The morning train ride had been crowded. But now, moving swiftly through the darkness, they saw no other people in uniform; indeed, they saw nearly no one at all. It took less than an hour to reach the edge of the administrative district. In that time, they passed through two vehicle checkpoints. At neither of those checkpoints did the guards leave the gatehouse to challenge them. The two dozen militants simply jogged past in their phony uniforms.

At the border of the administrative district they paused near a darkened checkpoint. "It should be straightforward the rest of the way," said Felicity. "I'll keep my radio on if you need me."

"You aren't coming?" asked Lieutenant Dumont.

"I've need to get to the Yellow Zone before it's completely engulfed," answered Felicity. "I have people there. Responsibilities. I have to help them."

They wished each other luck, and Felicity disappeared into the night. Layth, Dumont, Sridharan, and the militants walked the last few steps to the barbed-wire gate of the Administration District. Here, finally, they were challenged by the guards.

"Hold where you are!" A voice crackled over a loudspeaker. A floodlight illuminated them suddenly, shining from three stories up in an adjacent parking garage. Each person's exhaled breath was starkly visible in the cold. "This gate is closed. Use the main gate." The man's voice over the loudspeaker sounded short of breath.

Lieutenant Dumont walked forward and spoke commandingly. "We're from Chonthus Supplemental Security!" She pointed to her armband and waved her green tag. "We've got Green Zone clearance. Let us in!"

There were several moments of silence, then the voice came over the loudspeaker again. "Do you work for Armor or Homeland?" The voice sounded ragged. Panicky.

Jesus, thought Layth. *X must have started already.*

"We're independent!" called Lieutenant Dumont. "We only work for the Authority. Come on, pal; we're trying to do our jobs here." There was a moment of silence. "We're all in this together, right?" There was no response from the loudspeaker.

Layth looked up casually toward the floodlight. It was dazzlingly bright. In the parking garage above, hidden by the glare, there could be five or ten snipers. The militants were completely exposed in the open roadway. The uniforms were a good plan, but X's own phony uniform gambit had complicated matters. They were running out of time. Slowly, casually, Layth began to reach for his sidearm.

—⁄—

Juan's message—*Run*—was passed swiftly back through the line of escaping prisoners. A dozen childless people, in twos and threes, responded with the quickness of startled rabbits. By the time Addy realized what was happening, they were already disappearing into the nighttime haze along the beach. At least fifty people still remained, their faces creased with fear, confusion, and fatigue.

"Where can we go to communicate with my people?" asked Juan. But Addy was speechless. She stared out at the water. The surface, barely visible, rippled slightly with bubbles and debris. Addy had seen everything fall apart before. Flashing back to that day decades earlier, she—

"Addy!" said Juan sharply. "Where can we go? Where are your comrades?"

"Administration district," she blurted, almost without thinking. "They're headed to the admin district. We can use the transmitters there to contact your people. But I don't know the way."

"I do," said Sara. "I'll tell you the way."

"Evelyn is headed there," said Addy, "with the others."

"In that case," said Sara, "I'll take you there myself." The whole group followed Sara—who carried Sid on her back—along the gravelly beach to a disused waterside park, and from there up a darkened residential street.

"I don't understand," said Juan as they walked. "This administrative district, isn't it highly guarded?"

"With all the guards pulled to the triage districts," said Addy, "or deployed in the countryside, they'll be understaffed."

"There are still drones, no?" said Juan. "That might spot us?"

"Maybe we can sneak in," said Sara. "There's a woman with us who used to work as a cleaner in the basement of Triage Administration. They made her wash the quarantine cells and the operating rooms after they were used."

"Quarantine cells?" asked Addy, looking down to watch her step on the dark street.

"Solitary confinement cells, basically," said Sara. "As for the operating rooms . . . well, you don't want to know. The important thing is that she used a back entrance for menial laborers, and she can show us the way to—"

"Shh!" hissed Juan suddenly. "Find cover!" There was little in the way of cover on the street where they walked; Addy jumped behind a rusting dumpster along with Juan, Sarah, and Sid. Others simply pressed themselves against building walls or crouched near little bushes that had grown up from cracks in the pavement.

"What is it?" Addy asked. Their direction of travel intersected a larger, well-illuminated street half a block ahead. Juan pointed, and Addy followed his finger to the nearest corner where a large brick building stood, a department store built a century earlier. Just past the corner of the store she could see a dark shape on the sidewalk. She realized it was a pair of human legs, the rest of the body obscured by the structure.

"We must check it out," said Juan.

"Yes," said Sara, looking expectantly at Juan. "You're the commando, right? Get out your gun and do some recon."

"Actually, I'm a noncombatant," said Juan, "Under international law, I cannot carry a weapon and still qualify as a provider of humanitarian aid according to subsection—"

Addy rolled her eyes. "I'll do it," she said. She moved quietly along the edge of the building toward the corner. She looked back and saw, barely, several dozen shadowed faces watching her anxiously. She turned toward the intersection again. She could see the legs in detail now. Feet in polished black military boots, dark uniform pants. She slowly leaned forward and so that she could peer around the corner with one eye.

She scanned up the body. Black tactical belt, laden with handcuffs, radio, gloves, chemical sprays, ammo, gun. Then black shirt, a dark uniform coat bearing a private-security crest. And then, where the head should be, nothing—or rather, a lengthy red smear. The man on the ground ended at the neck. She followed the red smear and saw it was a tire track from an SUV that had driven over the man and directly through the main window of the department store, plowing through a stack of mannequins. The SUV bore the logo of Armor Security, and its windows had been shot out.

Addy looked up and along the silent main street toward the administrative district. Half a block away, the Green Zone gate was wide open; the street was scattered with more bodies, most in uniform, many in obvious pools of blood. Addy looked back toward Juan and beckoned him forward.

He examined the scene and shook his head. "Why would a security truck drive over a guard from another company? Why would they get in a gunfight with each other?"

Addy shook her head in confusion. She could see nearly a dozen bodies from where they stood, including one slumped out the shattered driver's-side window of the SUV in the department store. A woman with short gray hair, face covered in blood. Some of the blood from the top of her head had been channeled to the side by a scar above one bushy eyebrow.

Addy heard a quiet shuffling sound and turned to see Sara walking up to the corner, holding Sid in her arms. "Is it safe?" she asked. Addy raised her palms and wobbled her head slightly side to side: *What, exactly, is "safe"?*

Sara whispered something in Sid's ear and put him down against the brick wall of the department store. He covered his eyes with his hands. Sara leaned around to look. Her eyes brightened slightly. "They still have sidearms," she said. "Perfect." She began stripping the headless man's body of his firearm, ammunition, and flashlight.

Addy was about to warn of snipers, or suggest they try to find another way around, when a low whine began to echo across the city. It rose higher and higher in volume, then began to oscillate slowly in pitch. Addy was mystified. "What is that?"

"It sounds like an air-raid siren," said Sara. "But why would they—" She stopped herself and turned to look at Juan's face, which had turned grim.

"Backup," he said.

—◢

After Justinian departed, the guards left Evelyn's cell door open. At first, she thought this was an oversight; if only she could loosen her shackles she could simply walk out the door and escape. But it soon became clear that the open door was deliberate, a form of punishment—because through that door, Evelyn could see the passage of her fellow prisoners as they were transferred between cells or sent for "treatment." She saw a glimpse of her own near future.

It was a gruesome parade. A few of them could still walk, but many of them were pushed on wheelchairs or stretchers by masked guards. The few that could walk were attached to wheeled IV poles, which they were forced to push themselves as they shuffled along. One of the walkers was missing his arm below the elbow; it was neatly bandaged with an oozing yellow dressing. He didn't turn to look at Evelyn.

Another prisoner, a woman on a stretcher, was intubated and

attached to a portable ventilator; she stared at the ceiling as she was rolled by, an IV bag draining into a port just over her left eyebrow. A man in a wheelchair seemed to have a transparent plate mounted in the side of his skull; Evelyn thought she could see brain through it. Occasionally she could catch snatches of conversation from the staff—doctors?—as they passed by.

"He's a compatible donor. If we take the second kidney . . ."

". . . second nerve clamp may have been too much, she's gone non-verbal, but a cranial transect . . ."

". . .complete aphasia via removal of Broca's area should prevent the patient from acting out further . . ."

Many of the walkers moved with an awkward shuffle, their feet never leaving the ground, their movements jerky and birdlike. After a while, she realized the shufflers had flat boxes bolted to their skulls, a harness of wires that trailed down their spines or disappeared beneath their hair.

Another one of the walkers, quite gaunt, had nothing physically missing except for her hair. But she stopped in front of Evelyn's door and stood there staring at her, eyes blank, drooling slightly from her lower lip, until one of the guards sparked a shock prod to keep the woman moving. Evelyn felt deeply unsettled by the woman's gaze. There was something familiar about it.

At some point Evelyn didn't consciously register, the prisoners stopped passing, and the number of staff grew. They rushed past, and the snippets of conversation she heard became terse, even panicked.

". . . drones at the border about five minutes ago . . ."

". . . get staff to the air-raid shelter two blocks south . . ."

". . . *best* to leave the patients here until the situation can be . . ."

A few minutes later, the rush of staff ceased completely. Evelyn's door remained ajar, but she heard nothing in the corridor. She shuffled forward on the abrasive floor, pulling against the shackles, to try to peer further out into the hallway. Before she could see anything, the lights abruptly shut off. There was a brief, fading flicker in the light tubes above her cell, and then blackness.

In a distant cell, someone begin to shout wordlessly.

—✦

His hand sliding toward the grip of his pistol, Layth leaned toward Lieutenant Dumont and whispered. "I'll take out the spotlight. You get the others to find cover and direct their fire at—" Layth was interrupted by an air-raid siren from the building above.

A voice crackled over the loudspeaker. "You people can't use our bunker. Don't try!" The floodlight switched off, and distant sirens began to wail. Layth strode forward and tried the gate. It had been electronically unlocked and swung open when he pushed it. He beckoned to the others, and they jogged through the gate. Layth looked through the reinforced window of the gatehouse as they passed. He could see no one inside it. A mug, half full of foul-tasting "coffee," sat steaming on a counter.

They ran the last block from the gate to Electronic Countermeasures. Antenna towers and a smokestack loomed above the complex. They passed through the building's entryway just as the street lights began to shut off behind them.

—✦

"They're shutting off the lights," said Sara, "to make it harder for foreign aircraft to find Authority targets. We can make it the last few blocks to the admin district without being seen."

"Wait," said Addy, looking up as the lights of skyscrapers in the Green Zone clicked off building by building. "Who's targeting the city?"

"They aren't after the city," sighed Juan. At that moment, there was a bright flash overhead. They saw a puff of flame, and then an umbel of burning debris that quickly faded, like a not-very-impressive firework. A few moments later, there was a similar explosion near the northern horizon. "The International Fleet has sent in peacekeeper UAVs; they're shooting down YEA drones. They must have decided on a no-fly zone after my beacon. If only . . ." he trailed off. Another sharp explosion echoed in the distant dark. Suddenly, the streetlights near their intersection went out.

"We need to get indoors," said Addy. "It's raining drones, and we can't drag a bunch of malnourished children through a war zone."

"The whole city is a war zone now," said Sara.

"Can't they go home?" asked Juan.

"My home is gone. I'm not stopping," said Sara, "until we get to the Triage Administration."

"Fine," said Addy. She turned to the group, which was stripping the bodies of the dead contractors, arming itself. "Let's move!" She flicked on her red flashlight, and others turned on lights they had scavenged.

They went as fast as they could—limited by the speed of children, or people carrying children—through the gate. The back door of the Triage Administration complex was only a few blocks further. They found it unguarded and ajar. A cigarette smoldered where it had been dropped on the ground; a box of medical supplies had been tossed onto the pavement, spilling dozens of vials, syringes, and electrodes.

Addy shone her red flashlight onto the partially open door, which was marked with an enormous, peeling biohazard symbol. D WING ZONED RED, it said in all capitals. QUARANTINE. ENTRY FORBIDDEN. "That's creepy," she said.

Addy opened the door further and looked inside. Her light did little to penetrate the hallway within, which seemed even darker than it was outside. She could see a few overturned chairs in the gloom, their metal legs glinting redly from her light, and a sheaf of paper that had been strewn across the floor.

Beside her, Sara raised the pistol she had taken from a dead security contractor and pulled the slide back partway to check that there was a round in the chamber. She released it, and it clicked back into place, its metallic snick echoing in the empty corridor ahead. "Okay, Sid," she said. "Don't let go of me. We're going to find Evelyn."

—✦

"Here we are," said Sridharan. "Electronic Countermeasures wing. From here the YEA monitors all transmissions through networks both wireless and hardwired."

"Isn't it strange that there's no guard?" asked Lieutenant Dumont.

"They went to put down riots in the Yellow Zone," said Layth. "Or hid in a bunker, or they're fighting another security faction. But how do we get through this door?" Before them stood a solid steel door set into a concrete wall. A numerical keypad with a heavy, electronically actuated lock was mounted above a fairly standard-looking metal doorknob.

"I helped build the network in this building, a long time ago," said Sridharan. "The security system was notoriously touchy even then, constantly locking people inside the server rooms. Maybe they. . ." He prodded the dark keypad; nothing happened, so he reached out and turned the knob. The doorknob clicked, and—though it took two people to pull it—the door slid slowly open.

The inside of the server room was dim, warm, and quiet, though distant echoes implied a cavernous space beyond their sight. The pervading smell was that of smoke combined with the sweet acridity of melted plastic. But the odors were muted; if there had been a fire in this room, it was a long time ago. Beneath the smoke residue was a whiff of mildew.

As they filed into the room the floor was slimy beneath their boots, appearing damp in the beams of their flashlights. They heard a few computer fans running, but also the sound of dripping water.

"Jesus," said Layth, "what happened here?"

Sridharan played his flashlight across the server racks. Most were silent, unlit. "It wasn't like this before," Sridharan said. "Maybe the cyberattacks . . ." He just shook his head. The group picked their way through alleys between dark server racks. Layth kept his pistol in his hand, safety off.

"So," began Layth in a hushed voice, "you helped to design this place?"

"God no," muttered Sridharan, "I was a glorified technician—running wires, installing servers. Some of the same servers are still here; doesn't look like they've upgraded in years."

"What changed your mind?" asked Layth. "About working for the Authority?"

"This was before the Authority," said Sridharan. "I worked for the federal government. But after the Authority took over, some of the people who worked on these projects, who built them, objected to the Authority taking control of the servers. Those people started getting 'sick.' Getting quarantined. Not coming back. No one had to spell it out for me. It was like the pharaohs of Egypt, taking the people who designed their pyramids and burying them alive. I got the hell out."

"You still built a surveillance system for the government," persisted Layth in a whisper. "Routed all communications through a system that could monitor them."

"You've got to understand what it was like back then," said Sridharan. "There were no jobs. We were in a cold war with China, our biggest trading partner. Their hackers had penetrated our networks—business, financial, whatever. You'd have an engineering firm in Texas design a new oil pump, and before they could get to the patent office, China had already built a hundred thousand units and shipped them all over the world. How could we compete with that?"

"Industrial espionage," said Layth, as they threaded their way around a stack of servers that had been dismantled and sat in pieces on the floor.

"More than that," said Sridharan. "Cyberwarfare. Machines on the stock market worked faster than a human could blink. Some rogue, predatory algorithm could crash an entire stock exchange in five minutes, and it would take you five years of fiscal analysis to figure out what happened. We needed to monitor communications to prevent cyberwarfare. At the time, I thought the government was right, but now—"

"Hey!" hissed Lieutenant Dumont. "Cut the chatter!"

They reached the far end of the cavernous room. There were desks there, piled with cobbled-together computers, telephones, and printers. Each seemed to be a workstation, holding clipboards and stacks of index cards. Layth picked up a piece of paper. It bore handwritten notes on a phone conversation between two people in the Yellow Zone.

He shook his head. "We thought there was a goddamned artificially intelligent supercomputer in here," he sighed. "Recording all our calls, generating personalized propaganda on the fly. But they've been doing surveillance *by hand*. For years!"

"Come on, Layth," said Lieutenant Dumont. "We can't waste time."

"This stairwell," said Sridharan, "leads up to the transmitter control room. We should be able to shut down the jammers or send messages from there."

"Okay," said Layth. He looked over at Lieutenant Dumont, who nodded. "Let's go."

Addy found more flashlights in an emergency supply cabinet in the dark corridor of the Triage Administration basement. They were parceled out among the thirty or so people who remained in their party. Addy hadn't counted, but she was certain that when they left the triage camp there had been three times as many. Had so many people quietly peeled off to go back to find their families, to sneak back to their homes? Everything was a mess. It was more than she could possibly keep track of. Just like last time. Addy began to feel a twisting sensation in her belly that made her light-headed.

They shuffled single file through the dark corridor by the faint light of their few flashlights. The woman who had cleaned cells led the way, rarely looking up, not making eye contact with anyone, but guiding them implacably around corners and past thick steel doors. Addy followed her, with Sara and Sid next in the line.

Around every corner Addy expected to see something horrible: a guard leaping at them from the blackness, another body, or dozens of them. But their journey through the dark tunnels was uneventful. Eventually, their guide just stopped in front of a utility alcove—a little side room filled with mop buckets and cleaning products—and pointed forward. "Quarantine wing is that way. The rest of Triage Administration is upstairs."

"So, we need to find our way up?" asked Addy. She jogged forward a dozen yards to the end of the corridor. Through a tiny window in one door she could see a stairwell. She tried the handle; it was locked, and a very solid-looking key-card scanner was built into the door frame.

"I was never allowed to go up," said their guide. "Only into the cell block."

"Isn't that locked, too?" asked Sara.

"The cell block is only locked from the inside," replied their guide.

"We should fan out in small groups," said Juan. "Check the nearby corridors. There must be a way upstairs—a fire door, an emergency stairwell."

"Okay," said Sara. "Small groups. But don't get locked behind a one-way door by accident. Meet back here in two minutes."

"Wait a second," said Juan, tilting his head. "Do you hear that?"

⤔

In darkness, Evelyn felt around the abrasive concrete floor of her cell. She reached as far as her shackles allowed. She found nothing at first. But near the doorway her fingertips found something small and sharp that must have rolled in from outside. A needle, or part of an IV, perhaps.

From the corridor beyond, the distant shouting gave way to a pounding noise—a dull, arrhythmic pounding that came from bare feet slapping against concrete, bare fists beating against closed steel doors. And a wordless, muted chant.

She poked the sharp end of the needle into the keyhole of her wrist shackles. She had zero experience lock-picking but also had no other options. She probed the keyhole blindly. She felt the hollow metal of the needle buckle, felt a sharp pain in her wrist. Evelyn knew she had stuck herself with it. But she no longer cared.

She tried again from another angle, felt the needle bend and break. The remaining stub was uselessly short. "Fuck!" she said, and threw it into the blackness. "Fuuuck!" And she let out a long, wordless cry that mingled with a hundred other voices, reverberating dully between black concrete walls.

A faint light appeared in the hallway, visible indirectly through her open doorway. It grew stronger, and nearer. Someone with a flashlight was approaching. Evelyn tried to hide, but the shackles held her fast.

Layth kicked open the door of the transmitter control room, his gun raised. He found the room empty of people but filled with banks of computer equipment, desks, and workstations.

"Barricade the stairwell. Secure the room!" called Lieutenant Dumont. Fighters swept the perimeter. There was one main door, through which they had entered, and several secondary doors that they quickly barricaded with heavy steel desks. There was an antique-looking elevator door, but the controls were dark. On the exterior wall was a bank of floor-to-ceiling windows.

"Stay clear of the windows!" called Lieutenant Dumont. "Draw those blinds!" she added.

Layth spent a moment staring out the windows as the blinds were closed. Through a gap in the clouds he caught a glimpse of the full moon. He thought he saw a distant drone exploding, crashing into the glass façade of a blacked-out skyscraper, but he didn't have time to process what that might mean.

"Okay," Layth said, turning to Sridharan. "Do your thing."

"Err," said Sridharan, "what do you want me to do, exactly?"

"Start by shutting down the jammers," said Layth, "so we can use our radios again."

Sridharan tried tapping one of the workstation keyboards, where a dialogue box was flashing: "DRONES GROUNDED; NO-FLY ZONE IN EFFECT."

A login screen popped up. "Ahh, does anyone have a password?" Silence. He tried a few of the login-password combinations from Gwen. Nothing worked. Sridharan's hands were shaking with nervousness; it was unclear whether he would have been able to press the right keys even if he *had* known the password. "Okay, we'll try this a different way. Turn on your radio."

Layth switched on his handheld radio. It produced the same warbling, buzzing sound as when he had tried, and failed, to contact Addy on the container ship, though the sound was much stronger here, directly beneath the antenna array. Sridharan moved over to a tall bank of equipment standing along one wall. It was a nest of power cords and patch cables climbing across one another, a few neatly tied together but many looking haphazard. He spent a few moments peering at labelled dials. Then he began to pull cables, disconnecting pieces of equipment seemingly at random. Every few moments he would pause and glance at Layth's radio, listening to see if it were still receiving the jamming signal.

After what felt like a terribly long time to Layth, the jamming sound abruptly ceased. "There!" said Sridharan. Sridharan was perspiring heavily, his forehead covered in beads of sweat.

"Good," said Layth. "I was starting to worry you didn't know what you were doing." Sridharan gave a nervous, slightly constricted chuckle and sat down heavily on the floor as though he thought he would pass out before getting to a chair.

"Try calling X," Lieutenant Dumont said, "using the Chonthus band."

Layth switched the channel on his radio. "Come in, anyone," he said. "Can anybody hear me?"

—2

A bright flashlight shone through the doorway of Evelyn's cell. "This cell is open!" A woman's voice called loudly. "There's a person in here!" Then, more softly, "It's okay; we're going to get you out."

The voice was familiar. "Sara?" asked Evelyn in disbelief.

The flashlight pointed at her face for several long seconds before it dropped. "Evelyn?" Sara asked in a choked voice. Sara knelt down in front of Evelyn and cradled her face. She was shaking her head, slowly, and shedding tears.

Evelyn wasn't ready to cry. "You and Sid? Are you okay?"

Sara nodded. "Adita and Juan got us out of the camp and brought us here."

To her confusion, the submariner Juan appeared in her cell. "Cover your eyes," he said. There were a few bright flashes, and the shackles fell away from her wrists so that she could stand—well, in theory. In practice her legs buckled beneath her as soon as she tried. Juan found her a wheelchair and more dignified clothing.

Adelaide appeared a moment later. "You're Evelyn? I'm glad you're okay." Evelyn did not feel okay, but she didn't argue.

"Who is Adita?" Evelyn asked. "What's happening?"

"I'm Adita," Addy answered. "It's a long story. But some people are staying here to help liberate prisoners from the quarantine cells. The rest of us should go to the antenna control room on the top floor."

"I can show you the way through the building," said Evelyn.

Juan pushed Evelyn's wheelchair, with Sid sitting on Evelyn's lap, up to the large double doors marked **B WING ZONED GREEN. OPENING DOORS IS VIOLATION OF QUARANTINE.** The space beyond was fully illuminated. They pushed through, followed closely by the remaining group of about twenty former prisoners, many of them armed. A few had stayed behind to unlock the quarantine cells and offer what help they could to those inside.

"These are the archives," muttered Evelyn. "I worked here. Briefly." Stacks of file drawers stretched out before them. Directly in front of them was the long access hallway, several file carts parked haphazardly at its midpoint. At the opposite end of the corridor was a stairwell and elevator. "We just need to get there," Evelyn said, "and we can get upstairs."

"I smell smoke," said Addy, softly.

"I heard some of the doctors talking about a fire outside," said Evelyn. "Could there be—"

Then she heard a loud voice on the other side of the enormous space. "Get the rest of those files into the incinerator, now! The mob could be here any minute!" Evelyn's skin crawled. *Justinian.*

Ahead, a woman pushing a cart came into view, striding out from the stacks across the hall to the open door of the incinerator chute. She threw several files hastily into the chute before she realized that a crowd of people stood at the opposite end of the hallway. She stared at them for several long seconds, then yelled: "Director, it's a quarantine breach!"

A man stepped from the stacks and looked down the corridor. It was Stanley. He gazed at them for a fraction of a second before launching into action. "Philip, stairwell to the helipad, now!" Then he drew a pistol, pointed at the ex-prisoners, and opened fire.

Juan tried to pull Evelyn's wheelchair back through the doorway but was tripped up by the mass of people; Evelyn felt him fall. Sitting there, in the middle of the hallway, she saw everything. Addy ducked behind a filing cabinet and drew her pistol. Sara threw herself across both Sid and Evelyn. Half a dozen ex-prisoners raised their guns to return fire.

Justinian sprinted across the hallway toward the stairwell, flailing gracelessly with his walking stick. Several former prisoners shot at him. Stanley kept shooting, walking sideways to put himself between the freed prisoners and the director. The woman pushing the cart was hit once, maybe twice, and fell. An instant later, the director was in the stairwell and Stanley, the magazine of his pistol emptied, disappeared into the door behind him.

—⚭

Layth listened for a response on the radio; after several long moments he heard Felicity's voice in reply. "Glad you made it! Good job on the jammers. I'm trying to . . . get everyone connected in real time." She was winded, panting slightly over the crackling radio.

"We're figuring out the equipment," said Layth. "Soon we'll use the big antenna to transmit."

"Sounds good," huffed Felicity. "Let me . . . know."

"Why are you out of breath?" he asked, concerned.

"Just climbing . . . stairs . . . tall building," she answered. "Almost . . . at roof."

"Were you able to get a team into the Yellow Zone?" asked Layth.

"No," panted Felicity. Layth was gripped by a sinking feeling. "Didn't have to," Felicity added. There was a brief pause, and when she spoke again Layth could hear a sibilant burst of gusting wind over the microphone; she was somewhere high up. "By the time we got over . . . there had been a breakout at Central Triage." Layth heard her breathe deeply several times. "They learned about the fires over Samizdata . . . so they marched to the gate, there must have been seven hundred . . . they tore down the gates. Used fire trucks as battering rams."

"Hey!" called Layth, speaking to the room, "everyone listen!" He asked another question, then held the radio up so people could hear her response. "Did the guards at the gate open fire?"

"There were casualties . . . at the triage camp," said Felicity. "But guards at yellow gate . . . were afraid to shoot. There were only a few . . . most had hidden in air-raid shelters . . . or run from other contractors. The guards . . . knew the crowd would tear them apart if they opened fire. Overwhelmed. So they surrendered . . . the fire trucks got through; they're dealing with it now."

A cheer went up in the radio room. Layth keyed the microphone button so Felicity could hear the ruckus.

She gave a ragged, happy laugh in response, and her transmission came in more clearly. "The view up here is incredible. Thousands of people are in the streets . . . tens of thousands. The city is dark . . . but there's a sea of handheld lights. They're marching . . ." A moment of silence, then Felicity's voice became businesslike. "Heads up—it looks like they're marching toward the admin district. They're chanting; they sound angry. And they've got torches."

Layth was confused. "To cut their way in?"

"Not acetylene torches," came Felicity's crackling reply. "Like, *actual* torches. I think they want to burn down Triage Administration."

—⁄—

Addy emerged from behind a filing cabinet once the shooting stopped, gun in her left hand. Her swollen right hand throbbed from her fumbled, unsuccessful attempt to load a round into the chamber and turn off the safety. She could see that two of the escaped prisoners had been shot, and a Triage Administration bureaucrat lay slumped by the incinerator door.

Addy saw that both of the ex-prisoners who had been shot—a man and a woman she didn't know—had been hit near their sternums. Sara was directing first aid, but Addy doubted either would last more than a few moments.

Evelyn, with Sid still on her lap, began to roll herself forward in her wheelchair. Addy accompanied Evelyn to the body of the bureaucrat. "I knew this woman," said Evelyn. "Her name was Phyllis."

Addy picked up a sheet of paper from the floor. It described the results of an experiment in which a patient had been "nerve clamped." The text was accompanied by a wiring diagram. "They were trying to destroy evidence," said Addy, "of medical experiments. But why now?"

Evelyn just shook her head, but Addy couldn't tell whether Evelyn heard the question or not.

"We should go upstairs to the radio room," said Juan.

Sara appeared beside them, breathing heavily, her hands and face smeared with blood. "Evelyn can't climb stairs," she said, turning to Evelyn. "Maybe you should stay—"

"We'll take the elevator," interrupted Evelyn. "Our family will stick together."

Sara nodded, then went to the other escaped prisoners and picked a couple of volunteers, both armed. "I don't want to be surprised again. We just lost two people. You see someone in uniform, open fire. Don't hesitate." The volunteers agreed.

Addy, Juan, Sara, and the two volunteers entered the antique-looking elevator. Sara put Evelyn and Sid in the back corner, then pressed the button for the top floor. "Safeties off," Sara reminded.

Addy hefted her pistol and breathed deeply.

⟍

"I didn't copy that," said Layth to Felicity over the radio. "It sounded like you said they want to set the building on fire."

Lieutenant Dumont, who heard perfectly well, turned to three nearby militants. "Go downstairs to the storage rooms. Grab whatever bolts of fabric or cloth you can find and bring them up here." The three rushed off.

Sridharan, who sat at a workstation, reached over and touched Layth's arm. "I think I can get the main antenna to transmit, if you want to try."

"Felicity, I'll get back to you in a few minutes," Layth said into the handheld radio. "Call us with anything urgent."

He turned to Sridharan. "Are you ready to make the big broadcast?"

Sridharan put a memory card into one of the computers. "Ready to go."

"Send it out," said Lieutenant Dumont. "The people in the Green Zone need to know the atrocities their leaders have committed."

"And we need to know if our plan is working," said Layth, "if things have changed at the front. Can we call the Thistle?"

"Assuming they're listening on shortwave," said Sridharan.

Layth wrote down a frequency he had prearranged with Charlotte and slid it over to Sridharan. Sridharan twiddled some knobs to make the necessary adjustments and handed Layth an old-fashioned handset. "Remember," said Sridharan, "it's not encrypted. Anyone can overhear. Go ahead."

"Thistle, come in. Thistle, come in," said Layth. "This is Kraken calling. Respond." There was a long pause. Layth added, "There is currently a no-fly zone in place for drones; it is safe to transmit, over."

"This is Thistle," came Carlos's voice. His consonants were slightly slurred, as though he had been sleeping by the radio and just woken up. "What's your status?"

"Kraken has shut off jamming and controls one radio transmitter for now," said Layth. "The armbands are fighting each other or hiding in air raid shelters. We don't have long."

"Is Adelaide there?" asked Carlos.

Layth winced; he had watched the cargo ship be obliterated with Addy on it. "Not with me currently. What is your status?"

"Hold on," said Carlos. There was crackling and fumbling, then a new voice.

"Hi, Kraken," came Charlotte's voice. "YEA troops almost made it to Newbrook today but fell back. Left heavy equipment in the rush to get back to the city. We even liberated a group of prisoners from Elmira."

Layth smiled broadly. "You can tell our good friend"—he didn't want to say Gwendolyn's name—"her information was correct."

There was a brief pause before Charlotte spoke again. "I'm afraid Gwen didn't make it."

Layth's smile disappeared. All of his victories seemed temporary: He would stage an assassination, then be forced on the run. He would rescue a vital intelligence source, and a week later, she would die. As he tried to think of something to say to Charlotte, Felicity's voice came over the handheld radio.

"Do you know there's a helicopter lifting off from the roof of Triage Administration?" Felicity asked. Layth turned to Lieutenant Dumont in surprise; he was suddenly aware of a deep thrumming sound nearby, which had escaped his notice during the hubbub. He opened his mouth to reply.

Then the elevator doors opened, and all hell broke loose.

—⚡

The instant the doors slid open, Addy knew they were doomed. It had been too easy to get out of the prison camp, too easy to get into Triage Administration. Of course they would find their ultimate destination filled with dozens of YEA paramilitary officers in uniform.

Beside her, Sara pushed Sid into the sheltered corner of the elevator below the buttons. The other escaped prisoners in the elevator— obvious shock and horror on their faces—raised their weapons. Addy heard the deafening blast of a shotgun.

Addy's side had a moment's head start, but they were greatly out-numbered. Most of the soldiers in the room looked dully surprised; they weren't even holding their rifles, they ducked behind heavy desks and equipment for cover. One of the soldiers, however, was charging directly at them, running toward the open elevator doors, his arms raised to strike. Raising her pistol awkwardly in her left hand, she drew a bead on his chest and squeezed the trigger.

—⚡

When the elevator doors opened, Layth saw Addy immediately. It took him a moment to process that she was still alive. As the doors opened, he could see Evelyn, bloodied in a wheelchair, along with Sara and two ragged people he didn't know. He was about to greet them when they raised their guns—and he remembered his team was still wearing their phony uniforms.

He dropped the handset and raised both palms above his head. "Wait!" he shouted. No one could hear him; the entire room erupted into shouts. Someone in the elevator fired out into the radio room.

Layth could already see some of his side raising their rifles, saw Lieutenant Dumont looking in confusion toward the elevator.

He ran into the crossfire, his arms raised. "Stop!" he said. "Hold your fire!" Then Addy raised her gun and shot him in the chest.

—✒

Evelyn flinched back into her wheelchair as the shooting started and Sara pushed Sid into the corner. She felt so tired of horrors. Part of her felt like throwing herself overtop of Sid. Another part felt like throwing her body into the stream of bullets that was to come.

There was shouting, gunfire, and more shouting. The gunshots in the confined space of the elevator were painfully loud, and the doorway was hazy with smoke. Evelyn watched Addy fire her handgun and then pause, lowering it in disbelief. "Cease fire!" someone was shouting from the radio room. "Friendly fire!" Addy seemed to recognize the voice and echoed the call, grabbing the shotgun of the man next to her and forcing the barrel up toward the ceiling.

Evelyn heard only the ringing of her own ears. Then she leaned over to look through the elevator door and saw Layth lying on the floor, clutching his torso, blood already staining his hands.

—✒

Addy lowered her pistol and placed it on the ground. "Don't shoot!" she said, stepping out of the elevator. "We're on the same side!"

She walked the few steps toward Layth, who was coughing and gasping, his chest heaving. She knelt beside him and pressed her left hand firmly against a bloody wound just above his right hip. With her other hand she checked for blood on his chest, listened for the sucking sound of an incipient pneumothorax. But she found nothing. She looked into his face at the same time as she felt the firm layer of Kevlar beneath his phony uniform.

—✒

Layth winced as Addy pressed against his chest. He had never been shot before; now he had been shot three times at once. Through two of the shots had struck his bulletproof vest, they hurt more than the one bullet that had passed beneath the edge of the vest on his left side. It felt as though a truck were parked on his chest; he couldn't breathe, he was being crushed. He fumbled for the closures of his shirt and the vest underneath. Addy—whose initial look of horror had given way to concentration and resolve—helped him remove it, by which time Sara had arrived to help.

"You've broken some ribs, no doubt," said Sara. "But the bloody wound is shallow, it missed your kidney on the outside. If you can avoid infection you should heal up fine."

"If I can"—Layth coughed—"avoid getting shot by the actual enemy." Addy winced and began to apologize, but he cut her off. "How did you make it?"

Addy told him in rushed words how the submarine had rescued her but subsequently been attacked, how Juan had come with her. That Authority bureaucrats had been burning files in the basement, and two had escaped. Lieutenant Dumont, who had joined the circle of people kneeling around the injured Layth, looked at Juan and spoke. "We've been trying to contact people outside of Authority territory, but we don't know how to use all this equipment."

"I can put you in touch with my command," Juan said. "Just show me the equipment."

———✦———

Evelyn rolled herself out of the elevator, Sid crying softly in her lap, squirming disconsolately. His little feet scuffed her painfully abraded knees, but she was glad for his presence. He burrowed his face into her chest, covering his ears with his hands. She hugged him as hard as she could.

"Are you okay, baby?" she asked. He just kept crying. He wasn't injured physically, at least. She didn't know how he could answer her, really. It would take him years—decades?—to understand everything that had happened. She barely understood it. She patted him on the back. "I know, I know," she said. "It was very loud."

Sara came over and made as if to touch Evelyn, then remembered her hands were still bloodied. She washed them at one of Triage Administration's ubiquitous hand sanitizing stations. Then she returned to Evelyn, pulled up a chair beside her, and gently lay one hand on Sid's back and the other on Evelyn's cheek. Her hands smelled of isopropyl alcohol.

Sara made eye contact but didn't say anything to Evelyn for a long while—just gazed into her eyes and gently caressed her face. She smiled slightly, her eyes welling with tears. "How are you doing?" she asked.

"I don't even know," Evelyn said, her eyes reddened but dry. "I feel numb."

Sara nodded. "That's normal. But you'll be all right. Eventually." Sara looked around the room, which was filled with frenetic activity. Fighters were dragging crates of cloth into the room, people were shouting into radios, Dumont was calling out instructions. The first pink rays of a rising sun came across the rooftops and through the windows. Sara smiled slightly. "Somehow I think—I think everything might be okay, now."

Evelyn looked incredulous. "There are fascists everywhere," she said. "Who knows when those goons will stream back up out of their bunkers? We've got mass malnutrition and a society that hasn't functioned like a democracy for our entire lives. We've got global warming, soil erosion, mass deforestation. The city's infrastructure is falling apart, the land outside the city has been stripped to bedrock. And oh my god, the people in the basement, how can they recover, their minds, Mrs. Schmidt—"

Sara nodded more and more vigorously and finally interrupted Evelyn. "I know all that," she said. "But we're alive. And we're together again. Finally. We'll figure out how to deal with it."

Evelyn gave a dubious nod and sighed slowly. She said nothing, only reached out and pulled Sara close.

—⚡

Still flat on his back, Layth winced as a militia medic tended to his shallow gunshot wound. He raised his handheld radio. "Felicity?"

"I'm here," she said. "The crowd has nearly reached you."

"Any chance that helicopter was shot down by drones?" he asked.

"No, they made it over the horizon, going southwest."

"I think Justinian was on that chopper," Layth told her.

"—otherfucker!" she replied, cursing so loudly that her microphone clipped.

Layth waited for her to finish a string of obscenities. "We're going to be tracking that guy down the rest of our lives."

"No," answered Felicity. "Just the rest of his life."

Layth laughed sharply, to the chagrin of the medic who was trying to dress his wound. "How does it look?" he asked.

"Not bad," the medic said. "The bleeding should stop in a few minutes."

And lying there on the cold floor, Layth realized something very difficult: he was going to live. He was going to live; the Authority was going to fall. So many of the people dearest to his heart were dead, but he would live, and he would have to find some way to live without those pieces of his himself, in whatever new world they could make.

A sudden heat welled up in him, a pressure through his throat and his eyes. A moment later, Layth was racked with uncontrollable sobbing. The heaving of his chest sent jolts through his cracked ribs. He wept for his parents, for his dead comrades, for the gentler life he could have lived if the world passed down to him had been different.

The medic misinterpreted his obvious agony as mere physical pain and put a compassionate hand on his forearm. "I'll give you more analgesic," she said. "Breathe. Just breathe."

He inhaled raggedly, turning his face toward the windows and the rising sun.

—⧕

Addy listened to Juan speak in rapid-fire Spanish over the radio. After a moment, he turned to Addy. "We can get a data link," he told her. And he connected one cable to a laptop Layth's team had brought in.

A moment later, a face appeared on the screen. It was blocky and pixelated; video, but barely. Each part of the face moved slightly out of sync, as though the bandwidth were not enough. "We can improve that," Juan said, fiddling with the hardware.

Addy stared at the face. Her exceptional memory told her there was something familiar about it, but she could not yet place it.

"*Chhhee?*" came a voice over the speakers. The timbre of the voice was stripped away by overcompression, it sounded so tinnily robotic that she barely recognized it as a human voice. "Dee, is *chhh* you?" the face clarified, and suddenly she remembered.

"Simón." She smiled. His hair was grayer, but she knew it was him.

"*Chhhh* been a long time," he answered. He smiled, his image updating with a new frame only once or twice per second. The resolution improved a bit; she could see plenty of stripes on the epaulettes of his dark uniform.

"Looks like you've moved up the in the world," Addy said.

"*Chchchch* International Fleet," he replied. "Cyberwarfare and *chhh* drone command, stationed in the Saint Lawrence."

She frowned and shook her head. Only half of what he said was intelligible. "I guess we have you to thank for taking down the YEA drones."

He made his own confused face. "Can't hear *chhh* you are saying. Attack on *chhh*-manitarian submarine finally gave us the excuse *kekekeke* act."

"Are you coming with ships?" she asked. "More resources? International brigades?"

Simón gave her a pixelated, regretful look. "Our mandate is only"—his image froze for several seconds and then jumped forward—"limited resources. But now that we've reestablished communication, we can—" His image froze again.

Addy spun toward Juan. "This is ridiculous. Can we just do audio or something?"

"I can fix it!" said Sridharan, who joined the fiddling.

"*Chhhh*—s ridiculous?" asked Simón, looking worried. The screen image froze again for a moment, went black, and then resolved with improved sharpness. She could see his wrinkles now. "That's better!" Simón's voice had become clearer. "Now that we're in contact we can provide some outside assistance. But people in the disputed regions ultimately have to decide their own fate."

Addy had a hundred questions to ask. What disputed regions? What international force? Had Simón joined the military? It was impossible to concentrate with the hubbub in the room, with the growing sounds of chanting outside. Addy became aware that there was a massive crowd of people approaching the building in the streets below. Lieutenant Dumont was shouting more instructions. "Get those windows open! Just smash them; don't you see those torches?"

Addy concentrated and asked the question she was most afraid to ask. "What's it really like out in the world?"

He nodded soberly, his image smooth and crisp. "It's different everywhere, Dee. It hasn't been easy for anyone. Some places have gotten worse, like where you are. But some have gotten better, even *much* better."

"But did *we* make things better?" she asked. "Our work back then, did it help?"

"It's always hard to tell, isn't it? How the future could change from the smallest actions," Simón mused. "I believe we made things better. We bought time. Breathing room. We stopped one war. We didn't improve things as dramatically as we hoped. But we made room for a hundred other movements to flower. Some of them failed, but some of them are amazing." He smiled again. "You'll have to come and see." Then he was quiet and cocked his head, listening.

Addy listened, too. The crowd had arrived outside. Their angry chanting was thunderous now, frighteningly loud as it boomed in through the windows the guerillas had smashed open. Lieutenant Dumont was shouting. "Don't use the white cloth; we aren't surrendering! I don't care, use any color—use all of them! They're about to torch the place!"

"The tides always rise and fall for us," Simón said. "That's the nature of struggle. There is no guarantee, no permanent victory."

"'The work of the revolutionary is to plow the sea,'" Addy quoted.

"Exactly," answered Simón.

Addy watched a team of militants smash windows in front of her. They unfurled the bolts of cloth they had scrounged, letting them hang from the windows: silk and linen and wool in all colors—red and black, blue and green, pink and yellow, orange and violet.

The sound of the crowd faded for a moment; angry chants gave way to a confused buzzing. And then, from the murmurs, a single joyous shout. And another. Then the crowd burst into surprised and happy cheers.

"It sounds like the tide is turning in your favor today," added Simón. "Just remember, whatever happens: you are not alone."

Addy heard a cough and then a hoarse voice from the ground a few feet away.

"Help me up," said Layth from the ground. "I want to see." Addy reached down with her left hand and helped pull him to standing, let him put an arm over her shoulder. Together they hobbled to the windows. Everyone gazed out; Addy and Layth found a place between Evelyn, in her wheelchair, and Lieutenant Dumont, rifle slung over her shoulder.

The rising sun lit the rainbow of banners fluttering beneath their feet. As far as they could see the streets were filled with people, whose chants and shouts and cries rang through the urban valleys.

"Well," said Layth, tears streaming down his face, "how about that?"

24

2028

"Three cells," said Samantha in disbelief. "We just lost three cells."

Dee and her team watched the newscasts in dull horror. Kraken's methods of communication were safe but incredibly slow, so they learned of the disaster by watching it on CNN.

"This was bound to happen," said Security, cradling his head in his hands despondently. "We overreached. We should have quit while we were ahead."

The news video feeds switched among three locations. One was a pipeline pump station in Alberta where, according to the news, "police—tipped off by watchful neighbors—caught five anarchists pouring an abrasive into the pump lubrication systems. The pipeline is currently down for maintenance." Another was an Appalachian mountainside circled by helicopters, where "military search-and-rescue aircraft have cornered a small group of camouflaged figures who sabotaged the railroad equipment used to transport coal from mountaintop removal operations."

And, again and again, they cut to footage of a ten-story plume of smoke over enormous, blackened transformers. Fire trucks in the background sprayed gray arcs of water. Ambulances and police cars crowded around an overturned white van at the end of a muddy skid mark in a field of yellow grass.

"They must have known," said Media. "Someone tipped them off. Or talked. How else could they catch three teams at once?"

"Who did we lose?" asked Intel.

"Don't ask," answered Security. "Cell membership is still need-to-know."

The news anchor continued: "Police are calling this 'the biggest law enforcement mobilization in decades,' with military personnel in five countries participating. We go now to—"

"We were lucky before," said Security. "We took easy targets first, with fresh teams. Now they're exhausted, going after difficult targets . . ."

Overwhelmed by fatigue, Dee slumped into an overstuffed chair. Her limbs were made of lead, too heavy to move. Her fingers were sand, her lips dried meat.

Some expert in a suit was being interviewed on the television. "Domestic terrorists have taken advantage of unrest overseas to stab our country in the back. They want to use violence to impose their agenda on others. It's despicable. I just hope that the president and Congress will not be distracted by these cowardly attacks, that they will focus their efforts on consolidating our military presence in Asia."

"Will somebody turn that damned thing off?" said Intel.

Samantha got up and clicked off the television. "Okay," she said, "next steps. Has everyone in contact with the captured cells been warned to go deeper underground?"

"*Everyone* should go deeper underground," said Security. "We shouldn't stay here talking right now. We need to disperse and wait this out. If they've captured three cells *someone* is going to spill information. They'll track down others, compartmentalization or not."

"Don't panic," said Intel. "Dee, have you been in touch with the council?" Dee shook her head slowly. "Contact them now. We need them."

Dee shook her head again, slowly, staring at the table in front of her. "I can't reach them right now," she muttered.

"Have they left instructions?" asked Intel. "They've planned for contingencies, right?" Dee only shrugged.

"That's it," said Security, standing up. "We're burning time, we need to go."

"Whoa, hold on," said Media. "We lost action cells. But we aren't *done* here. We've had huge successes! There's a coal plant offline, arms factories down, two pipelines shut off. We still have our baseline capacity, logistics, intel, communications. We need to get our messaging out. Our own propaganda—"

"You're worried about *messaging?*" said Security. "I'm talking about prison. I'm talking CIA black sites. I'm talking about the hit men they hired to kill Gwen Gibson. That's what you need to worry about." He put on his coat and shoulder bag. "I'm going back to my cell. We'll relocate and lie low. I suggest you do the same. We'll try to regain contact later." He walked out of the room, and Dee heard the front door open and close. A moment later, she felt a wave of cool night air float past her ankles.

Media stood up, too. "I'm not giving up. But if it isn't safe to do my work here, I'll do it elsewhere." The others began to stand or gather their things.

Samantha went to Dee and grasped her elbow. "Dee," she whispered. "I know you're upset. Disoriented. We all are. But you need to do something. Everyone's going to leave." But Dee could only sit and think of the news footage, of the overturned van, and of Rebecca.

～

There was noise and pain. Explosions and gunshots. Tumbling, crunching, screeching. And then warm, blunt buzzing.

When Taavi came back to his senses, he was handcuffed to a hospital bed. His hand and face were bandaged to a ludicrous degree. One eye was covered entirely. Through his working, uncovered eye he saw flashes of brightly colored light each time he moved his head. He had an IV line in his right arm; his left was splinted, immobilized by layers of padding and plastic. He felt little pain, thanks no doubt to a strong narcotic in his IV feed.

Another person was in the room—a nurse, adjusting his IV pump. She said something muffled-sounding and offered him a drink of water through a straw. His throat was parched, and he accepted gratefully. He had barely finished swallowing when two men entered the room, one tall and balding, one short and hairy. He knew instantly that they were cops, despite their lack of uniforms.

"You were supposed to tell us when he was awake!" said the tall, balding one. He seemed to be yelling, but his voice was dull, as though the volume of the world had been turned down. The nurse said something; the man cut her off. "I don't care if he has a concussion, it's a matter of national security. Don't tell me about hearing damage or opiates, just get out of my way. Fine, *get* your supervisor!" The nurse left the room looking angry.

The short, hairy guy closed the door behind her and stood there. The tall, bald guy leaned over Taavi's bed and said something in a quieter voice. Taavi's own name? The short guy said something, made a plucking gesture next to his ear. The tall man reached to Taavi's uncovered ear and pulled out several pieces of white, cottony material. Taavi could suddenly perceive the subtle sounds of the room: rustling cloth, hissing ventilation, pulsing IV pumps.

"Look, Thorvaldson," began the tall man, his voice deep and slow. "Yeah, we know who you are. I'll level with you: You're pretty screwed. I mean, you're going to jail for a long time. Industrial sabotage, that's one thing. But charging a police blockade, setting off explosions? People got injured. People died."

Taavi's face twitched slightly.

"I'm sure you didn't want that. You seem like a good kid. But it happened. We have all the evidence in the world. They literally found the detonator in your hand, right? So, let's help each other. We expect more attacks, but I just want to save lives, okay? I don't care why you did it, for the polar bears, whatever. Politics is above my pay grade. But if you give me information, I can save lives, and it will look good for you when your trial comes. Understand? Are you hearing me?"

Taavi nodded—and immediately regretted it. It was technically true; he could hear the man. But that wasn't really what the man was asking, was it? Taavi felt a strange absence of anxiety at the presence of police, given how often the fear of them had occupied his dreams and idle moments. The concussion and the drugs were slowing his thoughts, undoing his training.

In response to Taavi's nod, the tall man smiled. "Good, we've got some understanding, we've got communication here. Now, Taavi, I know about you. I've read transcripts of your conversations with Corben and the rest, before you hit the road. I can tell you've got a good heart. You wanted to avoid violence, wanted to avoid hurting people, right?"

Taavi nodded again. That was true, wasn't it? He wasn't giving any information away.

"Taavi, the people giving orders in your organization don't feel that way. How much do you really know about them, Taavi?" Taavi pursed his lips. "We know a lot about the people who run Kraken. They aren't nice people, Taavi. Not like you. They've been lying to you. They're using you to hurt people."

Taavi said nothing. He thought of Dee. How much *did* he know about her?

"The people on this council, they don't care what happens to you. They've cut you loose. And they're going to hurt more people, Taavi—unless you help. Taavi, when is the next attack?"

Taavi took a moment to process all this. He began to realize, fuzzily, that the cop wasn't talking about Dee at all. The cop had bought the same crap story about the Revolutionary Council as the rest of them.

"What's the next target, Taavi? Tell me now, or it will be too late. What's next, Taavi?" Taavi said nothing. Just shook his head, slowly.

The hairy man by the door shook his head. "He's drugged to the gills. Turn off the narcotics." The tall man fiddled with the buttons on the IV pumps, then turned to the hairy cop and shrugged. "Just unplug it, just turn them all off." The tall man did, and the machines started beeping and buzzing.

"You're confused," said the tall cop. "I get that. Listen, Taavi. The people in the van are hurt bad. One is dead. Others are waiting for surgery, might not make it. The doctors need you to identify them. To get their medical records, their, ah—"

"Past medical history," put in the hairy cop.

"Like allergies. If the doctors don't know, they might give them the wrong drug, the wrong blood type. Then your friends die on the operating table. You don't want that. So, give us some names, Taavi. For your friends." Taavi frowned, silently, picturing Rebecca on a surgical table. Someone outside knocked on the door, then pushed it. The hairy cop kept it closed, put his weight against it. "Taavi, they're in custody. We'll know everything soon. But not soon enough to save their lives. Tell me the names of the people in your cell."

Taavi almost told him. Almost started to talk, when a doctor pushed the door open and began an angry exchange with the hairy guy.

The bald cop leaned forward. "Whisper them to me. They're almost out of time." His breath smelled of bitter coffee.

Taavi opened his dry lips. "Who died?" he whispered.

The bald cop looked at him. "The woman in front. The driver. What was her name?"

Taavi closed his eye slowly and turned his face into his pillow.

~

Helen woke when the sun rose. She got slowly to her feet; her bladder was tremendously full. She walked slowly toward her bedroom door and passed a window. Looking out toward the cabin's driveway, she saw that a new vehicle had arrived during the night—one of those modern-looking silver imports she could never tell apart. The vehicle she had arrived in was gone.

She went to the bathroom and voided her bladder, after which she spent several minutes sitting unnecessarily on the toilet. Just sitting. She flicked the room's light switch on and off a few times; the compact fluorescent on the ceiling did nothing. Power outage? She flushed the toilet. The toilet bowl drained, but no water refilled the tank. She tried the bathroom faucets, but nothing happened. Moments later, she heard an engine start outside. Another car? Water flowed from the faucets; the overhead light blinked on. A generator, then.

Helen went downstairs a few minutes later and found a strange woman bustling in the kitchen. Helen froze at the foot of the stairs. The woman glanced at her. "I turned on the generator," she said. "I hope I didn't wake you up." Then she paused. "That's not true. I'm glad you're awake. I'm in a rush. There's a lot going on."

"Who are you?" Helen asked, not sure of the proper protocol for encountering a stranger in one's safe house.

"Part of Kraken you aren't supposed to meet," the woman replied, rifling through a cabinet and pulling out a container of brown sugar. "Media."

"Medea?"

"Sure," said Medea. "Let's go with that. How do you take your coffee?"

"Milk and sugar," said Helen.

Medea checked the little refrigerator, pulled out a milk carton, and sniffed it. She wrinkled her nose. "Sorry. It'll have to be black. As in blackout," she added, gesturing vaguely to the outside. She emptied the milk into the sink. Then she poured a mug of coffee, mixed in some sugar, and put it on the table between her and Helen. "That's yours."

"Have we met?" asked Helen, not taking a step toward the coffee or the woman.

"Protocol says we never should. But with the blackout and arrests, we have to bend the rules."

Helen wanted to say *Protocol? Blackout? Arrests?* But she couldn't decide where to start. Medea poured herself a cup of coffee, drank a sip, and sighed.

"It's been a hell of a night," she said. "I'm surprised they haven't taken you out of here to someplace more remote."

Helen just stared. "I have no idea what you're talking about."

Medea looked quizzically at Helen and then raised her eyebrows in understanding. "You haven't heard the news, have you?" Helen shook her head. "Aaah. It's a long story. The network staged dozens of coordinated attacks in response to the war in the Pacific—the 'enforcement action' in the Pacific. Whatever they're calling it today." Helen just looked more confused. "Anyway, they were pretty successful—witness the blackout in this part of the grid, which also feeds several IRI projects. But three cells were captured, and mission control fell apart. People are going to ground. Et cetera, et cetera."

"So, it was a failure?"

"It's much more complicated than that," answered Medea. "Like your situation, right now."

"My situation is fucked up," said Helen.

"Yeah. I mean, watching your friend's dead body be burned to fake your own death? That's all *kinds* of fucked up," agreed Medea, more enthusiastically than Helen felt was necessary. "Sorry. I don't mean to seem insensitive. I'm trying to be matter of fact. I've got a lot to accomplish today, and if I don't get it done quickly I'll end up in jail. Or worse, have all my work be in vain, and so on and so forth. Also, I lost some friends myself recently, and if I stop moving I might not start again. Okay, next question!"

Helen hadn't asked a question and wasn't sure where to start.

"Your coffee's getting cold," said Medea. "Have a seat!" Helen complied. Medea drained her first cup of coffee and poured herself a second. Then she stood and began pacing around the kitchen.

"Here's the update that matters to you," said Medea. "I understand you were promised certain things by the network: safety, transport, resources. But the network's ability to provide may be compromised. More of a problem for you is that the person responsible for your well-being has been . . . incapacitated."

"What? Was she arrested?"

"The point is," said Medea, "the fixers who brought you here are occupied, and will be for the foreseeable future. There's no guarantee that they'll be able to come back for you, even if they want to. Oh, don't forget your coffee!"

"I don't care," said Helen, "if they come back or not."

Medea stared at Helen appraisingly. "Huh. I guess that's true, eh? Maybe I have more to offer than I thought." Helen raised her eyebrows skeptically. "It's like this: I need your help. You need my help. We can help each other. My branch of the network is intact. I can keep you safe and hidden, provide for you. You don't just have to wait for the cancer. You have options. We can give you a sense of purpose."

"What do you know about my purpose?" asked Helen.

"I know about your action with the heavy equipment. That was impressive, especially for someone working solo. And it was brave."

"Cancer courage," replied Helen.

"But I think that's not the kind of action you're truly passionate about. You want to connect with people, to *move* them, to build communities, to build movements."

"Is everyone in your organization a recruiter?" Helen asked.

"All radicals should be," answered Medea. "But you see my point. I can give you a critical role in our movement at this point in history— and sister, you need it."

"What do you want from me?" Helen asked.

"Simple," said Medea. "I need to connect with a certain audience, an audience currently on the fence, to make them understand what

Kraken has done and why it's important. Why it's right. For that, I need Gwendolyn Gibson."

Helen frowned. "Gwendolyn is—"

"I understand," said Medea. "I need *you* to be Gwendolyn, alive and free, depriving the right-wing vigilantes of their hit. Not a martyr. We're about to have a martyr surplus."

"I don't look anything like her."

"That doesn't matter," said Medea. "You have green eyes. Hair doesn't match, but you don't have much hair anyway. We can use wigs. But that's beside the point. You won't be on TV. You, Gwendolyn, are on the run, right? Hiding from death threats and vigilantes. You'll write at first. You're a good writer, and you knew her best—her mannerisms, her turns of phrase. You can write like her. You can make people—the people who listen to her—understand why Kraken is doing what it's doing. And why *Helen* did what *she* did. Both of which seem crazy to a lot of people, you understand."

"Wait," said Helen, "you want me to pose as my dead friend so I can write a politicized obituary for *myself?*"

"An obituary, great!" said Medea. "That'll be your first assignment."

Helen just shook her head. "This is a huge mess."

"The world is a huge mess," agreed Medea, finishing her second coffee. "Sometimes you have to do extreme things to make the world less messed up."

"I still have cancer," said Helen. "Even if I agree, I don't know how long I have."

"No one in this organization knows how long they have," said Medea. "I'm not being flippant. We'll help you get treatment, false documents. Move you someplace with good medical care. What else would you rather do? You can carry on your comrade's legacy, and your own. For as long as you want."

Helen reached out and took her first sip of the cooling coffee. "Sure," she said, shrugging. "Why not."

Dee and Samantha stayed at mission control in the hope they could keep things together. But by midnight, they were the only ones left. The departing promised to maintain communication—after things cooled off—but they went, regardless. They were spooked; they trusted their own cells much more than the roomful of strangers Dee had convened. Dee knew she would lose contact with some of the departed, possibly forever.

Dee worked until three in the morning to keep fragments of the network together, to ensure emergency channels of communication remained, to make sure action cells knew the fight was still on. She left nearly a hundred frantic dead drop messages, all typed to the background ambience of CNN. Samantha—who had barely rested in days—curled up in an easy chair and fell asleep.

And then, just after three in the morning, the news showed the photo of Rebecca from her driver's license and reported she had died in the van crash. Or had been shot while driving. Or both. The reports differed, but it didn't matter to Dee. She could do nothing after that—just stare blankly and shuffle papers. The word *guilt* covered not a fraction of one percent of what she felt.

Dee moved to the front room, lay on a couch, and tried to rest. She closed her eyes but could not sleep. After sunrise she sat up, pulled back the curtains slightly, and watched people in the neighborhood begin their morning routines. Small groups of kids walked past. A school bus paused down the street and then drove on. Individual commuters passed in their individual cars; carpoolers were so rare that she noticed when a vehicle with multiple occupants passed. She thought she saw a white sedan with tinted windows, full of shadowed figures, go by twice. Maybe three times? The idea sent a chill down her spine. She decided to wake Samantha.

In the other room she could hear the babble of twenty-four-hour TV news, the volume set on low. As she approached, she noticed Samantha was no longer on the chair she had fallen asleep on. Suddenly, she heard Samantha yell and the sound of breaking glass. Dee froze—were the cops smashing in the back door? She ran forward to see Samantha standing in front of the television where it was mounted on the wall, leaning forward and steadying herself with one hand.

The television's glass was shattered; fractures spiderwebbed from the center of the screen. "Samantha?" asked Dee. Samantha turned to face Dee. Dee's eyes widened, and she stepped back. Samantha's face was twisted and racked by emotion; blood was streaming down her face from a cut above one eyebrow. She looked terrifyingly enraged.

"They got him," Samantha growled. Through gritted teeth, she added: "They got Taavi."

"Did you smash the TV with your face?" Dee asked in disbelief.

Samantha ignored her and turned back to the television, the speakers of which were still emitting sound. Samantha grabbed the power cord with both hands and yanked as hard as she could, pulling the cord out of both the wall outlet and the television itself. Then she turned and rested her palms on the planning table. Blood began to drip and spatter onto the papers.

"Samantha, your face," said Dee. "You're bleeding everywhere."

Samantha closed her eyes and shook her head. "I don't care."

"Your DNA, Sam," Dee said gently. "You'll leave traces." Dee went to the kitchen. The cabinets were mostly empty, but she found a clean cloth and brought it back to Samantha. Samantha pressed it against her forehead and slumped into a chair without opening her eyes. Dee told Samantha about the car that had—possibly—driven by multiple times. "We need to get out soon," she said. Sam nodded. Her face had relaxed from its hateful rictus, but her lips were pressed so tightly together that they looked almost white.

Dee went to the front room and started a fire in the old-fashioned fireplace. The fireplace was one of the reasons the safe house had been chosen. She gathered all the takeout containers, notes, and scratch paper from the conference table—including those that Samantha had bled on—and threw them into the fireplace. She hastily wiped down the doorknobs, the faucets, the toilet lever, the light switches, and other surfaces she thought might gather fingerprints. She didn't have time to be meticulous, but she would hire a cleaning person over the phone, later, to get rid of the TV and scrub the place thoroughly.

Dee checked on Samantha after twenty minutes of frantic cleaning. "It's almost time to go. Show me your forehead." The gash was ugly and would surely leave a scar, but the bleeding had slowed to a trickle.

"Okay, you'd better get back to your cell. I have to meet with the Revolutionary Council."

Samantha rolled her eyes and laughed joylessly. "Come on, still with that? Drop the act. Taavi told me everything. Heck, I figured most of it out myself."

Dee showed no expression. "How many people did you tell? Is that why everyone left?"

"Everyone left because they're *terrified,*" said Samantha, "and unseasoned, and young. Fuck, you're probably younger than I am." Dee said nothing. Samantha continued: "I bet you don't even have your own cell to go back to, do you? All that courier bullshit. It's just you, isn't it?"

"I mostly work alone," allowed Dee. "And sometimes with . . . well, mostly alone, now."

"I followed you back to your house, once," said Samantha. "And to an old folks' home. You've got family there?"

"Wait, you *followed me around?*" asked Dee.

"Don't get all holier-than-thou," said Samantha. "You haven't earned that." She sighed. "We can still salvage something. Come with me to our logistics cell."

"I can't expose myself to more people," said Dee.

"Then work with me directly, and I'll work with my cell," said Samantha. "We all need to support each other to stay safe. If you're alone you'll get caught for sure. Heck, if *I* could figure out where you live . . ."

"I need to go home first," said Dee. "I have business to tidy up."

"We've got to go," said Samantha. "Now. Not back to someplace that could be under surveillance. Throw your phone in the fire, and we never look back."

"I have to make one call," said Dee. She put the battery in her disposable phone—not ideal, since the phone's location could be tracked. But the safe house would be cold long before anyone was investigating her phone records. She called the nursing home and left a voice mail for her father's doctor, explaining that she was out of the country due to a family emergency and authorizing him to give updates on her father's status to an imaginary cousin by e-mail. Then she turned off her phone and threw it into the coals of the fire. It withered into noxious smoke.

Samantha joined her in the front room and tossed bloody scraps of cloth into the fireplace beside the phone. She wrinkled her nose at the smell of burning plastic. Then she wrapped a clean strip of cloth over the still-oozing cut on her forehead before pulling a toque overtop.

"Okay," Dee said. "Let's get out of here."

—⟡—

"Dear Teresa," Taavi wrote, "thank you for your letter of March fourteenth. Sorry my response is so delayed. All prisoners in the special handling unit have their letters read and censored. There is a backlog because of overcrowding, so that takes weeks. And my ongoing 'trial' takes a great deal of time, although without access to the prosecution's evidence there is very little for me to do."

Taavi paused for a moment, rolling the stubby golf pencil between his fingertips. He rubbed the scar on his forearm, a set of faint white lines. He shifted his weight back and forth on the plastic lawn chair, trying to find a comfortable position. Then he leaned over his rounded steel desk and resumed writing.

"I'll answer your questions. First of all, no, I don't get an overwhelming number of letters right now; you don't need to apologize for writing. I appreciate it. They block many things from the outside. None of Apollo's letters have gotten through."

Taavi leaned back, raised his arms, and stretched his shoulders. He had been sitting in the chair most of the day, which always made his back sore. His shoulder and arm muscles were stiff; he had spent the morning doing as many push-ups and burpees as he could. He didn't have access to a gym, but he had enough room in his cell for simple calisthenics. He used exercises and stretches he had memorized from the booklet Rebecca had given him the first night he had stayed in that lonely motel room. He often thought back to that night, to Rebecca. He wondered whether he personally would have been better off if he had been arrested then, with Corben. Probably not.

"To answer your second question, my days are rigidly routine. We are locked in our cells for most of each day, including during breakfast. The doors are solid steel—not bars like Alcatraz or a movie prison—and so we can't interact much with other people. In the morning, I exercise in my cell. In the afternoon, I read books. In the evenings, I write my correspondence." He looked back at her letter and then added to his own, "Unfortunately, no, I am not allowed to go outside currently."

"The food is bad, but it could be worse. There are too many carbs, never enough vegetables. Actually, it would be easier to be a vegetarian here because then at least I could eat the meatloaf, ha ha. (There is not very much meat in it.)"

Taavi reread his last line and chuckled. His threshold for humor had fallen after six months in prison. His quiet laughter reverberated faintly against the beige cinder-block walls of his cell before being drowned out by the continuous background noise of television and argument from elsewhere in the cell block.

"I appreciate your offer to donate to my legal fund. My lawyer is well funded at the moment, compared to those of most prisoners. My time here has been . . . eye-opening. It would be better to donate to a general prisoner support organization. In terms of helping me: sadly, no, you cannot send me books or packages, though you can print photographs on regular paper and send them. I would appreciate photos of any outside scenes, nature, or wildlife. Also art.

"I would be very interested in radical writing about current events. We only get mainstream papers and magazines, and their coverage is shallow and capitalistic. I have been reading a lot of debate about Chinese purchases of North American energy infrastructure and would like more background on that. There have also been headlines about epidemics and antibiotic-resistant bacteria in the 'Third World' that have been blamed on a lack of drugs, but I would like to know, is that really the problem? Can you send me an analysis of links between disease and poverty, etc.?"

Speakers in the ceiling crackled on, and a voice announced, "Ten minutes to lights out." Taavi glanced up at the fluorescent lights recessed into the ceiling. They were nuclear bright; he never had to strain to read, at least. Shortly, the stark illumination in his cell would be dimmed to something like the light of a full moon.

"In response to your fourth question, no, prisoners in the special handling units are not required to work. Actually, this is an additional form of punishment, because life here is so monotonous and restrictive. In 'regular' units here, prisoners are required to work or attend 'programming.' They are paid only dollars per day, and room and board is deducted from their wage. It's the closest thing to slavery I have ever seen.

"It's difficult for me to answer your final questions, as my lawyer has been clear I should not discuss issues related to my charges or ongoing 'trial.' All my correspondence is carefully read by guards. Even vague information about my motivation can, supposedly, influence the outcome. Given that a sentence of life in prison seems to be the foregone conclusion, I'm not sure what difference this will make. Let me do my best to answer without giving my lawyer a heart attack.

"Basically, my answer is: No, I don't regret it. I would have changed a lot of things. I would never have worked with Corben. I wish we had planned certain actions more carefully, that we were less reckless. I wish that every day. But we always make mistakes. I guess that's okay as long as we learn from them. We as a movement, I mean—other people have to learn from my mistakes."

Taavi looked up at the buzzing fluorescents in the ceiling. He had perhaps ninety seconds before lights out. He began scrawling faster.

"What happens to me doesn't matter much in the scope of history. On the scale of the whole planet, I'm just one creature. Much worse things happen to eco-activists in Brazil, or gay activists in Russia, or Indigenous land defenders in Indonesia. I'm just one part of the struggle, and not an especially important one. But if we hold together, instead of splintering apart like *they* want, then we can still win. Dystopia is not inevitable. Catastrophe is not a given. We have a choice, and we can choose to fight.

"In solidarity," he signed, "Taavi Thorvaldson."

⚓

Every morning, Helen wrote a heartfelt letter to Apollo. She explained all her feelings, her worries, her thoughts about the world. She explained how much she missed him, wrote about what they would do if they were together again. Sometimes she went on for page after page. Then, at lunchtime, she would take her letter into the kitchen, open the woodstove, and burn each page into ash. It was simply too dangerous to send the letters.

Helen had spent two weeks in the cabin before they moved her. They just showed up with a car one day, Medea and a man named Jad who was sweet and quiet and had eyes like deep wells. Alternating drivers, they made one continuous trip across the continent to a rustic house in the northern Rockies, way back from the paved roads. Once December began, it snowed at least twice a week, and soon the snow was three, four, five feet deep. They made a point of not plowing the driveway. Medea and Jad spent most of their time tapping away on laptops but occasionally left on weeklong trips, about which they volunteered little.

Helen was strictly discouraged from openly contacting anyone she had known in her past life. On only a single occasion had they relented and arranged to send a printed letter (under a phony name) to Taavi, in prison. At least, she *assumed* they had relayed it.

They were serious about her new identity. They didn't even call her Helen to her face. They called her Gwen, or Ms. Gibson. She hated this at first but eventually got used to it. She even started to like it, as though she had sloughed off her old self—her own identity as the overworked nonprofit organizer, her old cancer-ridden body.

The cancer was in remission. It hadn't come back. Not yet.

Helen wrote a few undeliverable letters to the deceased Gwen, in the beginning, which she also burned. But by midwinter, Gwen was writing letters to Helen. It was Helen who had lost her life that night in November after wreaking havoc in the quarry.

By January, she was writing a letter or editorial almost every day, each of them signed "Gwendolyn Gibson." She was in hiding, she explained in the early letters, in the exile of self-preservation, her life constantly in danger. She wrote an abbreviated, fictionalized version of her escape that she gave to Medea. She doubted Medea ever passed it on to anyone.

She wrote letters to organizers Helen had known, to organizers

Gwen had known, to organizers on lists Medea gave her. She wrote to magazines, newspapers, websites, television shows, political officials. She wrote open letters, manifestos, and communiqués.

All of these built on Gwen's growing public profile, capitalized on her many radio and television appearances in the months after the petroleum-depot takeover. All of these emphasized the importance of radical solidarity, of direct action all of kinds from strikes to sit-ins to sabotage. And all of them were sent with a tiny picture of Gwendolyn attached.

At first, they were outdated photographs. But with little else to do over the long, cold winter, she revisited a childhood love of drawing. And she started to draw pictures of Gwendolyn—a new one each time, sometimes only a one-line sketch—as a kind of signature to send with each piece. A seal of authenticity, so to speak.

The truth was that Helen didn't look that much like Gwen. Helen was younger by a good ten years. Her hair was darker and straighter than Gwen's reddish curls. They both had green eyes, but of different shapes and shades; Helen's came from her central Asian ancestors, while Gwen's had come from Europe. But it didn't matter for the purposes of writing. People would assume that Gwen had altered her appearance in hiding, anyway.

Little by little, the illustrations she sent—the drawings of Gwen—began to look more as Helen had.

Time passed; the snow began to melt. One day early in spring, Medea leaned through the doorway of the room where Helen sat at her writing desk. Medea put one hand against the doorframe, the other on her abdomen, which was beginning to swell; obviously she and Jad had not spent the *whole* winter on their laptops.

"Gwendolyn," said Medea, "we'll have to move soon. Six months is long enough in one place."

"I can work anywhere," she answered, shrugging. Through death she had transcended Helen's limitations as a local organizer. She corresponded with people across the continent—around the world. She was coming to know the strains and eddies of global resistance with the familiarity of a Polynesian sailor navigating ocean currents far from the sight of land. Her isolation had heightened her sense of the big picture.

"You're doing an amazing job," said Medea. "Everyone is very proud—and very happy that you're so healthy." A single nod in response. "Is your writing going well today?"

She slid a few sheets of paper along her desk toward Medea. Medea picked up a news printout and read. "So, Philip Justinian got another promotion? That son of a bitch."

"I'm writing my latest column about him," she said.

"Is he that important?" asked Medea. "Sure, he's a sellout, a traitor, a collaborator. But is he worth spending ink on?"

"'If you want to rule, you must break your opposition down into tiny parts and pit them against each other,'" she read from her own page. "'Princes knew this long before Machiavelli. But Justinian understands it from both inside and outside. And that's what makes him dangerous.'"

"I look forward to reading it," answered Medea, turning to go. "Dinner is almost ready."

Putting pen back to page, she added a few more sentences. And then she capped her pen and placed it on the table.

She had become a skilled writer and correspondent. But she knew that she would never be happy shut up in little rooms in remote cabins. She looked enough like Gwen that with a haircut and maybe some makeup she'd pass with people who had never met Gwen in person. She would visit them—those who were not underground but who were radical. She'd help them network, give them courage.

She would be an exile in perpetual transit. She'd build an underground railroad for the new refugees and revolutionaries to come. She didn't know how long she could do it—her cancer could one day send her back to the hospital. Or worse. But it was a job she could do; something she would be good at. It was something to look forward to.

Gwendolyn would do it, for as long as it took. For as long as she could.

~

Dee looked out the passenger window of the jeep at the low, rolling mountains. They sped past pines that still held snow on their branches.

The sun was high in a blue sky scattered with cirrus clouds. Dee had just woken up, so her view seemed blurred, softened, impressionistic.

Samantha spoke to Dee from the driver's seat. "We need to get gas," she said. "Do you need anything?"

Dee shook her head. She turned to the little cooler between the seats and found a takeout container of leftover poutine. She ate it cold, using her fingers to pry apart stiff French fries fused by cheese and gravy.

"Did you sleep all right?" asked Samantha.

"It was fine," said Dee. She slept twelve hours a day. Mostly at night, but also in long, unpredictable naps strewn through the day. She made a mental note to look up narcolepsy when they had some Wi-Fi. Then she made another mental note to write that reminder on paper somewhere. Her mental notes weren't as reliable as they used to be.

Samantha pulled into a little rural gas station and got out to fill the tank. Her bangs had grown long enough to cover the scar above her eyebrow.

Dee picked away at the poutine. A few moments later, Samantha tossed a newspaper through the driver's-side door. "Here you go. Still another two hours to the meeting place."

Dee wiped her hands and picked up the newspaper. *Chinese Trade Disputes Hit NYSE,* read the main headline. In the aftermath of K-Day and an eruption of antiwar marches around the world, the conflagration in the Senkaku Islands had thankfully cooled down; the conflict between superpowers had shifted back to an economic and cultural cold war. Dee skipped the front-page story and flipped through to the obituaries, which she always read first.

A month after K-Day, a member of a captured action cell had died; he had killed himself in prison, supposedly. It was hard to say. Six weeks after that, she had found her own father's photo on the obituary page. *Long illness,* it had said. *Succumbed to antibiotic-resistant infection,* it remarked casually. The obituary ran long on her father's important role in the fair-trade movement. But the twist of the knife was only three words: *left no family.* It was months after that before she could pick up a newspaper again.

After checking the obituaries, she flipped back to the front page and read the pages in order: a few more stories about Chinese investment disputes, a plea from the World Health Organization and the United Nations for funding to deal with epidemics. A scattering of articles on the rise of leftist direct-action groups, and even more on the resurgence of right-wing militias. Dee found a letter to the editor from Gwendolyn Gibson, which she read through carefully, on the need for alliances among progressive groups. "Don't let them pin you down," the letter warned the reader. "You aren't just an 'environmentalist' or an 'antipoverty organizer.' Either we fight all oppression together or we all lose together.'"

"Anything interesting?" asked Samantha, as she returned to her seat.

"The economy's in the shitter," Dee replied.

"Ha. What else is new?"

"There's a letter from 'Gwendolyn' in here," Dee said.

"That reminds me," said Samantha, "I heard Media was pregnant." She started the jeep and pulled back onto the highway.

"Are you sure I need to know these things?" said Dee. "We shouldn't have more information than we need. And frankly, it's reckless to have babies in the underground."

"The Weather Underground had babies," said Samantha. "And come on; it's exciting! It'll be the first baby of our revolution. If we want to last in the long term, we need to be more than a network. We need to be a *family*." At the world "family," Dee turned to gaze out the window, stayed that way for some time as she watched the scenery pass.

The network had been in shambles since K-Day. It had split into branches, acting autonomously. One of the Intel cells had leaked a bunch of target analysis to the internet, which had sparked a new round of direct action that had nothing to do with Kraken. Aboveground organizers had chained themselves up at the same power plant where Rebecca had died, shutting down access for weeks. Two separate natural-gas pipelines had been shut off—using manual safety valves, not complicated robots—in a way that caused a cascading disruption through a whole network of fracking fields. Prisoner solidarity rallies had proliferated across the region. Dee felt from remote from it, but things were happening.

After a while, Samantha spoke again. "Do you want to start where we left off?" They spent much of each afternoon in deep conversation about the nuts and bolts of running a resistance network. Mostly Sam would ask questions, and Dee would respond at length, often drawing out a photo of a particular resister from a stack of black-and-white photos to jog her memory. In the beginning, it had been a kind of prolonged, unstructured interview. But as Samantha absorbed what Dee knew, the conversations had become more balanced. Dee would often ask for Sam's thoughts about a problem, or would give Sam an assignment to pursue with what was left of their network. "We were talking about esprit de corps."

"I should have given them more time to fuse as a group," Dee said, jumping as she often did back to K-Day and the mission-control group. "Maybe if they'd had a few days of rehearsal. Scenarios. Get them to know each other."

"It wouldn't have been enough," said Sam. "We recruited too much from among inexperienced people of privilege. It takes years to gain the character of a resister, not a few days of workshops."

Dee nodded in silent agreement.

"But things like K-Day can help people break out of a rut," Sam added, the cadence of her voice accelerating. "Other groups took action after K-Day that never would have before. More people understood the emergency, wanted to get involved.

"You know, the same thing happened with the nuclear disarmament movement in the eighties. An underground group called Direct Action blew up a cruise-missile plant in Toronto—some people criticized them, but it revitalized that movement, and nonviolent protests got even bigger afterward."

Samantha was relentlessly analytical, yet somehow her attitude verged on optimism. She had so much energy. The casualties, the arrest of Taavi and others, these things had heightened Sam's dedication. She wanted to learn from her mistakes instead of being weighed down by them.

Sam's drive and gentle positivity made Dee feel old—and reminded Dee of Rebecca.

"Let's talk later," said Dee. The truth was that since K-Day, and especially since the death of her father, her heart just wasn't in it. She knew the network was important, intellectually. She knew they had achieved something. But she could barely get out of bed in the morning. Her sense of failure was like a straitjacket cinched tightly around her body. Only Sam's regular prodding kept her from finding some dark corner of the world in which she could curl up like a dead spider and stop moving forever.

"When we stopped for gas this morning, I downloaded the messages from the last dead drop window," Samantha said. "They're on your computer."

Dee looked at her travel alarm clock, checked the timer. Indeed, the dead drop timer had recently reset. Dee had slept through the window. If it weren't for Samantha, Dee would have missed it entirely. She clicked over to the doomsday clock display. After K-Day, and the economic disruption that followed, they had gained about a year.

Dee pulled out her computer, booted it up, entered her passwords, and decrypted the first message. It was from Simón. They rarely chatted in real time anymore—it was too dangerous—but they did exchange short bits of text, steganographically hidden in images on the internet. The decryption program displayed a personal message to her.

"Dear D," it read, "I'm sorry to hear you have felt so despairing. Fallout from K-Day has been hard for everyone, and I'm sure especially for you. And what happened to your father. Don't give up. There is an old saying: 'The work of the revolutionary is to plow the sea.' Don't let these temporary waves overcome you.

"Things have gotten hot here, so I'm moving back south. It might be tough to get in touch for a while. I'll do my best to check in at the time windows when I can. Good luck to all of you. Love, Simón."

Plowing the sea, indeed. She saved the message—something she rarely did—and closed her computer.

"We should talk about money," said Samantha, rubbing the scar above her left eyebrow, "after the meeting tonight."

"We still have lots of money," said Dee.

"We gave a lot of cash to the Thistleroot Institute," Sam reminded her. "We have too many expenses right now. Also, we've been using this jeep a lot. We should get a new car."

"Sure."

"Let's get something cute. One of those electric Volkswagen Beetles."

Dee laughed, a rare occurrence. "We can talk about it." Dee leaned back in her seat and closed her eyes. Then she opened them again and looked at Sam for a second. "What's the date, again?"

"April twenty-first," answered Sam.

Dee nodded and closed her eyes again. It was her eighteenth birthday. She didn't tell Sam; she didn't want a party or presents. A nap would be gift enough.

As she tried to fall back asleep she thought about her future. She wondered if her revolutionary zeal would return. Surely someday she would feel better. For now, she felt each loss, each captured person, like a physical pain, like a knife in her chest. The sense of failure weighed on her, pushed her down into her seat, crushed her. Maybe she would quit. Retire. Go south and try to find Simón.

But no. There was still too much to do. She would help Samantha and the others, try to salvage something useful of her work. Try to help people learn from her mistakes. Live quietly, under the radar. If she had to she could leave the country, move to Australia. Her father had always liked Australia. If things got truly bad—if she were simply exhausted, if the economy collapsed to the point where she couldn't even get gas or travel easily—she could always go to the Thistleroot Institute. Just to take a break for a few months and recuperate before she went back out into the world.

In the meantime, she would do her best. She would do her best.